The Lovers

"Brimming with magic, *The Lovers* is a beautiful and sexy story that reminds readers of the wonder of the stars—and the power we ourselves wield to carve out our own destiny. An ethereal, delightful read!"

—Ashley Herring Blake, *USA Today* bestselling author of *Dream On, Ramona Riley*

"*The Lovers* totally delivers on its dreamy sapphic premise. This book wrapped me up in its lush setting, with characters that are as romantic as they are hilarious, and a plot full of tarot magic, deep sensitivity, and swoony, sparkly romance."

—Bridget Morrissey, author of *Anywhere You Go*

"Rebekah Faubion delivers a spellbinding story about love, authenticity, and the magic of the universe. Kit and Julia's chemistry was off the charts and had me rooting so hard for these two lovely humans finding their way in the world and back toward each other. Witty, satisfying, and enchanting, *The Lovers* absolutely dazzles."

—Taleen Voskuni, author of *Sorry, Bro* and *Lavash at First Sight*

"With a sizzling second-chance romance, atmospheric setting, and true insight into Zillennial influencer culture, Faubion crafts an engrossing love story that tackles the complexity of coming out in adulthood with deft compassion and proves that vulnerability and authenticity can open the doors to fate, love, and happy endings."

—Emma R. Alban, *USA Today* bestselling author of
You're the Problem, It's You

"Witty banter and swoonworthy second chances create a queer romance that is as fun as it is magical. Faubion's rich storytelling could make even the skeptic believe in soulmates."

—Liz Parker, author of *In the Shadow Garden*

"Deftly led by two of the most vivid, flawed, lovable, and compelling sapphics I've read in a while, this delicious second-chance romance will have you laughing, holding back tears, and believing in the magic of fate and the cards. *The Lovers* absolutely sparkles, and readers will be eagerly awaiting Faubion's next love story."

—Carlyn Greenwald, author of *Sizzle Reel* and *Director's Cut*

"A flawless second-chance romance that's sure to leave you grinning and kicking your feet, *The Lovers* explores themes of fate, agency, and living your authentic life, all while transporting you to a whimsical setting you'll never want to leave. This book should rocket to the top of your TBR. An instant fave."

—Jennifer Dugan, author of *Summer Girls*

"Faubion does a great job of creating the most delicious balance of caution and burn-it-to-the-ground chemistry between the two characters. . . . Faubion has a very cinematic eye, which is clear from the beginning of the story. . . . It's easy to get sucked into this world and these characters. . . . If you're looking for a good book to curl up with by the campfire and toast some s'mores, or to read while you sip your favorite seasonal beverage, *The Lovers* is absolutely the best choice. The cards say so." —Autostraddle

"Looking for an atmospheric second-chance sapphic romance? With a touch of fate and undeniable chemistry, *The Lovers* will make for a magical read and awaken the itch to purchase a new set of tarot cards to convince you that your fate is written in the cards." —The Nerd Daily

"*The Lovers* absolutely delivers on giving us some steam, some angst, and everything you're looking for in a fall sapphic story. . . . No matter if you're on the hunt for sapphic romance or just love a good soapy story, then *The Lovers* has your name all over it."
—Culturess

"If you like chemistry and angst in your sapphic romances, pick this one up." —Book Riot

"Readers will enjoy Faubion's novel about living and loving authentically." —*Library Journal*

Berkley Titles by Rebekah Faubion

The Lovers
The Sun and the Moon

The Sun and the Moon

and

the Moon

REBEKAH FAUBION

Berkley Romance
New York

BERKLEY ROMANCE
Published by Berkley
An imprint of Penguin Random House LLC
1745 Broadway, New York, NY 10019
penguinrandomhouse.com

Book design by Alison Cnockaert
Title page art: Sun and moon © EnkaArt / Shutterstock

Library of Congress Cataloging-in-Publication Data

Names: Faubion, Rebekah, author.
Title: The sun and the moon / Rebekah Faubion.
Description: First edition. | New York : Berkley Romance, 2025.
Identifiers: LCCN 2024056388 (print) | LCCN 2024056389 (ebook) |
ISBN 9780593640883 (trade paperback) | ISBN 9780593640890 (ebook)
Subjects: LCGFT: Romance fiction. | Novels.
Classification: LCC PS3606.A857 S86 2025 (print) |
LCC PS3606.A857 (ebook) | DDC 813/.6 — dc23/eng/20241122
LC record available at https://lccn.loc.gov/2024056388
LC ebook record available at https://lccn.loc.gov/2024056389

First Edition: August 2025

Printed in the United States of America
1st Printing

The authorized representative in the EU for product safety and compliance is
Penguin Random House Ireland, Morrison Chambers, 32 Nassau Street,
Dublin D02 YH68, Ireland, https://eu-contact.penguin.ie.

For anyone who has felt the particular pain of growing up in someone's shadow, not knowing if you will ever get your moment in the sun.

To me, you are radiant. You shine all on your own.

The Sun and the Moon

CHAPTER ONE

Cadence

Nature can't be tamed. Neither can a Connelly woman.

My mother's reason she would never marry, couldn't hold down a normal job, and didn't volunteer for the PTA. She was a wild thing, untamable, elusive—a wolf in the wilderness, not simply a woman. She wanted me to be just like her, and I wanted to be anything else. After years traversing the rugged landscape of North America, living among the untamed wilderness that has been claimed by man's hands, by land deeds, by acts of conservation, and, in many cases, by human greed, I have seen firsthand how the wilder the thing is, the harder it fights to remain free, even in the face of captivity.

If I am as wild as she always claimed, as wild as her, she really has only herself to blame for how things have turned out.

I crouch down, placing my hand on the edge of the rock in front of me. My eyes scan the plateau, looking for the creature. A flurry of white and gray, majestic and mysterious. It hasn't shown itself again, and I don't know if that's because Devin is a heavy mouth breather or because it's moved on already. I pinch my lips with the pointer finger and thumb of my other hand, signaling for Devin to shut his. He clamps them closed and then flips me off. He's holding the camera with the long scope, and despite the photographic evidence I've been able to capture on my iPhone, he remains skeptical.

I am happy to prove him—and our supervisor, Nika—wrong. There's fifty bucks and a day off on the line, after all.

Acadia National Park is home to a vast ecosystem of wildlife, protected within the boundaries of the park as best we can. The main predator to the natural world is human, tourists being some of the most destructive. The rangers created sighting competitions as a way to keep up morale throughout the year and keep eyes focused on the changes in the park that need our attention. I've never won, but this could be my chance.

The first snowy owl in October.

Even though it's September.

Which is why, of course, no one believes me. I cite climate change for bringing us a snowstorm that kissed Sargent Mountain with a dusting of white and might have urged the bird this direction early. Predicting the patterns of nature gets harder every year.

My mother would say it's fate that I saw the owl. A sign. A prompt for me to trust my intuition, lean on that still-small voice inside.

But I don't believe in fate anymore, and I never rely on my intuition.

So. Climate change it is.

"You can tell me if you're lying," Devin says.

"Don't be ridiculous." I wouldn't lie about this. I wouldn't lie about anything.

"Look, it's just convenient that you saw it on your own, is all,"

Devin says, fiddling with the long-range lens. "And you have an old-ass phone with a shit camera, so the pics are ragged." We're tucked into the tree line with a good view of the rocky summit where I spotted the owl yesterday while doing a trail inspection.

My supervisor, Nika, is encouraging me to start leading tours, giving instructional talks, literally anything more public-facing, because there's room for growth. But I didn't get into this job to be close to people.

The opposite, really.

I came here to get away from people.

"And your jabbering will undoubtedly scare it away," I tell him in a low whisper. Devin is what one might call a *work friend*. Someone I get beers with sometimes, who once invited me to a barbeque, and who tried to set me up with his sister before he knew me well.

Untamable as I am, dating isn't my strong suit.

You are a restless, wild thing. I shake the words away, just like I do every thought that gallops through my brain in my mother's deep, mellifluous voice.

Madame Moira, the enigmatic neighborhood psychic.

My mother.

My mind conjures an image of her rambling, supposedly haunted two-story Craftsman. Named Kismet—by her—because *all living things should have names* and because it's a place of business, not just a home. The neon sign on the wraparound porch advertises readings for $99.99 an hour; the formal living room's walls are lined with built-ins and packed with crystals, incantations, tarot decks, *anything* mildly metaphysical that she can sell to unsuspecting souls who walk through the front door.

Her home—my home, once—is magnetic and mythical in a

way that feels fairy tale–made. Her life once cast a shadow over every part of mine. Now she's mostly been reduced to memories that pop out in Technicolor when my vigilance drops.

I force my focus back to the cobalt-blue sky. Cloudless today and windy. The gray of the rocks contrasts against it in a beautifully stark sort of way.

"And it was just one?" Devin asks, still with that unmistakably skeptical tone.

September is the end of the snowy owl breeding season, which is another reason spotting one here this time of year is such a surprise. It's not migration time, really, which makes this bird's behavior odd.

Wild.

Or maybe just lonely.

The thought pings a soft spot between my ribs, and I almost wince. Too close to home, a place I try to avoid in theory and in actuality. I haven't been back to Kismet since Moira tried to convince me to take it over. Four years, the summer right after I finished my internship with the National Park Service and was offered a job at Crater Lake. She dismissed my achievement, claiming that Kismet was where I truly belonged.

"Just one," I reply.

Now Devin's eyes are scanning the ridge. We really can't get much closer, which is why we've come up here at peak daylight. Snowy owls are diurnal, which means they hunt mostly during the day—though, of course, not always. This one may well be hunting, and we'll have to wait to spot it until it returns to roost.

"Patience," I say, my brow hooking upward. "Or you could just leave the camera if you're bored." He scowls, tightening his grip on the Canon. It's the park's, but he acts like he owns it. And, granted, he did come to this job by way of a photojournalism major, but how hard could it really be to point and click?

"All good," he says, resting back in the camp chair he brought with him. He reaches over to unzip his pack, pulling out a bag of trail mix. "Hungry?"

With a shake of my head, I look back out.

Late September in Acadia looks like the beginning of an oil painting. Those first strokes of gold, red, umber sweep across the treetops, adding interest to the rolling green that leads out to the azure water of Somes Sound to the east and the ocean beyond.

That vast beyond is what drew me to Acadia. It's an island, the farthest north of all our country's national parks, easy to get lost in despite its small size.

College in Chicago wasn't far enough away from the all-seeing eye of Mount Moira. Even though I paid for it myself with student loans and grants and a scholarship or two, even though I didn't ask for anything—not even help with the semi-cross-country move—and even though I promised I'd call often, and did, for a while at least.

According to her, I was finding myself.

I had always been a searcher, but I *would* be back when I was ready to face my destiny. In her mind, that meant one day taking over at Kismet, learning to read the cards and the future for the people who came into the shop seeking guidance.

Chicago wasn't far enough away. Crater Lake wasn't, either.

No matter how far I got, I could still feel her eyes on my path. Probing, prodding, piercing—pushing me in the direction she wanted me to go regardless of my adamant refusal. It was only when I went no contact that I started to feel like I could live without looking over my shoulder.

Or, okay, not looking over my shoulder every day, at least.

Moira had her truth. A narrative for her life that centered on her intuitive ability and came at the expense of everything else.

Especially me.

Distance was the only solution.

I hear a buzzing sound coming from Devin's direction.

"You need to get that?" I ask as the buzzing continues. He must get cell signal up here. He tugs his phone out and I see the word *Ma* illuminated.

Devin's whole family lives in Bar Harbor. They're the kind of close-knit that makes my stomach twist up into knots. In each other's business, at one another's houses all the time.

Close. Real. A pack.

I've always felt more like a coyote forced out by her mange.

Only instead of mange, its emotional unavailability.

"Ma, I'm sort of on a stakeout right now," he says in a stage whisper that will definitely scare the more timid wildlife into hiding. I motion for him to cut the call—with the universal kill signal—but he stands in a huff and hands over the camera before tromping away down the hillside. His voice fades down the trail, and I'm left with the sound of nothing but the subtle shift of evergreen needles overhead as a breeze drifts over the mountaintop.

I rest the camera on my knees, tightening my hair into a low pony. The black curls cascade over my shoulder, and I swipe them back, feeling their weight hit the space between my shoulders. I raise the camera to my eyes, peering through the viewfinder.

"Where are you?" I exhale, letting the words dissipate through my breath, out into the air around me. People may not be easy for me to connect with, but animals always have been.

Wild things understand each other.

I hate myself for the thought, but then I also can't push it away. Don't want to.

Moira is a psychic. A seer in this almost supernatural way. Like in a Disney movie, or some picture book full of princesses, fairies, magic beans, and make-believe. It wasn't until I got older that I started to notice the gaps in her fairy tale. But there are parts of that story that even now—after all the disillusionment has settled—I cling to. Like a rabbit's foot for good luck or something. I want to be special, even if I don't want to be like her.

A streak of white screams through the blue.

"There you are." My lips twist into a smile.

I move my finger into position, the cool metal beneath my skin sending a jolt through my hand. The owl's wings are broad, swooping gracefully, and its talons open to hook the arm of a spruce perched right at the edge of the ridge. The bright white swath of its feathers is barred with brown through the wings and tail.

Not it, I think. *She*.

As she settles in, she swivels her head, turning her piercing yellow eyes in my direction. I am not foolish enough to think she's posing for me, but I snap the photo as if she were. She opens the hook of her dark gray beak to release a high, clear cry into the sky.

My heart leaps at the sound, an almost uncontrollable urge to reply. That is what freedom sounds like. I know because I've felt it time and again in the years since I walked away from Kismet. From my mother and her many premonitions.

I'm living a life I made for myself.

All by myself.

CHAPTER TWO

Sydney

Birdie.

A nickname from my dad. A pilot's call sign. For me it's become something more like armor. Along with my name badge bearing those sharp stenciled letters, *Sinclair*, and my pilot's wings of deep gold, I wear a delicate cobalt bird pin on my lapel at all times. As much a part of the uniform as my pilot's cap and oxfords.

Call it what you want. Good luck, superstition, ritual. Maybe it's my own version of a rabbit's foot or a four-leaf clover, maybe it's paranoia and my desire to feel grounded even in the air, but regardless, whenever I catch sight of the bird, I'm reminded that hard things are nothing new. I can do hard things. I can thrive under pressure, push through on fumes if I have to.

Birdie reminds me I already have.

My exhausted eyes meet their reflection in the first-class bathroom mirror and then drift down to my lapel. I adjust the bird pin with fingers still damp from washing my hands. We're about to start our descent toward LAX. This is my last flight on a ten-day schedule, the longest run I've had in a while, and just barely under the FAA guidelines for pilots' hours on duty and in the sky.

I meet my eyes again in the mirror. Sky blue. That's what my dad always says, anyway. Which I think is kind of silly. As a pilot—or former pilot now—he knows better than anyone that the sky isn't actually blue at all. It's not painted on the dome of Earth by a benevolent, creative God. We simply perceive it as blue because the light from the sun is white, which contains every color of the rainbow. As that light penetrates Earth's atmosphere it's scattered, and the smaller, shorter blue waves dominate our vision.

The sky is more than blue. Still, my eyes sure do match it.

Except, right now, my eyes are bloodshot and underscored with dark circles. Dry patches dot my skin. My blond hair is braided tight, low, and slicked back to hide the fact that I haven't washed it in a couple of days and really need to. I'm not one of those women who can go a week without washing and not look like a sewer rat. Last night's outing in the Village might not have been my worst idea ever on a layover, but my decision to booty-call my ex who lives in a walk-up in Williamsburg sure was. My choice to take that booty call to the next level is why I don't need to be in charge of my own love life.

I just fuck it up.

I keep telling myself that he won't be hurt when he wakes up—my eyes move to my watch to confirm that it's late afternoon in New York—*woke* up to find me missing. We were never that serious, even if he was the first guy I slept with in college. And the only guy I ever gave a blow job to.

Cunnilingus is just way more appetizing to me—

I pinch my eyes closed and tap my cheeks with the tips of my fingers.

I can do hard things. I did Gabe last night.

I snort. Even exhausted, I find myself funny. My eyes drift back open, landing on my reflection. I issue myself a *get your shit together* glare as I twist the handle to emerge into the walkway, almost straight into a young mom and her son. Giant brown eyes full of worry stare up at me from behind the fluffy head of a stuffed toy parrot. I scrunch my nose and offer him a tiny salute. His eyes crinkle. Nerves.

My left hand instinctively goes to my pocket, where I keep a few silver-and-gold pilot's wings at all times for moments like these.

"He's scared of the landing," the mom says. I look to her. Same dark eyes, same worry. "He thinks we won't be able to stop." My skin prickles at her words.

She shrugs, brushing her son's hair off his forehead. Her worry is clear, and almost admirable, but talking about crashing while on an airplane is bad luck. Especially this close to the cockpit. It's a universally accepted superstition among pilots—like taking a photo of the plane right before a flight or pointing to the sky. Bad luck, bad weather, all to be avoided. I squat down so that I'm on eye level with the little boy.

"Hi there." I scrunch my face, crinkling my eyes and nose. I know this to be a universally disarming expression. "I'm the pilot of this plane. My name's Sydney."

"I'm Henry." His voice is a squeak, small and meek like a mouse.

"Have you flown before?" I ask. He shakes his head. "Well, I have, *a lot*. And my dad has, too—he used to be a pilot before he retired." Retired early, way too early. And all because of me. I swallow the thought, forcing myself to stay focused. "I used to be scared, just like you. When he flew his planes, I worried, and whenever I went on one with him, I worried. I wished I had wings so I could do it on my own."

"Like birds do," he says. His eyes spark, and he hugs the parrot stuffie tighter to his chest. His chin presses to the top.

"Exactly," I say. I reach up to the lapel of my jacket, twisting it into the overhead light. "But I'm not a bird. That's why I wear this." And then I point to my pilot's wings. "And these."

"I have Rio," he says, lifting the bird up in my face. I chuckle.

"Perfect." I pull out a set of plastic pilot's wings from my pocket. "And, just in case you want a little extra birdy support." I hold the wings out in the palm of my hand. Henry's eyes widen, the fear leaving them as they take in the sight of the wings.

"For me?" There's wonder in his voice. I unhook the clasp and lift the pin toward him.

"May I?" He nods, the last of his trepidation melting away. I pin the wings on the collar of his t-shirt and stand. "There you go." I grin down, he grins up. "Now you've got wings."

"Thank you so much," the mom blurts, a relieved grin spreading her lips.

"Your safety is in my hands," I say, giving her a quick smile. "Please hurry back to your seats. We're about to begin our descent." I don't wait for her to reply before I push through the cockpit door, pressing it shut behind me.

I can do hard things. Landing this airplane isn't hard.

I'm the youngest female pilot in my company. One of seven in regular rotation. My copilots are almost always male, and older, and grouchy to the point of being passive-aggressively sexist about my role. I sped through college and flight school, worked hard to the point of exhaustion to get to where I am, but the challenge was never in landing the plane. It was never the mechanics of the work—always the politics, the pressure to keep the pace up so I didn't fall behind. To show Dad that his love of flying didn't have to die.

I take my seat, placing my headset back over my ears.

My finger lights the intercom. "We're beginning our descent into sunny Los Angeles, where the Santa Ana winds have blown in to welcome us with a speedy approach. I'm going to go ahead and turn on those seat belt signs, so if you're up and about in the cabin, please make your way back to your seats as quickly and safely as possible."

I take my finger off the intercom, as Stan, my copilot, says to me, "Turbulence over San Bernardino."

I caress the birdie pin on my lapel.

Nothing we can't handle.

CHAPTER THREE

Cadence

Nika lays a fifty-dollar Visa gift card in the palm of my hand and meets my eyes.

"Did she look like she was in distress?" Nika asks. The deep brown of her eyes always feels pragmatic and prescient at the same time. The *she* in that question is referring to the owl.

Devin and I returned to headquarters after I captured the picture and he grumbled about not getting to see the bird in person. Not my fault his heavy footsteps over dried leaves alerted her to our presence, scaring her away before he could get a look.

"She didn't. But she was alone as far as I could tell." I pocket the gift card. "If you want me to go back up there to observe, just say the word." Nika's lips pinch. She's got a strong face, full cheeks, and big, bright eyes.

"How thoughtful," she says, her tone playful but still authoritative. Devin snorts, dropping down into his swivel desk chair. She cuts him a withering look and he wilts. Her eyes shift back to me. "Can we talk in my office?"

A pit forms in my stomach.

"Of course," I say, my throat throbbing, but my voice remains stable.

The problem with loving your life, enjoying your work, is that at any moment, that work can be taken away or changed into something you don't love as much, that isn't what you wanted to do when you started but is somehow what you are expected to do if you continue.

I follow Nika to her office, watching her long, thick chestnut braid swish between her shoulder blades as she moves. Inside, she's decorated with mission-style furniture and a large painting of the Great Smoky Mountains, where she grew up. A photo of her family—wife, son and daughter, dog—sits on the shelf behind her. Nika is Greek. She comes from a huge family and is always bringing in leftovers to share with us in the break room or vegetables she grew in her garden for us to take home. She's funny and smart but also deeply intimidating.

I admire her.

She takes a seat at the desk, motioning for me to take the spot in front of her. I would much rather stand, but I don't think refusing to follow her instruction will garner me favor. I cross my ankles, the thick laces and rubber soles of my hiking boots scratching together with the motion.

She leans back in her chair, a more relaxed posture than I expect her to take if she is giving me bad news. I don't match her energy, choosing instead to sit up tall. She's got a discerning gaze. I can tell by the way her dark brows subtly shift as she watches me that my behavior is perplexing her. Which, well—good. I am perplexed as well.

"You have been with us for two years now," she says, steepling her fingers into a tent shape in front of her. I don't think it's a question, so I don't answer it. "And I barely know anything about you."

That is so not what I expected her to say. I blink, curve my brows into a squiggle.

"Is that required for this job?" I know it's not. She shrugs.

"Not in the slightest, but it does worry me how you isolate yourself. Not just from the public—even though you are more than qualified for an interpreter position." Park interpreter is what the guides who interact with the public are called in the National Park Service.

"I love what I do here," I say, the beginning of a plea rough in my throat.

Her expression softens. "That much is clear."

I don't know if she's wanting me to say more, to argue my case for why this introvert with an anxiety disorder who can't stand crowds—or people, really—should be allowed to continue to walk the trails and observe the wildlife instead of guide people through the park, explaining why the place matters.

So, again, I stay quiet.

"I have a daughter like you—smart as a whip but a bit rough around the edges," Nika continues. My eyes instinctively shift to the photo behind her—the dark-headed daughter. I don't see the problem with what she's describing, and also, her daughter looks plenty happy. "She prefers her solitude."

Preferring solitude is different from seeking it out of necessity.

"If this is because I didn't come to Fran's birthday party last week—"

"Or the Fourth of July picnic. You also didn't attend the retirement party for Bethany, who helped train you here at Acadia." I open my mouth to protest, but she raises her hand to stop me.

"Two years and you have attended one social event. Bird watching with the ornithologist from Cambridge."

"Birds are fascinating," I defend.

"I am well aware that you like them," she says with a smile. "Them, and most other animals that aren't humankind."

She's not wrong. I don't argue.

She leans forward, pulling her desk drawer open. She reaches inside to lift out a small navy-blue square envelope, then shuts the drawer with a click. She extends the envelope toward me, and it takes my brain a few seconds to catch her drift that she wants me to take it. With a jolt, I reach for it, my eyes trailing from her face to the words written on the front.

My name.

The swooping, chaotic script it's written in is immediately recognizable.

"What is this?" I drop the envelope back on the edge of her desk like it's a hot potato and I don't want to get caught with it.

"It was delivered here, and I'm assuming it's personal, considering . . ." She points to it as if the proof is in the visual. "And by your reaction, maybe unwelcome."

Return address: *Kismet*. The word dances through my brain, just like her swirling, twirling handwriting. I take a deep inhale and force my eyes to focus back on Nika.

"Very much," I say. The last thing I want to do is receive correspondence from my mother. I am basically no-contact with her now, but when I made the move to Bar Harbor, we were still texting, engaging in the occasional phone call. I told her about Acadia but never sent her my new in-town address. Her last known address for me was the rangers' housing in the park. I left that last year—too much community for me.

She could have done this on purpose. The thought menaces. Somehow, she might have known Nika would see it, be curious, try to talk to me about it since I never ever reveal anything about my family. It's stupid to think that. My mother isn't all-seeing, all-knowing, despite what she says at parties.

"It's from my mother," I say, a tightness in my chest. "We aren't on great terms." I reach out, grabbing it back up. The weight feels too hefty, like the contents contain a magic that makes it heavier than a regular letter.

"Ah," she says, nodding as she presses her pointer finger to her temple. "The address makes a lot more sense now."

"It's been strained for years, but I haven't spoken to her since I moved out of the rangers' lodging." I turn the envelope over. It's sealed with red wax. Stamped with a *K* for *Kismet*. The sight is an arrow straight to the heart. All the packages that are shipped out of the shop come with a note in an envelope bearing this wax seal. I used to help her with the task after school. She'd sit me down at the kitchen island and put me to work. I never did mind it, not even when I started to mind other things related to her work.

Nika is still watching me carefully when she says, "Do you think you'll open it?"

I blink because my eyes feel hot, stinging. When I look at her, I know she can tell I'm holding back tears.

"You don't have to," Nika continues. "There's a reason you've chosen not to communicate with her."

"I feel there's a *but* in there," I say, trying to smile. Nika's is genuine, definitely more so than mine.

"But if this is part of the reason why you shut people out, which is not sustainable long-term and leaves very little room for growth"—she doesn't mean my personal growth, not exclusively, anyway; this is a job that requires teamwork, and I am the opposite of a joiner—"maybe it wouldn't be a bad idea."

"Opening it isn't going to fix anything," I say.

"No, but it might start you on the road to fixing something," she replies. "If that's what you want."

I look back down at the envelope. Too heavy. Imbued with too much meaning.

"Thank you, Nika," I reply, uncrossing my ankles. "Is this all you wanted to discuss?" She observes me for a moment in that kind but stern way of hers before nodding, releasing me to leave the way I came in.

Letter from my mother clutched firmly in hand.

CHAPTER FOUR

Sydney

By the time I exit the airport, it's late afternoon. My shoulders and neck ache from the tension of that landing, which—no surprise—was a bit bumpy and not at all routine. Henry made sure to thank me for the wings again as he exited the plane unscathed. I made sure to clean my birdie pin with the cloth I carry in my sunglass case to wipe off the bad vibes. Born and raised in LA, I'm bound to be a little dubiously pseudo-spiritual.

It's basically a rite of passage.

I don't check my phone until I climb into the car. I have a voicemail from Dad, then a text that reads, Call me. Love, Dad. He signs his texts messages like a man much older than he is. At fifty-nine, Rick Sinclair is a salt-and-pepper-headed Phil Dunphy type. A young-at-heart magician in training, with bright eyes and a big sense of humor. He's been tragically lost without his Claire since my mom passed when I was thirteen.

Cancer, that cunt, claimed her way too soon.

It's us against the world, Birdie. Our mantra. Our edict. The creed of the Sinclair Trio, now whittled down to a duo.

There are also multiple texts from Gabe indicating that he did, in fact, get upset that I bailed on him before dawn, stole the last iced coffee from his fridge, and left the light on in the bathroom and pee in the toilet. In my defense, the pee was from three a.m., right after we fucked. I just forgot to flush. I drop my phone into my purse and crank the engine. I need a hot shower and a warm meal before I call Dad back or apologize to Gabe.

But let's be real, I'm probably not apologizing to Gabe.

Ghosting feels like the move here.

I pull out of the airport and onto the 105, passing the *Los Angeles Times* building on my right. There's something almost whimsical about a deco newspaper building greeting travelers to the City of Angels. Like it's trying to say something poignant about how our city supports dying industries to their last gasp. I find the building charming, but I also have to drag it every time I return home.

Home. It's funny, I spend so much of my time in the air that sometimes home feels more like a concept than a place. I don't know if I would have stayed in LA if Dad weren't still here—he's got his golf buddies at the club and his job as a tour guide at Universal Studios. He's caregiver to our family dog, a little Chihuahua mix named Chicken, and he loves his one-bedroom apartment that's rent-controlled. There's no way he'd ever leave LA, which means there's no way I will.

And fortunately, after four years working out of LAX for Dreamline Air, I don't really need to. It's prime real estate for a pilot.

What more could I ask for?

The thought gives me a familiar sinking feeling in my gut that will turn to gnawing if I don't dispel it fast enough. Don't get me wrong, I'm happy (she says with a smile that doesn't reach her eyes). On paper there is nothing wrong with my life. I have plenty of casual relationships of the sexual and the platonic variety. I have a father who loves me and has always supported my goals. I have a roommate/best friend who waters my plants and calls me on my shit.

I pull off the freeway, and the sinking feeling turns hollow, ready to eat me out and not in the fun way.

After Mom died, I watched Dad grapple with his grief, struggling to keep his eyes on the horizon and not the earth below. It changed my reckless, carefree teen years into something a hell of a lot more rigid. And when Dad finally did go back to work after his bereavement leave, he struggled to manage the time away in the air. Losing Mom changed his love of flying, turning it into something risky, and the fear of another tragedy couldn't be assuaged by all the pilots' superstitions and lucky charms in the world. He quit way before his pension was set to kick in so he could stay home and single parent. He never said it, but it was hard for me not to feel responsible.

Hard not to feel the weight of expectation that I follow in his footsteps.

That I carry on doing what he loved, since he wasn't able to.

Because of me.

I pull into my parking spot and cut my engine. I want to fall asleep right here, nestled in the cool leather seat of my Audi. But what I maybe want more than that is a scalding-hot shower, a face mask, and an overpour of pinot.

⌒

There's a tap on the bathroom door. Joe Lee, my roommate, a bisexual Korean American guy I met in college when he saved me from a laundromat one night. We then bonded because I was the only other out queer on our dorm floor, and we needed the solidarity. He moved to LA to pursue his dream of one day putting Botox in the rich and famous. He works as an aesthetician in a chic West Hollywood spa, but he still has his eye on Beverly Hills.

"Sydneyyy," he singsongs. "You've got heaps of mail on the table in there, and also I wanted to order sushi for dinner, but I didn't know if you had plans with your dad."

The steam has mostly dissipated in the bathroom. I have just finished placing a hydrating sheet mask on my face and plaiting my hair into two braids so it can start to dry with some wave. My hair is pin-straight otherwise.

I yank open the door. He's holding a glass of pinot in his rainbow-manicured left hand. His dark eyes lock on mine. "Sure, you can use the Korean egg cream mask I just got from K-Town and absolutely did not want to use myself."

"For me." It's not a question. I take the glass and scoot past him to walk back down the hall to my room and drop my dirty uniform in the hamper. I've put on boxers and a giant Van Halen t-shirt that I got from (stole from the closet of) this bartender I dated (hooked up with consistently for more than a week) last summer.

"Dinner?" he asks, not bothering to follow me down the hallway.

I need to check that voicemail from Dad—let him know I got in safe and sound. I grab my phone from the bed, then walk back down the hall toward Joe and pass through the doorway into the living/dining/kitchen combo. There's a wall of windows that look out over a small city park surrounded by shops. Culver City, Los Angeles (my locale), is basically a town within a city, and even though it's been bought up by Amazon, it's still managed to retain some of its original charm.

Though finding a restaurant that has a vibe that isn't decidedly *corporate in the wild* is almost impossible.

"Probably," I say, giving Joe a delayed reply to his question before taking a hefty gulp of wine and setting the glass on the circular dining table beside my stack of mail.

"I'm in danger of hang-er," Joe says, spinning his phone around impatiently between his fingers.

"Order whatever. You know I'll eat."

"That's the problem," he grumbles. "You're practically a competitive eater, and you don't believe in leftovers."

"No one believes in sushi leftovers," I say as I mindlessly begin fingering through my mail while I open my voicemail to check Dad's message before calling him back. Sometimes he says something important that he'll assume I'm already up to speed on.

Joe flops onto the couch just as Dad's voicemail begins to play.

"Hey there, Birdie. I know you're in the air now, so not expecting a speedy call back, but I wanted to let you know . . ."

His voice trails off. There's worry in the normally clear, chipper tone. He muffles the speaker, and I hear the faint sound of an obscured whispered conversation. My eyes drop to the table, wanting to have something to focus on while I wait for him to start talking again. What I find is nothing but a stack of catalogs. Sephora. West Elm. Sur la Table because one time I bought my friend Kendra a set of measuring cups and a cute apron. I, no surprise, am not a chef.

"Well, I think it's best, actually, if you hear it from me in person, but that's out of my hands. Since you should have the invitation by now."

My fingers come to rest, almost simultaneously as his words hit my ear, on a small navy-blue envelope with my name on it.

"Give me a call as soon as you get this, Birdie."

I let my phone fall from my ear to drop against the dining room rug. I rip the envelope from the table and flip it over to the seal. There's a small wax seal with a *K* pressed into it on the edge of the seam.

I tear open the envelope with trembling hands. There, surrounded by a whimsical Danish floral motif in blue and white, are the details of my dad's *ENGAGEMENT PARTY!*

To the woman he started dating a couple months ago. A woman he met on an over-fifties dating website (*Did you know there are apps for this now, Birdie?*). A woman I have never met, because I assumed that this relationship would end like all his other relationships after Mom's death:

Quickly and without much fanfare.

I scan the details as my vision narrows, the edges going dark with my adrenaline burst.

You are cordially invited to join in a weekend of
wine, wonder & winsome celebration of the engagement of

Moira Connelly & Richard Sinclair

on location in Solvang, California,
Danish capital of the US

I have to find out who *the fuck* this Moira is. There's no way they are in love. There's no way she didn't twist Dad's arm. My cautious father would never jump headlong into an engagement with a practical stranger and not tell me first—not unless there is something seriously shady going on.

"I ordered you a ten-piece sashimi, some fried tofu, some gyoza—" Joe lists before cutting off. "Whoa, you look like a deranged raccoon stuck in a trash can downtown."

My eyes trip up to his. Panic surges through me.

"Dad is engaged."

The words drop like a lead weight against the table between us.

CHAPTER FIVE

Cadence

When I think about my mother, a plethora of memories creep through my mind like a stalker in the night.

There's the one from when I was eleven and I had finally, finally made a friend at school. Sarah Wright, a petite blonde with glasses, who also loved animals. She didn't care that Moira was a psychic; in fact, she kind of liked it. She came to Kismet after school, wanted me to tell her what all the crystals were used for, show her what the contents of a tarot card deck looked like.

It shouldn't have surprised me that her mom was just as curious. It shouldn't have surprised me that she came one afternoon for a reading of her own. It shouldn't have surprised me when that reading ended her parents' marriage, blowing up Sarah Wright's whole life. Moira didn't care who the subject was, she just cared that she told them the truth as she saw it in the cards. She didn't care that most eleven-year-old girls wouldn't understand that decision.

Sarah Wright said she didn't want to be my friend anymore. She turned the other girls against me. Made me worse than a loner. Suddenly, I wasn't just the quiet girl who always volunteered to feed the class rabbit but didn't talk on the playground. I was the girl with the freak of a mom, which made me a freak, too.

The engagement invitation sits on the table in front of me, right next to the beer bottle I just finished emptying. The condensation pools on the wood, inching closer with every passing second.

My mother never worried if a thing should be said, because she was never around for the fallout.

I remember once this old guy with the saddest deep-set brown eyes came to Kismet looking for closure about his recently deceased longtime wife. I don't know what happened in the Reading Room, but whatever it was shook him right to his core—so much so that for days afterward, he came back, cash in hand, demanding she *look again*. Moira took his money every time, and every time this dumb hope would brighten his dim features, and every time she'd crush his soul.

Over and over and over until he finally gave up. Or maybe, he just ran out of money.

Solvang, California,
Danish capital of the US

I read the words again. Another thing that shouldn't surprise me.

It wasn't just one thing, one moment, one hurt that tore a rift between us, it was this one thing done repeatedly until finally it snapped us in two. Moira believed that my life and hers were intertwined, and an integral part of that involved me never straying too far from Kismet. Like I was a ghost tied to the place where I died, and she was the happily haunted homeowner.

There were lots of subtle ways she pushed her beliefs on me growing up—hints and games, loaded questions that made me feel guilty.

And then there was the prediction.

Laid out in the cards.

Irrefutable to a believer in the magic of Madame Moira. Which, at that time, I have to admit that I was.

Winter in LA is either rainy and chilly or sunny and warm. Seasons look different in SoCal, which means any resident with the means and motive will likely find themselves visiting the mountains to experience some variety. My mother was no exception.

Only her idea of a mountain vacay wasn't Big Bear or Tahoe, rustic Idyllwild or the majestic Mammoth Lakes. Since forever, Moira has been frequenting the "Danish capital of America," a kitschy, quaint town in the Santa Ynez Valley known for its charming Danish architecture, a plethora of boutiques, windmills, and Danish desserts, and—most important to Moira—an abundance of local wineries. She always stayed at the same hotel (the Hygge), where she had become buddies with the longtime owner-manager Sven Nielson, a second-generation Dutch immigrant with a love of his heritage and my mother's tarot card readings.

It was on one of those trips, on an especially blustery night, that she managed to wear down my normal resistance and convinced me to play querent in a tarot card reading by candlelight.

Wind whipped against the windows as she pulled out her deck of cards. The soft green background, with brown and plum nature-inspired accents, gave this deck an earthy feeling. Moira had seen me admiring it before—she'd brought it on purpose. She shuffled with ease. Her hands—slim and strong, most of her long fingers adorned with raw crystal and silver rings, her nails short and painted in a deep midnight blue, her favorite color—flipped the cards over and over themselves in a mesmerizing rhythm.

Cut the deck, she said, setting the cards down on the nightstand between her bed and mine. She insisted I always use my left hand. *Closer to the heart—better for the intuition*. She didn't ask me what my query was, but as the cards fell one by one, she decided she didn't need to.

The Fool: A fated new beginning. Spontaneity and adventure. Open-mindedness.

The Empress: A wise woman. Mother figure.

The Ten of Cups: Fulfillment. Happiness. Security. A homecoming. Love.

Are you looking for love, Cadence? she asked me, her deep green eyes shiny and searching. Even without the cards, the candle, and the ceremony of this ritual, Moira had a way of knowing things about you. Seeing truth you thought you hid well.

But seriously, what horny sixteen-year-old girl wasn't looking for love? Or at the very minimum, lust.

I had shrugged, wishing I had some surefire way to keep her third eye from prying all my secrets from their hiding places, but I already knew there was no escape. Not in such close proximity. Not without any shiny stuff to distract her.

She smiled. *Well, as long as you stay close by, you'll find a soulmate all your own.*

This tickled my brain, piquing my interest, turning me vulnerable. I wanted to know more. My mother had a reputation more specific than just *weird psychic witch lady who lives in the haunted house by the canyon and sells metaphysical shit out of her living room*. She was known to accurately and regularly predict soul-mates for anyone who came looking. *I can see the thread that con-nects souls seeking souls*, she said often, even though once I got smart, I repeatedly dragged her for appropriation of an Asian legend.

She didn't see it that way, no surprise.

It's all here, she said, touching the cards one by one. Claiming them, it felt like. *You'll meet your soulmate at Kismet, all because of me.*

I understood how she got that from the reading. I wasn't igno-rant of the cards' meaning. I had grown up watching over my mother's shoulder. Memorizing everything, inspecting and inter-rogating her interpretations against my own ideas.

Still. No part of me wanted to believe it.

And no part of me has ever agreed to it.

I pick up the invitation now, the memory of that night in Solvang ringing poignant and palpable. My eyes scan the details.

celebration of the engagement

My mind reels over the events that would have had to occur to make this outcome possible at all. Moira loved to predict soul-mates, but Moira had always said she would never be tied down. Not to anyone.

Not even my father fit the bill.

Not that I ever met him or know anything about him. She said he was a deadbeat and that he therefore had no right to a role in our story. I was always too scared to go looking for him. At first because I feared what I'd find if I did. And later because I feared finding him would prove her right, and the only thing I wanted by then was to show her how very wrong she was.

About everything.

So much would have had to change for my mother to get engaged. And even though the one constant in existence is change, my mother doesn't.

Wild things can't be tamed.

At fifty-eight years old, there's little incentive to turn over a new leaf and loads of inertia. Therapy might have taught me how to cope with my inherent and insatiable inclination to believe the worst about her, but the training of trauma runs deep.

This poor Richard guy has probably been duped. I don't know what possible ulterior motive Moira would have, but I'm guessing it's shitty and monetarily motivated. It wouldn't be the first—hundredth, thousandth—time she did something just because there was cash on the table.

Fuck.

Not a single fiber of my being wants to go back to LA—especially not since I will have to use some of my precious vacation time to do it, regardless of that extra day I just earned. But my stupid, dumb gut says I should. I can't let this go. I can't let her win.

And my hideous, voracious appetite to catch Moira in a lie is more compelling than my desire to never step foot in Kismet again.

I have to go.

Home.

Back to the lion's den.

CHAPTER SIX

Sydney

I'm pacing the floor, my stomach full of sashimi and gyoza and some of Joe's hamachi because he didn't order me enough considering the sheer amount of stress rattling my system right now, lighting up my limbs, firing through my brain, and making me absolutely ravenous. Every time I unlock my phone to call Dad back, my fingers freeze up as they hover over his name in my speed dial.

"Just call him," Joe spits from his reclined position on the couch, remote control poised in his hand. He's desperate to start the next episode of *Selling Sunset*, which he was in the middle of binging hard before my freak-out turned into a meltdown.

"I'm a horrible liar," I say, stopping momentarily in my pacing. Right in front of the TV. His eyes grip the screen behind me. "You know I can't hide anything in my voice."

"You aren't great at masking with me, or your dad, or Dr. Jackie," he says, referring to our shared therapist.

"Which is relevant considering Dad is the person I am trying to hide my true emotions from right now," I exclaim, almost dropping my phone into the mess of empty sushi take-out dishes, discarded soy sauce packets, and chopsticks.

"Don't you want him to be happy?" he asks, giving me a bewildered wave of his hands.

"Jesus, of course I do. That's not what this is about." He lifts his brows in disbelief and then flattens them almost as fast. "He just met this woman—online—and, what, a month later they're engaged?"

Now his brows turn into caterpillars of skepticism. "Try *three* months. You've been on the road a lot lately, so I get that your concept of time might be different than ours, but it's been three months."

"No way," I protest. He just nods. But I decide to double down. "Whatever, that's still fast."

"He's old, Syd. Time is running, there's a ticking clock, he's got needs. Who knows how long it's been since he's been intima—"

"Oh God, please *do not* talk about my dad's intimacy needs."

"Daddies have sex, too, darlin'."

"Ughhh." I shiver. "Don't say *daddy*." I almost throw up in my mouth.

"Daddy is a stone-cold silver fox." He's doing this on purpose now.

I mime vomiting, but it works to momentarily pop the crazy bubble. I deflate onto the couch beside Joe, who tugs me against him, his hand gently rubbing my shoulder. He smells like his spicy bodywash mixed with the sharp scent of ginger and wasabi on his breath.

"He's more salt-and-pepper," I reply, "but I get your meaning, weirdo."

"Call him. Hear him out. That's the mature thing to do, and

you know it." I roll my eyes. So mature. But I know he's right. The least I can do is let him tell me, in his own words, how this whole thing came about. I'm good at reading people, and especially good at reading Dad. I've had to. *Us against the world* was more than just a saying. Dad didn't have siblings, and his parents passed before I was born, so it really was just us after Mom died.

I lean up and unlock my phone. *I can do hard things.*

My finger taps his name, and Joe shoves at my ass, brows furrowed, remote pointed at the TV screen. "Other roooooom," he commands.

I shoot up, padding across the floor and down the hall as the call connects. I flop onto my bed and curl my legs up beneath me. One ring. Two rings.

"Hello there, Birdie," he answers. His voice is bright. A deep but friendly sound.

"Hey, Dad," I reply.

"I was beginning to worry," he says. I hear the trepidation in his voice. Now I feel guilty that I left him hanging while I had a (maybe slightly immature) freak-out.

"I needed a minute to process the engagement invitation in my mailbox," I say, and it takes all my focus and self-control to leave it at that. I just hope my voice is steady.

Unreadable.

"I can understand that," he replies. "And now that you have had a moment?"

This is the question I do not want to answer, at least not honestly.

Pull it together, Sydney.

My mind races. What can I say that will get him talking but won't invite much input from me? I do want to ascertain—at the bare minimum—the events, as many of the particulars of the story as possible, and try to get a read on his mood about the whole thing.

"I would love to hear the story of how this all came about," I say, raising my own voice to an octave that feels unnaturally high. I have never used the phrase *came about* in my life. Goddamn.

He laughs a big belly laugh. "Of course you would! It's a great one. On our first date, Moira said she knew the moment she saw my picture I would sweep her off her feet—a hefty order to live up to considering it has been a hell of a long time since I swept anyone off their feet." He chuckles again, and I swear to Christ it sounds like a girlish giggle. Is he high?

My mind doesn't know which part to latch on to first. The concern that my father has been drugged—probably shrooms—or that the woman, Moira, said they were destined. Who tells a person something like that? Especially on a first date when everyone—universally!—is supposed to be on their best behavior.

"But it wasn't hard to fall for her, to be her knight in shining armor," he continues.

Her knight in shining armor. The outdated nature of that phrase aside, shouldn't a single woman of her age be comfortable in her independence? I would hope that if I'm still alone at that age, I'm not seeking someone to save me from it.

I give a noncommittal "Uh-huh, that's so great" as I slide off my bed and over to my briefcase, unzipping it to reveal my laptop tucked inside. I yank it out and open it. Fuck, it's dead. As I fish around in my bag for the charger, Dad continues.

"We didn't play coy—who has time for that?" he says. I assume it's rhetorical. I shove the charger into the wall outlet. The computer slowly boots up once it's connected to power.

"It really has been the most seamless, joyful journey. I thought I was out of chances to ever feel this happy again." I'm tapping out the login password as he says this, which makes my stomach momentarily twist with guilt. "Moira said it was written in the stars that we find each other."

I bite back a snort.

"That's fun." I know I am not nailing the tone of voice I want, but the pseudo-spiritual phrases this woman uses are setting my teeth on edge. LA origins aside, I don't actually buy into this shit. "So, who asked who?" I cut to the chase because it's clear Dad isn't going to. My internet browser opens, and I type *Moira Connelly* into the search bar.

"It was really both of us," he replies. My finger hovers over the Return key.

"How can it be both of you?" I ask, a little too accusatory.

"Well, Birdie, I got on one knee and she got down there with me. The sun was setting. Chicken was curled up on her porch. We'd had a bottle of wine between us, and she'd been helping me master three-card monte," he says, referring to the well-known swindler street trick. "The perfect day. The kind of day I want to have for the rest of my life. I just dropped to my knee, and she laughed and joined me. She said no man was going to ask for her hand, but she sure could give it." He laughs. I snarl and hit the Return key to load up the search.

The results are instant and fairly prolific. I will have to wait to dive in until I have him safely off the phone.

"Well, this is really *something*," I say. *Weak, Sinclair, weak.*

"Oh, Birdie, it is. And we would love to have you for dinner tomorrow—a fancy place she loves in her neighborhood. I'll send you the details."

"Fancy?" I ask, still too accusatory. Fancy is what you do for an out-of-town guest, not your daughter. He wants me to be swayed. He knows I'm not yet.

This sends a cold trickle down my spine. I hate disappointing my dad.

My eyes flick over the Google search.

Madame Moira

Psychic

Self-published author

Kismet: metaphysical shop and portal to your destiny

There's that word again. *Destiny*.

"I'll be there," I say, clicking on the link that leads to Kismet.

⌐

The deep dive does not make me feel better about Moira Fucking Connelly putting a ring on my dad's finger. As far as I can tell, she is a snake oil salesman disguised as one of the Witches of Eastwick (probably Cher, because of the mane of black hair and searing green eyes).

"But for real, I need you to find out who does her work," Joe chimes in. *Selling Sunset* is still on in the background, but he has cleaned up the take-out debris to make space for me to set my laptop on the coffee table. "It's better than every single one of them." He points to the TV. "I am always in the market for a mentor."

"This is the woman marrying my dad, and she's wearing velvet," I say. "On purpose."

The photo on Amazon that accompanies her author page is

the same one as on the website for her metaphysical shop, right above the neon-purple button to *Book a Reading Now*.

It goes to a form. And as far as I can tell, it's only for in-person readings.

I stare at the photo. She's pretty.

"We don't know when this photo was even taken," I say. "Or how photoshopped it is—"

Joe points his finger to the screen below the pic where a photographer's copyright is displayed in tiny yellow font: *2023.* "And as an avid Facetuner of all varieties, I can assure you that this pic has been hardly touched. You can see freckles. You can see tiny crows."

She does have an ageless quality about her face, but not in a way that screams. If she's had work done, it was really by a wizard, because she looks closer to forty than sixty. She also doesn't look plastic.

Joe stands up and shuts off the TV, yawning and stretching like a cat.

"Bedtime," he says. "Busy day tomorrow—lots of foreheads to flatten." He smacks a kiss on the crown of my head. "Don't stay up stalking her too late."

I mumble a response that I hope passes as affirmation.

My phone chimes with a text from Dad, and I check the time on my laptop.

It's ten p.m.

He's usually asleep in his recliner by now. Still in his button-down and khakis.

Hi, Birdie, Moira and I are looking forward to seeing you tomorrow evening.

Then a photo appears of him and Moira sitting on the porch together as the golden-hour sun washes over their faces. I flip back to the pic of her from her website. Not only does she look almost identical as she did in 2023, she also doesn't look any more re-touched in this texted selfie from Dad.

Love, Dad.

There's a fist of guilt around my heart. I should at least give the woman a chance to make a case for her right to my father's heart. But that isn't stopping me from doing a little reconnais-sance of my own tomorrow morning. Kismet opens at eleven, and I'll be there with a disguise on.

CHAPTER SEVEN

Cadence

Kismet sits deeply and comfortably on a rolling half-acre lot. A dense fir tree curtains the roof, its long arms reaching around to cradle the edge of the river rock–accented front porch. Painted dark green, the trim a soft gray, it's more weathered than it was the last time I saw it. The front room on the second floor that used to be mine still overlooks the street, its curtains open and one of the windows slightly ajar. It has a perfect view of the Arroyo Seco Canyon and all her many whispering ghosts.

As a child, I would sit on the porch for hours, watching wildlife that lived in the fir or visited just to eat from the bird feeders or built nests under the safety of its needles in the spring. The swing still creaks in the corner. The door is still red. The roof looks in need of repair from all the affection the fir bestows on it.

This place was never just my home. There were always customers trailing in and out of the front living room: shoppers seeking crystals, tarot decks, Moira's tailor-made spell boxes, suitable for all occasions. There was Louisa, Moira's longtime best friend, who had a revolving door of boyfriends and a daughter, Lola, a girl a few years younger than me. There were the ghosts, which I never saw myself, but after hearing Moira's stories about them all my life, I was convinced they were real.

I've been back in LA over two hours—half of that spent in traffic on the way to the hotel—but it still hasn't quite sunk in yet. This place—this city, this house, the canyon behind me, the hills to the northeast—once, I loved it like a best friend. It was my stomping ground. Full of danger and wonder, hope and possibility. I don't know how long it took for it to change all the way, to become something menacing, more foe-like, but I know the reason why it did.

I shove my phone and wallet into the back pocket of my black jeans and tighten my denim jacket, hands in the pockets like that will ground me for the advance up the front steps. My booted foot against the wood sends a creak into the air, a startlingly loud sound in the quiet of this warm early-fall morning. A flock of doves let out a mournful coo as they fly to the sky.

I amble over the porch, fingers gripping the heavy metal door handle, nostrils flaring as I exhale my nerves. I didn't call ahead. I couldn't bear to hear the sound of her voice through my phone after almost four years of silence. She doesn't know I'm coming. This may be the last upper hand I have for a while.

Inside, the air is dense with incense; the light from the stained-glass windows that flank the door breaks through the smoke and dust. A bell dings and from another room—the kitchen, by the direction—and a young woman's voice calls, "Coming! Hold on!" I hear clamoring. "Fuck! My finger!" More clamoring and chaotic sounds.

My eyes trail over the living room, full to the brim with her wares. At the far end, an ornate maroon door is shut firmly. Above it on a hand-painted sign are the words *Reading Room*. Even though I can't see inside, my mind conjures the image. Rows and rows of bookshelves messily stuffed with her personal mementos, her journals, her decks, her favorite literature. A small round table, two chairs on either side, covered in velvet and lace. Candles. Incense. Moira.

A redhead with wide, bright eyes shoots out from behind the swinging door to the kitchen, yanking me from my revelry. She's sucking on the end of her finger, face screwed up in pain. When her eyes land on mine they go buggy.

"Oh my God," she exclaims. "Cadence Connelly."

"Hey, Lola," I say, unsure if I should wave or not. My hands jerk, clenching into fists in the pockets of my denim jacket.

"Thought you might be dead." Then her eyes narrow. "You're not, are you?"

Kismet.

Just like I remembered it.

"I'm not a ghost," I say.

"If you say so," she replies. We hold each other in a stare-off. She's twenty-six, maybe twenty-seven now. She's dressed in a midriff-baring Blondie t-shirt and denim shorts over stockings. She's got one ear pierced all the way to the cartilage. She has a nose ring, wrists weighted in clinking stacks of bracelets, and a tattoo of a poppy snaking up toward her rib cage.

Louisa, her mom, vanished when Lola was sixteen. Moira may know where she is but has never said. She let Lola move in, gave her a job. She wanted me to treat her like a sister, but I was in college when it all went down, and also, I've never been very good at that sort of thing anyway.

The whole family *thing*.

Lola lunges for me, and I instinctively jerk back, away, but she's wily, fast on her feet, and she grips me in a tight hug. Her hair smells of hemp and cinnamon.

"Welcome home," she says, tightening her grip. "Had to make sure you were solid."

She's the same Lola she always was.

I am the anomaly.

Lola squeezes once more before releasing me from the hug and walking over to the desk that also serves as a checkout counter for Kismet. She pulls the drawer open, removing that familiar navy-blue-and-white invitation. "I'm assuming you received yours." She waves it around as she talks. "And that's what has returned you into Los Angeles."

"*Ding ding*," I say as my nose catches a stronger smell of cinnamon and sugar.

"I'm baking snickerdoodles," Lola says as if she can read my mind. "I didn't know she sent you one—but I do know that she still talks about you all the time. Like you're on vacation somewhere, and at some point you're gonna come back. Return to your real life."

My cheeks heat, and I shift on my feet, fighting the rising urge to bolt back through the front door.

"I humor her, of course," she continues. "Because what else could I do? She's Madame Moira, all-seeing, all-knowing, and, for me, financially providing while I chase my bliss." She talks fast, her voice this husky, throaty tone that always sounds slightly congested or like she just woke up.

"Are the snickerdoodles part of that bliss?" I question. We never talk about Louisa, but I wonder if the snickerdoodles are somehow also her fault.

"Maybe." She smiles. "This week anyway." She leans back against the edge of the desk. "What I mean is, it's good to see you, Cade. Even if you're not really back."

"I'm not back," I confirm. My voice is clipped.

"Does she know you're here?" Her eyes shift to the Reading Room door.

"Not even a little," I reply.

And, as if summoned by the ghosts of Kismet in some sick loyalty to their master, the door to the Reading Room flies open. Moira emerges with a client, her hand placed soothingly over her shoulder. Her lips move, the tone too low to make out, and the woman nods, pats at her cheeks with a tissue. Without knowing anything about this woman—what brought her here or who she is—I feel certain Moira is helping her cope with grief.

They come here looking for answers. Who am I to deny them?

Kismet, Lola, Los Angeles, and me most of all—we've all physically changed with the time elapsed. We're showing the signs of our age, the growing pains, the weather, the experiences and heartaches. But Moira remains the same. Her black hair hangs long and shiny to her waist. Her figure is slim, draped in a flowy green dress, a floral shawl slung over her shoulders. Her high cheekbones and strong jaw have served her well as she's aged, acting as a framework for her freckled-but-still-glowing fair skin.

I turn away from Lola, wanting to face Moira head-on. Wanting to be ready, to feel sharp focus, have my feet firmly grounded so I can't fall off-balance. I see it the moment she realizes someone else is in the room besides who she's expecting to be there. Her nose twitches. Her green eyes—heavily lashed—blink rapidly as they lift, searching.

They land on me.

One corner of her lip edges up.

She releases the client, and her eyes shift to Lola as if to say, *Get ready.*

They return to me and hold. "The long-lost daughter returns."

The client, who is gray-headed and small-boned, snaps her attention to me as well.

"She looks just like you." Her voice has that elderly vibrato, and she clasps her hands together with awe.

"Spitting image," Moira says, a bit singsongy.

People always say that, but all I see are the differences. My smaller, slightly rounder nose, my more delicate chin, my curly hair.

My soul, her lack of one.

"Hey." The word feels weighty but also shallow. Entirely too small. Still way too heavy to hold. Her thick black brows—immaculately groomed—furrow, putting two small lines between them. *Hay is for horses*, I hear her say in my head.

"Lola, can you please help Elise with a tea bundle for emotional healing?" Moira asks, but she's still looking at me. Lola shoots up from where she leans against the desk still, watching us like we're a trainwreck. Which—fair. We kind of are. Her eyes dart back and forth, a wave of reluctance washing over her. She doesn't let it take her under. I'm sure she knows she can't argue with Moira.

That is a universal truth everyone besides me seems to agree on.

Lola guides Elise to the front living room, leaving Moira and me alone.

Together.

"I knew you'd come," she says. It's the only thing she could say, I guess, and yet I wish she had chosen different phrasing.

"That's bold. I definitely didn't have this on my bingo card for the year."

"You never were a very good gambler," she replies. My mouth purses. She moves, closing the small gap of distance that remains between us. I go stiff as she enfolds me in a hug, closing my eyes, trying to block out her scent—lavender and sage with a hint of citrus, probably lemon. All to ward off evil spirits or intentions that might try to come her way.

"Is Lola cooking something?" she asks. The question moves my hair, tickling my ear.

"Snickerdoodles," I reply. She releases me, sidestepping toward the kitchen. She doesn't motion for me to follow. It's just heavily implied in her energy that she expects me to.

I root into the ground, determined not to give her what she wants. Especially not without an explicit request. But the sound of Lola and Elise walking back toward the checkout desk and the smell of snickerdoodles growing stronger—likely because she's removing them from the oven herself—are why I move.

Or I tell myself they are, anyway.

I shove through the swinging door to the kitchen, and I am immediately smacked in the face with nostalgia. Years of sitting in this kitchen at all hours of the day, doing homework, stamping note cards with wax seals, brewing tea; late nights making margaritas (virgin for us kids) with Louisa and Lola as if we were the Owens sisters from the classic Alice Hoffman novel, or the Nicole Kidman–Sandra Bullock adaptation of it from the late nineties. A rectangular room, with a large cream-colored tile-topped island in the center. The backsplash is a lavender-and-orange combo. The floor is adorned with turquoise-and-cream linoleum.

Herbs hang in front of the window drying. Plants tuck into crevices and hang from crocheted holders in brightly colored pots.

The huge vintage stove, also turquoise, sits heavy and dominant against the opposite wall. Moira kicks the oven door closed, rising with a mitted hand holding a baking tray of perfect snickerdoodle cookies.

The smell is overwhelming. Moira plops the tray onto the burners on top of the stove and then turns.

"She's getting pretty good at the dough." She sets the oven mitt to the side, leaning down to touch the tops of the cookies with her finger. Testing their doneness. "But her timing remains shitty." Her eyes whip to mine. "You look well. Nice color in your cheeks."

She means my slight tan, which never lasts long and always leaves behind a few more freckles when it goes. She takes every inch of me in; her eyes don't move, and yet I know she perceives me. Catalogs every change I've made in the four years since I last saw her.

"I work in the great outdoors. I'm bound to catch some UVs."

She nods, and her eyes finally bounce away from me. "The house looks good, doesn't it?" She takes in the kitchen with a glance, a smile.

"The same, just older."

"I hope your next statement isn't that you could say the same about me," she quips. "I won't allow it." Her eyes flash with humor.

"You know you don't look older," I reply, biting back a smirk. "Still bathing in virgin blood?"

"Pssh, like there are any of those left in LA." Quick on the draw in every sense. She lifts a spatula from the ceramic pot beside the stove and begins shoveling the cookies onto a rack Lola must have set out before. "Just good old cold cream and clean living."

I almost believe her, except that her forehead doesn't move up and down with same dexterity it used to and her teeth have definitely been whitened. I run my fingers through my hair, a little self-conscious of the signs of my age. Thirty is respectably adult, but in her presence I still very much feel like a little girl, even if my cheekbones have sharpened and my eyes have set into some of their very own tiny spider lines.

"You're doing natural curls," she says as she admires my hair. I always longed for mine to look like hers—straight and impossibly shiny—but after years of fighting the frizz or frying it with a straightener, I finally gave in. My fingers brush the ends that fall right at my breast. "How was your flight?" She finishes setting the cookies on the cooling rack and walks toward me, a cookie in each hand. "Water? Iced tea?"

She hands me a cookie. I take it robotically.

"Not thirsty," I reply to her second question first. Her hand twitches, anxious for some activity. She settles on chewing the cookie. "The flight was long and expensive."

"I'm happy to pay you back for your travel expenses," she says as she moves toward the back door, where I know she probably has her purse slung on a coatrack. "Having you here is everything to me—"

"You are not paying for anything." Curt, no room for interpretation.

She stops in her tracks. Her eyes trail back to me. "If you're sure." She's already moving, though, back in my direction and away from her checkbook.

That was a little too easy. A thought pings through me like a pinball on a collision course. *Would that check have bounced if I'd let her write it and tried to cash it?*

"Then at least stay in your room, here—free and clear." She motions above her. "It's my yoga sound bath studio now, but I could easily get Lola to blow you up an air mattress."

"I have a hotel with a real bed and everything," I say, internally cringing at the thought of stepping foot in my old bedroom turned wellness retreat. Moira may have told people I'd come back any day, may have acted like the life I chose was little more than a detour, but it didn't stop her from taking the one space in this house that was once mine—to do whatever *I* wanted with—and turn it into another shrine to her desires.

She crosses her arms. My short, clipped replies are starting to bug her. The flare in her nostrils and taut shape of her full lips are proof. It gives me a little thrill that I have to contain from reaching my face.

"Rick will be thrilled to pieces to meet you—he likes to play skeptical. Keeps me grounded." Rick. The man she's marrying. The poor schmuck. "I told him you'd come, but he kept reminding me that even if you didn't, this weekend would be the perfect celebration of our engagement."

I can't pass up this chance to get her to talk about Rick, get some clues about who he is, what he does, whether he's a gullible sap or just a fool.

"Rick, right." I take a step toward the island, tugging one of the stools out to sit on. This concession will play well. Make her think I'm at least not about to bolt at any second. "How did you two meet?" Her lips twitch into a smile, but I can't tell if it's a reaction to my question or to my ass hitting the stool.

"You'll think it's silly of me," she says. Is Moira seriously trying to be coy with me right now? This is a new game. I crunch Lola's snickerdoodle between my teeth and chew. "I wasn't getting any younger or less lonely." Her eyes dart to mine. *Subtle, Moira. Really.* "And Louisa was always trying new men on for size, bringing them around here." Moira's eyebrow cuts up in a hook of annoyance.

"To be fair, Louisa abandoned her daughter and vanished without a trace. Maybe she shouldn't be your role model," I cut in. Moira smirks, a bit malicious, definitely conspiratorial. My face goes neutral. Can't let her get any ideas—I am not trying to be friends here.

"Well, *I* thought—what's stopping me from having a little fun?" She flourishes her hand in the air. "Lola helped me get on the app—"

I cough, spitting snickerdoodle crumbs from my lips as I exclaim, "You got on a dating app to find a guy?" The shock ripples through me.

She straightens, looking almost offended.

"Are you trying to say you aren't on dating apps?" she asks. I can't dignify that curiosity with a response, because it's not an innocent question. Moira wants me to open up about my life, to let her in on the status of everything, and—most importantly—to ascertain if I've found love outside the narrow parameters she gave me in that tarot reading when I was sixteen.

"I date," I say. "But we're talking about the love of your life here, not mine."

"Oh, Cadence," she says, her tone downshifting to something almost gentle. "He's not the love of my life." Her eyes sheen. My stomach clenches as the meaning of her words sinks in.

You are the love of my life, she might as well say.

The air in the room feels thin, as if we've just stepped up to a different altitude.

I push through the threat, zeroing in on a question to redirect us.

"What does Rick do?" My voice wobbles only slightly. Moira used to have a dramatic dimple at the right-side corner of her lip. It's mostly folded into the smile lines that have deepened in her skin, but I can still make it out as her lips quirk.

"He was a pilot for years before he lost his wife." Pilots make good money. In college I had a friend whose dad worked for Delta. "But when he became a single dad, he decided to quit so he could stay home to raise his daughter." Her eyes mist up, as if this story somehow makes him a hero and not just a decent human being capable of putting the needs of his offspring before his own desires.

Unlike some people.

"He works as a tour guide at Universal Studios right now and is studying to become a magician," she continues with a crackle of glee. "He's such fun, even if he still dresses like the manager of a furniture store most days."

I immediately imagine khakis and a pin-striped short-sleeve button-up. She pulls her phone out and shows me the two of them on her lock screen.

Rick is handsome in a *classically dignified white dude* type of way. He's got a clean-shaven face, close-cropped salt-and-pepper hair, a strong jaw, bright blue eyes, and a charming, effervescent smile. It's a selfie, so I can't see if he's wearing khakis, but I can confirm, the beige-and-light-green button-up is right in line with my imagination.

She pulls the phone back, turning it around to look at for another beat. Her face squishes up, her eyes adoring in a way that most people would call *swoony*, but I know better. Moira doesn't swoon. She doesn't feel vulnerable emotions like *need* or *dependence* or . . . love. Narcissism means she may think she feels those things, and she may be able to convince the unsuspecting of the fact, but I'm not one of them. I've been smart to her ways far too long.

Rick looks kind. Despite my continued desire to flee, I'm glad I came. Hopefully I can save this sap from being swindled or having his heart smashed to bits when he inevitably loses his usefulness.

I'm about to ask her when I'll get to meet him when I hear a *ding-dong* from the foyer. The chime that indicates someone has entered Kismet. Moira's eyes blink as she snaps out of one performance mode, readying for another.

"That'll be Gordon," she says, tucking her phone back into the folds of her dress where I assume a pocket must be hidden. "He comes once a month to get his energy cleansed. He works at a hospital." She leans in, lowering her voice to a whisper. "Morgue."

Our eyes lock. "Lucky he has you."

"Come to dinner with us tonight," she says. It isn't a request, technically, but it somehow doesn't sound like a demand. There's a waver in her voice. An uncertainty that makes a shiver shoot up my spine all the way to my ears. Moira wants something from me. "Rick will be there, and his daughter, Sydney." She emphasizes the *S* at the start of her name. "She's a pilot, just like Rick used to be. I haven't met her yet." Her hand flinches, like she's considering reaching out, but fortunately she doesn't. "I'll be outnumbered."

As if having me there would mean she has someone on her side.

I search her face. This close, I can see every freckle and line, the subtle shifts in tone, the hint of foundation and the pop of color in her cheeks. It all comes together to form a map of my mother's life in her face, a face that I used to search for any resemblance to my own.

Despite not wanting to offer an olive branch, I know I have to take her up on dinner. The sooner I meet Rick, the sooner I can figure out what's going on between them for real and find a way to drive a wedge there. Save him, or at least shorten his stay in Moiraland.

The sooner I can get back to my life.

"Count me in," I say just as Lola bursts through the kitchen door. Moira can't resist now. She grips my hands in hers, squeezing.

"Gordon's pacing," Lola says. "You told me pacing is a bad sign."

"Good to have you home," Moira says, winking.

But this isn't home. And she doesn't have me.

CHAPTER EIGHT

Sydney

I park my Audi under cover of a robust maple at the edge of the yard. The house is sprawling, but it's maintained in a haphazard way you'd expect of a self-proclaimed psychic medium, spiritual guru, and multi-self-published self-help author. My deep dive last night kept me up until the wee hours of the morning, which is why I slept through the alarm I had ambitiously set for seven a.m. It's now close to two, and after debating my ensemble for well over an hour, I am running behind on this whole stakeout thing.

I flick the visor down to examine my giant tortoise Chanel sunglasses. They may be overkill now that I see the place. It's not like I can actually disguise myself if I meet up with the matron. She's sure to have seen a photo of me—Dad loves to whip out his phone at even the whiff of interest in his pilot daughter. *Chip off the ol' block, my Birdie.* There's no way she got out of the first date without a slideshow.

Especially if the vibes were as intense as Dad made them out to be.

If I do meet her, I can feign that I'm here looking for Dad—who

I already know to be at the golf course shooting holes with his group of semiretired pilot buds. And it will give me a chance to get a one-on-one with the woman.

I yank the Chanels off and slam the visor back up, examining the yard. Patchy sections make up a few areas that sit under the cover of a dense, overgrown fir tree that looks like a fire hazard by the placement of some of the limbs over the roof.

The jacket is stupid, too. While it's a breezy sixty-two degrees today, it's not cool enough—or rainy enough—for a trench coat. Once I'm free of that, too, I'm left in a slim-fitting black boatneck sweater, dark jeans, and knee-high black boots. This works. I rip my keys from the ignition and grab up my tiny Valentino. Like 60 percent of my clothing budget goes to bags and shades, and I'm wondering if that makes me seem shallow.

I'm ready to climb out of the car, when the front door opens and a redhead dressed like an emo kid from the early aughts rushes out, down the steps to a hatchback parked at the corner. No idea who she is, but as soon as her car peels out, I climb out of mine and shoot up the path to the front door. There's a sign that reads *By Appointment Only*, but I can't imagine shopping falls into that category. At the very least, she must have an employee or something who watches the front while she's communing with the spirits or whatever the fuck it is she claims to do to read people's futures.

The doorknob is heavy, metal, ornately carved. I twist it, and the door slides open with a soft *ding-dong*, welcoming me. Alerting the staff, probably.

It reeks of incense, a smell I know well because I once dated a Reiki healer who never, ever stopped burning that shit. She had an exceptionally skilled tongue, which almost made it worth it to power through the smell. But not quite. Behind the scent of incense is one that's a lot more appealing: cinnamon and buttery, like a freshly baked cookie. The foyer opens up in all directions. Directly in front of me is a sturdy wooden desk with a laptop and a credit card machine sitting on top next to a sign that says *All Major Credit Cards Accepted* and then another sign right next to it with a QR code to Venmo. She's covered all her bases.

To the left, through a beautiful thick wooden doorframe, is what appears to be the main hub of her business. It's stuffed with products including physical copies of her books, and at the far end is a room with a red door, adorned with a sign that reads *Reading Room*, which must be where most of the swindling happens.

I'm moving toward that room when I hear a door open behind me with a swish. I swivel my head. A woman stands in the doorway, dressed in black jeans with ripped knees and an oversized denim jacket. She has the prettiest set of black curls I've ever laid eyes on. Her eyes are a simmering golden hazel; her skin is freckled and lightly tinted with a tan on the otherwise fair complexion.

She looks a bit out of place in the kitsch of this metaphysical shop.

Her eyes take me in, her face unreadable, but I do notice her attention focus momentarily on the key chain still dangling from my fingers. The bisexual flag, my little airplane, the *Can a gay girl get an amen?* charm, a fave line from that Reneé Rapp–Megan Thee Stallion collab moment.

I fight the urge to smirk.

"Can you help me?" I ask her when she doesn't offer. Her eyes trip up to mine. There's an indecipherable emotion in them. Alarm mixed with interest. A flash of intensity that makes my skin zip with electricity.

"Are you here to see Moira?" she asks. Not *Madame* Moira. *Interesting.*

"Is she here?" I answer her question with a question.

"She's with a client," the woman replies. "I don't work here, so if you need to make an appointment or buy something, you'll have to wait."

What is she doing here if she doesn't work here?

"Believe me, I am not interested in buying anything." I flick my eyes to the Reading Room door.

"The employee just stepped out—should be back any minute."

"This place is wild," I say, because even though I don't believe in mystical things—science and reason explain existence just fine for me—there is something about the air here. The way the aroma sparks your senses, sending them off-kilter. "It's not like I imagined it would be."

"Imagined it?" the woman asks, suspicion now edging its way into her even, clear, and bright voice. "You came here because you imagined it?"

"Not *because*, per se, but I did have an idea of the place before I showed up," I reply. I feel like we're discussing two separate topics, and whatever she is saying is setting her nerves on edge. She steps forward, planting those intense eyes on mine. My curiosity, once piqued, is an insatiable beast. I lock eyes with her, which sends a thrill of heat through my stomach before it pools between my legs.

Closer now, I can see the brown and gold mingling in her eyes; I can't ignore the heat coming off her, either.

"You don't have an appointment, then?" she asks.

"No, sorry, I didn't realize I needed one to stand in the foyer," I reply. Her lips thin.

"But you're here because of Moira?"

"I guess you could say that I came here because of her."

There's a noise in the other room. The creak of an old doorknob turning.

Someone is opening the door to the Reading Room. Good. This woman was clearly not planning to let me have an audience with the madame, and I didn't come here just to get weird with a stranger who is also a major hottie.

Despite how invigorating I do find the experience to be.

"Fuck," the woman curses under her breath.

"Excuse me?" I barely get it out of my mouth before she grabs me by the waist with both hands—strong, long fingers, short nails—and yanks me behind the swinging door she recently emerged from.

"What the actua—" Her hand clamps over my lips.

We stumble into a brightly colored kitchen, where she drives me up against the refrigerator, pushing me bodily (hers against mine) taut to the door, her breath coming fast and hot on my cheek. I struggle (a little, for show mostly), which causes her to tighten the grip she still has around my waist. My body surges with attraction.

She's clearly nuts, but my libido doesn't seem to care.

"I'm sorry," she whispers, eyes wide with panic. "But she absolutely cannot see you in the foyer right now. No matter what."

I bite her hand, forcing her to release my lips with a shiver.

"What the hell?" she growls, wiping her hand on her jeans and glaring at me hard.

"*What the hell* is right. You just assaulted me in a place of business, psycho."

"I'm not psycho, I'm trying to prevent my mother from saying *I told you so* this early in my trip."

My brain locks in on a few details contained in her statement. *Mother. I told you so. Trip.*

"Are you Madame Moira's daughter?" I ask, trying to see the resemblance and mostly failing. The black hair and freckles, maybe, but where Moira is sharp and mysterious, this woman is soft and vulnerable. Every feature wide, plush, gentle.

I vaguely knew Moira had a daughter, thanks to my deep dive on the internet, but most of the photos online—which are pulled from some of Moira's books—are from when she was a teenager, and in those, she had a pixie cut and looked rather impishly grunge.

Very different vibe.

"Afraid so," she says. She looks genuinely disappointed.

"Then you're here because of the engagement party."

Her brows shoot together. "How do you know about that?"

My lips twist into what I hope is a devious smile. "I'm Sydney, Rick's daughter."

"The pilot."

As recognition settles over her face, she also seems to remember that she is still holding me hostage against this refrigerator, her hand tight and warm around my waist, her tits pressed up against my shoulders since she's a few inches taller. She releases me, taking a step back.

"We should talk," she says, just as the sound of a woman's voice travels through the door. Raspy and deep, with a slight indistinguishable lilt that could be affected or could just be the remnants of an accent.

"Cadence?" comes the voice. A name.

Her name.

"Are you back there?" The voice must be Moira's.

Candence points toward the back door, holding her finger up to her lips with a big-eyed plea. Whatever's going on here, I have to find out. And—okay—I'm a bit taken in by the desperation in her face and the way her curls tuck around the buttons on her jean jacket. I give her a swift nod, pushing off the refrigerator and walking as quietly as possible toward the back door. Cadence is on my tail, so silent and stealthy she makes me think of how a cat moves across a countertop minefield.

I'm reaching for the door handle when her arm shoots around me, grabbing it first and giving it a hasty twist. I nearly tumble out the door, with her close behind, and she pulls it closed behind us with a light puff.

"That way," she says, her voice still low. She never stops moving, so neither do I. "I know a place."

"Then you'll explain your psychosis?" I ask.

"Something like that."

My eyes eat up the view as I follow her around the edge of the yard to a small gate in the fence. Her hair color reminds me of the way the sky looks at midnight. There's a certain sheen to it, a glow almost, and as she moves, the thick tendrils shift, some taking on an almost aubergine hue. She's tall, with long and lean limbs, a trim but sturdy silhouette. Her ass is taut. Her fingernails aren't painted. I don't think she has on much makeup, either. Not that she needs it.

She's gorgeous in this rugged *I just came in from the trails* windswept and wild sort of way. But she also seems to have some kind of mommy issue that could help me unravel the reason for this marriage—maybe even enough to stop it altogether.

If it needs to be stopped, that is.

The gate opens up to an alley that we take around to a side street, where a small SUV is parked. "Get in," she orders. I cross my arms. "Please."

"Only if you promise not to murder me."

Her eyebrow, just the left one, curls up. "I always thought it was stupid in movies when people did that." She yanks open the driver's-side door. "If I was going to kill you, what difference would a promise make?"

She drops into the driver's seat as a thrill wriggles through me.

CHAPTER NINE

Cadence

Sydney Sinclair sounds like a stage name. If I didn't already know she was a pilot, I'd think she was an actress, seconds away from her big break.

She's that gorgeous.

Tan skin, dirty-blond hair, big blue eyes, and pouty lips. Her body is ridiculous. Curves for days, a compact frame, immaculately manicured nails, and chic style. Basically the opposite of me in every way imaginable.

The reality that I'm attracted to her makes me feel a more intense urgency to convince her to maintain the secret of where we actually met as long as possible. Moira will sense my interest—it's hard to imagine a person who *wouldn't* be interested.

"You two need anything else?" the waitress asks. Her eyes slip over Sydney.

Interested.

"We're all set," Sydney replies, flashing a toothy smile. The waitress looks desperate to linger. But I have a case to make.

"Thanks so much," I say too curtly. "We'll let you know if that changes."

Her mouth tugs closed into an almost scowl, but it does the trick. She walks away, swinging her tray, mousy-brown ponytail bobbing.

"Alright, I'm all ears," Sydney says. "Explain yourself." She takes a sip of her lavender latte. A rim of foam lingers on her upper lip, and she uses the tip of her tongue to lick it away

I force my focus to her eyes, away from her lips. "First of all, I would like to apologize for grabbing you back there. That was inappropriate."

"But kinda fun," she says, winking at me. I blink, too stunned to speak for a second. The ease she seems to have—with me, the waitress, simply *existing*—makes my brain feel itchy. "I'm just curious why you freaked out so fully and then rushed us out of the house before I could get a look at your mother."

"More like before *she* could get a look at *you*," I correct.

"Okay, intriguing," she says. Her lips turn down at the edges in what seems to be an almost perpetual frown shape. When she curls them up, the effect is mischievous.

"If you say so." I'm trying to figure out where to start—*how* to start—and taking a drink of my green tea feels like the way to stall. There's a need for transparency here that I am not used to giving in to so easily. "Moira, she's the reason I grabbed you. She's the reason I do a lot of the things that I do—questionable or not."

"Your core wound." She flips her hair. The silky strands cascade into a deep side part, and she tucks a thick section behind her ear.

"I don't know what that means."

"I took a screenwriting class in college," she says, leaning forward to set her cup back down on the saucer. The golden light streaming in through the window makes her eyes look almost navy. "It's a term that is supposed to refer to the past pain that drives a character's choices and actions."

I'm almost taken aback by how accurate it is.

"Oh," I say, fiddling with the edge of my cup. "I guess, yes. Moira isn't the pain, necessarily—but a lot of my choices stem from trying to prove her wrong." It's strange to admit it out loud, especially to a virtual stranger.

But maybe even more to myself.

"Like in the case of today's *choice* to grab me by the waist and shove me against the fridge with your tits?" she asks. Her tone is playful, even if she's still trying to dig up the motive for my screwy behavior.

"I reacted first and thought later," I reply, brushing over the word *tits* as if it weren't uncomfortably evocative, "which is unusual for me." I pause again, trying to summon the courage to carry on down this path. "You'll think it's ridiculous."

"Try me," she says. "I might surprise you." She lets her eyes settle on mine, her gaze softer than before.

She'll be the first person I've ever told this story to.

I have to ignore my mother's voice in my head trying to tell me this part is significant. *Soulmates can't hide the truth from each other.* If I believed there was such a thing as a soulmate—fate, destiny, any of it—this would really be a problem.

"Moira is a psychic reader," I start, and Sydney shifts, elbows on the table, eyes pinned on me. She's settling in like I'm about to tell her a fairy tale. Grimm as it is, I wouldn't call it that. "She built this lore for herself among the people in her life: her clients, readers of her self-help books. She could give you closure to your grief, answers to queries you couldn't otherwise find. But if you were seeking love—looking for that thread that was tied to the soul of the person who would complete you—Moira could find it. She could see it, or at least the path to it."

Sydney tucks her hand around the nape of her neck, leaning into it for support as she listens. Her gaze is unwavering. "Soulmates. She makes money predicting soulmates." Her phrasing is a *choice*. My lips kick up into a tentative smile.

"I never asked her about mine, but if there's one thing I can guarantee about Moira—at least where I'm concerned—that was never going to matter."

What *I* wanted wasn't the point.

Her face twitches. Where I'm going with this is starting to dawn on her.

"I haven't been back to LA in four years, and before that it was sporadic." I pause, breathe, focus. "When I did visit, I tried to steer clear of Kismet."

"Wait," she interjects, straightening. Her hands cup the coffee mug. "You didn't visit your home because of something she predicted about it?" She blinks. Understanding sharpens her features. "A soulmate thing." Her nostrils flare.

Her hands drop from the coffee mug. One finger turns inward, pointing to her chest.

"I don't believe in soulmates," I say swiftly.

"But she does." It's not a question.

I lean back, nodding, answering anyway. "When I was sixteen

she predicted I would meet my soulmate at Kismet all because of her."

The heaviness of this information sits between us for a second, charged, almost electric with the way it changes the energy.

"Why would you risk coming back here, then?" she asks. "Going there at all."

"The engagement invite." I take another sip of tea, letting the soothing aromatics fill my nostrils. "She sent the invite to my old address, which just happens to be on-site at Acadia National Park, where I work. My supervisor gave it to me." I leave out the part about how she encouraged me to consider facing my issues with it—with my mother—in order to become a better, more well-rounded employee.

"You work at a national park?" I can't decide if she sounds surprised or impressed.

"I'm a park ranger," I say, unable to suppress the sense of pride in my voice.

"Ah, so that's what this *just came in from the trails* vibe is about."

"In what way do I give off that vibe?" I grip the edges of my denim jacket and tug it around me as an example of my neutral, not-trail-like style.

She points two fingers at me, sweeping them up and down. "Have you looked at yourself in the mirror? You're wearing hiking boots. You've got a *Save the Forest* enamel pin on your denim jacket." She grins. "Your hair is windswept and wild." The word *wild* twists through my gut, so loaded and still so welcome as it trips from her lips.

"LA is a very outdoorsy place." I clamp down on the exhilaration.

"But, like, in the *REI membership, hike Runyon Canyon* kind of way." I want to be offended, but I'm not sure why. She's not wrong. "So you're suspicious of this engagement, too?"

"*Too?*" I can't keep the surprise out of my voice this time.

"You first." Another cock of her brow. A clear challenge.

"Moira never wanted to get married. She was adamantly against it for herself, claiming her soul needed to be free, not bound to another person." This gets a guffaw from Sydney.

"She's a trip," she grunts.

"You have no idea." There's a twinge of pity in her eyes. It doesn't linger, but for a moment I see understanding reflected there. "Marriage, commitment," I plod on, resisting the urge to spill everything. To add *fathers* to the list. I don't want to unpack all of my trauma and inner thoughts for this woman. "The whole *till death* and *true love* thing wasn't for her. So, what? Suddenly that's changed?"

"You don't think so?" she asks. "You said you haven't been home in four years. You don't sound like you're on the best terms." She shrugs, playing devil's advocate now, when seconds ago she was readily agreeing that this betrothal is fishy. "Maybe she's changed."

"Moira doesn't change."

She looks me over, nibbling the edge of her lower lip as she considers. She crosses her arms and leans back, a more defensive, less vulnerable stance.

"My dad hasn't dated much since my mom passed," she says, her tone more guarded now than before. "And when he has, the relationships usually fizzled out pretty fast. But not this one. It went so fast that I haven't even met her yet, and sure, I've been busier than normal lately, but . . ." She pauses, nostrils flaring. Annoyed, I think, and maybe it's with herself. "He didn't tell me it was serious, which makes me even more sus."

"How fast has it moved?" I ask, because I genuinely don't know, and because I think it could be a clue to Moira's motive.

"Like three months? They went from meeting up for coffee to my dad basically living with her." She crosses her legs, pretzeling up as she leans forward. "He's bringing Chicken for sleepovers and sunset dinners."

I'm confused, and I don't try to hide it. "*Chicken?*"

"His old-man Chihuahua."

"Moira hates dogs," I counter. And many other living things that require her attention for their survival. "There's no way."

"Well, Chicken is a nonnegotiable," she says. "And she's getting all cozy. He sent me a pic showing them snuggled up."

"The speed of the relationship is a red flag to me." I am cautious to a fault when letting people into my inner world, my life. It takes time to build trust, to really see the truth of another person clearly enough that I can be sure letting them in will be worthwhile. That level of trust is something I haven't achieved in a long time, not romantically. Not even with friends—not really.

I came by this trait genetically.

"No offense, but it's hard to imagine my dad being the one to ramp up this timeline. At least not without hefty encouragement," she continues, treading carefully. I don't think she wants to offend me by outright suggesting my mother could be that outside influence or that the reason for the red flag timeline is rooted in Moira's malicious intent.

"Moira must have a reason for pushing this forward so fast. That's the only explanation." I say what she is scared to. She is taken aback.

"What reason could she possibly have?" She's searching my

face for a clue. It's the first time I've felt shitty about my suspicions. Thinking them is one thing, admitting them out loud feels like it makes them all the more plausibly true.

"I have a hard time believing love is driving her decision to get married."

"What, like she's conning him or something?" She outright cackles at the suggestion. But when I don't immediately dismiss it, her expression tightens. "You're serious?"

"There's no way to know for sure without doing some investigating, but . . ." I pause, feeling wholly ridiculous. What am I, a private eye? "I haven't been here in four years. I didn't come here to celebrate."

She curls her lip again. Mischievous. The spark in her irises is just as sneaky.

"You came here to break up the engagement."

As soon as the words leave her mouth, I recognize them to be true. I hadn't fully thought of what I was doing here as that direct, but it is. There's no other way to say it. I came here because I don't trust my mother, and if I can prevent another person from getting unwittingly yanked into her orbit, sucked through the event horizon into her black hole of a personality, then I must.

I know too much not to.

"Cadence," Sydney says. Hearing my name in her mouth shakes something loose. A dormant feeling. A sleeping beast. Our eyes lock—heated, honest. "What's the plan?"

"You want to help me break them up?"

"Call me *partner*," she says. "Let's break this case wide-open."

A thrill scampers up my spine, the heat of it curling around my ears and warming my cheeks. A partner. Someone who gets it, wants in. Someone who puts themselves in the fray with you and promises to have your back.

I don't believe in soulmates. I won't acknowledge that the Universe might be trying to turn Sydney into mine.

But a partner? I wouldn't mind that.

Even if it's only for a week.

CHAPTER TEN

Sydney

The plan is simple.

Like the most iconic little black dress.

Like an exceptional martini.

We're going with a classic bait and switch.

Tonight at the *meet the fam* dinner, we'll start by getting them to open up about the progression of their romance. I'll prod Moira about her business, using the very real truth that I don't know anything about it and I'm curious how someone can make a living doing what she does. Her self-published books aside, it seems the bulk of her income comes from Kismet. We'll push for a timeline with hard facts. Have they set a wedding date? Are they planning on having a ceremony or eloping? Anything we can use to gather clues about the fast track they've put themselves on.

"They'll probably both cite their age," Cadence had said as we plotted. Poking holes in the plan, prodding it, looking for flaws. *Vigilant* and *earnest*. Those were the words I thought as I observed her mind at work.

Her warm hazel-gold eyes were molten; her voice took on this manic, urgent rhythm.

Vigilant because she's always had to be. A feeling I relate to more than anyone knows.

Us against the world isn't exactly a mantra that makes a kid feel secure.

Sure, Dad was there for me growing up—I'm convinced it was the best he could do. An old-school kind of guy, he wasn't great at feelings. He wasn't great with periods and mood swings, and there was an Airbus-size gap in his knowledge about everything from proper bra fits to how to handle broken hearts, but he never missed a parent-teacher night and he never forgot to sign a form or attend a band recital.

He was there in a lot of ways that count, but not in many of the ways a girl needs as she becomes a woman. Vigilance can become the coping method even when you look like a messy, devil-may-care, *youngest female pilot in your airline* type of gal.

"We'll ask them why bother at all, then?" I replied, shrugging and smiling. Playing it like I was the one who would bring the chill to this duo. "The excuse for that one is a lot less obvious." Her eyes crinkled at the corners with her smile. The levity in her face didn't last long, which was good, because the way her skin flushed beneath her freckles made my stomach feel off-balance.

Pilots constantly experience our equilibrium going out of whack. We're masters at maintaining balance against all odds. I just wasn't used to the tilt while sitting at a metal bistro table in a Pasadena coffee shop where origami cranes hang from the ceiling and the windows are painted with an elaborate rose motif.

Now I flip my phone out of my purse to check the time. I'm the first one to the restaurant despite my preference for always being a cool ten minutes fashionably late. My nerves got the better of me while I was getting ready. Joe got into my head about traffic. I worried there wouldn't be parking. It was a mess in my head, and the only solution was to act. Lean into the nerves; that always gets me through it.

The sidewalk is damp from a light mist of rain; shadows and light play on the ground. The Eastside really isn't my scene, but this little strip of road is the main drag in the neighborhood, and it shows in the variety of shops, bars, restaurants, and even a movie theater lining the road. The restaurant entrance is down a quiet street off the main drag, on the second floor of a brick deco building, with a balcony that overlooks the hustle and bustle. I'm waiting downstairs for literally anyone else in the party to arrive.

I have half a mind to hide out in the bushes until they do.

I open my texts, considering starting a thread with Cadence. She gave me her number so we could coordinate or communicate under the radar from our parents. I saved her in my phone as Ranger Girl and have convinced myself (almost) that I did so simply because I didn't want either parent to know I was texting her, in the event they got a peek at my phone. I tap the icon for her fake name and open a text box.

Hey, I'm here already, I start to type.

No, that will make her think of me as both punctual and impatient. And it's not that either of those labels is wrong, per se, it's just not how I want the Ranger Girl with the wild hair and the sad eyes to think of me. I've never been late to a flight. Never been one to go with the flow. I just don't want anyone to know I'm that way.

"You beat me," a voice—Cadence's voice—says. I look up to see she's halfway down the block and moving stealthily. My breath gets caught in my throat, like a bug I'm about to choke on.

Cadence has tamed her mane into a low ponytail, the curls smooth and soft as they billow over her shoulder in a cascade toward her chest.

She's paired a hunter-green button-down blouse made of some kind of gauzy, clingy material with dark jeans and simple loafers.

Ranger Girl can sure clean up nice.

"Google got the estimate wrong," I reply, dropping my phone back inside my purse. My mouth is parched—I wish I had a drink. Thirst is *totally* the issue here. I take a couple of steps, meeting up with her on the sidewalk, a few feet from the entrance to the restaurant.

She's wearing a sharp swoop of black liquid eyeliner and a simple nude lip. Otherwise, I can't detect a stitch of makeup.

"Have you heard from your dad with an ETA?" she asks. Her hand tucks into the hip pocket of her jeans.

"He isn't a big texter, and he never, ever would distract himself while operating heavy machinery," I reply, smirking. "Especially with what he considers precious cargo inside." Her lips pinch. The annoyance gives me a tingling thrill in my stomach. "What about your mom?"

"She texted me to confirm I hadn't changed my number," Cadence says, still gritty from my needling. "Which was an unpleasant reminder that the last text convo between us ended with me telling her to get out of my life."

"Ouch." I make a sizzle sound. "That's gotta sting."

"Her, maybe," she says. "It just made me reevaluate my decision to come here at all."

"You can't bail on me," I say, lifting my brows in warning, "partner." The last part comes out too late and a little strangled.

Her lip kicks up at one corner, and she fits me with a penetrating stare. It's easy with those simmering eyes.

"It's not like we made a pact."

"Pinky swear me." I lift my hand in a fist, my pinky erect and ready.

"What are we, eleven years old?" she asks. She's incredulous, but her mouth is fighting against a smile. There's a chuckle at the back of her throat that's evident in her voice. Her eyes focus on my finger, which I am not moving. It's silly, but there is a small part of me that wants the stupid reassurance that she won't run off and leave me to untether our parents alone.

Security is never a guarantee, not even with the steadiest of people.

I wiggle my finger. She rolls her eyes.

When our skin connects, there's a *zip*. Static electricity in the air, maybe, or some other spark I don't feel safe naming—not even in my own mind. I twist my finger around hers. Locking us together in this scheme.

Just the scheme, I tell myself. *Nothing else.*

Our hands drop back to our sides, and I'm unsure what to do with the lingering energy zipping over my knuckles. The *click-clack* of women's shoes and shuffle of men's loafers from down the street jerk our attention from each other.

Even if I didn't know them, even without my suspicions, these two as a pair make no visual sense. Dad will forever cosplay the off-duty *Gen Xer on the cusp of boomer* airline pilot.

Moira, in the flesh, embodies the modern witchy motif.

Not fully Morticia but headed firmly in her direction. The hair is long, board-straight, and raven black. Like, almost illogically so considering her age. She must dye it on a semiregular basis to combat the appearance of grays.

Tall and slim like her daughter, but where Cadence has rounded features—a button nose, wide eyes, curvy lips, and a defined but still somehow soft jawline—Moira is all angles and lines. Catlike green eyes, sharp cheekbones, chiseled like a statue. She's in a flowy dress with a bright pattern; around her neck is a black stone hanging from a thick silver chain. Every finger has a ring on it.

They approach with their hands clasped, and Dad leans over to press his lips to Moira's ear. She throws her head back, releasing a bright, melodic chuckle before lightly slapping his chest. He grabs her hand, holding it over his heart.

The chai latte I had on my way over threatens to make a return. I flick my eyes to Cadence to see, yep, she's watching with the same look of abject horror painted on her face.

Dad finally looks our direction.

"Good, you both made it," he calls out to us. His smile is broad, toothy, and his eyes sparkle with joy. I almost feel bad about what we're planning to do when I see the expression on his face, and I have to remind myself that it really is for his ultimate good and happiness (and possibly safety and security).

He releases Moira's hand when he reaches us so he can scoop me into a swift hug and peck me on the cheek. He's wearing some kind of overly masculine–smelling cologne. Spicy and manly and so not his usual fresh-soap style. It sets my teeth on edge, another out-of-character move. He pushes me back, looking over my face. His eyes are just as blue as mine, just as incorrectly sky-like.

"Birdie, Birdie," he says.

"Daddy-o," I reply. He chuckles, and then his eyes shift over to

Cadence and Moira's arctic greeting. Cadence stands with her hands stuck down in her front pockets, her shoulders stiff, her eyes on her mother. Moira doesn't reach out to touch her, though the energy that radiates from her makes me think she's itching to. Her eyes rove up and down her daughter's face to her curls, to her hands, and then, without any warning, over to me.

I don't look away, even if inwardly I flinch and my heartrate skyrockets.

"You must be Sydney," Moira says, her voice rich and cavernous like a canyon. It's a sound that almost gives me vertigo, throws my skillful equilibrium off-balance.

I know she's a psychic, but is she also a witch?

I grapple for the right move, suddenly in my head about her putting a spell on me. I extend a slightly shaking hand toward her. "I must be." She swipes at my hand.

"We're about to be family," she says, placing both hands on my shoulders and tugging me in for a hug–air-kiss combo. And I just fucking *go with it*.

She's definitely a witch.

Her smell is an earthy combination of something sharp and herbal mixed with a sweetness that reminds me of buds in spring, carried by a dense, thick scent that reminds me of the way smoke billows in the air.

"And I feel like I already know you," she continues, pushing me back but not releasing my shoulders. "What with how much Rick has talked you up." I am desperate to pull away but immobile. She twines her finger through a long strand of my blond hair and then places her hand back on my shoulder. "Youngest female pilot in your company. You must really love what you do."

There's nothing wrong with what she says. But still, it hits my adrenals like a warning. Because when I lie in bed at night, unable to sleep from my inner clock being fucked by the changes in time zone, I wonder if I actually love what I do or if I just do what I do well because I never gave myself another option.

"It's a dream job," I say, my voice too pinched. Her brow does the tiniest twitch, there and gone. She knows I'm lying. *Witch*. First thing tomorrow, I'm going to that crystal shop near my apartment to get something for protection.

No, I will not feel silly about it.

"I see you two have already met," Dad interjects, moving toward Cadence with his hand extended. This does the job of breaking Moira's grip on my shoulders since Dad has to practically push through us to get to Cadence. "But I haven't yet had the pleasure." His eyes shine, friendly like always, just like his tone of voice, but there's also an edge of mistrust in them. Not as wide-open as usual. "Rick Sinclair."

Cadence lets the ice around her thaw enough to shake Dad's hand.

"Nice to meet you," she says to him. Her eyes trip to mine. "And you."

That was the other thing we agreed on at coffee. Beyond the scheme to break them up for the sake of my father, Cadence asked me to keep the circumstances of our original meeting a secret from Moira. I agreed—it works better for our plan if they think we haven't met before anyway. They won't expect us to be working together, two strangers.

But the soulmate thing doesn't matter to me. No matter how hot I may think Cadence is.

Soulmates are for fairy tales. I prefer the drama of reality TV.

"Same here," I reply to her, letting my eyes linger for just a second on hers before tearing them away to our parents. "Shall we? I think we're about to be in danger of unforgivable lateness under LA restaurant law."

Dad takes Moira's hand, and she lets him lead her through the door.

CHAPTER ELEVEN

Cadence

They seated us on the balcony at a table for four. The neon-green light of the movie theater sign glows against the dark sky. They've lit a candle and turned up the heater, and in the dance for seats, Sydney and I ended up next to each other, across from my mother and Rick, like two teenagers at a family dinner.

My phone buzzes with a text.

I tug it out of my back pocket to make sure it's not from one of my coworkers. I originally slotted myself off for three days, not intending to stay through the engagement weekend in Solvang. I had hoped I could come here, blow up whatever plan my mother was working on with this guy, and bolt home. But now that Sydney is a factor—strictly as a partner in this scheme—I don't think I can run back to the mountains to avoid the debris of this relationship explosion. I'll have to finesse the situation a lot more now, which will require a longer time frame than initially expected.

It's not Devin texting back to confirm he's covering my rotation on the trails for the next few days. It's not Nika, who I briefly checked in with before booking my flight and who had the decency not to press me on the reason for my sudden departure, though she likely assumes it had something to do with the letter I received. A part of me wanted to tell her more—take the opportunity to connect.

A very small part.

The text is from Sydney.

I put my phone under the table ledge, opening my menu to serve as a buffer so I can check it without prying eyes.

> You catch more flies with honey

I want to cut her a glare, but I'm acutely aware of my mother's attention. I glance up to see she's perusing the menu, chattering with Rick about appetizers, but that doesn't mean she isn't also perceiving my every move.

I settle on sending the annoyed-face emoji instead.

> She'll know something is up if I get friendly

> Just suggesting you ease up on the vinegar douse

Three blinking dots.

> Slowly let the sweetness in

"Should we grab champagne for the table?" Rick asks, breaking us from our covert convo. "This is a celebration." So earnest.

He looks like a male version of his daughter, except for the salt-and-pepper hair. Big, doe-like blue eyes, a downturned mouth, wide, glistening smile that draws you in, strong jaw, and strong presence.

"Wouldn't you agree, dear?" Rick turns to my mother, the term of endearment hovering in the air like a wasp.

The waiter arrives just in time for her to smile back, wink, and say, "I'll never turn down some bubbly."

"A bottle of your finest," Rick says to the waiter.

"Or maybe just a bubbly that you couldn't buy at the gas station," Sydney chimes in. "No need to break the bank on us, Dad." Clever girl. This is such a good icebreaker, immediately getting the pretense that we can't discuss money or other more personal topics out of the way. Setting us up to launch our scheme.

"Let him spoil us," Moira says, looking at Sydney. "Who's it gonna hurt?"

Sydney's face doesn't ever slip from the sanguine expression—that go-with-the-flow energy she is so good at giving off. But I can feel her nerves jolt, an electric current, a Spidey-sense that practically makes the hair on my arm stand at attention.

The waiter looks uncertain until Rick's face cracks open with a smile, a laugh rumbling in his throat. "Finest champagne it is."

"And some whipped feta with honey," Moira adds. "Extra naan." Her eyes travel to me. "Anything to add, Cadence?"

"You seem to have it covered," I reply, closing my menu even though I haven't decided what to order for my entrée. My stomach is a violent storm. I might just stick to liquids. I turn my attention to Rick as my mother's eyes bore a hole in the side of my face. "Thank you for the champagne, Rick."

For a second, no one speaks. Whether because this is the most

I've said at one time since we've all met or because the awkwardness of this situation is finally starting to dawn on the parents and now they aren't sure how to surmount it so we can enjoy our dinner. I ball my hands into fists against my thighs, letting the short tips of my nails dig into my palms. As a rule, I rarely try to lead conversations in social settings. I'm much more content to ride out the ebbs and flows of empty silences if that means I can keep my input to a minimum.

"Moira, Dad told me you two met on that dating app for the over-fifty crowd," Sydney says, her voice easy and charming. I'm struck immediately by a bolt of gratitude that I'm not trying to tackle this thing alone, relying on my skills—or lack thereof—of communication.

"Silver Sweethearts," Rick pipes up, reaching across the tabletop to take Moira's hand, right between their sets of silver cutlery.

"Silver Sweethearts," my mother repeats, lifting her free hand to rest it on top of their clasped ones. "Although, I joined through the website—Lola helped me, as you know, Cadence." She focuses on me. My eyes, my reaction. She's trying to position us as having communicated about this before, like a normal mother and daughter would.

"I'm sure you didn't give her a choice." I'm surprised when the words leave my lips, and even more surprised when she laughs.

"There's always a choice." Light flickers in her eyes, brazen. This is exactly what she wants. While I push connection away, Moira runs headlong into it. "But even without Lola's support," she continues, "I felt that soul-deep certainty that always accompanies an intuitive hit from the Universe that it was the right thing." She lets her gaze drift over to Rick's face. It settles, stays, turning into something almost gentle. All the hard lines, those sharp cheekbones, her piercing eyes—all tender. For a second she looks more like me than ever before. "And look at us, within a day Rick had sent me a nudge."

"And she had messaged me to get a cup of coffee."

The waiter reappears with a bottle of Bollinger, hitting the pause button on the rest of the story as he makes a big show of removing the metal cap on top of the cork.

"Shall I do the honors?" he asks Rick. His teeth gleam. "Or would you prefer to take the reins?" He lifts his brows in question. Rick releases my mother's hand to raise both of his in the air, waving them dramatically in surrender.

"I couldn't, I couldn't. You're the expert," he says, flashing a smile that's somehow even more charming than the young waiter's. Something tells me Rick very much *could* and probably *would* find some way to make it magical if he did. But he's letting the waiter do his thing—not trying to steal the show—and I can't help but feel a surge of respect that he is.

The waiter positions his thumb at the rim to pop it open, then works it slowly from the confines of the glass until it slips free without bubbling over.

"Bravo!" Moira chimes in. "Didn't waste a drop."

Historically, my mother is a red wine drinker almost exclusively. I've never known her to do bubbles or whites, and as a rule, sweet is always out.

"Is it spilling or just toasting with an empty glass that's considered bad luck?" Rick asks, taking a glass from the waiter's hand and passing it over to Moira.

"Bad luck isn't real." The words, said in unison with my mother, create a harmony of her deeper tones with my brighter ones.

"You don't think so?" Rick asks as the waiter passes another glass to me. I follow Rick's lead and hand it to Sydney. Our eyes meet briefly as our fingertips touch.

I seal my lips, happy to let Moira chime in first. She was the one who taught me that the events of your life aren't determined by luck.

But by action.

"And you do?" Moira asks, sounding surprised but giving him a little wink. It's weird to see her playful in this way. Caring, like she wants to make sure Rick is in on it with her, but I have a hard time believing she's not setting him up somehow.

The waiter retreats, leaving the bottle to the side of our dining space, tucked neatly inside a bucket of ice.

"Pilots are some of the most superstitious people on the planet," Rick says. He looks at Sydney, mouth spreading in a grin. "You still wear the little birdie?"

"Every time I fly," she says. "Wheels aren't going up without it."

My hands go clammy. Something about this makes me feel trepidatious, but I don't know why. It's like the way it feels when a storm is brewing in the distant sky. Crackling, darkening, but still not close enough to make you batten down the hatches.

"And you live by this superstition . . ." Moira offers that Mona Lisa smile of hers, the one that seems to say *I know something you don't know, but I'll never tell.* "Why? Because you have reason to believe, or because you don't?" This question could be for either of them, but my mother only directs it toward Sydney.

"I don't get the question," Sydney says with a cultivated boredom. "Sorry." Shrug.

My mother doesn't flinch.

"Let's see," Moira says, setting her champagne flute down on the table. Her fingernails tap the stem once. "Sometime in the past—before you started wearing the *little birdie*?" She quirks her brow in question.

"A birdie pin I got her," Rick says, sounding proud. "Because she's my little Birdie girl."

"How sweet," my mother says, her eyes drifting to Rick briefly, softening momentarily, before returning to Sydney. "Sometime before you started wearing the pin, you either had an experience that made you believe you needed this charm to keep you safe, or you didn't, and you began wearing the charm as a precaution created from a shared belief. Between you two, possibly?"

I watch the Sinclairs for their reactions.

Rick's eyes shimmer with love, adoration, a little bit of dazzled wonder. It becomes clear that he's been taken in by not only her beauty but also the air of mystery about her; Moira has captured his imagination. Something she is especially gifted in doing. This is a ride he wants to take, no matter how uncomfortable it gets.

Sydney's posture has stiffened. Gone is the boredom, the shrug she was able to deliver only a moment ago. She's on alert. And she's right to be.

"It's not hard to figure out. Dad was a pilot. He said pilots are superstitious. I'm the daughter of a pilot who became one."

"But you don't question it?" Moira asks.

"It's not that serious," Sydney says, clearly trying to maintain her chill demeanor.

"Oh, but it is." My mother's fingers graze the curve of the glass. "People seek out patterns, hold on to charms and mantras, interrogate tarot cards, all as a way to try to safeguard against a future that is unknown."

"If this is some part of your sales speech—"

"Birdie," Rick interjects, and then smiles awkwardly, nervous Dad mode engaging.

"I just mean, sorry—you're a psychic. Don't you sell certainty based on the superstitious, pattern-seeking nature of human beings by reading their supposed future?"

"No one sells certainty." She smiles again. "But I do offer a *certain* comfort to people who seek my help."

Sydney leans forward, the shimmery gold of champagne bubbling in her glass as she moves.

"Right. Fate and destiny and all that jazz is kind of your bread and butter," she says, her eyes sparkling. I press the rim of my glass to my lips in an attempt to hide my smirk.

"My bread and butter?" Moira repeats. There it is again. Mona Lisa intent on playing her games. "What a funny idea. I suppose if we want to put it in such crude terms, my bread and butter is more . . ." She twists the champagne flute in her hand, thinking. "I would say it's selling something more like hope."

Jesus Christ. I'm wishing we had launched into this conversation after the broken first-sip rule of toasting. Hearing my mother talking about herself like some kind of healer makes my stomach sour.

Sydney snorts. "And how is that different from my little birdie pin?" She flips her hair over her shoulder.

"I didn't say it was." Moira crinkles her nose.

Mayday! Mayday!

Sydney's lip does a little twitch. It's a tremor of nerve running through her face. "You said bad luck wasn't real, but you yourself are basically a charm against it for anyone who comes knocking on your door."

My mother's eyes gleam with pleasure. There's nothing she loves more than talking someone in circles until they come out on the other side believing in her powers of otherworldly perception.

"What do you imagine a person who comes to a psychic seeking information about, say . . ." Her voice trails off, as if she's thinking of an example, but I know good and well that she's not. Her eyes slide to me, and I glare back. "Their soulmate? What do you think they are actually hoping to find?"

"A time, a date, and a place," Sydney quips. I am impressed she's holding her own against direct questioning from a soul devourer.

"Funny." My mother's chuckle is melodic. "Really, though?"

Sydney considers her. Really looks at her.

"Answers," she says, finally. "You tell them what they want to hear. Of course that gives them hope." Sydney shifts in her chair, leaning in. "Just like my birdie pin makes me feel safe when I'm in the air."

"You don't question that, but you do question me."

"I have to question you," Sydney replies.

"Birdie, come on, now," Rick says, giving her a very *dad* look that says, *Don't embarrass me.*

Moira pats his hand, never missing a beat.

"Of course you do," my mother replies.

I have the distinct urge to step in and help Sydney. Take some of the heat. My mother is aware Sydney doesn't trust her—and it has nothing to do with how she makes her money. Or at least it's not solely about that for Sydney, who is clearly protective of her dad, even if that should really be the other way around. All of this has been Moira's way of getting her to admit it.

"Shouldn't we toast?" I say, holding up my glass in a desperate attempt to remind them that booze is considered social lube for a reason. "The existence of luck may be debatable, but my thirst isn't." I lift my glass, and Rick seems to be the only one listening. Moira and Sydney are locked together like birds of prey battling it out midair for a carcass.

"Questioning is a good instinct," Moira says. Sydney's face pinches in annoyance and what appears to be a whiff of disdain. "Everything should be questioned. Examined and inspected."

That's rich coming from her. As far as I remember, Moira believes in absolute truth.

Hers.

"We should probably toast to the four of us," Rick says, sounding nervous. He's looking at me for help.

"Not everything needs to be questioned," Sydney says, her eyes laser focused on Moira.

"Why on earth not?" my mother asks, the edges of her lips playing with the idea of a smile.

"Because some things are too important to pick apart." Sydney leans back. She looks like she's questioning something right now, and she really doesn't want to be. A curiosity rises in my mind, wanting to ask what it is.

"When people come to me looking for answers, that doesn't mean I tell them what they want to hear," Moira says. The Mona Lisa smile is back in full force. "But they aren't afraid to ask. They are there to listen, to work in collaboration with the Universe." She raises her glass. Ready to toast on her final words.

Round one is over. My mother may not know what game she's

playing, or that she's also going up against me, but she definitely knows one is in motion.

"Everything that is meant for you will find you," she finishes.

"Hear! Hear!" Rick says, audibly relieved as he twines his fingers with hers.

He clinks his glass with Moira's before turning to us. The last thing in the *universe* that I want to do is toast to a Moira win. When I look over at Sydney, I can tell she feels the same, but any other action would make us look like jerks and could potentially alert both of our parents to the notion that we aren't one hundred percent behind this engagement.

"Cheers," Sydney says, her voice flat.

"Bottoms up," I offer.

The musical chime of glass on glass signals the end of round one.

Moira is now in the lead.

CHAPTER TWELVE

Sydney

Dread snakes its way around my throat as I replay the night's events.

Dad tugged me aside right after the meal. Seconds, that's all we had to chat alone.

"What a ride that was!" he said, looking invigorated and enthused. "You like her, right? I mean, since she answered your questions?" Hardly! But I didn't want to disappoint him. Not when he's clearly smitten and all I have are bad vibes and the testimony of a perfect stranger with her very own vendetta.

It's after midnight. I'm still recovering from days in the air, still disoriented about what time zone I'm in, exhausted as fuck, but even after two Benadryls and a dose of melatonin, I'm wide fucking awake. I feel responsible for how the conversation derailed so completely, never managing to get on track with our original plan. Cadence tried to warn me about her mother. The cultish way her personality curls around you like rope and ties you all up in knots. I never should have let that conversation escalate as far as it did. I thought I had it under control, but, wow, did I think wrong.

I don't really know why it got under my skin so fast, either. But it was like from the moment I met her, she had some sort of dirt on me, like she was a journalist with a scoop. I just couldn't put my finger on what the scoop was. I felt weirdly exposed and defensive, like I had to prove I was stable and happy and exactly where I want to be lest she try to advise me on a better way to go.

I do not need advice—I am doing *just fine*.

We never got on topic after the toast, and I feel shitty about it.

Moira won't be easy to break, even with Cadence here setting her on edge. It's crazy to think I went that deep with her—talking about belief as if it were casual dinner conversation. I don't do that shit, not normally. But Moira pushes the boundaries.

God, I need sleep. My eyes ache, my skin feels tight. Nothing is working to quiet my mind. In my experience, there is one thing that almost always does the trick when nothing else will. I flip over, yanking the drawer of my bedside table open and pulling out my vibrator. Small, discreet, and pink, with the best sucking action known to woman. A little release might do the trick to carry me off to dreamland. I clutch it in hand, falling back against my pillows.

Everything that is meant for you will find you.

Fuck my mind for that betrayal.

How am I supposed to get off with her words echoing in my brain?

The conversation with Moira more than rattled me—I'll admit it. To myself, anyway.

I've dated around enough to know that I don't have a clue what

I'm looking for in a romantic partner, but I've otherwise always felt pretty sure-footed when it comes to everything else. It really bugs me how she poked at my belief in the little birdie pin. Sure, it's a fucking superstition that I inherited from my dad. Just like my blue eyes or my spatial awareness. Why does it feel like she was saying so much more than that?

And why do I care?

I shake my head and let out a groan.

I am right where I need to be. Successful, independent, living the dream. Single and mingling. And sure, maybe it gets old going from person to person, but the idea that I could find someone I would want for more than a few days or weeks isn't an idea that I've entertained as plausible.

It's not that I don't want it. Of course I'd like a partner to do this thing with. It's more that I don't want to rely on a person, because even your person can leave. Mom didn't choose her exit from our lives, but that didn't change the nature of her absence. She was gone, and it was *us against the world*. Just Dad and me.

I've never found another person who I thought could become a different *us* with me. An *us* all my own.

So I leaned on what I knew best. The *against the world* mentality.

Joe is the closest I've had to a partner, and we're the farthest thing from romantic. Always have been. It's nice to have him around as a roommate. Low stakes but still valuable in a way most every other relationship I've been in isn't.

I curl my fingers around the vibrator and close my eyes, willing myself to conjure up literally any image that might get me off.

But what comes is *much* more complicated.

Black curls hanging wild. Long, lean limbs. A taut but supple backside that looks good in a pair of jeans. Skin like sugar. Lips like roses.

Cadence Connelly should *not* invade my brain in this way. There's danger in entertaining the fantasy of her. Not just because of the very real stakes of our scheme to split up our parents, which, should that succeed, would make any kind of connection between us tenuous.

You don't do long-term anyway. The voice in my head taunts as my mind's eye slides over the slope of her hips. The devil on my shoulder isn't wrong. Even if this line of thinking very much could be.

But then there's the soulmate-prediction elephant in the room. Huge and hulking despite the two of us adamantly and openly declaring we don't believe in the concept. The shiver through my center, settling cold right behind my belly button, sends my eyes flying open.

Questioning is a good instinct. Madame Moira fucking strikes again.

My hand releases the vibrator, and that anxious restless energy coils around my thighs. No relief on any front. I get up, yank on my Ritz-Carlton bathrobe (stolen after a one-night stand in Vienna), and venture out into the kitchen. Maybe some chamomile tea will do the trick.

Joe is in the kitchen making himself a late-night Kraft Mac & Cheese snack. He's standing over the stove, face above the lightly rolling water to get the pore-opening benefit of the steam. I watch him for a second with his eyes closed, his lips slightly open.

Joe was the first person I told I was bi. He was an inexperienced Midwestern bi baby himself, barely out. We bonded over the experience, shared dating horrors over Slurpees at two a.m. At the time, I was just starting to come out of my sexuality shell, and I didn't yet understand how my queerness would affect my sexual experience. The broad spectrum of attraction, the way I approached intimacy—it was all a big question I was trying to answer.

Still am, if I'm honest. Romance is a whole other layer. You can feel attraction and not experience love. You can experience love and not feel attraction. Joe would say that my Sagittarius Venus just thrives on adventure, and maybe he's right.

Sometimes I fear that it's deeper than that. That if I found the right person, I would still itch to get away from them, eventually fuck it up.

Wind up on my own again.

"You're staring at me," Joe says. His eyes open, the dark row of lashes sticking together in little clumps from the steam.

"Oh good, you're awake. I was worried for a second that you were sleep cooking again," I snark. Deflection is one of my favorite forms of coping.

"You joke, but you also benefited from that little brush with sleep psychosis."

"Your snooze brownies were exceptionally yummy." I scoot onto one of the kitchen island stools.

He pours the pasta into the rapidly boiling water. "Glad you're up. This way I won't have to eat alone." His eyes settle on me, and I know I've been caught. I can tell by the way his lips twist into an almost frown.

"I'm fine." I try to head off the concern.

"Anything but," he says. "After you came home cosplaying Oscar the Grouch, I was happy to let you brood in your room for the night. I planned to draw it out of you by whatever means necessary in the morning." He stirs the pasta mindlessly. "This is better."

"Just because it's after midnight doesn't mean I'm going to be any more forthcoming."

Now he does pout out his lower lip.

"You'll sleep better if you spill it."

The problem with spilling it is I would have to know what *it* is that I want to spill. And right now the feeling is more like a nebulous orb floating in a bowl of cosmic goo. Dark matter from the core of reality.

"I don't know what's actually gnawing at me," I say in a burst of irritation. "But it's driving me fucking crazy."

Joe grabs the milk and a few slices of plastic cheese (more Kraft) from the fridge. I eye the extra cheese. He shrugs. "What? My toxic trait is that sometimes I eat literal garbage, and I like it better than Nobu." I cackle. "You're no different, Ms. Mama Zuma's Revenge Habanero Chips with a Dash of Tabasco." He mimics barfing.

"Don't knock it until you try it."

"I did try it. I had heart palpitations."

He starts mixing the milk and cheese packet together, spooning out a little pasta water as he does. "You're veering off when you should be baring your soul." He plops the cheese in the milk mixture and sticks it in the microwave for thirty seconds.

"It's something we talked about at dinner," I say, but it feels like even those words are being excavated rather than offered.

"Who talked about it?"

"The psychic," I say, pausing to watch for his reaction. In a calculated move, he turns around to grab the colander. "And me."

"So a convo between you and the woman you're treating like a pariah for falling in love with your dad"—he dumps the pasta out—"has you all shredded up?"

"Do you know why you're here?"

"Like, on this planet?" He makes a yuck face. "Pretty sure it's because May and Daniel Lee boned."

I cackle. "You know good and well that's not what I mean."

He rolls his eyes. "I don't think about it like that. Like there's some grand master plan and I'm meant to figure it out." He adds two pats of butter to the noodles, then points at me with his knife. "Do *you*?" He dumps the sauce over the top and stirs. I fidget with discomfort over the direction this is heading.

"I am tonight." I sigh deeply. His brows cinch.

"Because of the psychic?" he asks.

"Have you ever talked to a psychic?"

"No, not my thing. Though I think my mom got a saju reading for me when I was a kid." When my face makes it clear that I don't know what he means, he elaborates, "It's a Korean form of reading your fortune." I nod. Makes sense and sounds interesting.

"Did it say anything about soulmates?" As soon as the question leaves my lips, my head feels light and weird. Questioning everything also means questioning my belief in *that*.

"God, probably, but I don't really believe in soulmate messaging," he says, spooning servings of pasta into bowls. He gives himself a heftier portion. "Even if I did, like from a purely romantic, daydream, pie-in-the-sky sort of place, it wouldn't change the way I live my life."

I tuck in to the bowl for a bite. "Why wouldn't it?" I ask around my chewing. Joe takes a bite, chewing slowly. Buying time to get his words just right. The Scorpio comes alive at night. He's at his most philosophical, most intense, most thoughtful.

"Because love is still a lot of work, whether it's with someone the universe fated for you, or whether it's just someone you choose and keep on choosing."

He's always known deep down that he wants to get married, have kids, settle into a little bungalow, and barbecue on the weekends. He doesn't have a gender requirement for his happily ever after, but he knows that he wants it. Me? The only thing I know for sure is I'm terrified to love a person so much that my life becomes partially theirs.

"Sometimes I forget how poetic you get after the witching hour," I say, deflecting the uncomfortable feelings rising to the surface of my skin.

"And I forget how emo you get," he says with a snort.

I shovel a few bites, one after the other, into my mouth. Trying to push the image of Cadence out of my brain again.

It's illogical, almost intrusive, but somehow I feel myself letting her get under my skin when I should be guarding my peace with an arsenal of fire. All of this stuff has me questioning more than I want to. The only way to shake the feeling is to say it out loud.

"If I tell you something wild, you have to promise not to be weird."

"You know who you're talking to, right?" he replies.

"Exactly." I wait. He rolls his eyes.

"All right, I promise," he says, raising his left hand and placing his right one on his heart.

"When Cadence—"

"The park ranger daughter of the woman you want to send to the other side of the galaxy?" he interjects. I nod.

I decide to deliver the information as succinctly and swiftly as possible.

"Cadence believes that when she and I met at her mother's shop, we fulfilled a soulmate prediction Moira gave her as a teenager, and it's freaking me out in the context of everything else."

Joe blinks at me. His lips drop open. His dark eyes narrow.

"*In the context of everything else*," he says, putting dramatic air quotes around the phrase. "You think she's hot."

"No—well, yes, but that's not the point at all."

"It sounds very much like the point."

"I just told you her psychic mom predicted the exact scenario we met under, and this is the part you choose to fixate on?"

Joe screeches, tossing his head theatrically. When he brings it back upright, he smiles. Genuine and open. "Sweetie, you don't even believe in long-term relationships."

I want to defend myself. I want to argue.

"And what if this whole time I've been wrong?" I set my bowl down on the countertop, dropping my fork back inside with a clink. Joe sets his bowl down and comes around the island to swivel my chair so I'm facing him. He places one hand on each shoulder, dropping down to look me right in the eyes.

"Then you change your mind," he says tenderly. "And you invite in whatever new truth you want to embrace."

Change is my least favorite word.

Not for how it sounds or the way it rolls off the tongue. It's the way it grips me right in the throat like a clenching fist. It's the way it sends shoots of electricity from my heart to my stomach to my fingertips and toes. The flight response that has nothing to do with landing a plane.

Horrible, terrible, incredible.

Coming right for me no matter how hard I try to avoid it.

CHAPTER THIRTEEN

Cadence

Well, that plan got fucked.

Sydney's text, sent moments after we left the restaurant last night. She followed it up with an apology, which she didn't need to do. It isn't her fault Moira bent the conversation to her will. I spent the rest of the night until I passed out worrying my mother's probing her about her beliefs, digging at her surface to try to see what was underneath, would spook her. Sydney doesn't seem easy to scare. She also doesn't seem like a person who likes to be fenced in.

That conversation was barbed wire meant to trap.

I just can't figure out if my mother is setting the trap solely for Sydney or for us both.

I can't even examine the notion that she knows Sydney and I met at Kismet—there's no logical reason to think that she would. But the spooky terror my mother dredges up in my soul isn't based on logic, reason, or any of the things I hold most dear. It's a deeper root, the kind you can't just pull out. One that, in order to fully understand, you'd need an advanced degree in psychology and an endless well of time and patience. Neither of which I have.

I won't give in to the gnawing at my brain trying to convince me she was manipulating Sydney into discussing cosmic concepts because she knew how we met. Where we met. And even why.

You'll meet your soulmate at Kismet, all because of me.

The specificity is a coincidence.

Sydney is not a romantic interest.

As if on cue, a black Audi rolls up to the curb opposite my rental car, and the bodacious blonde who is very much not in question climbs out. Dressed in painted-on jeans and a flouncy cobalt-blue sweater that hangs off one shoulder, exposing it bare. She closes the door with her ass because her hands are full with two to-go cups and her purse. She scans the road before crossing in front of my car to the passenger door.

She falls into the seat, the scent of rose and jasmine filling the car, likely from her perfume. She whips off her sunglasses, tucking them into her hair glamorously. She lined her upper lid in a shimmery golden brown before sweeping it with a similar coppery color. The combo, multiplied by the sweater, turns her eyes sapphire.

"Okay," she says, thrusting a cup toward me. "Green tea with honey and lemon."

I take it, openly baffled. "How did you know my order?"

Only one corner of her lip curls. "The coffee shop yesterday," she says. "I pay attention to details, Ranger Girl."

"Ranger Girl?" Apparently the only sentences I can muster this morning come in the form of questions.

"Trying it out," she replies, taking a sip of her coffee. "Ranger Girl." She says it again, the other corner of her lip curving up. "I like it." I can't tell if it's the nickname or her little twist of a grin that sends a thrill straight through my center. Regardless, I take a deep drink of my tea to drown out the sensation. "Tell me we're not just staking the place out," she says. "Not after last night."

Her lips flatten—all whimsy gone in a flash. I can feel her disappointment pulse through the air. I'm hoping the plan for today will help dispel the lingering bad taste of last night from her tongue.

"We very much are not *just* staking the place out," I reply. "We're going to follow Moira while she runs errands."

Her eyes narrow. Interested, but skeptical.

"How do you know she's going to be running errands?"

"I called Lola," I say. "Told her I wanted to come by to go through some old stuff in the garage but didn't want Moira to be around while I did it."

"And that didn't send up any red flags?"

"She's acquainted with the bad blood between Moira and me. It would probably be more of a red flag to her if I was actively seeking out one-on-one time."

"A legendary feud," she says. The phrasing stokes those same warm embers in my stomach.

"Lola has her own mother issues," I reply, trying to tamp down the heat. "She's empathetic to the cause."

"Unfortunate that she relates," she says, fiddling with a tiny loose thread on the edge of her sweater. All I know about Sydney's mom is that she passed away, leaving Rick to raise Sydney alone for the rest of her teenage years. I don't know what it would be like to lose a mother, especially that young, especially if you were close to her. It feels like a tricky topic, considering my mother is still very much alive and until this week I was actively choosing no contact. There's a difference in removing a person from your life and having that person taken away.

I'm staring too long. I flick my eyes back toward Kismet, sip my tea.

"But it's convenient," I say, voice rocky.

"Glad she's on your side," Sydney says, a subtle shift in the way her voice sounds. It's like she doesn't want to let the mother talk get to her. Like she's shoving it away, burying the emotion rising up. The pain.

To me, other people's feelings are like the ocean's waves, treacherous, consuming, fascinating but overwhelming. It's been that way as long as I can remember, and it's made everything from my friendships to my romantic entanglements rife with complexity.

Shutting people out is just easier. A fact that, I can admit, may not entirely be my mother's fault, even if it's been made more complicated from the force of her influence. My mother connected my own skill with empathy back to an inherited psychic ability.

Back to her. The origin of everything.

And then she used that to try to convince me that becoming just like her was my path to success. Kismet was supposed to come to me at some point, but when I told her I didn't want to do what she does for a living, that inheritance was snatched back as fast as it was offered. I guess, except in the event of her untimely death. But even then, I'd expect her to have planned for it.

She'll have seen it in the cards and willed the place away from me in spite.

"Lola told me Moira has a few errands to hit in town before the weekend." I have to lock all the rumbling thoughts and feelings firmly behind a steel door. I shouldn't be daydreaming about Kismet or the life I could have had if my relationship with my mother were different.

I can and will focus on the task at hand.

"So you want to tail her?" Sydney's voice is underscored with new energy. I feel relief as the conversation moves along. "What makes you think we'll learn anything worthwhile? Her errands could be, like, the dry cleaner and Trader Joe's."

"Because one of her errands is the bank," I reply. "Lola talks a lot."

Her lips tug toward a smile and she sits back in the seat. "Well done, Ranger Girl."

There it is again. That bolt of heat. The nickname-smile combo is lethal. Addictive. I don't immediately shut it down, even if I probably should. Her shoulders drop down into a more relaxed stance, and she sips her coffee, calmer. She looks toward Kismet, her eyes raking over the facade.

The face, as Moira has always called it. Kismet has always felt especially alive. Serving the community as it does, all those people coming in and out, all that energy flowing through the doors, seeping into the wood beams.

Living, breathing, and completely unique.

"Did you always live here?" she asks, not looking away from the house.

"I was born on the Westside in a tiny apartment. Midwife, no drugs, all her." I wouldn't believe the story if not for the framed photographic proof displayed proudly on a shelf in the dining room. Grainy, just her on a bed of blankets, holding a new, gooey me.

"I was a hospital baby. Epidural and induced. Late to my own birthday," she says, her smile soft but a little sad. She looks back to me. "That's what Mom said."

"Early and angry, according to Moira," I reply, pointing to myself. She laughs, a bright sound that breaks up the heaviness in the air.

"Honestly, I could see it." Her eyes take me in, and I wish there were somewhere to hide away. "How long until you moved to Kismet?"

"I think probably two or three years. My earliest memories are on the porch, looking up at that tree." I point to the fir, hoping it will push her focus back to the house and off me. It works. Her eyes trek the expanse as the memory crashes into me of many hours spent alone with nothing but the company of that *wild thing*.

You and the tree aren't that different, you know, I hear Moira say from somewhere far away, as if the words approach on the wings of a bird seeking shelter in the very same tree. There was something about the wild parts of this suburban world that always felt more real to me than the concrete or the shiny skylines ever could.

"She opened Kismet when I was still in diapers," I add, desperate not to get lost in these feelings.

"What a bizarre place to grow up," Sydney says, her voice pensive. "Don't you think?" She looks back at me to confirm.

I'm taken aback by the question.

Growing up, I was the weirdo at my school. The girl with the psychic mom. The girl with no dad. The girl with no friends besides the trees and the creatures that live in them. But it wasn't like anyone ever asked me how I felt about it all. It wasn't as if anyone ever wondered if this was what I wanted my childhood and adolescence to look like.

"Sorry," she says, likely course correcting due to the way my face scrunched up when she asked the question. "I just mean having so many people in your space, like, all those strangers in and out, the way they must have acted toward Moira—or you."

"No, you don't have to be sorry," I fumble through. "No one's ever asked me what I thought of it." Her eyes droop as understanding registers. It blasts through me like a warm breeze. I have to swallow the frog of feeling in my throat. "I'm just surprised."

She nods, waiting for me to pull myself together. Giving me space to put years of loneliness and isolation into words.

I look back to the house because it's easier than looking directly into Sydney's eyes.

"It was lonely, even though it was always full of people," I start, surprising myself with how easily the words do come. "None of them really paid attention to me, and if they did, it was only because they were interested in Moira and the guidance she offered them." It's hard to dam the flow of feeling now that the water's broken free. "I was just another component to her mythology, like a talisman she would sell in the shop. Her daughter, *surely magical herself.*" I furrow my brow, telling it as if it were a direct quote. My eyes sting; I don't know why this is making me want to cry. "They were always disappointed when they were wrong."

The front door swings open.

Moira steps out, dressed in a loose-fitting linen pants-and-blouse combo. I'm jolted back into myself and immediately slouch down into the seat out of view. Sydney ducks with me, her head coming close to mine as we try to pretzel behind the dash. We listen for signs she's leaving. I chance a look at Sydney as we wait, anxious and uncomfortably aware that I just bared my soul without an ounce of hesitation in a truly out-of-character brush with vulnerability.

I'm surprised to see her eyes bright with the remnants of moisture—they almost glow. I'm terrified when they land on mine, her breath and mine so close that they mingle, the flush in her cheeks robust.

"Showtime," I say before she can show me just how deep her own empathy goes.

There's the sound of Moira's engine, the screech of her tires peeling away from the curb.

"Ready, Ranger Girl." Sydney has the decency to let the moment rest. Even if I may never recover from the aftershocks of allowing so much honesty to shake loose or how easy it was to entrust her with it.

⌒

The bank is a deco building right next to a West Elm and a California Pizza Kitchen. Sydney and I parked at a meter around the corner before slinking out of the car to follow her inside.

"I should have worn something more incognito," Sydney says as we approach the doors. The windows are heavily tinted like most bank buildings, so it's hard to see inside. I stop Sydney at the door, tugging her around to the row of begonia bushes that flank this side of the building. The magenta blooms waterfall over her head, reaching around her like a hug.

I can understand the inclination.

What? I shake the thought out of my head.

Focus. I twist my hair into a tight bun in the hopes that hiding the curls will help hide me from Moira inside.

"How do we want to do this? One at a time? Together?" Sydney asks, sounding simultaneously nervous and exhilarated. She's wearing these square Chanel sunglasses in a gray tortoiseshell, the lenses almost as dark as the windows of the bank. It's impossible to see her eyes.

Moira is observant when she's in control of her surroundings, but out in the world, *aloof* wouldn't even begin to describe the level of untethered she is. When I was growing up, she regularly got distracted by existing and ended up being late to everything from school pickup to swim meets to my graduation ceremony.

"She won't be looking for a tail," I say, convinced we can get in without her noticing.

"I don't think we should both go in, even so. Two of us lurking around the corners of a bank? They'll think we're casing the place."

"Us?" I give her a look of disbelief.

"It's a bank. They keep money in there. They're weird about anybody standing around glaring at their customers," she argues. "We could easily be a Zillennial Thelma and Louise."

"I am not a Thelma or a Louise."

She grins. "You sure about that?" I roll my eyes and she barrels on. "I can go in as the eyes and ears."

"You're going to draw the eye a lot more than I would." I flick my eyes up and down over her. Impossible to look away from, easy to notice.

"You're her estranged daughter who lives out of town," she counters, hooking the curve of her waist with her hand in a pose of indignance. "If she sees me, I can just say that I bank here."

I don't like the idea of her going in alone and potentially getting caught in the jaws of the beast, but I can't deny the validity of her argument. Moira might be suspicious of her story, but she's less likely to question her on it since she's trying to impress her as part of whatever con she's working on her dad. She wouldn't want to make waves with Sydney, at least not in the obvious way. Waves with Sydney would spell trouble with Rick—of that I am certain. He may be smitten, but he's been her devoted dad, widowed and raising her on his own, a lot longer than he's been worshipping at the altar of Moira.

"Okay"—*fuck*—"okay, you're right," I have to concede. She buzzes, her body doing a shimmy of glee that is almost pornographic with her standing so close to me. She tugs her glasses down, tossing me a devilish look.

"Wish me luck," she says, brushing past me toward the entrance.

"Text me," I call after her. "Updates." She turns, glancing over her shoulder, giving me modern Jessica Rabbit.

"Aye-aye, Ranger Girl."

And for the third time this morning, a burst of heat zips through me, warming all my chilly corners, turning my gray shadows gold with light.

CHAPTER FOURTEEN

Sydney

The automatic sliding doors part to let me inside. As soon as I cross the threshold, I change course, gliding around the bank of partitions where patrons fill out deposit slips. *Paper deposit slips*. I wasn't aware they even made paper deposit slips anymore. All my checks are direct deposit, and on the rare occasion when I actually need cash money, I just go to the nearest ATM and stick in my card.

I give the room a sweep with my eyes as I come to stand near the popcorn machine. The smell of stale butter fills my nose, and I'm tempted to grab one of the premade bags inside. It's a sickness, my affinity for garbage food—*Ooooh, they also have cookies?* Maybe I'll change banks—

"Ma'am, can I help you?" asks a pinch-faced man with a silver comb-over and garish sweater–vest-jacket combo. I'm offended by the insinuation in his tone and his tight expression. Yes, I am lurking like I'm staking out the place—no need to be rude about it. I shove my Chanel sunnies up into my hair so he can get a look at the irises.

"Just deciding on a flavor," I reply. "Of cookie."

"Do you need help with that?" His eyes cut deep. "Or with anything else?" His focus is on my glasses, probably clocking the brand name. He swims in my vision as I try to see behind him to find the one woman I need to get close to in a sea of people.

"I . . ." I say, stalling with a pause as my eyes search behind him. "No, I don't need hel—" I cut myself off when my eyes home in on my target. Across the room, Moira is being seated at a desk by a sturdy Black man with an excellent beard. "Actually, I do. I would like to open an account." My eyes snap to his, which immediately widen with his smile.

Cha-ching, they seem to say.

"Oh, of course, I can absolutely assist you with that. Right this way," he says, straightening his tie, his glee barely contained. I left my purse in Cadence's car, my wallet and ID inside. If opening an account gets any further than preliminary chitchat, I'm in trouble.

He motions for me to follow him, and I'm falling immediately into step, eyes on Moira's position, thoughts on my Louis Vuitton in the front seat of that rental SUV, when I feel a text come through in my back pocket, distracting me.

"Oof," I gasp, as I nearly topple into my escort.

"Your cookie?" The banker points to the tray of picked-over baked goods that still look incredibly delicious somehow.

"Right, can't forget that." I reach for the nearest one, which looks like it's probably oatmeal raisin, and he clears his throat. His eyes widen as his head gives an almost imperceptible shake. My fingers twitch, hovering, uncertain now.

"Peanut butter," he says. "Trust me."

I almost laugh at the straight-faced seriousness he delivers his warning with. But I grab the peanut butter instead. He starts walking again, with me close on his heels, in the direction of the section of desks.

"Let's get you started, Miss . . . ?" he asks, searching for my name.

"Sydney," I say. "Nice to meet you"—my eyes drop again to his name tag—"Duncan." Robotic niceties aren't usually my thing, but they are almost always required on the job. Pilots have to be perceived as kind and reassuring while also maintaining strict boundaries with everyone on board. I've developed the skill despite my aversion.

My professional smile is legendary in my fleet.

I turn it on for Duncan and let him lead the way. I need to get close to Moira so I can eavesdrop, but I don't want to get close to her on the way. Which is what it looks like will happen if we keep walking in this direction, at this trajectory.

I do a quick scan of the surrounding desks. They're all separated by privacy dividers without being closed off. In the one directly next to her, a couple sit with their chairs close, the man's arm slung over the woman's seat. They're talking to a brunette banker. Any one of them would get me close enough that I could try to listen in, but I don't want to cross behind and beside her to sit down.

I catch up to Duncan. "Which one's your desk? I need to pop into the restroom real fast." I flash my pearly whites. He blinks in the glow and then points toward the desk that's situated directly on the other side of Moira. *Jackpot.* Except I'll have to sneak into the cubicle from a different angle if I don't want to be seen by her.

"Excellent," I say. "Can you point me in the direction of the facilities?"

"Just on the other side." My eyes trail over and up to the simple black rectangle marked *Restrooms* dangling just beyond the sea of desks.

Fuck.

There is no direct line to them that doesn't put me potentially in her sights. My brain whirs, the cogs spinning fast, trying to think of a solution. All I want to do is ascertain something, anything, about why she has to come to her bank a day before leaving for a weekend of wine and good times in the Danish capital of the US.

All I want to do is not fuck up the plan again.

"Great," I say, stepping off before I've actually figured out what I'm going to do. "I'll be right back." I can feel him tracking my every move, and I can't blame him for his renewed suspicion. Nothing about the way I'm acting is communicating *trustworthy future customer*—it's rather more like *low-level heist decoy who's starting to rethink her line of work*.

I can't go to the bathroom now, because any route I take that isn't direct will surely get me detained for questioning by Eagle Eyes. *I'm going to have to get caught by Moira.* The thought dawns on me just as Duncan clears his throat behind me. I can feel him readying a query, and even without looking I imagine him raising his hand, finger lifting. My hovering anxiety is way too squirrelly for the inside of a bank.

It's unthinkable what I'm about to do. But it's the only way.

My cell buzzes again. *Sorry, Ranger Girl.*

"Moira?" I call out. Heads turn around the room. "Wow, that is you." I step forward, painfully aware of Duncan edging close, ready to pounce.

Moira turns with absolutely no urgency at the sound of my

voice. Her eyes lock with mine, momentarily searing, before she adjusts her gaze. A smile spreads her cheeks to show off all of her bright, straight teeth.

"What on earth." She says the words in a tone that I would describe in any way *except* for *happy to see me*. The banker has a few papers laid out in front of him. As I near, she stands to greet me, blocking my view of the desk.

And my eyes catch on the dark form of her daughter entering from the south side of the lobby.

CHAPTER FIFTEEN

Cadence

The great thing about banks—universally—is the fact that they always have large leafy plants in their lobbies. Perfect for hiding behind. I slip behind the fiddle-leaf fig to the right of the doorway. It's healthy, clearly being cared for correctly—I mentally tip my hat to the employee who must be responsible. My fingers brush the lush oversized green leaves that spring from the thin trunk and make a great disguise for my face and hair. Even with it pulled back in a bun, I know I'm recognizable to my mother.

From here, I have a full view of Sydney, but only a rear view of Moira. Sydney's features have taken on the overexaggerated roundness of a liar. That bright, too-open expression that is trying to look as if it could never conceal anything in an attempt to conceal everything. There's something happening with the banker who was following close behind her as she stops whatever path they were heading on, presumably because she realized it wouldn't yield her what she wants and decided on a plan B that is probably more of a suicide mission.

It involves talking to my mother, so it must be.

She hands back a cookie and dismisses him, an action that makes his already pinched features turn in on themselves in a sour expression.

Now it's a back-and-forth between my mother and Sydney. The man Moira was meeting with stands, moving away from the desk and the papers on it. My eyes quickly scan the space. There is a clear path through the desks to the one directly behind his. If Sydney keeps Moira engaged, I could potentially sneak into it and get eyes on those documents before the banker puts them away.

I don't have time to wait it out, and I can't send Sydney a message to keep Moira's attention focused on her. I just have to hope she and I are on the same page about the goal of today's mission and that she will instinctively know to act as a diversion in any way she can manage.

She's talking animatedly, and the banker with the cookie is walking away now. The other one is distracted at a bank of printers and other ancient-looking office machines. It's now or never. I step out from behind the fiddle-leaf fig and into the fluorescent lights. As casually as possible, I walk toward the nearest empty desk cubicle. There's a half-wall partition between it and the desk directly beside it, which is occupied. I catch a few words about percentage rates, a snippet of a woman saying "that does seem high," and then I'm gone, moving diagonally across.

I have to make a quick pivot over to the next desk when I notice there is a woman sitting at the one I was aiming for, silently eating her lunch and scrolling on her phone. She is so absorbed in her yogurt parfait and—I glance at the phone, which is propped up against her desktop computer—a cat-riding-a-skateboard video that she doesn't notice me nearly barreling into the partition separating her desk and the next.

I crouch in this two-sided cubicle, listening. I am closer now to my mother and Sydney, but not so close that I can make out the whole convo over the hum of noise in the bank. There's something about places that are supposed to be quiet. To me they always feel loud.

Or maybe it's just the anxiety that I will draw attention to myself in a space where you aren't supposed to draw attention to yourself that makes the inside of my head feel all buzzy.

"That looks important," I hear Sydney say, her voice laced with blatant curiosity. I wince. There is no reason to believe my mother's senses won't be on alert with the sudden appearance of her future stepdaughter—wow, first time I've thought those words. Never want to again.

"Business," Moira replies. "You and Rick with your day jobs don't know what it's like being an entrepreneur." *Insufferable, but okay.*

I rise slowly, peering through the little window in the partition between the desks to see that the banker Sydney gave the cookie to is on his way back to Moira and Sydney, leaving his desk—an opportune spot for spying—open. From there, I expect that I will be able to get a look at the papers Moira came here to discuss.

I shimmy across the carpet in a hurry, momentarily squatting, ear to the partition, listening.

"As soon as I know, you'll know," Sydney says. I slide up to see Sydney is taking a business card from the banker whose desk I'm currently hiding in—fuck, fuck, he looks like he's planning to head back this way—when I feel eyes on me and freeze.

But it's Sydney. Momentarily our gazes meet through the glass.

"Duncan, could you also grab me a water?" Sydney calls after him.

I catch the tail end of a smirk on her face as relief floods through me.

Partners. The word, the pinky promise. The thing we're somehow doing despite the insane circumstances.

I force myself to focus, immediately dropping my eyes to the papers on the desk. They look vaguely *loan-like.* Legal paper size. There at the top is some information about the property address—Kismet's property address. These could be loan documents about Kismet, which doesn't make sense to me. As far as I know, my mother doesn't have an active loan on the place. When I was fourteen, she had a big bash—invited some of her regulars, including Louisa and Lola before Louisa bailed on her whole life.

I remember it clearly because Lola and I hid out on the roof with a thermos full of hot chocolate and some desserts we swiped from the party.

I remember because Moira called it her *Debt-Free Dream* and made everyone pull cards about their own financial futures.

Kismet didn't have a loan on it years ago. But does it now?

I'm about to get a closer look when Sydney says, "I am a little curious about what it takes to start your own business and especially to run it successfully for so long."

The hairs on my arm stand. *Alert.*

"And I'm a little curious about what your future holds," Moira says.

No. *Fuck.* My eyes shoot to Sydney. She looks taken aback but not on high alert. She *should* be on high alert.

"My futu—Why?" She blinks.

"You seem to have a lot of questions about it yourself—whether you want to move, buy, or sell? Change careers? Love?" I am struck by two simultaneous thoughts. *I didn't know she was thinking about changing careers. But maybe Moira did.* And *the game from last night isn't over*, she's just been waiting to make her next move. "I'd love to give you a reading." Her hand grips Sydney's. "On the house."

My heartbeat shoots up, sending a whir of blood rushing past my eardrums.

"I've never had a tarot reading before," Sydney replies. Her voice quivers, a different curiosity laced through it.

"I'd consider it a high honor, then, to give you your first."

Moira whirls back to face the desk and her loan docs, and I just barely drop below the glass before she sees me. "I think we have what we need here."

A flurry of texts from Sydney make my phone buzz repeatedly.

> I left my purse in ur car

> gonna ride to kismet with ur mom

"If you could just forward everything to the email I gave you . . ." Moira's saying.

I text back: do not let her give you a reading

"I will happily finish my end of this over the weekend," my mother's voice continues.

I have to, Sydney replies back. Follow us

"I Ubered," Sydney says, and I assume our chance to text has ended. Meaning my chance to talk her out of this disastrous idea is over as well. "I just realized I left my purse in the car."

"I hope they can recover it," Moira replies, looking alarmed.

"I'll have to use the app and see if the driver will meet up with me somewhere," Sydney replies. "Can I catch a ride with you back to Kismet?"

"Ready when you are," my mother says.

Oh, I bet she is.

⌐

For the second time today, I find myself hiding behind a plant. This time I'm outside my childhood home, crouched in the begonias, looking in through Moira's Reading Room window. I parked down the street where I could see the front of the house but couldn't be seen by them as they pulled up beneath the jacaranda tree near the curb and parked. I still don't know what Sydney learned about the reason for Moira's bank visit, since she wasn't able to text me without drawing the Eye of Moira to her, and now I have the added anxiety of worrying that Sydney has been saddled with the difficult task of surviving a tarot reading without revealing our secrets. I should have been the one to go in instead of her.

I could have easily walked right up to Moira and asked her what the bank meeting was about. I could have insisted she be square with me, and even if she refused, played coy, tried to dodge, I could have played the indignant daughter and forced myself into the conversation.

I could have, and maybe I should have, but when Sydney suggested she be the scout, it felt logical, reasonable, like teamwork,
which isn't something I'm used to having offered my way. I wasn't
the girl chosen first in gym class—not because I wasn't athletic but
because I was a weirdo. I wasn't the girl people wanted as a study
partner or to sit with at lunch. I've always told myself it's because
I prefer my solitude, but even I know that isn't the whole truth.

I've never been seen and loved without condition. Not by
friends or classmates.

Not even by my own mother.

After that whole thing with Sarah Wright, and then all the
times after, I realized it would be a lot easier to never get close to
people. If I don't get close, don't care, the eventual rejection can't
hurt. From then on, I didn't bring friends home in order to avoid
my mother meeting their parents and ruining their lives. Keeping
people at arm's length, or even farther, is easier than closeness—
even if closeness is what I crave.

Too much empathy, not enough armor.

There is a sliver of room exposed through the window I am
trying to peer through, so I can tell that they have entered
the Reading Room and haven't yet taken their seats. The table
where Moira does her reading is in view, even if their heads will
be obscured behind the window shade. None of the candles have
been lit yet, Moira hasn't grabbed her deck, and I can see Sydney
standing in the doorway as if waiting like a vampire to be invited
inside.

It is typical of my mother to insist on giving a person who has
never otherwise expressed interest in the mystic arts a free, un-
requested tarot reading in a thinly veiled attempt to learn more
about the person for her own benefit.

I press my fingertips to the edge of the outer windowsill, feeling the coarseness of the wood grain. It's a familiar sensation, one I remember well from when I was a little girl who wasn't allowed in during my mother's readings. I turned a lawn chair into a stepladder so I was high enough to peer through. I made up stories about what was happening in the readings when I could only see the cards, the hands shuffling, the shifting of torsos in chairs.

"Cadence?" Rick's voice comes from behind me, startling me into the begonias. Flowers find their way into my mouth as I flop backward in surprise, nearly losing my balance completely.

"Rick!" I exclaim, spinning around on one foot and gripping the side of the house. *Fuck fuck fuck.* We can't be chatting here at the window with them right on the other side. I know from years of haunting this spot that sound from the outside carries. I've been discovered more than once and reprimanded for it.

He's wearing a Universal Studios–branded blue button-down with a matching navy-blue windbreaker over it. Beside him on the lawn is a skittish-looking brown-and-tan Chihuahua attached to a thin leather leash.

"You must be Chicken," I say, climbing from the bush and crouching toward the creature. Maybe if I fawn over the dog, his owner will ignore the weirdness of finding me in the bushes outside my mother's house.

"You know about Chicken?" Rick asks, his voice immediately bright with a mix of pride and surprise. I extend my hand, palm down, fingers curled, for the dog to sniff.

Which he does, staring straight into my eyes as if reading my mind.

You're up to something, the look seems to say. But then his tongue whips out from between two gnarly teeth to take a taste of my hand. Whatever I'm up to, he's decided not to be bothered by it.

I know about Chicken because Sydney told me about him, but I can't very well say that when Sydney and I supposedly met last night and the topic of Rick's dog did not come up during dinner.

"Moira mentioned him," I lie, feeling more confident in the falsification than in the real story. Moira never mentioned the dog, but Rick is less likely to question that. And if he does, I can always double down should Moira deny it.

"She did?" He beams. The dog doesn't budge. I stand, coming face-to-face with Rick.

He has a sharp, strong jaw and the brightest blue eyes I've ever seen. His have more silver tint than his daughter's, which are almost violet. He has tan skin and a sturdy build. A dignified, handsome older guy, almost stodgy until he smiles and mischief takes over his face.

Which is what he's doing now.

He grabs up Chicken to smack a kiss on the top of his head. "I got this fella when Sydney's mom passed. Scrawny one-year-old rescue with the saddest eyes you'd ever seen," he says, pressing his nose to the dog's head affectionately. Chicken looks anything but sad now. In fact, he's got a bit of a belly on him, indicating the plush life he has likely led since leaving the shelter. "I thought he would be good company for Sydney." His lips twitch down, a momentary frown.

There's a ping-pong of feeling in my chest at the thought of young Sydney needing this dog as a distraction from the loss of her mom.

"And she named him Chicken?" I ask, biting back a smirk at the idea.

"That was a joint effort between us. The pup was scared of everything. Couldn't even walk him at first because even the slightest surprise sound would set him trembling." He scratches beneath Chicken's little chin, where I can see a plethora of gray hairs have sprouted in the dog's beard. "On one of the walks, after a particularly bad reaction to one of the police helicopters always flying overhead"—he rolls his eyes, and I snort a laugh; citizens of Los Angeles are united in their hatred of the LAPD, but especially of the LAPD surveillance helicopters that are constantly patrolling even the more suburban neighborhoods—"Sydney picked the shaking beast up, clutching him to her heart, and said, *You're just the cutest little Chicken.*" His eyes are fully misting up. "And the rest is history."

"But he lives with you and not Sydney?" I clarify.

"He's an old man," he says, setting him back down on the grass to sniff. "And as an old man myself, I understand what he needs. Plus her schedule is more unpredictable, takes her away for stretches." He shrugs. "Makes the most sense for him to stay with me."

"Well, and now Moira," I add.

"I do stay here an awful lot, with my lease up at the end of the month and everything. Easier to make the transition slowly rather than all at once." He flashes me a smile. "Old-guy stuff."

"I get it," I say, and I can't help but smile. "I'm more set in my ways than most people my age. Living alone for so long kind of does that to a person."

He nods, his eyes steady on mine. "There's nothing wrong with wanting stability."

I don't need him to approve of my choices, but it feels nice that someone does. I don't want to linger on the feeling, or in this conversation too long, so close to the Reading Room window. But it's not a bad idea to engage Rick in conversation—he might inadvertently drop some important clues about the bank docs or their relationship.

There's a part of me that wonders if the documents I saw her working on today are related to her sudden interest in love and marriage. Rick is a stable guy. With a good, steady income. And he's a former successful pilot who likely has a 401(k). Even though he retired from piloting early, it's more likely that a buttoned-up guy like him would have socked away funds, would have good credit, would be a better candidate for a loan than Moira.

Her one good financial move was paying off the house. But as long as I've known her, she's spent carelessly, traveled extensively, and not treated her credit as something to maintain.

I start walking around to the front of the house. "How are you feeling about this weekend? A big engagement party. I can only imagine what the wedding will be like."

He follows, Chicken sniffing as he does. "The party was all Moira's idea. I would have been happy just getting hitched at the justice of the peace and then telling our dearest friends and family." He chuckles. "But she hadn't ever planned on an engagement, let alone a wedding, and she wanted to do it all the way up."

We reach the porch, and he unhooks Chicken, who runs up the steps to the screen door and scratches. With surprising agility for a self-proclaimed old man, Rick takes the steps two at a time and lets Chicken inside.

"You don't have to do all this if you don't want to," I say. Maybe Moira is trying to swindle a big, lavish engagement party and wedding out of him merely for the spectacle. She loves being the center of attention—this isn't the craziest theory I've had so far.

He turns. "I don't mind a little pageantry."

"Oh right, I know you're kind of a performer—"

He waves me off. "I wouldn't call me a performer. But *you* can call me one if you like."

My laugh is a fast burst, surprisingly genuine. It's easy to see who Sydney learned her skills of communication from. Rick radiates charm, just like his daughter.

"I don't know if I have enough proof to give you the title," I reply, surprising myself with how easy the banter slides from my lips.

"You busy?" he asks, eyes sparkling.

Confusion wars with intrigue. I do want to stay here to try to swoop in at the first possible moment and thwart whatever scheme Moira is trying by offering a reading to Sydney. But I also want to see if spending more time with Rick will yield more fruitful insights.

"Not really?" I reply, my voice trailing up in question. He laughs, scaling back down the stairs to meet me on the walkway where I'm still standing.

"Wanna join me on an adventure?" he asks, extending his arm, the elbow crooked like a gentleman.

There haven't been all that many men in my life. A couple of boyfriends, a few bosses. There were no best friends' dads to act as my surrogate father. No father. And, of course, the few men Moira did date throughout the years never stuck around long enough to get comfortable.

I tuck my palm into the crook of his elbow with hesitation. He pulls me into his side in this paternal way that makes tears prick in my eyes, and we head off together as if this is totally normal, as if I am not the estranged daughter of his fiancée and he is not the man I am trying to save from marrying the woman he thinks is his soulmate.

CHAPTER SIXTEEN

Sydney

The Reading Room at Kismet is designed as a sacred space. Moira left me alone inside while she went to the kitchen, claiming a cup of tea and some biscuits were just what we needed to connect with our guides. I think her blood sugar was just taking a midday dip and she needed a caffeine-and-cookie boost. Which is totally fair. I can't blame her, and also, *same.*

The room is rectangular. The long wall directly across from the doorway is lined with built-in bookshelves that frame a window with a shallow window seat. There's a plush carpet in a swirl of deep jewel tones, another wall lined with bookshelves, only this one holds tarot decks and other occult artifacts. At the center of the room sits a round wooden table covered in velvet and lace, with tall-backed chairs on either side. Overhead is a stained-glass light fixture like nothing I've ever seen before. A pendant in cerulean and iridescent glass etched with a dandelion flower design that winds around the fixture as the dandelion seeds shoot out as if blown in a wish.

At the far edge of the room is a heavy wooden desk in front of more shelves. On those shelves are some colorful wooden boxes and trunks, small enough that they can fit in a bookshelf and a little out of place in how organized they appear.

They must be more function than form. They very likely contain secrets she doesn't want on full display. Probably private business-related docs.

Cadence texted me that Moira was discussing something financially related to the Kismet property, and this was a red flag to her since the property has been paid off for years.

I want to make a swift and certain beeline for the desk, but I'm aware that Moira could come back any second. I will have to find a way to sneak back in here when she isn't paying attention. I walk toward the bookshelf nearest me, scanning the shelves with interest. Moira sells tarot decks in her shop outside, some I see here neatly organized. These must be her personal decks, ones she uses for clients or for her personal readings.

There are candles, dried herb bundles, and some beautiful crystals she has set up in clusters around the shelves. But most notable to me is the framed photo of Cadence. It has to be her—the rambling dark curls and haunting hazel eyes are unmistakable. She's sitting on a tree branch that hangs over the roof of Kismet, her long legs, knees knobby, dangling on either side of the branch. She's holding on with one hand, but in the other she holds something.

My fingers twitch, moving of their own accord toward the frame to pick it up, draw it closer for a better look.

A bird. Cadence is holding a bird in her open palm.

The sight causes a strange lifting sensation in my stomach.

The hand holding the bird is open, palm up to the sky. The bird sits inside the palm, and Cadence's smile is calm, a settled, soft fix to her round features. The bird isn't a parakeet or budgie. It's not the kind of clipped-winged creature you might expect to see sitting in the palm of a young girl's hand.

It's a tiny jewel-headed hummingbird. Not easy to catch, harder to hold on to.

"It flew right to her." Moira's voice startles me, and I nearly drop the frame. I turn to see she's holding a tray of teacups sitting on saucers and a plate of cookies. The cups are a delicate china, mismatched. My stomach growls at the sight of the cookies.

"A hummingbird?" I ask, setting the frame carefully back in place on the shelf.

"That's right," she says, walking to the table with the tray. She pulls a leaf from the left side and situates the tray on top all in one fluid motion.

I don't know if I'm supposed to move from my spot yet, but my gut says she's coming over here. She's not done taking this opportunity to talk about Cadence.

My instinct is confirmed when she crosses to where I stand and picks up the framed photo. Her eyes are gentle as they take in the image of her daughter. Sadness etches her features, and I imagine it's likely she's thinking of that time. A time before Cadence left home, left her behind, stopped trusting her and her premonitions, stopped letting her dictate her story.

"A wild thing," she almost hums. "She always had this way of making nature feel comfortable." She brushes her thumb over Cadence's face in the picture. "Something in her understood the same something in nature. Kindred, connected." She looks up, as if driving the point of her words toward me. She seems to be implying that I am a wild thing and Cadence and I should understand each other.

The annoying thing is, she isn't wrong.

I couldn't say it out loud, not with how wound-up Cadence is over the circumstances of our meeting, but she has this way of making me feel like my feet are on the ground. Like I could land and stay for a while.

Probably the same way the hummingbird felt in her hand.

I can't follow this train of thought. Not just because I don't think there is anything about me interesting or intriguing enough to usurp the permanent distaste Cadence has for her mother's soulmate premonition, but because this close to Madame Moira I feel exposed. I don't believe in supernatural forces any more than I believe in Santa Claus or God, but I am starting to believe in the power belief can wield. And Moira is a person who has been imbued with presence thanks to the many people (including herself and her skeptical daughter) who do believe in her ability to see the future.

Or, at the very least, the answer about the future they seek from her.

I don't want to follow a train of thought about how grounded her daughter makes me feel, because I'm afraid that she'll somehow know—read my mind, feel my feelings, whatever.

"It's crazy that it let her catch it," I say, trying not to sound too invested.

"Her," Moira says, and I realize she is correcting me. "The hummingbird was a her."

At that, I decide to move this whole thing along. At least away from the topic of her daughter capturing in hand the fastest-moving bird in nature.

Birdie.

Stop seeing coincidences and reading them as signs.

"Those cookies look delicious," I say, walking to the table in a few fast strides and grabbing one up. "Snickerdoodles."

"Lola is in a baking phase," Moira replies, following me to the table.

I turn the cookie over between my fingers.

"She's the one who got me on the dating site that led me to meeting Rick." I nod, acknowledging recognition of the name and why I would know who she is.

"The wild card," I reply. Her lips quirk. Referencing a direct quote from her daughter was probably not my most genius move. "Or something like that."

"Exactly that," she says, but thankfully doesn't dwell on it. "And she is. Cadence isn't wrong there. But Lola's been loyal, sticking around even though she could leave if she wanted. Nothing's stopping her."

"She likely appreciates that you let her . . ." I look to the cookie, searching for the right words. "Follow her interests while on the clock."

"I don't own her time, not even when I'm paying her. People do what they want no matter how tightly you hold on." This is an audacious statement coming from her considering everything Cadence has said. "Last month it was painting. Before that, learning French on Duolingo, *merci*," she says in a flawless accent. "Lola is like a daughter to me. I don't mind her searching, especially here, where I can keep an eye on her." There's some undercurrent to her words, as if there's more she wants to say on the topic but not more she wants to reveal. "She could so easily get off track."

Whoa, the puppet strings are showing.

I bite down on the cookie, reaching for the chair to tug it out from under the table. Can't say anything that might put Moira on the defensive.

"Tasty," I say, sliding into the seat. "Your instinct to let her do her thing is paying off."

Moira chuckles, tugging her chair out as well. "My taste buds don't complain. Just my waistline." She motions to her svelte figure. I can't figure out what the fuck I'm supposed to believe is suffering there. She drifts into her seat and picks up her teacup. She rests against the pintucked velvet cushion covering her high-backed chair.

I give her a tight smile and keep my backbone stiff as I reach for my own cup. The tea has a rich nutty color, the smell reminding me of fall. Crunchy leaves underfoot, spice in the air from all the baked goods. We sip our tea, and her eyes never leave my face.

"I see a lot of your father in you," she says thoughtfully.

"I get that a lot, especially from people who didn't know my mother."

"Diana." She says my mother's name in the same thoughtful tone. "I saw her—Rick keeps family photos around of the three of you." She sets her teacup down and picks up the deck of cards sitting out on the table. In all the conversation and preliminary snooping, I didn't notice she had set them out.

The backs of the cards are a pale green with a cream border that looks like vines. In the center of that is a tree with a thick woven trunk, deep roots that connect to the vine border below, and a lush crown that spills into the border at the top and sides.

"That's not the same thing as knowing her."

Moira's hands flick, sending a cascade of cards up in a controlled arc. Her long fingers work the deck into a rhythmic shuffle, and my eyes drop to the movement, sticking like glue as the cards sift into and through the spaces between one another.

"So how does this work?" I ask. I wish I could get the focus off me and onto her but that doesn't seem likely as long as I'm supposed to be the subject of this tarot reading.

"You're the querent, and that means you can ask whatever you like of the cards," Moira says, pausing her shuffle to rap her knuckles against the bottom of the deck like she's knocking on a closed door.

"What if I don't have a specific question?" Or, more accurately, a question I can say out loud.

"It's not required," she says, leaning forward in this conspiratorial way that puts me on edge and makes me instinctively want to mirror the move. With all her clear narcissistic tendencies and my blinders-off awareness of her ability to utilize her charm to bend the will of those around her, my resistance isn't nearly as strong as I would like.

My understanding of how she hooked my dad is starting to get more defined.

"But if I may be so bold . . ." *Ha!* She doesn't do coy well. My brows jump, and she sets the cards on the table between us. "I sense you have some unease about the future." Her eyes are pools of endless dark water. "Cut the deck."

My hand moves, my brain screams, and the only thing on my mind is *What if she's right?* Not just my unease about the future, which feels fucking plausible and like it shouldn't come as a shock to anyone at all that I reek of uncertainty like it's bad BO. What if she's right about Cadence and me? What if Ranger Girl is my goddamn soulmate?

You don't believe in soulmates.

Questioning things is a good instinct.

Shut up!

I lift the cards without grace. A chunk comes up, a few slipping from the bottom back to the stack below, and then I set down the cards in my hand. Why is my hand trembling? I curl my fingers into a fist and shove it between my thighs.

"Which one?" she asks. "The stack you pick is the one we draw from." She's guiding me more than I expected she would, but she isn't giving me the answers, either. This is in my hands, not hers.

I let my eyes drop to the two stacks. I don't know why this feels like a critically important decision—it's just tarot cards. A parlor trick akin to one my dad would do in our living room. A coin behind the ear, a bunny in a hat. Tarot itself was invented as a playing-card game, glorified only by the adaptation of the deck into occult practices. (Yes, my deep dive on Moira Connelly led me to the tarot page on Wikipedia.)

This isn't fate. The universe isn't speaking. Yet the weight on my chest reminds me of the first time I set foot in a cockpit. Newly minted badge on my breast, 160 souls in my hands. Destiny right at my fingertips.

No, not destiny. *Obligation.*

My eyes flick up to Moira again, and I point to the stack that was on the bottom—the one the few cards dropped onto after I cut them. She touches the stack I point to, and I can't tell by her face if she approves or not. I inwardly scold myself for caring. She lifts the stack and sets it on top of the other one, pulling it back toward her but leaving it resting on the table.

"Does the order they come out in have a specific meaning?"

"Oftentimes I'll do a three-card reading for general energy. It could represent past, present, future; it could be the potential on your path." At the word *potential* my skin tingles. Just the finger-tips, but it's potent enough to notice. "That one?"

She flicks her eyes over my face.

"I mean, who doesn't want to hear about their potential?"

"Well, the potential of your path, currently, as of this moment in time," she corrects.

"You mean, what we see could change?" I ask the question—breathless for the answer. *What is happening to me?* This spiritually curious person is not me. I've never even read a horoscope, though Joe insists I am *such a Libra it's scary.*

"Depends on you—what you do with the information the cards present."

"And not what you tell me to do?" My lips leap into a smirk. She isn't swayed.

"I'll have my own interpretation, but it's up to you what you do with it."

To me she extends agency. To the girl out front, Lola, she teth-ers a long leash. But to her daughter she narrowed the vision. Claimed ownership of her future. Told her, point-blank, that her soulmate would only ever cross Cadence's path because of her.

"I'm ready," I say with a nod.

She brushes the cards with her fingertips before flipping the first one over toward me. It lands upright. The first thing my eyes grip is the name.

Two of Cups

The words are written in a cool, deep blue, and there's a treat-ment on the card that makes it look antique. Not sepia, but just a careful fade that feels vintage. The border is done in the same vines as I noticed on the other side of the cards, but within the border the background is a soft pink-and-blue-and-purple wash. At the center of the card are two figures—two women, I realize upon closer inspection—each holding a cup in hand as they face each other.

My eyes jump back and forth between the two women as heat creeps up my neck where it warms my ears. Something about this card is giving gay love. Love is love. You are about to be in love.

I don't love this for me. But still, my heartbeat patters. A faster beat, the yearning kind.

Without saying anything about the first card, Moira flips over the next one.

The Sun

The words are written in a soft, shimmery gold this time, and they have been given the same antique treatment, that same winding vine border, and the background is done to look like a soft blue sky, below which rolling hills expand to the horizon. In the center of the card is a woman curled into a ball, the long gold tendrils of her hair fanning out in a shape that mirrors sunbursts. She glows, her face illuminated as if from within. I stare into her face. Her expression set in a smile, her eyes focused forward, on the future.

Moira flips over the next card.

The Moon

Shimmery silver letters, antique treatment, winding vine border, only the background of this card is the inky blue of a night sky. There are purple and silver swirls at the edges and what looks like tiny starlike dots in the deep color. In the center is a woman curled into a crescent moon shape, cloaked in her raven hair, illuminated from behind with a silver glow.

I look between the three cards, fighting the thoughts in my head as they scream, *This reading is about you and Cadence!* Me, the Sun. Her, the Moon. Us, together in a romantic way, with our cups running over with . . . lust? Desire?

Love?

I swallow the panic and hope it will stay down long enough for me to get through this.

"Interesting spread," I say with a frog-like croak. I will myself to look up at her face. She's not looking at me, though. Her attention is on the cards, her expression pensive. "I have no idea what any of this means," I prod, the panic threatening to rise back up.

"Where would you like me to start?" she asks, looking up at me finally. I know she can read the fear on me. I just hope she can't pinpoint why.

"How about this one?" I point to the first card I pulled out. "Start at the beginning, I guess?"

She runs her finger over the edge of the first card. "The Two of Cups is a soulmate card."

"You sure you haven't rigged this deck?" I say with a scoff. Her smile is Cheshire.

I'm playing it cool, but inwardly I'm screaming. I *do* believe in coincidence. Happenstance that leads to moments that feel like they were meant to be. After all the questioning I've been entertaining despite my better judgment, it seems now I can't escape my very own Madame Moira soulmate prediction.

"You're not in the market for a soulmate?" she asks. There's almost no inflection in her voice. Unlike yesterday, when she prodded me toward a conclusion through our conversation, right now, she has an almost neutral tone. Like she actually wants me to make my own mind up.

I shrug. Match her energy, keep it neutral.

This nonanswer is enough to send her eyes back to the cards.

"You're the Sun here, and this person you'll love, they are the Moon," she says, moving the cards closer in proximity. "There is a story here that describes that push and pull, the give and take, much like these two forces in our skies. One cannot exist without the other."

Moira's words stick in my head, brambles of a rose with thorns aplenty.

"So, like, opposites attract?" Cool as a cucumber, even if my brain is on fire.

The first thought I have is a dangerous one.

Cadence and I aren't just extroverted and introverted. I don't just have sunny blond hair, and she doesn't just have hair the color of an inky starless sky. We aren't only opposites who could very easily attract. We're opposites who could very easily *go together*. Like sweet ice cream and salty French fries, like laughing so hard you cry, like pairing leather with lace or polka dots with stripes. We don't make sense, but we may be even better together than apart.

Moira sits back in her chair, looking me over with eyes like an X-ray. She's got this calm that feels otherworldly.

Or maybe I'm just in the eye of the hurricane.

"When the Sun and the Moon are together in a tarot reading, they are a powerful combination," she says, and my adrenaline shoots into action. There's that whirling, swirling, dragging me off the ground to toss me around in the sky. "The cards are transformation with balance. They are light burning away confusion. They are hope"—she touches the Sun card—"and intuition"—she touches the Moon—"working together for the hand of fate."

Fate.

Almost every decision I've made about my life since entering high school has been planned to the letter, no room for magic or fate. I became an overachiever with very little space in her life for deep feelings and even less space for divergent paths. Partying and dating casually have been my vices of choice to deal with it, and I'm just not sure why I can't sit still, can't commit, can't be grounded for long.

But maybe I'm ready to find out.

CHAPTER SEVENTEEN

Cadence

M y only visit to the Universal Studios theme park was with the one friend from my adolescence who Moira never managed to get her hooks into. Hannah Zhou. She was the new student at school, and she mistook my loner status for approachability when she befriended me the first day of eighth grade. From Singapore originally, her family immigrated to the States when she was two, first to New York City, then Washington, DC, for her dad's work. Their move to LA was supposed to be temporary, which made me feel less terrified about being her friend. She and her mom had committed to seeing all the theme parks, big and small, that SoCal had to offer.

Disney, Knott's Berry Farm, Legoland, and, of course, the Los Angeles mainstay, Universal Studios. They went over Thanksgiving break and invited me along. All my memories of it—and my brief but potent friendship with Hannah—remain the only fond ones I've retained of the entirety of my eighth-grade experience.

"Take a seat right up front, Cadence," Rick says, pointing to a spot up ahead inside the tour guide's carriage. The empty white-roofed, navy-blue-sided open-air tram emits a low hum, ready to set off toward the throngs of guests waiting to board for the tour, one of the most popular "rides" in the park. There are sections to the vehicle, and Rick and I will sit in the second. The front is where the driver sits, a woman named Flo, who is communicating with Rick through a walkie, saying that we're about to head toward the gate to pick up passengers.

Rick is giving me a free ride and an up-close view of his showmanship. I'm hoping we have some downtime to chat during the parts of the ride that don't require he have his microphone on.

I drop into the seat, crossing my legs. He climbs in through the other side, swiveling his neck to look at me. "Don't forget to keep your hands and feet inside the vehicle for the duration of the tour."

"Noted," I say, raising my hands dramatically before folding them in my lap. Someone calls over his walkie-talkie, giving him a green light to proceed.

"Thanks for letting me tag along," I say. "I haven't been here since I was a teenager."

"Can't abide that," he says, cheery but affronted at the same time. "How old were you?"

"Fourteen. Fall of eighth grade," I recite, thinking about the awkward long-legged girl desperate to win a toy from the *Simpsons* carnival.

"They've added a lot to the tour since then. You're going to love it," he says with pride.

"Can't wait," I reply. His smile is broad and comes easily. Like resting bitch face but a whole lot happier. "When I rode it back then, I loved the part where Norman Bates follows us onto the road. And seeing all the bungalows and the active soundstages."

"You're an LA kid," he says a little dreamily. "Makes sense that

you love movie sets." Sometimes it's easy to forget just how much
of an LA kid I really am. Having left it behind a long time ago for
college, and then having stayed away as I worked up to a full-time
position with the National Park Service, I don't feel as connected
to the place where I was born as I used to. I like to keep my origin
story—and not just the psychic-mom part of it—a secret at work.
Which means I don't often chat about how firmly my roots lead
back to LA.

We are now in line, queuing toward the stalls that hold the
waiting customers. Rick takes a gulp from his giant water bottle—
a Stanley, as if he were a millennial mom.

"How long have you been doing this job?" I ask. I know he left
piloting full-time when Sydney was in high school, but I'm not
sure what the trajectory was that took him from commercial airline pilot to tour guide at Universal Studios. It can't have been a
straight line. It's a fun gig for someone with a performer's itch
who doesn't want to act, sure, but more a *retired guy looking to stay
sharp* job than a career path.

"I was a consultant for a while on sets," he says, adjusting his
aviators on the bridge of his nose. There's a smidge of white lotion
staining the corner, and I bite back the urge to chuckle. He's such
a buttoned-up guy in appearance, and then he'll have these chaotic elements that feel totally incongruent to the image he proj-
ects. The poorly applied sunscreen being one of them.

The car eases forward until we're one away from loading up.

"That's so cool," I blurt. He chuckles, not surprised by my reaction. There I am being an LA kid again. "What did that entail?"

"They'd hire me to read scripts, give notes on aviation-related
elements. Sometimes I'd come out to live sets and give feedback. I
never flew for a film or anything, but I did explain how to look

like you know what you're doing in a cockpit to Ryan Gosling one time." He lowers his aviators and turns to look at me, making sure I can see his brows waggle. I snort. Ryan Gosling is quite the charmer, I have to give him that.

"Very cool guy," he adds brightly.

"Glad to hear it," I say, smiling.

Flo eases the truck forward before putting it firmly in park to let the families, solo travelers, groups, and couples file on board safely. I feel eyes on me, knowing my presence at the front of the car is an anomaly. Even if it's their first time on the tram ride, even if it's their twentieth.

A little girl wearing a Rosalina t-shirt and carrying a star purse climbs on and takes the seat closest to the front, forcing what I assume is the rest of her family—a grumpy-looking dad in socks and sandals, a younger sibling inexplicably wearing goggles, and a mom with a visor on to block the sun—to sit there as well. The little girl is the only one who looks properly excited for this ride.

I turn my attention back to Rick, since the rest of the loading process will take a few minutes and I don't want to drop the thread of his tour guide origin story.

"You were telling me how you became a tour guide," I say in that leading way that hopefully gets him going again.

"Ah, right!" he says with a snap. "The whole consulting gig paid well but was pretty inconsistent, as you can imagine, and while I had my 401(k) for retirement and I had money socked away, I got restless between jobs and wanted something more to fill that time."

"And your mind went to tour guide at Universal Studios?"

"I was on a set—I'll point it out when we pass by today—and the tour came by. I could hear the guide chattering about the history of the studio, saw all those happy faces, and it reminded me of my wife and me bringing Sydney here every summer break. It felt like a link to the past, simple as that."

The welcome video starts playing, introducing the ride, and I know we won't have much more time to chat before he has to turn on the mic and charm the customers.

"What was she like as a kid?" The question blurts from my lips, surprising me. This is not the kind of investigation I'm supposed to be doing right now.

"Birdie?" he asks, chuckling.

Birdie. His nickname for her. *If she was a bird, she wouldn't be easy to catch.* The thought makes my stomach seize. As if I want to catch her, hold her in my hand, hold on to her forever.

"She was a spitfire," Rick continues. "Smart, but not just with her academics—which she, of course, excelled at. She had this keen ability to notice details, never missed anything, never let it go if you tried to pull one over on her. Transparent to a fault, horrible liar." I bite back a laugh and pass it off as a cough. Her skills have improved only slightly as she has gotten older, but I don't see that as a bad thing. Normally, at least. For the purpose of our scheme to root out Moira's motive for marrying Rick, I wouldn't mind a bit more finesse.

"Did she always know she wanted to be a pilot?" I ask. I've wondered how much of that decision was for herself and how much was because she felt guilty her dad retired early. I can't see Rick's eyes behind his aviators, but the set of his jaw goes rigid at the question.

He's saved from answering by the sound of the instructional video winding down. Time to turn on the charm. He flicks on the mic, and his lips rise into an automatic, larger-than-life smile.

"Hello, hello, everybody, and welcome to the world-famous Studio Tour at Universal Studios in beautiful Hollywood, California!" This greeting gets a chorus of cheers from the audience, which feels like the appropriate word for the people taking this tour. "Are we excited to be here, everybody?" More cheers. I glance around at the family on the front bench seat. The Rosalina stan is clapping animatedly, her father and brother look like they've started to fall asleep, and Mom is nursing a cup that is likely full of one of the park's many alcoholic beverage offerings.

Smart woman. I wish I had thought to grab one on the way in.

Rick goes through his own safety and housekeeping brief, and once everyone has more than thoroughly assured us that they all have a pair of 3D glasses, we're off toward the lot. He removes his aviators now that the camera is on him, and with every bit of history he reveals (most of which I somehow still remember from the one visit in the eighth grade), the mood of the audience becomes more unified. Everyone listens, laughing at his jokes—which are plentiful. Even that sleepy dad and boy in the front start to perk up.

But for me, watching him charm the audience only dampens my mood.

He's more than a nice guy who's worked hard all his life. He's a man who approaches the world, despite all its flaws and all the ways he's been wounded, with the hopeful optimism of a dreamer. If I weren't absolutely certain Moira was up to something, I'd almost believe they were made for each other.

I inwardly kick myself at the urge to give in to the idea that soulmates aren't just a ruse my mother uses to make money. But entertaining the idea that soulmates might really exist isn't something I can let myself do. Then, my mother would be right, and all her pushing, prodding, and manipulation would come into question. Fit beneath that rose-colored light, I would have to start to question whether running from Moira's premonitions was really the right path for me at all.

~

An icon of the Universal Studios backlot tour, the 3D Fast & Furious—Supercharged portion is a favorite of most people, but I have a tendency toward motion sickness. We're midway through the chase sequence when I finally have to lift the glasses from my nose for relief.

My eyes immediately catch on Rick's cell phone, lit up in his hand, as he types out a message rapid-fire with both thumbs. I shouldn't peek. No matter the objective, a person's texts aren't the business of a prying onlooker. Even if I'm trying to help with my nosiness.

But I do look, knowing full well that a text he feels the need to reply to in the middle of a tour is probably urgent. Might even contain a clue.

The text thread is with GREG ✈ and from the fast glance I can manage to get of the screen, I see it's about money.

The word alone is a cold block in my stomach.

> **GREG:** Hey bud—Pam and I are a go for this weekend, but she's on my case again.

> **RICK:** She has the right.

> **GREG:** She does, she does. Where are you at on that loan?

Rick is typing his response, so I read it in real time.

> **RICK:** I'm grateful for your help, you
> know that, but we're not to any firm
> numbers yet—though should be
> soon.

He sends it. Waits. And then when he sees those telltale three blinking dots, he adds: Moira promises it will all sort out.

And then he signs the text with his name like it's an email.

If there was a pit in my stomach at the mention of money, this last exchange feels like a fist clenched around my throat. They've known each other for three months. What financial situation could the two of them have gotten tied up in during that time? Rick doesn't seem like an impulsive individual—speedy engagement to my mother notwithstanding.

Whatever mess they're in, all signs point to Moira as the reason why.

CHAPTER EIGHTEEN

Sydney

It's the morning we're supposed to leave for Solvang for the start of Dad and Moira's engagement celebration, and I really could have used a decent night of sleep. Two nights in a row lying awake for hours with my mind racing is hard enough to handle when I am coming into it well-rested, but after being in the air for the last ten days, I'm haggard on a whole different level.

When Moira finished with my reading, I was so shaken up that I didn't wait around after. I did text Ranger Girl to see where she'd gone, only to discover she had taken a ride on the Universal Studio's backlot tour with my dad and learned some *interesting info* she'd have to tell me about in person.

I decided to head back to Culver City, got stuck in rush hour traffic, then ate dinner in my room watching reruns of *House Hunters International* to cope.

Joe was home, a new guy on the couch beside him for the Netflix part of their Netflix-and-chill session. I didn't want to third wheel any part of that and also really didn't want Joe to immediately read the conflict on my face and make me explain what was up.

Because something was definitely up, and it was largely to do with my personal tarot reading delivered by my dad's fiancée. Madame Moira really knows how to take a girl with a few superstitions and a whole lot of emotional baggage and turn her into a bumbling, questioning, soulmate-imagining idiot.

I got less than two hours of sleep, am running on caffeine and carbs, and am pulling up to Kismet half an hour late.

I tug out my phone and glance at the itinerary Dad and Moira sent over in a mass-bcc'd email to all the guests attending the engagement weekend. They reserved a block of rooms through a special rate Moira secured with her connections at the hotel, removing a roadblock for most of the guests considering the last-minute nature of the invite. Guests are able to check in and pay the remaining balance on the room, but with the discount, it's a steal.

I flick my tired eyes over the itinerary.

Friday
Arrive at the Hygge 2–4 p.m. *(strongly suggested)*
Wine Tasting at Whimsy Winery 4:30 p.m.
Opening Ceremony of the Danish Days Festival 7:30 p.m.
Axe Throwing and Brats Directly Following

Saturday
Danish Days Festival
(see website for detailed list of activities)
Cheese and Wine at the Hygge 2 p.m.

Sunday

Engagement Brunch

Food, Wine, and Dancing at Whimsy Winery

A whole weekend of "fun," and me without an ounce of energy to enjoy it.

Or thwart it.

I secretly hoped they would leave without me, and then I could drive down alone and clear my head.

Dad is still loading the trunk of his Subaru Forester, which means, unfortunately, my plan is foiled. The back is wide-open, so I can see they've piled in oodles of luggage—more than two people could possibly need—and by the looks of it, there is still more on the sidewalk waiting to go inside. I climb out, my almost-empty Starbucks in hand. I slide my sunglasses into the neckline of my sweatshirt as I approach Moira and Dad.

"You know we're only staying for the weekend, right?" I say, causing them both to turn in my direction. Dad's face immediately breaks into his larger-than-life smile, and he tugs me in for a hug. Moira doesn't move from her spot on the walkway, but she offers me an air-kiss. I force myself to stay calm and neutral.

I tell myself to stop thinking about the reading right the fuck now.

"This isn't all ours," Dad says as he reaches for another floral-patterned duffel. "We're taking Lola's bags since she's riding up with her *friend*"—Dad says *friend* like it means anything but the definition of friend—"Hawthorne, on his motorcycle."

"Love, you said you would play nice with Hawthorne," Moira chides with a chuckle. I am completely lost. Moira can tell. "Lola calls him her *situationship*. Rick refuses to acknowledge the word or the man."

I guffaw. "Come on, Dad. Get with it." Dad shakes his head adamantly.

"I'm old and stuck in my ways," he says.

"You just got attached to Lola's last situationship, and she was gone after a week," Moira says, shaking her head. The look in her eyes is pure adoration. It's hard to believe this look could come from a person conning my dad out of money. I decide I absolutely will not dwell on the uncomfortable way that thought makes my stomach sour.

"So I'm on my own, then?" I ask.

"You don't have to be," Moira replies. "Cadence needs a buddy."

The front door opens, and Cadence emerges carrying a very content-looking Chicken. My eyes slide over her, taking in her travel gear—loose jeans rolled up at the cuff, a pair of high-top Converse in red, a cap that says "Tree Hugger" in maroon, and a faded t-shirt advertising Yosemite.

We meet on the sidewalk, and even though I am acutely aware of Moira's gaze tracking my movement toward her daughter, I manage not to buckle beneath the pressure. As soon as I'm visible, Chicken's tiny tan tail begins wagging like wild.

"You're very on-brand today," I say, motioning to her *every-thing*. I reach out, treading dangerously close to Cadence's chest, in order to scratch Chicken on the top of the head.

"When you work in the parks, you shop in the parks," she says, her eyes trailing to my hand. Chicken twists around, trying to swipe my palm with kisses. "I get a discount."

"Ah, does it extend to friends and family?" I ask, and then add with a lift to my left eyebrow: "Partners in scheme?" I'm pleased to see the edge of her lip kick up. She has beautiful, soft blush-colored lips. Without gloss, they're a matte mauve, a pretty pink with just a little hint of brown.

"Speaking of, they're all full up over there." She nods toward Dad's Subaru. "Wanna carpool?" The question causes a jolt of nerves in my stomach. Alone with her in a car for two hours sounds simultaneously heavenly and horrifying.

The Moon. The Sun. The Two of Cups.

"Sounds like a plan," I say. "Your rental or my Audi?"

"As much as I'd love to ride in high style—" I interrupt the compliment with a blurt of laughter. She gives me a quizzical look that quickly shifts to playful suspicion. "That's exactly why you bought it. It's a status car."

"This is LA, people know you by your car."

"See?" she says, rolling her eyes.

"We can take the Audi." I shoot her a mischievous look.

"I'm paying for the midsize sedan, so we might as well use it."

"If you're sure," I reply.

"Don't tempt me," she says with the tiniest growl. I feel it right between my legs.

"I'd let you take the wheel," I press. Right out here in the open, where Moira and Dad can see. It feels reckless.

And wonderful.

The sun filtering through the tree dances in her eyes, bouncing off the messy curls she's tossed over one shoulder.

"Get your bags." Her voice has a new breathiness to it. "I gotta deliver this fella back to your dad." She turns hastily, and I watch her walk away.

I toss the coffee cup in the trash bins by the road on my way back to my car to grab my duffel. Cadence still has my purse in her car, which I have tried not to think about since that also means she has my driver's license. Driving home yesterday without it after sneaking away from Moira's hawkeyed glare was anxiety-inducing enough.

I should tell her about the reading—I'm sure she'll ask. I *have* to tell her, but no part of me wants to reveal the soulmates of it all. She might bail on me, the coincidence of that too much for her to bear; she might not, which could be a more terrifying proposition.

My mind wanders over the scenario for a brief, steamy second before I snap myself back to the moment and to the real concern. How to not lie and also not tell her the truth. This is part of why I couldn't sleep last night and what I spent some of those waking minutes trying to figure out. At first I thought maybe I'd just sub in a different card for the Two of Cups—which seemed to be the one that really set off the whole *your soulmate is on the way* bit. How hard could it be? What harm could it do?

But that feels too close to outright lying, which isn't something I want to do at the beginning of a friendship—or whatever this may be.

Stop that right now.

I discovered in my traverse of the Wikipedia page about the Two of Cups that the card doesn't have to represent romantic connections, but it can be about any kind of connection. Even business. And with us partnering up, I feel like that's the natural non-lie lie to go with. I just hope she buys it.

I swing my duffel over my shoulder and turn, only to find Dad standing there, now holding Chicken, a pleading look on his face.

"What's up?" I question, nervous at the way his face contorts.

"Got room for this gent?" he asks. My eyes drop to Chicken, whose tongue sticks out from the space between his first canine and his front tooth. He's missing a couple of little teeth there, and sometimes his tongue sneaks out unbidden.

"Why are you asking it like it's a huge favor?"

"You know how Chicken's bladder is now," he says. Chicken needs to pee every half hour, like clockwork.

"He's just like a girl," I quip. "But I'm riding with Cadence, so it's up to her." I can already tell where the question will end up, though. *Cadence the Animal Whisperer.* Ranger Girl will surely want the pee machine in her presence, window down so he can bite the wind all the way.

But Dad isn't focusing on that part. He's looking at me with a curious, goofy gaze.

"Why are you being weird?" I start walking, hoping it will shake him from this state.

"Just glad to see you two are getting to know each other," he says. "Moira's missed having her around here—maybe you could put in a good word for her coming to visit more often."

"Dad, we barely know each other. Why would she listen to what I have to say?" I ask, lowering my voice as we're getting closer to where Cadence is standing near Moira.

"You can be very convincing when you want to be," he says, and I don't miss the slight innuendo in his tone. I stop in my tracks, tossing him a glare, which he sidesteps to peck me on the cheek. "Just think about it." He rushes off before I can say more, moving toward Cadence, who takes Chicken from his hands so fast it's almost comical.

She lifts Chicken up to nuzzle him cheek to cheek.

My heart skips a beat. Unpermitted but not unwanted.

CHAPTER NINETEEN

Cadence

Sydney's laugh is like a sunbeam. Warm and glowing, golden, somewhere safe to curl up and nap. When it appears because of something you've said, it's hard not to feel like you could do anything. Emboldened with energy, alive with purpose. I feel silly and overdramatic as the thought takes shape, but at least she doesn't know I'm thinking it.

"Dad has never invited me on a tour," she says, her laughter dying down. Her smile clings to her face. "Now I know why."

"I didn't even know people still kept photos in their wallets," I reply. I had told her about how fast he whipped out pics of her when he heard there was another pilot on board the tour car. He was retired, with a daughter Sydney's age, and Rick was in a mood to show off. "The guy looked like he was about to choke when your dad said you were the youngest female pilot in your fleet."

"Bragging rights," she says, clearly just as impressed with herself as her father is.

"This guy's daughter is a dental hygienist," I reply.

"Important work for sure," she counters.

"True, but no one likes going to the dentist," I finish.

"I actually find it relaxing. And mine still gives me a lollipop when I leave cavity-free." She grins to show me her cavity-less pearly whites.

"I always thought it was weird the dentist gives candy out. Like, do they care about teeth or not? Pick a side." She laughs again, shorter and sharper, but just as warm.

I had to bring the mood up after I filled her in on the weird text chain between Rick and Greg—who I learned from her is also a retired pilot (LA is lousy with them), one of Rick's old buddies, and will be in Solvang this weekend. At least we know we now have another angle to our sleuthing.

Chicken pops up from the spot on Sydney's lap where he's been curled in a ball since the drive started, wrapped in a baby blanket covered in ducks and clouds.

"Uh-oh," Sydney says, running her palm over Chicken's head and down the length of his spine. Her eyes flick up to the road and she grabs her phone.

"Pee break time?" I ask.

"You made it almost a whole hour, buddy," she says in a baby voice. Chicken turns a groggy gaze on Sydney and licks her right on the tip of her nose. The affection is gentle and sweet, like you'd expect from two bonded best friends.

"We can pull off in about half a mile," she says, pinching to zoom out on the map so she can see locations. We're going through the hills around Malibu right now in an area called Calabasas, one of the wealthiest cities in the United States, with more celebrities per square mile than Beverly Hills. "There's a little park not too far from the road. Yelp reviews are decent. Lots of grass." She looks directly into Chicken's eyes. "Plenty of lush grass to do your business."

Her care that Chicken has a plush place to pee is giving me the warm fuzzies. Most of the people I have dated have thought my interest in nature, both flora and fauna, was quirky at best. Even dating people within my field didn't mean we would immediately have a connection on that topic. And if we did, the stress of that close proximity to my work made getting close outside it a lot harder.

My vigilance is something I'm proud of, even if I know it comes from growing up with a mother who made herself the main character and expected me to perfectly act out the supporting role in her life.

Sydney programs directions to the park, and I follow them, winding through a few neighborhood roads—beside some fancy big-ass mansions—toward the mountains. We have to detour about five minutes, but when we pull up, it's clear the extra time was worth it. The area is framed at the back by the mountains in the Topanga State Park. Quiet, with a small playground and a walking path. I turn into the parking lot, which is only populated by a couple of other cars. Sydney hooks Chicken's leash to the metal toggle on his blue collar and opens her door to climb out.

I shut the driver's-side door and take in the view.

Sydney wore a pair of skintight yoga pants and a lightweight Burberry sweatshirt. Her hair is in a messy high bun, making it look even more like spun straw, and her face is mostly free of makeup, with the exception of mascara and a nude gloss. Her shape really is an hourglass, a full, swooping, curvy hourglass. She bounces around the green with Chicken, trying to convince him to go ahead and do his business.

"I think he wants to stroll," she says, looking my way. I'm glad I have sunglasses on so she can't see how my eyes are fixed on her.

I meet up with her on the grass, and we walk in a diagonal toward the park, slow and plodding so Chicken gets his fill of sniffs in.

"You never told me what happened with Moira and your reading?" I ask, nervous. I sound it, too. She takes the corner of her lower lip between her teeth and nibbles. "Yikes, that bad, huh?" I brace for something bonkers, some tale that's authentically and dementedly *my mother.*

"No, it really wasn't," she says. Her eyes aren't hidden behind shades; she doesn't look right at me when she says it.

"You don't have to try to spare me—nothing could possibly surprise me."

"Oh, really? Would you be surprised to learn she had a photo of you in her Reading Room?"

"She has a photo of me?" This does give me pause.

"You didn't know?" she asks.

"Where was it? Her desk or the altar?"

"What the hell is an altar?"

"The shelf with the crystals and candles. She used to keep a photo of a villa in Tuscany there," I reply, shoving my hands in my pockets. I feel suddenly chilly even though the temp hasn't changed.

"So it's, like, for manifestation?" Sydney asks.

"I'm surprised Ms. Left Brain Pilot knows about manifestation," I goad her.

"I'm from LA. It's like the bible of the West Coast." She grins, and I laugh, which startles Chicken out of his pee stance. "That's where it was, yes. Surrounded by crystals and candles."

"Great, good to know she's crossed yet another boundary I set for her."

"You set a boundary that she wouldn't manifest for you?" Her nose scrunches up with confusion, but the smile on her face lets me know just how silly she thinks that is.

"I told her not to do any spells to try and bring me back to LA."

The word *spells* does seem to throw her a bit, but not so much that she dwells on it.

"I don't know if it was *that*, but you were younger in the picture, and you were holding a hummingbird in your hand. You looked . . . happy." She pauses, blinking, as if trying to conjure it from memory. "Happy and free."

My mind is flooded immediately with the memory of the day I took that photo—or, I guess, the day Moira took that photo of me. Without prompting from Sydney, I realize I want to tell the story, and somehow, I know she wants to hear it.

"My bedroom window was right next to that tree branch," I begin, glancing to her face, looking for a reaction. Her eyes settle on me. "There had been a young female hummingbird building a nest outside of the window. Right where I could see it, and she didn't seem to mind when I watched."

Chicken stops at a patch of dandelion, and Sydney doesn't prod him to move along too quickly.

"I can't believe that she let you watch her," she says, urging me on. Interested in a story just about me.

"I couldn't, either, and I got *really* invested. Like, *didn't want to go to school for fear I'd miss something* invested," I continue. "But, of course, I did go to school, and one of those days she vanished. I watched all night, the next morning, but she didn't come back. I was sure something horrible had happened to her—I got obsessed and started trying to, like, *solve the mystery*. Looked up everything

I could about hummingbirds' mating habits and nest-making habits—they can be really vicious, especially during mating season."

"Fair. It's probably pretty brutal out there."

"Like, even mating itself can take a dark turn." She makes a *yikes* face and I match it. "But there was no way to know what had happened, and that nest was going to sit outside my window forever as a reminder, because I didn't want to move it. Like, what if she came back?"

"This is devastating," she says, and she really sounds like she means it. But then, her brow quirks up. "But in the photo . . ."

My smile spreads, pleased at how invested she's getting. "The next spring, a hummingbird showed up at the same spot. She was a little plumper, bigger, older-looking than the other one." Understanding breaks like dawn over her face, and her mouth falls open in awe. "And she used that old nest material, which was still there, though a little weathered, to build a new one."

"You think it was the same bird?" she asks, her voice round with awe.

"I read that sometimes adolescent females will practice building nests before they are ready to actually use them. When I was in college, I did some volunteering at the Cabrillo National Monument in San Diego, and the rangers there had observed the habit in real time."

"She was doing that," she says, her voice happy. Chicken barks at the change in her tone of voice. She bends, ruffling his ears. "So why was she in your hand in the photo?"

"I hung a feeder outside my window so she didn't have to go far for fuel. I spent a lot of time in the tree, or near the tree, and one day she just came up, that *zzzz* of her buzz drawing me out of the book I was reading, and I just knew. She wanted to sit with me." A lump forms in my throat as I try to recount this part of the story. "I was alone a lot. I think she might have known I was lonely."

Her expression falls. My eyes drop from the sadness in her face to see her hand twitch, almost lift toward me, like she wants to reach for mine.

I have the urge to close the gap.

The sound of pee softly pelting grass below yanks both of our attention to Chicken, who has finally, with incredible comedic timing, decided to do his business.

"Good job, sir!" Sydney congratulates him, doing a little cheer. His stoicism is iconic. She snorts, then her eyes trail back up to mine and her smile contracts a little. I force a smile, trying to brighten my expression to something less Eeyore. "Cadence." She says my name, lets it sit in the air like a smoke cloud between us. "I would have liked to climb that tree with you. Just FYI."

She whirls, walking back toward the car a little too fast for the ancient Chihuahua on her leash. I stand in a daze, hoping the high in my head will clear before I make it back behind the wheel.

CHAPTER TWENTY

Sydney

We're about to turn onto the main drag of Solvang and are greeted by a craggy stone pillar holding a blue-and-white sign that says *Welcome to Solvang* in ornate Danish letters (what else would I call that blocky script?), and right below, it indicates that the village center is a half mile ahead. Cadence hasn't brought up the reading with Moira again. Neither have I. After her story about the hummingbird picture, we ended up spending the rest of the drive talking about anything but her mother. Or my father.

Since we met, their relationship has loomed like a storm cloud over us, big and ominous, ready to burst and ruin our plans. Our plans being to ruin theirs—but whatever. It was nice to talk about ourselves, to share bits of who we are in this moment and how we got here. I learned that her supervisor wants her to start leading tours, which is a promotion of sorts, but she's torn since her favorite part about working for the parks is being with nature. Not humans. Which I get, but I think she should go for it, and I blurted as much.

"You do?" she asked me, a quizzical expression on her face.

"Sounds like the tours are an important part of furthering visitors' understanding of the park, which seems like a vital way to help bring in donations and support conservation." I don't know why I felt so confident in offering her advice—she doesn't exactly seem like the type to revel in listening to the opinions of others.

Her smile let me know she didn't mind hearing mine, which sent a butterfly wing fluttering through my tummy.

I learned she likes lobster rolls but doesn't like lobster by itself (*shells freak me out*), and she doesn't eat beef or pork; she was a vegetarian for years and sometimes still toys with going back. She lives alone, and she's single.

That last part I may have found a bit too interesting.

This kind of one-on-one is something I usually reserve for therapy, or Joe when we're both feeling existential or lonely. It's not usually the kind of conversation I have with people I'm attracted to. And despite my best efforts, I can admit that I am definitely, not maybe, attracted to Ranger Girl.

From the passenger seat, I've had a prime viewing spot to take in her unusual beauty. Her cheeks are smattered with dark freckles, a sharp contrast to her fair skin. Her long, curly black hair seems to have a life of its own with the way it twists and moves and drifts and tangles. In profile, her long, dark lashes whisper against the skin on her cheek when she blinks. Her chin is her most delicate feature, dainty but defined. The perfect shape to clutch in hand and tug close—

I blink away at that.

Attraction is one thing. Acting on it is another.

At least I have the road ahead to focus on. We're now entering the village, heading toward the center. Many of the buildings that line either side of the main road toward the town center were built in the Danish Provincial style, with thatched roofs and charming facades featuring board-and-batten siding in a variety of colors to match the buildings. There's a mixture of brick and other more modern buildings sprinkled in, but all of them have worked to streamline the aesthetic. Through a courtyard that leads to another section of shops, I can see one of the village's famous windmills.

It's a slow crawl through the village center.

Cadence pushes out a puff of air through her nostrils in annoyance.

"What?" I ask. "I don't love that sound."

"I just can't believe she planned her engagement weekend on Danish Festival weekend. The village is going to be unhinged and booked to the brim," she says with a growl. I *do* like that sound. Jesus, I'm a mess.

"You think there's a reason?" I say.

"With her, there's always a reason."

I flick my eyes up the road to see the sign for our hotel becoming clear. It's called the Hygge, after the Danish word used to describe something that invokes a cozy, contented feeling of well-being. Which is anything but the way either of us feels as we turn off the road—struggling through a throng of people crossing—to enter the hotel parking lot. Cadence pulls under the porte cochere and cuts the engine. A young man dressed in a navy-blue vest, fitted white button-down, and navy slacks opens her door.

She lets out another deep huff. I don't think about it. I just reach out.

My hand presses to her shoulder in solidarity, but the burst of heat that shoots through my center sets me off-kilter. She turns her face up, and her eyes catch mine. The heat pulses between my legs as I hold the look.

"I'm glad you're with me this weekend," she says in a low voice that cracks right at the end.

"Checking in?" the valet attendant interrupts. Cadence's lips work into a swift smile, which she leaves plastered on as she turns to the attendant, climbing out but leaving the keys in the car.

My head drops back against the rest and my eyes close. "Me, too," I reply to her, too late, barely audible. She doesn't hear me. My eyes peel open and drop to look at Chicken, who now stirs on my lap, realizing the car has come to a stop and no doubt needing to pee again. I brush my hand over his head.

"Uh-oh, buddy," I say. "None of this is good."

~

The Hygge is the physical manifestation of that word's intended design. At least, this lobby is. Cozy fur throws, plush couches in neutrals, a glowing fireplace with two rich velvet chairs in a classically Scandinavian design. The light-washed wood floors are covered in artfully laid rugs with blue, red, and white Danish prints.

As we approach the front desk, we meet up with some of the engagement party attendees, as well as Moira and Dad, who are standing side by side at the front desk. Dad is noticeably quiet in the shadow of Moira, who is busy yapping with a tall sandy-haired man who looks distinctly like a real-life version of Anna's love interest in *Frozen*.

"Sven," Cadence says, quiet enough that only I can hear her. I press my hand to my lips to hold in a guffaw. "I know, he literally looks like a cartoon character."

"I was just thinking about the guy with the reindeer in *Frozen*," I reply. "Isn't his name Sven?"

"I think that's the reindeer," Cadence says, her lips threatening a smile.

"Honestly, he kind of resembles the reindeer, too."

There's the smile. The way it lights her eyes is intoxicating.

Moira throws her head back in a cackle at something Sven says, and Cadence fills in the blank after my quizzical expression. "She's been coming here since I was in middle school; she's ingratiated herself to everyone with a pulse."

Cadence is biased against her mother, something that I understand comes from years of feeling powerless, or at least feeling like she doesn't have autonomy from her mother's strong personality. But even with the bias, her assessment of Moira feels pretty fair. She has a way of making you forget your own boundaries in favor of the ones she lays out. I never would have agreed to a tarot reading from some random psychic—not even as a party trick or in a tipsy state of being.

I glance over from Moira and Dad to see that Greg and Pam have arrived. They have a son my age, so I am well acquainted with them since many of my teenage summers were spent lounging in the pool in their backyard. Greg is a distinguished-looking man, with close-cropped silver hair and a strong jaw. Pam is a small-boned and pretty Black woman, with shoulder-length braids and a kind smile. I've always liked her way more than her husband.

I lean over, pressing the tips of my fingers into Cadence's wrist. The contact sends shoots of energy up the length of my arm. When she turns her face toward mine, the heat of her breath hits my cheek.

"Greg and Pam, two o'clock," I say, my mouth going dry. This close, I can see a dimple indenting when her lip twitches up. It makes a half-moon right at the corner. I force myself to focus by removing my fingers from her wrist and edging my face out of the proximity of her breath.

"Do pilots have some sort of dress code?" Cadence says in a quiet voice. A chuckle rumbles in my throat, and I have to swallow it back. "Could have picked him out anywhere."

"Until the rest of Dad's pilot friends arrive, and then it's like a *Where's Waldo* situation," I quip. She flicks a glance to me.

"You don't dress like part of the club," she says, allowing her gaze to travel over me. Everywhere her eyes touch is a stroke of heat.

"Cade." A younger woman's voice breaks Cadence's focus from me, rescuing me from a near collapse under its weight. We both look toward the sound to see a redhead whose voice is high and bell-like, a contrast to her grungy, nineties-inspired cutoffs, flannel, and crop top, which reveals a tattoo on her abdomen. She's accompanied by a guy the size of a redwood tree approaching. Her face has this wide-open quality about it that makes her look younger than she probably is. Her eyes flick from Cadence to me and then back.

"She's in rare form," the redhead says. She's looking at Moira when she speaks.

"Rare in what way?" Cadence asks.

"The exceptionally Moira way." The redhead grins, and Cadence groans.

Cadence's eyes drop to her legs. "You'll freeze, you know."

"The winds aren't that bad yet," she replies.

"The temp drops fast," Cadence counters.

It's clear from their exchange that there is substantial history between them, but it feels more familial than romantic.

"And you're Lola," I break in as the thought enters my head and then immediately leaves my mouth. I extend my hand, and Lola ignores it.

"Sydney, the pilot daughter," she says brightly. She grabs me in an unexpected embrace. She smells of cinnamon and sugar, and I remember she was experimenting with baking cookies recently, but somehow she feels like the type of person who would just always smell like that.

She presses back, and then motions to the man-tree beside her. "This is Hawthorne. My plus-one."

"Hawthorne," Cadence repeats his name as if searching for the rest of it.

"That's it," Lola says.

"Named for the author," Hawthorne says, his voice a rumble of thunder through my bones. Lola leans into him, but with her petite figure, she only reaches the middle of his chest. The logistics of this pairing baffle the mind.

"We have a theory," Lola says. She and Hawthorne lean toward us. Cadence and I instinctively reciprocate. This move puts our bodies even closer. The light press of her arm against mine is almost all I can think about. "This is a hell of a lot of trouble for an engagement party." Lola raises both her thick copper eyebrows.

Without her saying the rest, my stomach drops. A cold pit forms in its place.

"You don't mean you think they're secretly getting married this weekend?" Cadence asks, sounding appalled. Lola bites her lip and nods.

"They invited, like, fifty people," Lola continues. "I saw the guest list. And plus, this romantic setting—"

"Solvang is hardly romantic," Cadence cuts in.

"We're surrounded by wineries and cute inns, it's practically a Hallmark movie," Lola says, scrunching up her face in annoyance. Cadence leans back, as if by moving away from Lola she can get away from this possible scenario.

"There you two are," Moira calls to us. She motions for us to come over. Cadence looks like she wants to stay put, Lola makes her wide eyes wider, and Hawthorne stands erect like the old-growth tree that he is.

"Come on." I tug lightly on the edge of Cadence's t-shirt, and I could swear she leans in. Against me. It doesn't last long, but I know it happens.

"There's a problem with your rooms," Moira says.

And for the second time in two minutes my insides become a tundra.

CHAPTER TWENTY-ONE

Cadence

They only have one room available.

I keep repeating the words in my head, trying to alchemize them into something different. I had assumed Moira, in her infinite psychic-ness—and her certainty that I would come to this party—would have gone ahead and booked me my own room. I don't mean to sound entitled or anything, and it isn't my preference, it's just what my mother would normally do.

So not only is this a disaster, it's suspect, as it goes against behavior I have come to expect from her. My mother is the type of person to plan a dinner reservation without confirming you're available and then make you feel like shit if you can't make it. The Hygge is her haunt. The spot she stays in every time she comes to Solvang.

"You're telling me that you forgot to book me my own room?" I ask through gritted teeth.

"I forgot to call in the whirlwind of your arrival," she says, tapping her room key on the counter. Impatient. I can read on her face the subtle shift from amused to agitated as it happens in real time.

"And there's nothing available, not even for you?" I ask, not trying to flatter her, though she definitely takes it that way. Her smile creeps back out, chasing her annoyance away with the flames of her ego. I cross my arms to shut out her happiness as it bounds toward me.

"The Danish Days Festival brings in thousands of extra travelers," she replies. "So, as you can probably imagine, the whole town is full."

I open my mouth to argue, because in a tourist town like this, there has to be something available. An Airbnb at the very least—even if it's not ideal. But Rick gets in there first.

"Well, Syd wouldn't mind letting you bunk with her," he says, and then turns his crystal-blue eyes to Sydney. I swear to God, the look that passes between them is loaded. He practically pleads. My mind is glitching over his use of the word *bunk*, like we're two girls at summer camp and not two gay girls with heaps of chemistry and a stupid soulmate prediction fucking around with our heads.

"Oh, what a wonderful idea, love," Moira says, gripping Rick by the arm and tugging him in for a kiss on the cheek. He beams.

I am at a loss for words, but thankfully Sydney isn't.

"If that's the easiest option," Sydney says, holding her dad in a glare before shifting her eyes to me. "As long as you don't snore."

That is not what she was supposed to say. She was supposed to be as surprised as me, shaken to her core. The chemistry was supposed to make her proximity-conscious. She shouldn't offer her room. She can't possibly think this is actually a good idea.

I can't sleep near enough to her that I can imagine what it would be like to sleep *with* her.

"I don't snore—"

"Ah, then it's settled," Moira interrupts me before I can protest any more. She turns to Sven, who has been silently watching this exchange, doing nothing to try to stop it. "We've solved it. Let's get them checked in!"

While they're distracted, I turn to Sydney.

"You don't have to do this," I say. Not *we shouldn't do this*—which we shouldn't. Not *I can find somewhere else to stay*—which I am sure I can even if it's a couple towns away. But when my eyes find hers, I forget the panic. I forget the lone-wolf girl with no one to have her back. Because Sydney's eyes are like deep water I could let myself float in. They cover me in comfort like lapping ocean waves used to when I was a little girl. They seem to say that this is going to be okay.

Because it's not just *me* going through it.

It's *us*.

"It's just two nights, Ranger Girl," she says. "And as far as anyone knows, we're not women who could be soulmates." She coaxes her lips into a tiny smile, and I'm fixated on the way the left corner kicks up higher than the right. Crooked and perfect.

Moira turns back to us, holding a small paper envelope with our room keys and instructions on how to navigate our way there.

"Sven will have your bags brought over," my mother says, her eyes steady on me. I feel like she's waiting for something, but I can't imagine what. I clutch the keys and lift my brows.

"We better get settled in, then," I say, holding her green eyes with mine.

"Shuttle to Whimsy Winery leaves in thirty minutes."

"We'll be there," I say, giving her a tight smile.

"You remember the dress code—"

"I have plenty of business casual—"

"No hiking boots—"

"Mom, stop." The name, *Mom*. Her eyes sheen immediately.

"It's nice to hear you call me that," she says, and she doesn't seem to care that Rick and Sydney are close enough to hear and are definitely watching.

"Reflex," I say. She nods almost imperceptibly. I walk off in the direction of the doors that lead to the courtyard connecting the lobby to the rooms.

Sydney and I stand in front of the one queen-size bed sitting ominously in the center of the space.

"There's only one bed," she says. I hear a chuckle in her voice.

"She booked you a queen, not a double." It still isn't sinking in.

"To be fair to your mom—"

"Let's not—"

"She didn't know I would be sharing a room with you," she says, and I swear to God, now she is most certainly holding in a laugh. Not a chuckle; a full-on guffaw.

"You don't think she knew—"

"Cadence, she isn't psych—"

I whirl on her, my mouth flying open in an O as she clamps her hand over her lips and crumples, unleashing her laugh into the room and all over me. It's sunshine, warming everything, and I have no defense against it.

She drops to the bed and falls onto her back, giving me the most insane view of her body prostrate against the white hotel linens. Her hair is coming loose from the high messy bun and streaming out in rays. She rolls onto her side, looking up at me. Her body makes a perfect hourglass shape when standing, but it's even more aggressively clear just how scandalously flawless her shape is when she's lying like that. Her full, natural-looking breasts peek from her shirt. Her ass spreads against the bed, her thighs pressing to touch each other.

Her eyes blink, bright with humor.

"Why are you looking at me like that?" she asks, her expression settling, softening. I have no idea what my face is doing.

"What am I looking at you like?" Heat pools in my cheeks. It races down my spine. It gathers between my legs in a pressure I wish I could ignore.

Want is unmistakable, inconvenient. It's making me lightheaded.

"Like you want to kiss me." Her voice is steady. My eyes trip to her lips as if I'll see proof of that word, *kiss*, floating there. "You're looking right at my mouth."

I blink, ready to dispute her assessment, but I can't. Because there's no denying it. I was looking at her mouth.

I would kiss her if she let me.

She grips me by the hand and tugs me onto the bed beside her. I let myself fall, rolling against the cool linens and ripping my baseball cap off. My hair flies out, wild around my head, and she tucks her face close to it, moving some of the tendrils.

Playing with them.

The tips of her fingers caress the dark strands, twisting the ends around her pointer finger as her eyes flutter up to me, shining with interest.

I am not someone who thrives under the weight of attention,

always preferring to sink back to the edges of a room, seek the darkness outside the spotlight. But something about the way Sydney Sinclair bestows attention doesn't make me want to shrink away.

I become a fern on the floor of a forest, stretching her fronds toward the sun.

"What if I said you were right?" I say, twisting around to prop up on my arm. So far, she and I have managed not to lie to each other. So far, we've been transparent. We've worked together. We've made pinky promises and landed on partnership.

I don't want to pretend with her. A realization that terrifies me as much as it thrills me.

"*Are* you saying that?" She raises her arm, curving it behind her head until she's propped on it. I'm at a slight advantage from my more upright angle, and I feel more physically in control, even if emotionally I'm a buoy in a stormy sea.

"What if I am?" I let myself look at her. Really *look*. She doesn't shy away from my gaze. She shifts just her face so that she's looking up at me. Her skin is a soft golden tan, the kind you'd see on a girl in a sundress at the beginning of summer. Kissed with color and almost shimmering.

"I'd be surprised," she says, taking her lower lip between her teeth. Small and white, straight but not perfect. One of the front teeth kicks out a tad, overlapping the smaller one behind it. "But I'd be lying if I said I haven't thought the same thing." Her eyes trail over my face like she's tracing an outline. "If you said that, I mean."

I swallow a hard lump that's formed in my throat.

"I can't say that," I reply, but I am desperate to inch closer.

I haven't wanted to kiss someone in a long time—so long that

I almost forgot what the desire feels like. She rolls to her side, drawing a section of my hair between her fingers.

"Then don't say it," she says, eyes on my hair with a hunger. "You can just *do* it."

"I don't know what it means if I do."

"Does it have to mean something?" She lifts her gaze.

"The soulmate thing—"

"But neither of us believe in soulmates." The shoulder of her sweatshirt slips down to reveal creamy tan skin and a neon-blue bra strap. Her eyes land on my lips, and my hand itches to reach for her waist, cup the small of her back, and pull her against me.

Feel the weight of her body, not just her gaze.

"We could try it," she says, and her lip curls. She has a small, slightly pointed nose, which she scrunches as her smile spreads. "It might be fun."

Fun. I could kiss her just for fun.

"It doesn't have to mean anything about our souls," she breathes. This close I can feel the heat. I want it to consume me. *For fun.*

"No strings," I say, but I'm not thinking about the kind that mean obligations or commitment, payment or puppetry.

I'm thinking about the string tied from one soul to another.

"Just how I like it." The words leave her throat with a growl.

All I have to do is lean in and our lips will touch. She wets hers. Now they glisten, enticing, inviting. "Okay," I whisper.

"Okay," she consents.

Her hand twines in my hair now, up to the nape of my neck, fingers stroking skin as our breath mingles in the tiny expanse of space between us.

My hand snakes around her waist, flattening my palm to her

back, pressing her closer. I resist the urge to squeeze her flesh, run my hand over the generous slope of her ass, cup the curve at the bottom.

I focus on the smell of her skin, fresh air and spice and sunshine. Her nose touches mine in a gentle nudge, waiting for me to do the rest.

And so I do. Slowly, slowly.

And then all at once.

I take her lips hostage, mine fitting over the soft, supple curves of her pout. My tongue slides past that cute crooked tooth, searching. Tasting. Coffee and mint, a little salty and sweet and so warm.

A small primal noise rumbles from my throat.

Her hand cradles my head, and she closes the gap between our bodies just enough that I can feel all her ample curves against my longer, leaner lines. Her tongue touches the tip of mine, her hips press into mine, amplifying the ache that pulses between my legs.

Knock knock knock.

Our faces whip apart, but our bodies stay in tandem.

The sound is coming from the hotel door.

"Who the hell would—" she nearly spits. I love that she hasn't let me go yet. Makes me hopeful she doesn't want to—isn't regretting what just happened now that we've been interrupted.

"Valet," I reply. "They haven't brought our bags yet."

"Oh fuck." She turns back to look at me. Her lips are a deeper shade of pink. She grins. "Let me get my cash for a tip." Her eyes drop to my mouth. "Fuck." But she smiles when she says it. "Coming!" She lifts herself off the bed and walks across the room to where her purse sits by the coffee machine on the dresser. Her yoga pants are riding up a little in her ass crack, adding definition to the outline.

Jesus Christ.

I sit up, crossing my legs and leaning against the end of the bed to ease the throbbing.

She opens the door to reveal the same valet attendant from when we arrived earlier. He's got a cart with her duffel and my rolling suitcase sitting on it, as well as the bag containing Chicken's food and water bowls, treats, and the ziplock plastic bag of dog food they packed him for the weekend.

As far as I know, Chicken is staying with Moira and Rick, not us, so that will need to be returned.

Us. We are staying in a room together, but we are not an *us.* We are trying to make sure her dad doesn't get swindled, but we are not a *couple.* We just kissed like starving people loading up plates at a buffet, but we are not *hooking up.*

The valet drops the bags just inside the door, and Sydney discreetly hands him a folded-up dollar bill in an amount I can't see before she shuts the door and turns around.

My eyes can't get enough of this view.

And then on the dresser her phone begins to buzz with a call.

CHAPTER TWENTY-TWO

Sydney

Whimsy Winery is on 250 acres of land in the heart of Santa Ynez. The rolling hills feature rows and rows—innumerable to my eyes—of grapevines. The sky is dotted by fluffy whisps of cloud against the cobalt blue that matches my irises. The early-arrivals crew—or, really, on time by the *suggestion* in the itinerary—that's gathered are Moira's and Dad's closest friends. A pre–engagement party wine tasting and tour of the grounds. This is where the party will take place on Sunday for brunch.

Or, more specifically, the barnlike barrel room that I can see just at the edge of the rolling hill is where the party will take place. It opens onto a limestone dance floor. It's a popular wedding destination, and this winery is the one Moira has regularly frequented on her visits to Solvang, a fact that I learned on the short ride over with Cadence.

Lola and Hawthorne's assessment that the engagement party might be a wedding in disguise is starting to feel a hell of a lot more plausible.

Cadence sidles up to me and hands me a glass of the vineyard's signature white blend. I resist the urge to down it in one gulp. I can't decide if it's the potential wedding-not-engagement that is causing my inner spiral or if it's the heated kiss on the one bed in the room I'm sharing with my partner in scheming that's doing it.

We had to get ready in a hurry. Dad called to let me know he was bringing Chicken's bed to our room so he could stay with us because we're on the ground level and, to quote him, "He misses you, Birdie, you know?" I had to roll my eyes at that one. I think Chicken mostly misses the fact that I am a whore for snuggles and he can always get a treat from me even though he's supposed to be on a diet. I am pretty sure Dad just didn't want to cart him around all the time.

Chicken mostly sleeps now, anyway. Something I hope will rub off on me but probably won't.

Not with my other bedroom buddy.

I flick my eyes to Cadence. She changed into a pair of dark jeans and a loose-fitting green-and-white button-down, those same loafers from dinner the other night, with her hair in a loose braid. The way she looks laid-back and put-together but also, like, still windswept and a little wild—it's really sending me.

No strings. Her words, my idea. One I am always so happy to find out the person I'm about to kiss is willing to agree on. It's such a theme of my romantic relationships that it's almost a joke and not worth mentioning, and it means the closest people in my life almost never get a look at the people I date, let alone a meet and greet.

So why am I fighting the urge to text Joe right now just to tell him I kissed a girl?

"This is a wedding venue," Cadence says, taking a sip of her wine, her dark eyes gliding over the rows of grapevines.

"We need a plan," I say, gulping my wine so that I almost

choke as it flows free and fast down my throat. I recover with a cough, which draws Cadence's eyes to me in alarm.

Don't look at her mouth, my mind commands.

So, of course, my focus drops right to her lips.

She has this Cupid's-bow upper lip, deep and plump, swooping over her lower lip, which is slightly bigger and softer. I know now just how cozy her mouth on mine feels. I can't unknow it.

One cannot exist without the other.

That's what Moira said about the Sun and the Moon in my tarot reading.

That's what a soulmate is.

"Totally," Cadence agrees, and we both force our focus on each other's eyes, not mouths. "We have two possible sources of information here."

"We need to find out more about Kismet, the loans, the state of things," I add on. "And we need to find out more about that text thread with my dad and Greg."

"I think Lola is our best bet for info about Kismet. She's worked there forever, and Moira considers her innocuous enough that she might be more likely to drop her guard."

"Impressive," I say, bringing my wineglass to my lips for another drink.

"Plus, people just tell Lola things—she's a Scorpio," Cadence quips. The look of horror that immediately crosses her face after the word *Scorpio* leaves her lips nearly makes me choke.

"Was that Freudian or just your true colors shining through?" I gasp.

"Old habits die hard," she growls, lifting her glass to press back her smile with the rim. "The air in Cali brings out the mystic in me."

"Uh-huh. Next you'll be telling me that my aura is purple." I laugh outright.

"Shut up," she says through a chuckle she clearly wants to smash. "Can we focus, please?"

"Sure thing, you cute little astrologer, you," I reply, and almost, very nearly reach out to tug her in for a kiss. I catch myself just in the nick of time and turn to look over the guests, tamping down the urge as it surges through me like a current. "So Lola or Pam and Greg." The frog in my throat hopefully isn't too noticeable. "Those are the targets."

"I know if I can get Lola alone, I can get her talking."

"I thought Scorpios were steel vaults with secrets."

Cadence is fighting back the cutest smile ever. That crescent-moon dimple is in danger of popping right out and making me want to kiss it. "Her chatty Sagittarius rising isn't."

We both take sips of our wine as we chuckle.

"Pam has always had a soft spot for me," I say, and my stomach flips for a way less fun reason than wanting to tangle my fingers in Cadence's hair.

Greg and Pam were my parents' closest friends. Their son, Luke, and I were besties, too—until we hooked up senior year and, no surprise, I wanted it to stay no-strings-attached. But in the year before Mom passed, when Dad was still flying and we didn't yet know how truly awful things were about to get, Pam was kind of a rock for me and Mom. And, of course, her swimming pool and the fact that she always had Hot Pockets in the freezer didn't hurt, either.

"Good. Then, what do you think about a divide-and-conquer strategy?" Cadence asks with a teeny waggle of her brows. I grin.

"Excellent, Ranger Girl," I say, extending my glass for her to cheers.

We walk in the direction of the rest of the party. Everyone has full to semifull glasses of wine, which means everyone is likely about to disperse to explore the grounds. I have to get in with Pam and get her walking off on her own.

Moira, Greg, and Dad stand in a group with another couple I don't recognize, who must be friends of Moira's. The woman from that couple and Moira are currently having an aside, while the man and Greg have become absorbed in one of Dad's newest tricks. He's been trying to master different sleight of hand illusions using cards, and recently he's focused on a trick called the Four Appearing Aces.

They are engrossed, or at least actively humoring him.

Pam is only halfway engaged. Her other half is heavily invested in her wineglass.

I approach, waving to get her attention and flashing her a smile.

"I haven't had a chance to say hi," I say, opening my arms for a hug before I even reach her. She brightens as I approach, letting me wrap her in a light embrace.

Pam is your classic LA suburbanite. A little frumpy but still trying to stay hip since she lives near a city obsessed with youth. Her recent switch to shoulder-length braids makes her look fresh.

"Wanna walk around the vineyard and gossip?" I say in a low, conspiratorial tone that makes her chuckle. I extend her the crook of my arm.

"You know the answer to spending time with you is always *yes*," Pam replies, taking my arm.

We set off down a winding walkway that spills us out into the vineyard. The sun is just starting to edge toward the hills, so the light is slightly less harsh than it was when we first arrived. I know I can't broach the subject of the texts Cadence saw between Dad and Greg, not outright, so my armpits are sweating and not because it's hot. I wore a bodycon gray t-shirt dress, steel-toed Alexander McQueen booties, and a loose-fitting denim jacket because it's actually quite a cool afternoon.

No, the sweat is my pits' reaction to my brain telling my mouth it has to be reserved. Lie if need be. I'm here for answers, and I won't get them with blurting. But I *can* nudge her about what she thinks of Moira. Maybe if I let my skepticism show, she'll be more inclined to spill some beans.

"It's really beautiful here," Pam says, eyes misty as she looks out on the horizon.

"It's great that Moira knows the owners so well. Probably got them a discount on the party," I say, taking a ginger sip of wine. Pam's lips tighten ever so slightly.

"She seems to have a way with people, doesn't she?" To someone who doesn't know Pam, she'd sound neutral. Admiring even. But I can read between the lines, and what I'm getting from her is far more emotional.

"I have to confess," I say, pausing just so. She cuts her eyes over, ready for my tea. "I was really thrown by the engagement invitation. I hadn't even had a chance to meet her because of my schedule."

"It didn't surprise me in the least," Pam replies as we take a turn at the end of this row of grapevines, walking along a path that leads us toward the barrel room, where the engagement party will be held.

"Really? It's not like Dad to move that fast," I say, letting the hurt bleed through in my voice. Because it does really hurt that he made this massive decision without coming to me first. Maybe it's childish, but I feel like that whole *us against the world* thing should apply to him, too.

"Oh no, I agree with you there, Sydney. I just mean it's not a surprise that it happened lightning-quick—not to me, anyway. Not after I saw the two of them together," she says, and actually, *what the fuck?* Her voice sounds all dreamy and soft. There's no way she actually thinks Moira is good for my dad.

I fight the urge to throw a fit. I am a grown-ass adult woman with a career and a 401(k) and a whole apartment and rent. (Okay, I split those last two with my best friend, but rent in LA is high.)

"When did you see them together?" *Pam and Greg met Moira before me?*

"Last month, right before they got engaged. Greg had some things . . ." She struggles a bit over the word and I take notice. "To chat with Rick about, so we stopped by his place and wound up splitting a bottle of wine with the two of them. Played cards."

"And you left that impromptu meeting feeling good about her and Dad?" I am stuck on this. It's kind of derailing my fact-finding mission. She and Greg met them a month ago! Dad didn't tell me it was serious! He didn't tell me they'd gotten engaged!

What else isn't he telling me? Even if Moira isn't conning him, the fact that he kept this from me makes me feel confused and angry—I just don't know exactly who to direct that anger at.

"She's good for him," Pam says, just as we reach the entrance to the barrel room. It's got a big distressed sliding back door, in stark contrast to the soft peachy white of the stucco building. "I haven't seen Rick this happy in a long time."

My face falls. I feel the features tumble, and I see the evidence of it in Pam's expression. Her brows knit and she tugs me in for a side hug.

It totally deflates my balloon of angry confusion.

"Rick needs someone to help him keep his life straight. He always has," she says. "You had to take that on after Diana passed, and you handled it well." Tears sting in the corners of my eyes at the compliment, or the mention of my mother's name, or a little bit of both. "I'm glad you can let go a little now." She tucks my cheek into her palm, gently caressing. "Maybe find your own happiness that doesn't depend on making sure he's okay."

I clench my teeth and try for a smile. She chuckles.

"You don't have to like change. But that doesn't stop it from calling."

"Right, well," I stammer, but I can't commit to an argument, and Pam knows it. Fortunately Greg calls her over with a wave and a "Sweetheart" and says to meet him at the sommelier station, rescuing me from having to say more on the topic. My brain ping-pongs between the dissonance of the idea that Moira makes Dad happy, could actually be good for him, be what he needs, and the tiny little sliver of info about the night she met Moira at Dad's.

Greg had something to discuss with Dad. And that something is probably what that text thread Cadence saw is about. What happened to get Moira involved? It could be why this engagement feels so rushed. I hope Cadence learns more than me from her trek around the vineyard with Lola.

CHAPTER TWENTY-THREE

Cadence

Hawthorne has abandoned Lola and me in our walk through the grapevines after he met the vintner and learned he could go see the machine where the grapes are smashed. He smacked a kiss on Lola's cheek, requiring him to nearly double over because of their height difference. Even though my main objective in this one-on-one with Lola is to try to get information about Kismet out of her, I have to admit, it's nice to be in her company. In a lonely childhood, Lola was often my only friend. Even if the three-year age gap meant we never shared any classes in school and were usually out of sync in our development.

"I didn't see you come by yesterday to go through your boxes in the garage," she says, in the beat of silence that follows her explanation of how she met Hawthorne and why she isn't calling him her boyfriend: They met at a Ren faire where she was working a friend's jewelry booth as a favor. He works at the Ren faire and is leaving soon for a circuit in the Midwest. *He's good in bed and he's nice to me, but I know it's temporary.* She sounded surprisingly melancholy when she said that last part.

"Oh," I say, trying to think of an explanation that isn't an outright lie. "I ran into Rick, and he invited me to take a backlot tour of Universal."

She nods approvingly. "Getting to know the future stepdad. I dig it."

I balk openly at the use of the word *stepdad* to describe Rick, which garners a laugh from Lola.

"Calm down," she says, her voice breaking over the chuckle. "You don't have to call him that or anything."

Technically, she's correct. He would be my stepdad, but I find it difficult to wrap my brain around that reality for more than one reason. Thinking of a man as a stepdad because he's marrying my mother, who I have been estranged from for years, feels weird. Moira only gets the label *Mom* when I let my guard down. Even if they wind up married, it's not as if I'm planning to come back into her life in a more consistent or permanent way.

But beyond that weirdness, there's the whole thing about how I never knew my biological father, have never called any man *Dad*, and don't plan on starting now.

It's not often that I think about him, the man who helped Moira make me. Not as an adult, anyway. There was a time when his secret identity used to intrigue me, serving as a mystery to fill the space in my childhood and adolescence. But Moira thwarted me at every turn, refusing to let me seek him out; she made finding out his identity a source of tension between us.

I used to care about easing the tension in any way possible. Walking the tightrope she hung for me. And even my realization that I didn't want to do that anymore—even if it meant I barely saw her—didn't make me any more sure I could find him without her help. It's a cruel joke to know your trust in a person is eroded so deeply that you don't want to answer their calls but you still *deeply* fear that one day they'll actually stop calling altogether.

"He's a nice dude," Lola is saying. She's smiling, and I know I should smile back. I should agree with her. It's the socially appropriate response. I suck at socially appropriate responses, but I don't disagree with her about Rick.

"He is," I reply, seeing a window of opportunity opening up. "I don't understand what he sees in Moira." It won't surprise Lola for me to say something like that.

"You mean besides the fact that she's an ageless beauty and thoughtful communicator," she says, and the way her lips jump and flatten in rapid fire makes it clear she's messing with me.

"Did she pay you to say that?" I retort. Lola owes a lot to Moira, but she isn't fooled by her. Despite everything she's been through, Lola has always had a strong sense of self, one Moira doesn't mess with. My mother made sure Lola finished high school. She gave her work and freedom.

Two things she never seemed to want to give me willingly.

"Cade, come on, when was the last time you saw her like this?" Lola flicks her eyes up, looking over the rows of grapevines to where Moira stands with Rick. She's smelling the grapes. Rick is looking over her shoulder admiringly, with Chicken on a leash sniffing the same vine, just closer to the ground. Rick leans in, nuzzling her ear with his nose. She giggles, turning to close her arms around him in an embrace. The whole display sets my nerves on edge.

"I've never seen her like this," I say. "That's why I'm suspicious." Lola halts at that, face jumping in surprise.

"What do you mean *suspicious*?"

Fuck. Way to step in it, Cadence.

"I'm always suspicious of her," I say, trying to save it with my signature bitterness. "I have good reason to be."

"Okay, I won't argue with you there," she says, looking back at the two of them. "But they're in love. I can tell by the way she's changed at work."

At work. The mention of Kismet is such an organic gift that it could be considered a blessing from the Universe. If I still believed that the Universe was in the habit of granting me favors.

"You'll have to fill me in," I reply, trying to snuff any audible expectation out of my voice. Lola takes a drink from her wineglass, and I follow her lead.

"She's just not as intense about retaining clients, getting new clients. It's almost like she would rather go on lunch dates with Rick than do a reading for a stranger."

"So if she isn't working, is Kismet in trouble?" The bank papers for Kismet could be related to the business and not the house. I can readily admit that I don't know enough about these types of things to be able to tell the difference at a glance.

"I don't know about that—it's not like she lets me look at the financials—but her attitude has been different. That's all I'm saying. And I do kinda get it."

"Because she's in love?" I cut her a look of disbelief. She elbows me lightly, starting to walk again. I don't follow right away.

"Because her industry is changing like crazy." She turns back to look at me but doesn't stop moving. I have to follow her. "People can get a psychic reading on an app. They can order crystals from Amazon. Why would they trek through LA to a spooky house in Pasadena just to sit with her in person?"

"Loyalty?" I question. Despite everything, the idea that my mother might be pushed out of a profession she's been in for over three decades gives me a sinking feeling. Who is she without the thing she's worked so hard to make her whole identity?

Who am I if not estranged from her because of that?

"*Hello*, have you met the internet?" Lola guffaws. "There's no loyalty there. Sure, she has her clients, but she doesn't offer Zoom readings, and she's not on any of the apps."

"Have you noticed a drop-off in her clientele?"

"There's been a drop-off in everything to do with Kismet," she says. We round the end of the row of vines just as Moira and Rick reach the ends of theirs. I feel her eyes on us, watching, and my paranoia spikes.

Lola seems to experience the same creepy sensation, because her volume shifts down to almost a whisper. "It just wouldn't surprise me if she was planning for her second act."

She catches sight of Hawthorne emerging from a large outbuilding with the vintner and waves. Her smiles cracks open her features. She looks genuinely happy to spot him, but she's probably also grateful for the excuse to escape this conversation.

"With Rick?" I question. I know she's going to read my skepticism as something to undercut Rick, even if that's not how I mean it. Her eyes narrow.

"No offense, Cadence, but why do you care?" I'm surprised by the sharpness in her voice just as much as I'm surprised by the question.

"Of course I care." I don't know why, but I feel the sudden urge to defend myself.

"Really? You left LA, you don't visit, you've made it clear that none of this matters to you." Her words feel like a slap. I have to double down; it's the only way I know how to put up my armor.

"Moira and I don't mesh. It's better for us to be in each other's lives as little as possible."

"*Is* it better?" Her massive eyes shouldn't be so cutting. But her normally doe-like expression becomes a knife. "Or just easier?"

"Lola, that's not fair," I say, surprised by the sting.

"Not fair? That's not the only thing that isn't fair." She turns to go.

"I'm sorry about vanishing on you," I say before she walks away. Because I did. It's the truth, even if I never saw it that way before now, and even if I don't have any idea how to possibly mend it.

"I'm used to it," she says. A truth that crushes me. "I get that you need to shut her out—I do." She drains her wineglass in what I assume is an attempt to drown her feelings. "I don't mind her overbearing bullshit, her thinking she knows everything because the cards said it or she *vibed* on it." A snort tempers her words. I feel a smile creeping my lips up. "It never bothered me, but I know it was hard between you two. I know she wanted something from you that you couldn't give her—or maybe it was the other way around." She shrugs. "I don't get it, but that doesn't mean I don't believe you're doing what you think will protect you—or something." She pauses, looking me over. "But you could have called *me*. I was there, not going anywhere."

I should say she's right, let her know that I miss her, too. But I never told her I appreciated her growing up, and it's really hard to start telling her now.

"It was easier to put Kismet in its entirety behind me."

She nods, as if I've said exactly what she suspected and she's not mad, she's just disappointed. "So why are you here now?"

It's rhetorical, which becomes clear when she walks away without giving me a chance to explain. I watch her move, with a stiffness in her posture as she crosses a section of grapevines to meet up with Hawthorne. I turn in the opposite direction, not sure what to do with myself.

Lola's hurt pricks beneath my skin, and as much as I want to ignore it, I can't. When I left Kismet behind—put LA in my rear-view mirror and tried to lose every number, box up every memory—Lola got thrown in and closed off without me ever considering another option. It's true that I was lonely as a kid, as a teen, but I often forget that Lola and I had a lot in common. We both had messed-up relationships with our moms, and we were both only children. But even though we could have had each other, we never really figured out how.

Or I just didn't try hard enough.

I scan the area, my eyes stinging, my heart aching, until I see her.

Sydney.

She's emerged from the barrel room, her hair down from her high bun and streaming free in the light breeze. It's foolish how much seeing her calms me down. How I want to tell her what I learned about Moira's work, but I don't want to leave out the part where I realized I was a shitty friend to one of the only people in my life who really feels like family. This longing to be seen by her is a new sensation, one I am unfamiliar with wanting.

One that scares me more than whatever scheme Moira is trying to pull. More than her being right about my soulmate.

Even more than her knowing she might be right.

CHAPTER TWENTY-FOUR

Sydney

Dad finds me outside the barrel room as confusion over my own feelings wars with a desire to keep my cool, and any words I might have get caught in my throat. Dad finding happiness, feeling secure in setting down roots with another person, is harder for me to accept than who the person is. He spent years struggling with the loss of my mom, and watching him go through that—seeing how it stripped back the persona of stable father and exceptional pilot that had always been there—has had no small effect on me.

I'm not holding on to the whole *us against the world* thing as a strict rule of life. It's more that the mentality of placing myself in constant opposition with my world is why I am a twenty-eight-year-old who has never had a long-term committed relationship. It's not that I can't do it. It's not that I don't want it deep down. It's that having that would mean running the risk of getting hurt so deeply by losing it that I'd also lose my way.

Lose myself.

Lose my job and security and control. Just like Dad did.

"It's beautiful country up here," Dad says, and I flick a quick look at him. Dad isn't a fan of nature unless it's a birdie on a golf green. That whole adage of how golf is a good walk spoiled, he doesn't believe it. That's his preferred way to engage in a stroll.

"It's beautiful," I say, and even though I'm grappling with big feelings, I'm nothing if not an excellent compartmentalizer. You can't be a good pilot without the skill to shut away outside distractions.

Lola's proposition that this engagement party is actually a wedding is stuck in my head.

"It's a lot of trouble for an engagement party," I say.

"It's what we want," he says, shrugging. "If you can't get what you want when you're our age, when can you?"

"Fifty-nine isn't old, Dad," I reply. I don't think this is a late midlife crisis, but if it's even a little bit about that, then reminding him he's still relatively young can't hurt.

"It's not young, either," he says, flashing me a self-deprecating smile.

"Tell me you're not marrying this woman because you feel old."

He laughs me off, not offended, and clearly not swayed.

"I'm marrying her because she makes me feel young," he says, winking at me. We have the same bright eyes. The same strong jaw. That same sense of mischief. But his soft, squishy heart breaks easily, and mine is walled up like Rapunzel.

Dad continues. "I would think you'd be starting to come around, at the very least because you and Cadence seem to be hitting it off."

This assessment throws me. "How do we seem like that?"

He looks at me like he's surprised by my surprise. "Birdie, I know you. I know when you like someone." He pauses, his smile drooping slightly. "I know when you don't."

I refuse to acknowledge that I understand his meaning.

I refuse to acknowledge any of this.

"Rick, love!" Speak of the devil. Moira approaches, full wine-glass in hand, eyes cutting through me like lasers. "Can I steal you for a walk through the kitchen? They've prepped appetizer samplers for us."

"Excellent," Dad replies, extending one hand for her to take while the other presses to his belly to feign hunger. "A snack before we head back for the brats at the festival is just what I need."

"You're joining in the festivities tonight, I hope, Sydney," Moira says. It feels like an order. I'm not sure what festivities there are that I'm expected to take part in, but I'm guessing if I say no, Dad will go all wounded puppy dog and Moira will have an argument prepped and ready for why my decision isn't the right one.

"Wouldn't miss it," I say. My eyes instinctively slide away from Moira, seeking focus on the movement behind her. Cadence approaches with a wary expression, which she quickly wipes clean before Moira realizes she's behind her.

"It's the launch of the Danish festival tonight, so there's all kinds of fun events. Axe throwing," Moira says, looking at Cadence as if this should be of interest to her. Ranger Girl that she is, I expect she's right. "Torch parade, concert, beer and wine, something like twenty-five varieties of bratwurst." Moira pauses, a smile lifting her lips. There's a look of vulnerability that fixes in her features only when Cadence is near. The piercing, cool focus she wears in almost every situation drops, revealing softer eyes and a lighter clench to her jaw. I realize all at once that with

Cadence, Moira doesn't look like a predator on the hunt. She looks like a mother protecting her young.

"Apparently anyone can participate in the axe throwing," Dad chimes in with a little thrill. The look Moira gives him is another one of surprising gentleness.

Turning to me, seamlessly, her gaze sharpens.

"We purchased some tickets if you're interested," Moira says in a subtle correction to Dad. "Cadence was always exceptional with an axe."

Cadence can't fight the smile at this surprising praise. "I did okay."

"You won a gift certificate to the beer garden one year," Moira replies.

"Which you cashed in on my behalf," Cadence says.

"Well, you were sixteen. What did you need at a beer garden?"

"A pretzel and a sampling of their collection of artisanal mustards," Cadence lists with a subtle smile. There's tension between them, taut as always, but there's also something else.

Camaraderie. Shared memory.

Family.

The word makes me ache for Cadence, who has untethered herself from the family she had here and acts like she's cool with being such a loner. But no one can do this life thing completely on their own.

"I stand corrected," Moira says, turning her gaze to me. "What do you two say?"

Cadence shifts her weight subtly toward me. It feels like a reminder that we're in this together. And again, my heart aches because I want her to have someone. Maybe I even want to be that someone. The urge to reach for her hand, twine our fingers together, is strong. I can't give in to it no matter how much I might want to. I said no-strings-attached to the kiss.

It's the first time I haven't wanted that.

"I'm in," I say. "But I'd really like to freshen up back at the hotel first."

Moira's face brightens, and she points in the direction of the winery's visitor center.

"The shuttle is here for our use—you two can head back," she says, taking a small pause to look back and forth between us. "Freshen up." Her tone doesn't shift, but the energy around the words feels electrified. I have the distinct urge to run away, or attempt a lie, though I'm not sure what it would be about. Just something to make this sensation of being seen lessen in intensity.

I show her my teeth. "Perfect." Then I look to Cadence, willing her to catch my drift and bail alongside.

"Do you want us to take Chicken back with us?" Cadence asks, her eyes dropping to land on Chicken's tiny tan head. He's currently sniffing a scrub of what looks like lavender. The vineyard has planted rows of lavender alongside some of the grapevines, but this little struggling plant was like a shoot from a seed on the wind.

"Ah, thanks for looking out for him," Dad says. He's smiling big at Cadence now, who looks surprisingly pleased herself. "He's enjoying himself too much—we'll just drop him by before we head out to the festival. That way he'll be good and sleepy and won't get too anxious being left alone."

It's hard to read Cadence—she seems especially skilled at masking her feelings—but I'm starting to pick up on subtle shifts. That Cupid's-bow top lip flattens against the lower, causing the natural curl of her lips to straighten. It's small, the disappointment, but I see it. And the fact that she feels it in relation to my old dog causes my stomach to do a flip-flop.

"Well, then," I say, trying to shove that feeling way down, "we should probably head back." Cadence nods in agreement and bends to ruffle Chicken's ears, then we both turn to leave. The parents are watching—the pressure of their eyes is heavy.

CHAPTER TWENTY-FIVE

Cadence

There was a random couple celebrating their twentieth anniversary on the shuttle back, plus a chatty driver, who homed in immediately on the fact that he could engage Sydney in conversation. My resting bitch face made me exempt. But that also made it difficult to talk to Sydney about my conversation with Lola. However, it did give me plenty of time to spin out over the way Sydney smelled (warm and bright and earthy) and the way her knee was bumping mine with the movement of the vehicle. It gave me plenty of time to fixate on the fact that the whole purpose of my being here was to thwart Moira's nefarious plans, and now I'm worried her plans may not be as malicious as I want them to be.

Okay, so it's not that I *want* her to be a conniving con woman out to swindle Sydney's dad. Especially not when Rick looks at her as if she's hung the moon. It would be tragic to see him hurt by her, to be proved right that she can't be trusted with another person's heart. But a reality in which Moira is in love with another person and not just in love with the use of them for her purposes is one I don't know how to live in.

Wild things like us aren't made for easy love.

Another Moira-ism. Even after she predicted my soulmate would appear on the doorstep of Kismet all because of her, she didn't let me forget that just because a person is your destiny doesn't mean that being with them will be easy. A common misconception is that soulmates are guaranteed a happily ever after like we see in the movies. The kind of connection a soulmate brings isn't always the kind that settles down beside you for a long-haul life together.

Moira never believed she had one, but that doesn't mean she isn't willing to preserve her comfort with a kind man's help. Maybe that's all this is. Not a con, per se, but a solution to her own fears about the future. A funny idea for a woman who claims to *know all* through the spirit.

The shuttle ride was just long enough to let these feelings fly to the surface but not long enough for me to get centered, grounded enough to know how I feel about this potentially new spin on our breakup scheme.

"My brain is on fire," Sydney says as the shuttle pulls away and the random married couple trips off in what I assume is the direction of their hotel room. She looks stressed and distracted, something I can very much relate to. "I feel like I need a shower just to wash the flames away so I can think straight." She cocks a hip. "Also, the grease. I feel grody."

I laugh at the word. She looks heavenly to me, but I don't say that. Not with my lips anyway. My eyes take a trip over her, looking for anything at all that could be considered *grody*. The idea of being in the same hotel room as Sydney while she takes a shower is going to undoubtedly cause me to enter another spiral.

"If you want to go back to the room to get some space," I say, because I can't bring myself to comment on the whole concept of her naked and wet in a shower in the room we're sharing, "I don't mind making myself scarce." I pause, trying to get a read on her. Her eyes aren't settled on mine. Is she nervous? Now that we're back here, is she remembering our no-strings kiss and regretting it? "The hotel has a good bar—I can go hang out there for a while."

She inhales, scrubbing her fingertips in her hair, which makes the smooth strands stand on end from the friction. "Yeah," she says, gripping a section of her hair and twisting. Her eyes drift to mine and hold. The force quakes through me. "If that's what you want."

What I want is to slip my tongue in her mouth.

To twist my hands in her hair and tug just enough that it exposes the soft, supple skin on her neck.

But what I don't want is to give in and regret it. To play with this fire and get burned.

By her or by Moira when she finds out.

She may not know about how Sydney and I met, but that doesn't change the circumstances. We can say there are no strings, but who are we to tempt fate? The more we give in to these wants, the harder it will be to untangle.

"I'm a little thirsty," I manage to say without choking. Her lips tug against a smirk. Heat floods my cheeks, chest, ears; it blossoms between my legs, and I have to get away. "Enjoy your shower." I spin away, walking through the double doors that lead into the lobby before she can say or do anything else.

Jesus Christ. Get a handle on it.

The hotel lobby is buzzing with people checking in, some of whom I recognize as friends and clients of Moira's, which means, fuck, I wish I had a hat—

"Cadence Connelly!" a woman wearing a sun hat and a linen

ensemble calls from the chair near the fire. I cannot duck out fast enough to escape — she's already walking this way. I stall in place, and for some reason I smile, forced and tight, and then I lift my hand to wave. Her face splits into a pleased grin.

I hate that even though I've been out of Moira's life for years, I still feel a pang of responsibility to play the part of dutiful daughter with her friends.

This woman, Adria Sloane, has been coming to Moira for weekly readings ever since her first husband passed when she was in her forties. Her LA-ageless face makes that seem like less time than it actually is.

She tugs me into an uninvited hug and smacks air-kisses to either cheek.

"How long has it been?" Adria asks me when she pulls back from our greeting. I wish I could say that I don't know, but I have a distinct memory of the last time I saw her. It was during a neighborhood yard sale to raise funds for the animal shelter, and Adria bought my record player, that I was selling in an act of rebellion. Moira wanted me to leave it behind when I left for college. I wanted to do anything else.

"Since the year I left for college," I reply, already trying to edge my body out of her grip.

"Can't be!" she exclaims. "I haven't seen you since you graduated?" Her mouth hangs open in disbelief.

"It's true." I nod, reassuring her.

"How is that possible?" She smacks a hand to her hip in another show of shock.

"I haven't been back . . ." I fight the urge to soften the statement by adding *much* to the end. It wouldn't be true, but it would lessen the likelihood of more follow-up questions.

"Not at all?" Her face falls. Fuck, this is going to backfire. Lie it is.

"Much—I haven't been back much." I shrug, trying to look and sound as casual as possible. My soul dies a little with every second I spend in this ever-growing facade. "Busy, and work took me far away."

"Ooooh, anything exciting?" *If I say no, will she let me leave?*

"Unfortunately, nothing too glamorous. I'm a park ranger at Acadia—"

She swats me. "Get out!" *Gladly.*

"Yeah, anyway—"

"I love Bar Harbor in spring." Her face goes immediately wistful. I cannot let her get onto a new topic, even if it is one I am normally interested in.

"Oh, me, too," I say, looking over her shoulder where I can see through the large double doors into the bar. Sitting at a lounge table are a blonde and brunette who look about my age. Jackpot. They will provide the perfect cover for my escape. "I was just meeting some old friends at the bar, Adria." I nod in the direction of the couple and she follows my gaze.

"Oh, of course, go, get caught up!" Every sentence is either exclamatory or questioning, with almost no in-between. "I should really freshen up, shouldn't I?"

I smile, tight again, though thankfully she doesn't notice. She lets me scoot past in the direction of the couple who are not, in fact, people I know at all. But since I can still feel her watching me, I have to do the unthinkable.

I drop down into the spare seat at their table.

"I am so sorry," I say in a low voice when they both look over at me. "I told the woman back there in the sun hat that I know you two."

The blonde, who is sitting across from me with a good view of the lobby through the doors, cuts her eyes over my shoulder. Her mouth twitches.

"She's still watching," she says, leaning over so her lips aren't visible to Adria. "I'm Kit, this is Julia. Let's get you a drink so she isn't suspicious." She has bright green eyes that remind me of fresh spring grass. It's only when I look down at her that I realize.

She's holding a deck of tarot cards in her hands.

"You brought tarot cards to a bar?" I ask, and Julia snorts. I cut my eyes over to her. She has a completely different vibe. Serious aqua eyes and a strong, straight posture. Her hair is shoulder-length, with a fade shaved on one side showing off a row of silver in her ear.

"She's a tarot reader," Julia says. "She always has a deck."

Panic snakes its way through me. These two can't be here by coincidence. Not on the same weekend that Moira is holding her engagement party.

"You look like you just saw a ghost," Kit says. She holds the deck in one hand, raising her other and smiling. In seconds, a waiter is at the table asking for my order, and I mumble out something about a gin and tonic, to which the blonde says, "Do you want lime with that?" And I think I nod.

"Please tell me you're here on vacation or something?"

Julia twerks her brow. "You tell us why you're being weird."

"My mom is a tarot reader," I say, because *psychic* is not a word you just throw out midday in a bar. Kit jolts, a smile making her pretty face glow.

"Madame Moira?" she asks, and her hands do what looks like a robotic shuffle of the deck. A habit, maybe, but that's when I notice the delicate amethyst ring on her all-important left finger. My eyes trip to Julia. She's wearing a sapphire ring on the same finger. It's similar, though the band is thicker, weightier.

"You two are a couple," I say, sidestepping her question with my observation.

Julia's fingers reach on instinct toward Kit, who leans toward her. It's like they subtly lay claim on each other while not taking ownership or control. It makes my cheeks ache with the sweetness.

"We just got engaged a month ago," Kit says with a shy smile.

"Hold on, Kit," Julia says. "Is Moira your mom?"

I take a heavy breath, just as the waiter returns with my gin and tonic.

"She . . ." I struggle, a fish on a hook. ". . . is."

Kit nearly drops her deck. "I can't believe this." She looks to the brunette, who is frowning now. Her face drops. "Why are you making that face, Julia?"

She doesn't snap out of it right away.

"She was acting shady about your cards. I'm just trying to figure out why the daughter of a psychic would be surprised to see a tarot reader with their deck out in public."

I roll my eyes. Clearly this woman is not going to make anything easy for me.

"I wasn't so much *surprised* as I was *freaked out*. My relationship with tarot is a little rocky," I say, followed by a deep and generous drink from my glass.

"Your relationship with tarot?" Kit asks, her hand tightening around her deck. "Or Madame Moira?" Her big eyes seem to see through me, right to the vulnerable center I like to keep walled away and hidden.

"No offense, but baring my soul to strangers isn't really my thing."

"Oh," Julia chuckles. "I get that—really. But you will."

Now it's my turn to quirk my brows. "Excuse me?"

"You'll tell her," Julia continues with a sly grin. "People love unloading their problems on Kit."

Kit blushes pink and says, "You don't have to tell me."

"I've had years of practice not talking to people."

"And you're still amazingly bad at it," Julia jibes. Kit shoots her a look, soft lips with tense eyes. As if she's trying to say *be nice* without saying it out loud.

"I assume if you're here, you must be clients. Because Moira really isn't known for befriending other members of the mystic community."

"Oh no, she's not." Kit shuffles the deck. *Swish swish swish.* My gaze lands and sticks, watching her hands, the amethyst ring, the row of bracelets catching light, the gold foil on the edges of the cards shimmering. "We aren't clients, though."

I'm curious and I shouldn't be. If I give in, I fear she'll get the whole story out of me without much prodding. I can tell this woman has a special knack with people—though not in the same way Moira does. Not manipulative, not like a power struggle. She just feels like the kind of person you want to trust, and if you do, you won't regret it.

"If you're not clients, then how do you know her?"

Kit smiles, shuffles her cards. "We met her on a dare when we were twelve."

"At Haunt O' Ween fair in Old Pasadena," Julia interjects.

"She gave us a joint reading, even though we didn't ask for one," Kit continues.

I raise my brows. "Sounds right."

"Yeah, it was weird," Julia says.

"So weird, but kind of fun," Kit adds with a wink at me. "And it stuck with us for . . . forever, honestly."

"Because she predicted that you were soulmates," I say, a cold pit forming in my gut.

"Twin Flames." Julia this time, her voice softer than before. Her gaze travels to Kit, landing and setting up camp. "Mirrors to each other. Destined to break apart, with a promise that we would always find our way back to each other."

Jealousy twinges in my gut at the way she relays this. For everyone else, Moira provides a story that makes their soulmate prediction feel like a fairy tale. For me, she inserted herself in the story like a fairy godmother with a bad attitude.

"And it happened." Kit takes over again. "We were best friends until we became more. Then I freaked out and ghosted Julia right before I left for college. It took us ten years, but we found our way back." Her eyes travel to Julia as one of her hands, the one closest to her fiancée, releases the deck and reaches out. Their fingers twine.

More spikes of jealousy prick in my stomach. This time at the sight of their closeness. I drown it with some gin and try to get control of my face. When Kit looks back at me, I can see that I'm not fast enough by the way her blond brow quirks with concern.

"We went to the festival last year, but she wasn't there," Kit says, plodding forward despite my expression. "Julia would have been happy to leave it at that"—Julia taps her nose, *nailed it*—"but

I kept thinking about it, how it felt like this loose end, so I googled her."

"What a trip that was," Julia slides in. She's drained her beer, and her eyes search the room for a waiter. "I bought one of her books on Amazon."

"I read it," Kit jabs and Julia snorts.

"You outlined the highlights for me, babe."

Kit rolls her eyes good-naturedly and turns her attention back to me. "We booked an appointment so we could tell her she was right."

Their being here is starting to make sense now. If they told her about the success of her reading, there's no doubt she invited them here to make her look good in front of Rick's friends. I can only imagine that the buttoned-up retired-pilot crowd he likely invited will be coming here with a hefty dose of side-eye about his new fiancée.

"You're skeptical," Julia says, and I realize my face must be out of control, showing my thoughts again in a very uncharacteristic way. Her eyes glance over me, reading me with a whole different set of skills than Kit's.

I shake my head. "Not of the story. I've been her daughter my whole life; I've heard a lot of those stories."

"Then what?" Kit queries. The cards in her hands get one more shuffle.

She's been readying them for you. I feel the thought, force my focus away from the cards and back to the tarot reader's face.

"There's this girl." The words drop from my lips, too heavy to hold inside anymore. "And despite my better judgment—despite the very real truth that she fulfills my own soulmate prediction"—I pause when Kit's breath catches in her throat—"despite the fact that everything in me wants to stay far away from anything that gives Moira more power in my life . . ."

I look between them for a sign of surprise, but what I find is that both of their faces fix in very different—though no less transparent—expressions of understanding.

"I think I'm falling for her."

Kit's lips curve up.

Her eyes rest on mine, caring and sure. She extends the deck in her hand.

"Pick a card."

I'm tugged, like a rope has been tied around my hand, like my body is possessed. My heart pounds as my fingers reach to cut the stack of cards into two sections. I rest the one in my hand on the table next to Kit's wineglass. My eyes drift back up to hers, awaiting instruction.

"Which one?" she asks me, her voice steady, reassuring. I point to the stack in her hands, too breathless to speak. Too shocked that I'm doing this at all. She places the stack I picked on top of the other, her hand hovering above the cards for a second. Her fingers give a little wiggle.

She flips the card over to face me.

The Ten of Cups stares up from the table. And my heart leaps. This card can only mean one thing.

The exact thing I'm trying to avoid.

CHAPTER TWENTY-SIX

Sydney

Should we stop the scheme?

In the heat of the shower, as steam cocoons me with my thoughts, I can't stop questioning our whole plan. Which is really fucking annoying because I'm already questioning more than enough at the moment without adding this on top.

But. Fishy as all of this is, I can't shake the feeling that it may be fishy only because we want it to be. Because Cadence and I are hardened unromantic messes who have degraded our belief in true love so completely that we can't acknowledge it could happen to anyone for real.

I haven't seen Rick this happy in a long time was Pam's assessment of Dad. If he really loves Moira, who am I to stand in the way? After everything he went through with my mom, and then with raising me alone, his assured happiness would be a huge weight off my shoulders.

Maybe even a way for me to start healing a little myself.

When a girl loses a mother before she's out of training bras, there's a lot she loses out on. Stuff no one tells her, teaches her, even knows she needs, because it's stuff only a mom can know. Growing up with a mom like Moira, it's not the same as growing up without a mom entirely, but there is something about the way Cadence holds herself so tight—like someone who hasn't ever been hugged hard enough, held long enough—that is so familiar to me.

We're opposites. *The Sun and the Moon*. But we aren't that different at our core.

I wonder: If we could stop looking for pain, would it be able to find *us* after all?

I twist my damp hair into a loose braid and swing it over my shoulder, taking one last look in the mirror. I need to talk to Cadence about this.

I need to tell her I like her. That thought comes crashing out of nowhere, but I can't reject it, because it's true. I do like her.

I'll talk to Cadence. I'll just tell her all of this.

I may need a drink, too.

I grab my room key and my purse on my way out the door. She said she was going to the bar, so I trek back through the courtyard that connects our bank of rooms to the lobby. It's a gray cobblestone area dotted with seating arrangements, each around its own firepit. Some of the hotel staff are prepping the space for the evening, fluffing the pillows and setting up the firepits for guests to enjoy.

She may not like me back.

I know she finds me hot. The memory of her lips on mine, her hands gently but firmly gripping my back, is proof alone that the girl wants a taste. But with all the soulmate mess in her head and the mommy issues in her heart, I don't know if she'll be willing to give me more than a taste. And I don't even know what I mean when I say that, either. I just know that I don't want Ranger Girl to hike out of my life without at least letting me try to figure it out.

I walk through the doors into the lobby, and my eyes search for the way to the bar.

I'm going to tell her I like her even if it makes me desperate to run the other way.

Confidently—at least I hope that's what I'm giving with my walk—I enter the bar and scan it. I spot her almost immediately, sitting at a low lounge seat right in front of the bar with two women. Cadence's hair is down—I see the hair band she had it tied back with around her wrist—cascading in a swoop over her back like tangled vines. She's listening to the blonde with clear interest, but her expression isn't happy exactly.

She looks like she's about to cry. Or run.

I approach them, hoping that if I'm interrupting something uncomfortable, she'll be happy for the help. But I stop short a few feet from the table. Sitting on top of the deep chestnut wood is a stack of tarot cards, a soft pink with gold accents. One is turned upright to face Cadence. I have to strain to get a clear look, but I'm able to make out the words written around the border.

Ten of Cups

I step back, scooting into a booth by the door. There's a half-eaten plate of fries and water glass dripping condensation onto the table, but it's empty. I swipe open my phone and tap the internet icon to do a quick search for *Ten of Cups Tarot*. I tap the first link and scroll down to the description of what it means when the card is upright, since that is the position of the one in front of Cadence.

The Ten of Cups represents the embodiment of
happiness, joy, commitment, and fulfillment with
your family or your romantic partner.

My head spins with this first sentence, but I force myself to
read on.

This is not a card of selfish indulgence or success.
It is one where that love is shared with others, an
experience that can only come after learning to love
oneself, proving that true happiness comes from
forming authentic bonds with others.

The lonely girl with the hummingbird out her window pulled
a card that represents finding a fulfilling bond?
My eyes snag and stick on one of the final sentences in the description.

This card can indicate that the querent is
experiencing a sense of happily ever after—of
family, of harmony, and of the truest, deepest love.

My eyes shoot up, across the room to Cadence.
Never have I believed in the power of the cards.
Never have I looked to the Universe for guidance or dreamed
of a soulmate kind of love like you hear about in stories.
But looking at her in this gold-infused light, I can imagine it.
For a moment, a breath, it's almost like I see it.
Her soul and mine intwined in a cosmically coordinated dance.
I pocket my phone and take a deep breath, centering myself

before I approach again. With that tarot card pull and my new, fuller understanding of it, telling her I like her is taking on a whole new meaning. A bigger meaning, with the heft of a hand of fate that I never really believed in before but am now entertaining more by the day.

But then, I suppose if I was truly honest with myself, it's not like I'm immune to what is maybe irrational belief. My pilot superstitions have always felt more normal than not, largely because within the community it's rare to find a pilot who doesn't have a preflight ritual at the very least and a whole set of rituals on board at the most.

As I near them again, I see that the blonde has the deck in her hands now. She's reincorporated the Ten of Cups into the stack and is tucking it away inside her purse.

Her eyes trip to mine, a recognition in them that surprises me.

Cadence twists to see what she's looking at. Her eyes land first on my hips, then trail up the length of my torso, over my braid. They rest on my lips and then eyes. The whiskey color of her hazel-gold irises shines.

"Hey there," I say, my voice coming out wobbly, with a rough edge of want that I really wish I could erase. I flick my attention to the couple she's sitting with. "More old friends?"

"More like new acquaintances," Cadence says. "Kit and Julia are here for the engagement party." Cadence looks at them with this pointed tension in her face. It makes me a little self-conscious, like they were talking about me before I arrived.

A thrill zips up my spine at the thought. I know from my reading with Moira that the person who gets the tarot reading—the querent—also comes to the cards with a question they hope to get insight about.

Could I have been what Cadence asked these cards about?

The brunette, Julia, is signing the check as Kit stands, hooking her purse over her shoulder with a smile. She flicks her big green eyes back and forth between Cadence and me, her lips lifting into a quick there-and-gone smile.

"Gotta get changed for the festival," she says, motioning to her ensemble as if it's an example of what not to wear. "I have a whole outfit planned."

"And I am her Instagram boyfriend," Julia says, closing the leather booklet over the credit card receipt.

"The price you pay for being engaged to an influencer," Kit says. "As much as I'm hoping it won't be that way too much longer." Julia reaches for her hand, clutching it to pull her over for a kiss.

"You can quit anytime," she says, nuzzling her cheek with her nose.

This public display of affection would normally make me break out in hives. So much closeness out in the open for everyone to blatantly see, and with such ease. But with Cadence nearby and that tarot card's definition swimming in my mind, I find myself wondering what it would be like to be so in love with someone that I can't resist taking them in my arms no matter who's looking.

To feel that for someone, truly—that feels like a foreign concept.

I drop down in the seat Julia was just occupying as she and Kit walk away with a "hope to see you there tonight" and a wave. My eyes find Cadence's across the table. I'm debating whether to ask her outright about the card, when she lifts her hand and nods. I turn to see she's motioning the waiter and I realize that there are way too many people in this bar for any kind of real conversation.

"They were setting up some firepits outside in the courtyard," I say, whipping around to face her. "Might be easier to talk there." The waiter arrives to take our order.

"Can we take our drinks to the courtyard?" she asks with a sly smile.

⌒

With our drinks in hand, we head out of the bar and back in the direction of the courtyard beside our room. We're not more than a few steps outside the doorway when we hear familiar voices trickling our way from somewhere nearby. I stop Cadence by placing my hand on her forearm.

Dad and Moira. I mouth the words. She nods, eyes shooting in the direction their voices are coming from. It's definitely rude to eavesdrop, but it also feels a little like a divine gift. If I believed in those, which . . . wish I was less wobbly on that one than I currently feel.

We edge around the corner to where a tall shrub creates an entrance into another courtyard, likely leading to their room. We have to crouch down to look through the shorter manicured bushes that form the wall around the courtyard.

Moira is sitting on one of the outdoor couches surrounding an already-blazing firepit. Dad drops down beside her and takes her hand gently in his.

"You're doing everything you can," he says, bending to try to snag Moira's eye contact.

"I don't know if it's enough," Moira says with a sniffle.

Is she *crying*?

I flick a glance toward Cadence to see that she has gone stiff beside me. Rigid as stone.

"I can tell when she looks at me, she's not really seeing me now," Moira continues, the distress in her voice making it brittle and unfamiliar. All that robust bravado I've gotten used to hearing in it doesn't come through right now.

"She will, though. She came here, didn't she? Just like you hoped," Dad tells her. He brings one of his hands to her cheek, where he brushes away what appears to be a tear.

"She did," Moira replies, finally looking up into Dad's eyes.

"My everything," Dad says, as if it's a term of endearment. Moira's frown momentarily lifts. "This is the beginning of a new chapter for all of us. Don't give up."

He presses a kiss to Moira's lips.

"Oh God," I whisper. Cadence is already scurrying away, keeping low to the ground as she rounds the corner.

"How did I get so lucky?" Dad says.

"You didn't," Moira says. "You got exactly what you were fated."

Their cackles follow me away.

CHAPTER TWENTY-SEVEN

Cadence

I burst into the courtyard and take a hefty gulp of my cocktail.

She's not really seeing me now.

An iconic performance, one for the ages, except for the fact that I don't know who the hell it was for. The way she was talking makes me think she's been honest with Rick about our relationship. Even if she can't take the blame for how her narcissism drove me away, she doesn't seem to be pretending to be innocent, either.

She sounded like someone who has worked on herself.

Who has *changed*.

"Cadence," Sydney says, stepping into the courtyard behind me. When I don't immediately turn, she walks around.

The flames dance in the center of the firepit, their orange glow a stark contrast to the slate-gray stones surrounding them. Their light plays around all over the curves of her body. We're the only ones out here. I assume that's because everybody else is probably getting ready for the festival kickoff or already making their way over to the center of town for a good seat to view the opening ceremony.

"Cadence," she says again, looking up at me standing awkwardly over her like a wraith. "Do you want to sit down?" I flick my eyes to hers. The cool blue, the soft, swooping lashes, and the wide-open way she's looking at me immediately take the edge off my anxious spiral.

"Yes, okay," I stammer, dropping down into the seat and setting my cup on the table. After a second, she moves around to sit beside me. Her weight on the cushion makes me roll toward her, almost into her. My hand drops to the couch to steady myself, but at this proximity, it's impossible to keep my fingers from grazing her thigh. The tips slip beneath the swell of her muscle. The weight is delicious, and it's hard not to imagine what it would be like to turn my palm up, reach my other hand around to get a good grip. Her eyelids flutter, the soft lashes lifting. She wears mascara and some eyeliner in a deep burnt gold that brings out the darkest shade of navy in her irises.

"You smell incredible," I choke out. It's the wrong thing to say. I don't know why I say it. I am really freaking out.

"I think we should stop the scheme," she blurts. It's not what I'm expecting her to say, so I pop back. Far enough that I can see her more fully. Her body language is tense. Her jaw tight, her back taut.

"You do?" I ask, but I'm not that surprised somehow. "What about the pinky promise? What about the bank docs and the weird text with Greg?"

Sydney's expression droops. "Can't part of the pinky promise be that we decide together what to do?" She's a little breathless. "I don't think she's conning him."

"That's because she's a pro," I reply, but I can't quite commit to it.

"You don't sound so sure yourself," Sydney counters, and her voice has an edge of defiance in it. "She sounded really upset back there. And my dad seems to be in on that part at least. What if there's not more to it?"

"Fuck," I breathe. Antsy, I take a drink, feeling the twinge of acid on my tongue and wondering if it's the lemon or the realization that all things really can change.

Even Moira Connelly.

"What did you learn from Lola?" Sydney presses.

"She thinks Kismet could be struggling financially, but she doesn't know that for sure," I say, and it feels like a concession.

"So the loan docs or whatever, those could be something related to Kismet? Which doesn't mean she's swindling my dad or something. People take out loans all the time."

She's right. I know she's right. And more than that, there's the other part of what Lola said. The part where she asserted that Moira is happy. She's changed since meeting Rick.

Something that lines up—at least in theory—with what we just saw between them.

"What about the shady text with your dad and Greg?" I press her.

I'm not ready to let go of the idea that Moira is conning Rick. That Moira isn't following her truth like always, and, like always, at the expense of those closest to her. That Moira could meet someone and fall in love and get to live happily ever after. Not after all she put me through growing up. Not with how she's fucked my brain over about relationships—all kinds of relationships, not just romantic ones.

People were pieces on a life-size chessboard. This can't be different.

She's not really seeing me now.

"Pam said there was something between Dad and Greg, but that was going on before they met Moira. I don't think it has anything to do with her, Cadence." Her eyes search me.

"Aren't you curious what that is?" I ask.

"Sure, but I can talk to Dad about that anytime."

It's not the first time in my life that I'm struck hard with the reality that I don't know what it's like to actually *trust* your parent. Like Sydney trusts Rick. I am caught in the thought, just like she's caught by the light of the setting sun. This courtyard is shielded, so all the cool stone makes the light almost lavender behind her. Her face is lit with the orange of the fire.

Her nostrils flare. "I think they're really in love. Dad seems to be, anyway. Pam has known him since before my mom passed away." Her voice is aflame. "She hasn't seen him this content in a long time."

Mention of Sydney's mother takes the wind out of the sails of any argument I'm readying. This topic feels like the kind she doesn't readily talk much about, especially not with someone she barely knows.

"Why do you hate her so much?" Sydney asks in a tender sort of way.

A fist around my heart. *Tight, tight, tighter.*

"I don't." I shake my head, tears threatening. "And that's what always sucked about being her daughter." It's like a weight lifts from my chest as I say the words out loud. "She was like the sun, and I lived my life like the phases of the moon." Sydney's face twitches, a wash of some intense emotion brightening her eyes. "When she shined her light on me, I was full. Illuminated.

Making big waves. But that wasn't all the time, and eventually I got sick of the dark side."

Sydney's hands drop to mine. I don't pull from her grip.

"But that's not true now," she says, her eyes serious. Her soft pink lips turn down. "And maybe it's not the only thing that's changed."

The planes of her face take in all the light from the fire.

"You think they're really in love," I say softly, looking deep into her gaze.

"I think I don't want to waste what little time I get with you trying to figure it out."

She's pinned me with her eyes. I am lost, swimming in the sea of their blue. Drifting. Content. Until my brain catches up, alerting my body to the warning bells of what she's just said.

The no-strings kiss.

The comfort her presence brings even though she's little more than a perfect stranger.

"What are you saying?" I need her to spell it out. As much as I have conditioned myself to fight any and all influence of Moira in my life, the urge to know Sydney better is a powerful magnet to the hardened metal heart in my chest.

"I like you, Cadence," she says. Deliberate and pointed. She reaches up slowly, easing her fingers toward the wild tendrils of my hair. When I don't pull away, look away, her mouth curves, and her fingers twist into the strands. She tangles them up until she reaches the nape of my neck, her thumb brushing my jaw where the tender skin behind my ear is taut across the bone.

With control she tips my chin up so my lips angle toward her.

"I want to kiss you again." Her breath bursts over my lips. They tingle, tantalized by the sensation.

"Kiss me." The words are barely more than a breath.

Her lips capture mine.

It's not a hostile takeover. They open slightly, pillow softly, before I feel her tongue slip between my lips, and I release a moan as they open to welcome her in. I am a willing captive to her mouth, losing myself to the sensations that spark all over my body. The heat pooling between my legs. The tweak of my nipples. Her fingers brush the sensitive skin at the nape of my neck, sending shivers *down, down, down*.

I don't think about how quickly and ferociously I reach out to grip her waist. I just do it. Tugging her toward me. My palm snakes up the curve, and the other slides down to where a single fingertip slips between the hem of her shirt and the waistband of her jeans to graze smooth, warm skin.

A giggle rumbles in her throat.

Our lips break contact and my eyes open.

"Fuck, you can kiss," she says. My lip gloss glistens on her lower lip. Her pupils are dilated, fixed on my mouth. There is a hunger I recognize in her expression. Like a wolf on a hunt in the wild. It is anything but feral; rather, it is the gaze of a creature who understands they are a predator tasked with great power.

She could devour me whole, and I wouldn't want her to stop.

"Our room is just over there," I say, because though I am desperate to see where this goes, I am not exhibitionist enough for a full-on make-out session in such a public place. I low-key fear that Moira and Rick will walk through here on their way to drop Chicken off in our room and we'll be too *involved* to notice.

She runs her hand down the length of my arm, making me wish I were wearing a tank top just so I could feel her skin on my skin. Her fingers lock with mine. Perfectly, they fit together.

Easily, our palms connect. Standing first, I tug her up, and she lets her body collide with mine. I am intoxicated by the feeling of her soft curves melding against mine. Her breasts soften against me, her thigh presses to the space between my legs.

I nearly buckle at the fresh contact, but fortunately she doesn't maintain it for long. Without breaking her hold on my hand, she pulls away, leading me off toward our room. We abandon our cocktails, happy to be intoxicated with each other it seems.

If I let myself think too hard about what this means for me, I will crumble.

I don't want to crumble. Like her, I know I don't want to waste whatever time we have together. Because even without the breakup scheme factoring in, there is a clear ticking clock on this connection.

No matter what happens this weekend, I return to Acadia and a job that I love. A life I've built slowly, meticulously, all by myself.

A lonely life, sure.

But a life I can control without tarot predictions or the helpful hand of fate.

CHAPTER TWENTY-EIGHT

Sydney

We tumble into the room, practically tripping over ourselves to get the door shut behind us. I am not one to overthink sexual attraction, but this feels like so much more than just a physical connection. This is a want that cuts to my core. A desire to *know*. A longing to see and be seen. It's wild to think that my dad finding new love might actually be the key to me finally having my own big feelings for someone.

Cadence grips me by the hips and whips me around to face her. Her lips smash into mine, a new hunger unleashed from her tongue. She licks the inside of my mouth and drags me bodily against her, pressing her hips into mine. Her hands are explorers, and I want to tell her they have my permission to search.

"Do whatever you want," I say, breaking our lips apart.

My own hands can't stay still as I push her jacket off her shoulders. It forces her to let go for a second so that it can fall to the ground behind her.

"Are you sure?" she asks, but she's buzzing with desire, and I'm aching for more.

"Get back over here," I order her, and she complies.

She crashes against me, using her hand to gently push my chin up so she can tuck her face into my neck. Her teeth graze the skin, sending shivers through me, and my nipples stand up, tightened with desire that races through my body right to my soul.

Her fingers touch my braid and then hook the small hair band holding it together and yank it off. My hair falls free, and she works her fingers into it, and there is something so sensual about the act that moisture springs to my eyes. Her hand runs down the length, grazing over the curve of my breast, then winding around to my waist.

Pressure pulses between my legs, hot and urgent with want.

Her hand tucks under my shirt.

"Take off my bra," I command. Her eyes connect with mine. Her mouth is swollen with kissing, lips open like she wants to consume me. Take a bite of me. Take many. I want to touch myself to take some of the ache away, and this look on her face isn't helping.

Her fingers find the clasp of my bra. She unhooks it. My breasts spring free, and her hand comes around, grazing the skin. She cups the mound, lightly squeezing, and then her fingertip grazes my nipple, and a shudder of desire releases from her lips.

She traces my nipple; it's hard against her touch.

With her other hand she starts to work my sweater and bra up, and I happily comply, raising my arms overhead to help her remove my clothes. Cool air hits my skin. Her eyes devour the sight of my breasts, and her tongue slips out, wetting her lips.

She buries her face in my breasts, mouth open, tongue slipping over skin to taste my nipple. My eyes roll back in my head, and my hands burrow into her hair.

"That feels so good," I whisper.

"God, your tits are perfect," she says before getting a mouthful of nipple and flesh. Her tongue flicks the taut skin.

"You're good with your tongue," I say, nearly gasping.

"You have no idea," she says. With that, we're moving to the bed. She kicks off her shoes, fussing with the laces for a second. I'm glad I'm wearing booties that come off easily, because it gives me a chance to watch her move.

Her hips are trim, her torso lean, I wonder what she looks like without any clothes.

I reach over, touching the button on her jeans. She leans down, kissing me softly and leaving space for me to work the button free. Drag the zipper down. Tuck my hand into the curve of her warmth and feel just how wet she is.

"It's been a long time for me." She whimpers as my finger brushes over the fabric, pressing the mound of her pleasure like it's a button.

"For what"—I kiss her—"it's worth"—*kiss*—"you don't seem out of practice at all."

She smirks against my lips.

And then there's a knock at the door.

She pulls back, her eyes immediately going to the bedside table.

"Goddammit," she says, her breath a hot burst against my cheek. "The Danish festival starts in ten minutes."

Another knock, this time followed by the sound of my dad's voice.

"Birdie, we have Chicken here!"

"Do you think they went on ahead?" This is Moira.

We pull apart, scrambling up from the bed.

As quietly as possible.

"They wouldn't forget Chicken," Dad says with confidence.

"Fuck," I almost whisper. "I *did* forget Chicken." Cadence shakes with a chuckle. I cover my boobs with the cups of my bra, flicking my eyes up to Cadence's. She's wearing this deeply forlorn expression. "It won't be your last chance with them," I snort.

She blushes. Her pants are buttoned, and she drops to the bed to shove her shoes back on. "Can women get blue balls?" she asks.

I whip my sweater over my head, biting back a cackle.

"Coming!" I call to them. I quickly check myself in the mirror. "Anticipation makes everything better." She looks up, and our eyes meet in the mirror. Want zips like an electric current between us.

This thing happening with her is something.

Special.

Wild.

Real.

I force my breathing to neutral, and she nods, letting me know she's ready for me to open the door. I can't get too in my head about this, because if I do, I will definitely stop us from ever figuring out why the Universe—or whatever force exists beyond our will, if any—has pushed us onto each other's paths. And if this is what it feels like for fate to work her magic, then I don't mind so much if she does.

CHAPTER TWENTY-NINE

Cadence

We've been stuck side by side with my mother and Rick watching the opening ceremony of the festival, but in my head I'm still back in that hotel room with Sydney. My mind flits over images of her as I stand, the back of my hand pressed against hers in the crowd.

Her tan skin like silky cream, soft and supple in my hands.

Her mouth, pliant and plump, her tongue hot as it lapped mine.

The way her voice tipped over into a command. The force of her hands gripping my hair.

I've never toyed with the idea of someone being made for me. Another human put here who will embody my desires and needs. I can't say with any amount of certainty whether she is that for me. But for a second my mind toys with the hope. Bats it around like a cat with a toy on a string.

The Danish Maid is crowned, and the festivities officially begin with the sound of triumphant cheers. The crew gathered around us is made up mostly of Moira and Rick's invites—Pam and Greg, Adria, Lola and Hawthorne. I don't see Kit and Julia, but I expect they're somewhere in the crowd. I secretly hope we don't cross paths again while Moira is around. I'd hate for her to get the opportunity to gloat over her successful pairing.

Still, I'm glad I met Kit when I did.

The Ten of Cups is a card I never wanted to see again. The weight of my mother's interpretation of it from my soulmate prediction felt impossible to carry, so it was shackled to me, and I was left dragging it behind me like a ball and chain.

Just because she predicted it doesn't mean she holds your fate in her hands, Kit said. *Catalysts don't decide a lifetime loving each other. Your choice to work hard at it every day is what does.*

She used herself and Julia as an example, but I knew the *you* in the sentence was me. If I wanted to let my feelings for Sydney become more than a passing attraction, whatever came after would sink or swim because of the actions, the choices made by Sydney and me.

Lola surprises me, coming up from behind. She bumps me on the side that isn't pressing up against Sydney, and I turn to see a sheepish smile and hopeful but apologetic expression on her face. I want to tell her she has nothing to apologize for.

I want to tell her she was right.

"I sent Hawthorne ahead of me to get in line for axe throwing," she says. "I figure we can all cut if he's there."

"Right," I say, searching inside myself for the cool ease Sydney is so good at, which I struggle to ever exhibit. "Unlikely that anyone would challenge him to a fight."

"Based on looks," she says. "Little do they know he's fully a pacifist."

I grin at the idea of sequoia-size Hawthorne hugging it out instead of throwing a punch.

"Should we get our axe-throwing tickets from the parents?" Sydney asks, moving her hand from its place bumping against mine. Lola's gaze latches on to the now-empty space beside my hand, and her left brow hooks. I lock on to her gaze before she looks back at me. I try to send telepathic signals for her to play it cool. *Please.*

"You wanna ask them, Sydney?" Lola says, a tiny smirk twisting her lips. Fortunately, Sydney doesn't seem to notice the moment passing between Lola and me.

"Sure thing," she says, walking off in their direction. My eyes follow her for a second before returning record-scratch fast to Lola.

"Were you two holding hands?" she asks, a little too loud for my liking. I press into her, grabbing her by the wrist and giving it a light squeeze.

"Not so loud," I say, cutting my eyes toward Moira, Rick, and Sydney.

"Why does it matter if they hear? It's not like you're forbidden from hooking up with the adult daughter of the guy marrying your estranged mom," Lola says, thankfully lowering her voice to a volume that doesn't carry so easily. "Maybe not the most advisable decision, but—" She stops dead when her eyes meet mine.

"Don't," I try, but she's putting the pieces together.

Lola knows me well, a truth I wish didn't run so deep.

"Hold the fucking phone," she exclaims in a whisper-scream. "How is it possible? You two met at dinner, not Kismet." I give her a tiny headshake. "Explain, motherfucker."

"We met while you were out getting us coffee," I say. A scowl twitches over her features, making them all pinch up.

"That's why you weren't there when I got back." She smacks

me on the arm with just enough force that I feel it through my thick denim jacket. "And you didn't run straight for the hills?"

"What good would that have done?" I ask. "Her dad is marrying Moira. Running would only remove her from my life if I never came back."

"Seems like a perfect excuse." Her voice ripples with sarcasm.

"Not when I came here because I don't trust Moira to begin with."

She cocks out a hip. "I knew it was more than just generalized concern."

"Okay, yes, I was sus, and I came here to expose her."

"You came here to make her pay," Lola says. She's not pulling any punches, and I don't blame her. My behavior may have been grounded in good intentions, but my heart wasn't in the right place. I can admit that, embarrassing as it is.

"So what if I did?" I say, but as soon as I do, and before she can reply, we are interrupted by Sydney's immediate approach. She's holding four red tickets in her hand and wearing a grin.

"Wrangled all of us a chance," she says, smiling ear to ear. "Dad didn't want to give one to Hawthorne on account of your situationship status."

"Oh geez," Lola exclaims, her vitriol now focused on Rick and not me. "I really did a number on him when I broke up with Wednesday."

Sydney snorts. "Like the beloved television and comic book character?"

"In more ways than one," Lola replies. Sydney chuckles. Thankfully it looks like she's dropping both the Moira vengeance plan and the topic of me and Sydney's developing *whatever this is*.

For now.

Dancing around the whole soulmate prediction would be bad enough, but getting into the ins and outs of our hookup is more complicated territory. Sydney and I haven't had time to talk about it between us, so I really shouldn't be talking about it with Lola.

Sydney doles out our tickets, giving two to Lola, and we all head off down a narrow side street that leads to the area where they have set up the axe-throwing arena. I'm tall for a woman, and so is Moira, so it's easy to see her across the crowd. Easier still to feel her gaze traveling along with me.

At some point I will have to talk to her. I can't avoid it forever. Not if I truly am abandoning the scheme, letting this whole ride go to its natural conclusion. Accepting that the conclusion might be her grand romance with the father of my intended-by-the-Universe soulmate.

Sydney steps up closer to me when Lola breaks off from us, spotting Hawthorne in the line winding its way out of the axe-throwing tent.

"Is it true?" Sydney questions. I'm thrown, worried that somehow my inner monologue made it out of my mouth.

"Is what true?" I ask. *Don't knee-jerk the response. God, her skin shimmers.*

All along this courtyard they've set up real fire-burning lanterns lighting the way to the tent and providing ambiance to the many food and merchandise vendors who have set up shop. Across the cobblestone courtyard, they've roped off a section for brats and beers, expanding from the normal beer garden to accommodate the heavy crowd.

"Moira's claim that you were an excellent axe thrower once," she says.

"Oh," I say, huffing a laugh through my nostrils. "She's a liar." Sydney's expression twitches at the word. We are abandoning the scheme, and maybe that means she wants to give Moira a chance at character redemption. I decide to brush past the look, and tell the story with as little Moira slander as possible.

"I got lucky," I say.

"You don't believe in luck." Sydney's eyes narrow.

"Touché," I reply, fighting a grin. "The toss was all aerodynamics. But she *had* told me I would win if I got on the platform."

"Ah, I get it. You want to pretend it had nothing to do with that." Sydney nods, not surprised. I really wish I weren't so predictably wounded.

"It was my idea, not hers," I say with a flare of defensiveness. "I was angry with her about the soulmate reading and was ruining her trip as a result. So when she realized I had interest in the competition, she ran with it. She wanted me to stop brooding, and she thought if I won, I would. So she told me it would happen. She could see it or whatever."

"And you took that to heart," Sydney says. Somehow she doesn't look surprised.

"Hope leads to action. Luck has nothing to do with it. I fucking believed in her despite all the bullshit."

"And then you won," Sydney replies. She raises her brows.

It was a nightmare having a mother who is the center of her own universe, but there *were* times when my wants aligned with hers perfectly.

In those times, she was my fiercest ally.

"Yeah, my least favorite kind of win." I tread lightly back over the memory. "I spent most of the afternoon watching others trying. Studying their form. Watching the way weight was shifted from left to right and the angle of the handle when it left their hands."

"Ooooh, tell me more," she says in a playfully seductive tone. It sends a thrill right through my stomach. I chuckle nervously, hoping I can deliver more goods.

"There's a bravado to throwing an axe," I say, and she leans in just enough that I can smell the sharp citrus scent of her perfume. "A certain steadiness is needed. I guess I had that. Because when I threw it, it landed dead center in the bull's-eye."

"I bet you were beaming," she says in a breathless sort of way.

"For a second I was definitely shiny." We're nearing the line now. I don't know where my mother and Rick are in the crowd, but I can still feel the pressure of her awareness nearby.

"And she let you shine?" Sydney asks, her voice dropping, mood shifting.

"She took my prize and got her free beer—which she didn't even want," I say, nibbling my lip. "Told everybody about the win. Talked me up like I was some kind of axe-throwing prodigy—so stupid, but people ate it up. They were drunk."

"She made your win her win."

I nod, relieved she seems to understand. "And I remember thinking, I could just decide to not let it bother me. I could play my own game, one where I didn't have to respond to her poking and preening. It was the first time I realized I could do that."

She presses her hand to my shoulder. Her eyes trip over it, and I know she's spotted Moira somewhere in the distance.

"Cadence." She says my name softly, like a secret. "You think of her as having all this power over you and that you have to do all this stuff to assert yourself, but maybe that's not the whole story."

I try to tug out of her grip, to get defensive, but her hand courses down the length of my arm, where she clutches my hand for the briefest moment.

Our eyes lock.

"What if you had just as much power over her all along?" She steps off, letting her words seep through my pores. Knowing they're having their intended effect, rattling the cage I've locked myself inside of for so long.

Power and love, two things I've always felt my mother held in spades against me. But if she didn't, if she wanted my love, my acknowledgment, my approval, that might change how I framed our shared history of heartache. It might make it possible to let go of the fight-or-flight that has reigned supreme in my life. It might be enough to convince this lone-wolf girl to find a pack, or at least a mate she can walk beside.

CHAPTER THIRTY

Sydney

We're all gathered inside the tent now, with Hawthorne at the front, readying his tree-trunk body to take the platform for a throw. Moira and Dad found us in line, each of them holding a cherry Danish. "Eat dessert first, feel regret never," Dad said, taking a huge bite. To which I grumbled that he should have had the decency to get his daughter one since he was going to show up here taunting her with it anyway.

I'm trying to see their relationship through a different lens now.

But honestly, they aren't the couple taking up the most space in my mind.

I keep trekking back over the clandestine make-out session we shared in our hotel room earlier. And even though Chicken is making himself comfortable in the room, so we aren't totally alone in there, his awareness isn't enough to deter us tonight.

A sleeping old-man dog who's hard of hearing isn't a roadblock.

"Wait, Hawth, you should get some advice from Cade," Lola

exclaims right before Hawthorne steps up to the platform. My eyes instinctively shift to Cadence, trying to catch a reaction, but I'm distracted by Moira in my periphery. There's a glint in her eye, a sly smile spreading her lips. The legend of Cadence throwing the axe is one Moira takes pride in, that's clear, but the look in her eye rubs me the wrong way.

The axe-throwing moment doesn't matter for the reason Moira seems to think it does. It wasn't a win because of the momentary glint of glory.

To Cadence, it was a moment when she realized her autonomy was within reach—emotionally at least—and that's huge. It just sucks that it seems like she never got to feel her mother's pride for the life she built for herself, by herself, when she left LA.

It hits me, sudden and swift: I've never heard Moira ask Cadence about her life.

Cadence deserves to be asked. To have a spotlight just because of who *she* is.

"I literally threw an axe one time." Cadence is sheepish in the face of attention. "I'm not an expert."

"Perfectly," Moira pipes up. "You threw it perfectly."

"But that's nothing, right?" I say, the words rising in my throat before I approve their release. "You're a badass park ranger. Your outdoor skills have probably majorly exceeded that by now."

Cadence's eyebrow quirks, a pointed look that's a mix of confusion, amusement, and gratitude. I lift my shoulder in a barely perceptible shrug.

"Throwing an axe isn't an outdoor skill," Cadence says with a grin. "But I can start a mean fire with nothing but sticks."

"See?" I look back to the group, all of who are giving me bewildered stares. "Badass."

Hawthorne is the only one not paying attention; he's lost interest in the conversation and picked up the axe. I'm suddenly weirdly aware of the way Moira's eyes trek from me to her daughter and back, but thankfully her attention is forced away when Lola plunges back from the platform and into her.

Something like anguish flits through Lola's eyes as she looks up at Hawthorne. Moira grips her with a strong, supportive hand. The dichotomy of this woman is really something to behold.

Hawthorne runs his hand down the length of the handle, fits his palm loosely around it, and raises it over his head. I remember from Cadence's explanation that one of the factors of the axe's aerodynamics has to do with shifting the weight from left to right and releasing the handle at the proper moment.

Hawthorne exerts brute force on the throw, launching the axe across the hay-covered arena and burying it *not* in the wooden bull's-eye at the far end but in the giant stack of hay bales that make up the backdrop.

"Fuck!" the pacifist exclaims, spinning around with a grunt. Men really do turn into beasts when competition and weapons are at hand. His eyes trail to Dad, who stands there as stoic as a philosopher. Rick gave him one ticket. He isn't a fan of this new situationship for Lola. There is absolutely no way he'll grant him another try.

Hawthorne stalks off the platform and past Lola in a brooding silence. Her cheeks flush to match her red hair. Cadence reaches out, a soft hand on her forearm. A gesture of friendship. Lola looks at her with big eyes, clearly embarrassed and trying not to show it. Cadence turns to the platform, lifting her red ticket between her two fingers.

If I wasn't already falling head over heels, I definitely am now.

She whips her jacket off, pushing the sleeves of her t-shirt up to reveal her chiseled biceps. She cracks the knuckles on her left hand, then her right, and grips the axe. Her fingers caress the wooden handle, thumbs running up and down the slim spine. My mouth goes dry, all the moisture in my body flooding between my legs at the sight. She grips the end lightly, not choking it out or white-knuckling. She plants her boots to the spot; her long hair drifts around her shoulders and looks like a waterfall of curls down her back.

She lifts the axe up, drawing it gently back so that the blade is momentarily parallel with her shoulder. Her trim hips, long legs, and sturdy, well-defined arms form a perfect languid line. Even though there are other platforms in the tent where other people prep their own throws, it feels as if the attention of the whole place has turned to Cadence. I hold my breath. Lola reaches for my hand, twisting our palms together in anticipation.

Cadence releases the axe with a swoosh.

The blade buries itself in the wood. *Thwack.* Dead center, right on the bull's-eye.

Lola and I jump up, cheering her. "Holy shit, that was hot," Lola exclaims.

I couldn't agree more.

Cadence spins, looking down from the platform, eyes sharp like blades. They find me, holding my gaze. Heat swells between my legs as I flush at the intensity of her eye contact.

And my mind begins plotting our escape.

CHAPTER THIRTY-ONE

Cadence

Sydney looks like she's about to pounce on me when I step down from the platform. I should feel impressed with myself that I can still do it, no instruction needed. I shouldn't care that now Moira is recounting the original axe-throwing tale to Pam and Greg, emphasizing her role in it. I shouldn't be embarrassed by the attention, the cheers of *fuck yeah, good throw* coming from onlookers as they pass by.

As soon as I near Sydney, all of that drifts away. The noise in my head gets quieter, shifting into a single palpable feeling instead.

Want.

I don't care that I met her at Kismet all because of my mother.

It doesn't matter that she could be my soulmate, and that must mean fate isn't a fallacy.

Because like Kit said when she pulled that Ten of Cups, the catalyst isn't what decides a lifetime of love. It's not the thing that makes a soulmate a partner. Not even the Universe has the power to do that, not without the help of the querent.

"We should make ourselves scarce," Sydney says in a low voice as we turn to watch Lola take the platform. She's trying to mimic my stance and almost nailing it.

"Wanna get food?" I ask, but my eyes say *bedroom*.

"I could definitely eat," she replies, a naughty uptick to her lips.

Lola lifts the axe into position with hesitance. "Why don't you head over to the garden?"

Leaving together at the same time will warrant an explanation. May get us tagalongs. If she skips out ahead of me, I can just feign needing to go lie down or something. They won't know we're together, and we won't have to make an excuse as to why we left at the same time.

She gives me a wink, taking her lip hostage between her teeth. I force my focus to Lola and let Sydney slip away. I ignore when she is stopped by Rick asking where she's off to and she says, "Need some air." Lola releases the axe with just the right amount of force, I can tell as soon as it starts to spin. The blade makes contact with the wood right at the edge of the target, but it sticks. She flies up, clapping, and whips around to look at me.

She searches for my approval like I'm an older sibling, someone whose opinion matters. I'm surprised by the ache in my chest when our eyes meet. She hops down from the platform, and I extend my hand for a fist bump.

"Almost in the target," she says in a self-deprecating tone.

"Better than most of the guys in the place." I mean specifically Hawthorne, and she knows it. She grins at my slight of him. The shelf life of that relationship just got a hell of a lot shorter.

"Where's Sydney?" Lola asks, looking around me like she expects her to be right at my side.

I see an opportunity to pull her into this for some amity,

something I think she'd appreciate and also something that could genuinely get me out of here faster. I lean in, lowering my voice.

"She bailed, and I'm about to follow her." Lola gets my drift immediately. Her smile is bright and easy.

"I'm glad you're letting her in, Cade. With how you met her and everything," she says, not saying the why of it out loud. I'm grateful she doesn't, but a small part of me tugs toward her, wanting to spill my feelings. Wanting the connection I never valued before.

"I'm scared," I whisper, giving in to the moment even though it's just as scary as anything else happening. Her eyes shine, and she grips me by the hand.

"Good," she says. "That means you care." I watch as her attention shifts behind me and then her eyes widen pointedly. Moira and the rest of the crew must be edging closer. She pulls me to the side and whispers, "Go" and "Good luck," and I bolt without looking back.

Whatever they all think is happening, I do expect that Lola will be able to deter them. She's always been clever, and it's likely that skill has only improved over time. I shoot out through the exit of the tent and into the cool night air. It hits my skin with a burst, drawing goose bumps to the skin. I yank on my jacket and search the space for the hot blonde of my dreams.

I catch sight of her across the cobblestone, standing in the light of one of the firelit torches. Wind catches her hair. Her skin glows a warm gold. I'm tugged toward her as if the string tying our souls is being reeled in to draw us together. She catches me with her eyes, turning her body my way. A smile cuts her features, awakening the butterflies in my stomach.

She likes me.

She wants me.

"Hey," she says, her voice dropping into a low, raspy tone.

"Hey," I say, unable to contain my grin.

Feeling happiness because of another person isn't something I've experienced in a long time. I'm surprised by how it lets light into the darkened corners, airing out those shadows, warming up the confusion that comes from walking all alone for so long.

I reach out for her hand, and she fits her fingers in between mine, pressing our palms together. Without a word, we walk away from the crowd.

The overhead light above our hotel room doorway has drawn some little brown moths to the glow. As we near the door, she leans over, pressing a kiss to my cheek. I turn my head to capture her lips with mine, cupping her chin in the palm of my free hand. She smiles against my mouth.

"Where's your room key?" she asks, and I take the break in our kiss to inhale the scent of her skin.

"Back pocket," I say, tasting her neck with my teeth. She giggles, a light, airy sound, before reaching around to the pocket of my jeans and fitting her hand inside for the key.

With a swipe, we fall into the room together, our lips breaking apart for a moment while I fuss around with the light switch on the back wall. The jangle of metal tags reminds us of the Chicken in the room. He stands up, looking bleary with sleep, and stretches. His long pink tongue curls out as he yawns.

"He probably needs a bathroom break," she says, her eyes drifting to the puppy pad sitting unused next to his bed. She turns, gripping me by the waistband to peck another kiss on my lips. "Wait."

With a smile, she grabs Chicken's leash and hooks him up to take him outside. The door slides closed, leaving me alone in the room for a beat.

My thoughts swirl. This isn't somewhere I ever expected to be. Not after I ran so far away from anything that could lead me to this path. In all my resistance to my destiny, I never once entertained the idea that meeting a person in the foyer of Kismet could ever make me feel like coming back home. But not to the home I had to leave because it was never mine, never really safe for me.

To a home where I belong. To someone, with someone.

The door swings open, and Chicken is the first one through it, his little waddle from the arthritis in his hips making him almost bob across the threshold. Sydney follows, praising him for doing his business. He runs over to me, licking my hand a few times before circling back around to his bed.

I walk over to the sink to wash my hands of spit and whatever grime I've carried inside with me from axe throwing. In the mirror, I see Sydney's reflection as she tucks Chicken into his bed, covering him over with a blanket and placing his stuffed drumstick toy in beside him.

She exhales a sigh. Crossing to stand beside me at the sink.

"Are you sure you want to do this?" I ask. Maybe because I can't imagine a reality where this girl actually wants me and isn't already rethinking this whole thing.

She turns to face me.

"If you want consent . . ." she says, not a full sentence. She lets it dangle. Her hand raises to my hair. In a slowly deliberate move she brushes the strands off my shoulder. Her fingers graze the skin of my neck. She leans in, pressing her lips there, light and closed, little nips of contact as she moves up toward my ear. She opens her lips against my skin and breathes, "You have it."

I turn, gripping her at the waist and pulling her into my body until every gap closes between us. Our lips lock and our tongues twist. She pulls her mouth away, the absence dragging a groan from my throat.

"I need to wash my hands," she says, and then tosses a glance over toward the bed. "Go sit." I have never been one to do as I'm told, but I'd take orders from Sydney any day. I break my grip on her and walk over to the bed, dropping down on the edge.

From my vantage point, I have a perfect view of her hourglass shape. She's still wearing her jeans and sweater; her hair is down, lightly waving from the effect of the braid she had it drying in earlier. The mirror light is glowing softly, the only light we have on in the room. Her ass is plump, a perfect peach at the top of her curvy thighs. When she reaches up to dry her hands, her eyes catch sight of me watching her in the mirror.

"You're staring," she says.

"I won't apologize for it," I reply. She turns, leaning against the counter. Her face is momentarily in shadow. "I've seen the view from the top of Pikes Peak. On a clear day you can see five states from the summit." I let my gaze drift over her curves as if they are mountaintops. "You may be more beautiful."

She steps out of the shadow cast by the light at her back. Her expression is misty, surprise and desire mixing in her face. Cheeks flushed.

I almost gasp. "Definitely more beautiful."

"Does that mean you want to fuck me?" The word, *fuck*, slices through me. I press my thighs together to ease the ache between them. "Because I want to fuck you." Her eyes drop to my legs. "I want you screaming my name."

The power in her voice is the hottest thing I've ever heard.

She walks toward me, taking slow and deliberate steps as she removes her sweater. Her bra is a dark purple with lavender flowers, the cups barely holding in her ample breasts. Her cleavage mounds, a perfect crease that blossoms from the lace edging. I want to bury my face in her cleavage.

"You're having all sorts of thoughts," she says. "I can practically see your mind spinning."

"Your body is a lot for me to process." She's closer now, I could almost touch her.

"Tell me what you're thinking." It's a gently firm order.

Her jeans hit right at her waist, the button dipping into a small V where her navel peeks out in a crescent at the top. Her generous hips and tits accentuate her waist's smallness.

"I was thinking I want to lick your cleavage and bury my face in your breasts." Heat rushes to my cheeks, the ache in my pleasure palpable. But now that she's closer, there's such a flood of desire, thoughts and feelings and longings, it's almost overwhelming. "I want to grab your ass, one cheek in each hand, get a mouthful of your breast and take tiny bites out of your stomach."

I have to force my eyes up to her face; I'm a little scared to see her reaction.

Her lips have dropped open, and her eyes are dark with a look of pure lust.

She bends down so her breasts are right in my face and takes my left hand in hers. Slowly, she lifts it to her ass. I wait, happy to let her lead. She places the other hand on the other cheek. "Go. Ahead."

Her breath pounds against my forehead.

I grab a handful, yanking her onto my lap. Her breasts are right below my chin. Just out of reach of my mouth. Her eyes and mine are level, and I focus on the deep rim of navy outlining the cerulean. She wraps her arms around my shoulders, her legs around my hips. Her breasts push against me, and I'm wishing I didn't have a shirt on anymore. I'm wishing there was nothing standing between her and me becoming *us*.

In every way possible.

"Hey." She brushes my lips with her thumb. "Where'd you go?"

"Sorry," I say. "It's awfully loud in my head."

She presses her forehead to mine. I run my hands up the length of her back, savoring the feel of her skin under my hands. Her lips touch mine tenderly.

"I'm terrified," she says. "I haven't felt like this—" She cuts herself off. "I was going to say *in a long time*, but that's just swagger." She presses another gentle kiss to my lips. "I don't know if I've ever felt like this before."

It takes some of the sting out of my own inner turmoil to hear her say she's scared, too. Scared because she feels so much, just like me. Scared to feel as much as she does, because it's foreign, so unknown.

"At least we can be terrified together," I say.

Our eyes connect, and I'm struck by how I've never thought about it before. How true it is when they say that the eyes are the window to the soul. And if that string is tied from her soul right to mine, I wonder: If I looked in her eyes long enough, would I be able to see it?

And I realize: It wouldn't matter.

Soulmate, not soulmate.

Sydney is who I want.

CHAPTER THIRTY-TWO

Sydney

Longing isn't something I usually equate with having a hot woman between my legs, but that feeling underscores this lust, shading my ravenous need. Because pleasuring her body isn't enough. I want to taste her soul.

I cover her lips with mine and am pleased when she opens them to my tongue, letting me in. My hands work down her back, finding their way under her shirt, and I am happy when she breaks our kiss to let me ease the fabric up and off. Her bra is black, simple cotton. Her breasts are perky and full, a good handful. I pepper kisses on her neck as her hands travel up my back to where the clasp on my bra is closed.

"Can I?" she says, leaning her head back so I can plant kisses on the soft skin near her earlobe. I nod, breathe a "Yes." She works the clasp free with one hand while the other comes around to help me remove the straps.

My bra falls between us, and she tugs it out of the way. With a groan, her hand cups my breast. "I could spend all day here," she says. "All night." Her pointer finger and her thumb close around my nipple, tweaking the sensitive skin until it makes me moan. Sitting on her lap like this, it's easy to press my need against her hips. She buries her face in my breasts, tonguing my nipple before taking the flesh, areola and all, into her mouth. I gasp as pleasure ripples through me, as she writhes against me. Her hands slide up my waist, into my hair, and around my neck, leaving sparks of electricity like a path across my skin.

"I want to see you," I say, easing back from working my mouth over her neck. I twist off her lap, and give a playful tug of the thin black strap holding her bra up. She laughs as it drops down. I reach around, undoing the clasp.

She lets it fall to the ground next to mine.

My eyes get stuck on her breasts. Skin like crushed seashells, with a tiny birthmark near one nipple. Her areolas are small, the nipples plump, tan. I take one in my hand, and it's a perfect fit. With my tongue I trace the ridge of the areola before using the tip to taunt the nipple. She quivers, groaning as I take the whole sweet thing in my mouth.

"Oh God," she says, followed by a soft cry. Her hand reaches between her legs. I move my own hand over hers, applying pressure. I feel her warmth through her jeans.

But I want to feel her wetness.

I release her breast from my mouth. "These have to come off now." Her eyes roll open and she laughs.

"Go right ahead." She smirks. I make fast work of the button, standing up to help ease them off her hips. Her black underwear slides off a little with them, and I tug them all the way down.

I stand there, topless, surveying her naked body with hungry eyes.

Her long legs and tight stomach. Her breasts that naturally

fall to either side, perky and plump. Her bush, full and black. All the expanse of her skin in soft cream peppered with dark freckles over her chest, her arms, her cheeks. I lean in to kiss her on the lips, taking her breath and her tongue in my mouth. When our lips break free, her hand moves to clutch the waistband of my jeans, thumb caressing the metal button.

"Your turn," she says. She tugs me against her, releasing the clasp on my jeans, dragging the zipper down. She takes my nipple into her mouth, swirling the tip of her tongue around, taunting it with the edge of her teeth. She leans back, spreading my pants open so she can see my underwear.

"Lavender lace," she says, practically licking her lips.

"Well, I am a gay girl, you know." My clit aches for relief, and my voice quivers with want. She grabs at the waistband of my pants and tugs, working the skintight fabric over my ass. I help her along until I'm standing there with only my underwear on. Her finger traces the waistband, runs down to the center. I ease my legs open. She fits her hands against my warmth.

"Fuck, these are drenched," she says, starting to work her fingers against my mound. I almost buckle, my knees nearly giving out. I fall against her, my tits hitting her face, and she moans, burying herself between them.

We plunge onto the bed together, twisting until we're all tangled up. I nudge my thigh between her legs, seeking contact with her wet warmth. When my skin grazes her heat, she lets out a moan and starts to rub against my thigh. One of her hands is still between my legs, but the other grabs for my ass, roping my underwear to pull them down. She draws her hand from between my legs, letting my underwear slip out of the way.

Her fingers spread my pussy, touching my swollen clit and

then sliding lower. She enters me with a gasp. I grip her ass and press her against me, angling my thigh for optimal friction.

As she works her finger inside, her palm applies pressure to my clit. Stars flood my vision as the intensity builds beneath her hand. Her finger slides in, moving in a rhythm with the motion of her hand, and I squeeze my legs together. My hand dips into the space between us as my finger slides over her want, slipping inside to feel the velvety warmth.

Her eyes roll open and fix on my mouth before dragging up to meet my gaze.

"I want to taste you," she says, and the force in her voice sends fresh heat between my legs. She lifts her hand from my pussy and touches the tips of her fingers to her tongue. The sight of her sucking me off her fingers like some sort of delicious treat turns me ravenous. I attack her neck with the edge of my teeth, devouring her as I move down, over her breasts and the hard cut of her abs, until my mouth reaches her bush and my fingers spread the lips open.

She takes a sharp inhale.

"Can I?" I ask her, dying to get a taste. She squeaks a "Yes." My mouth closes over her sex, and my tongue slips inside her where my hand was just exploring. Her fingers fist into my hair as her hips buck up. I work over her clit, tantalizing the tender, sensitive skin with my breath and my tongue. I lift up, sliding my finger inside her again as she reaches down to pull me against her. Our breasts press together.

Her thigh slides up between my legs and then her finger slips into the gap. The pressure is almost more than I can bear.

"I'm close," I gasp, my lips in her hair. Oh my God, my whole body is lit up, from my skin all the way to my soul.

"I am"—she breathes out a whimper—"too."

I open my eyes to see the rapture on her face. Her cheeks glowing, her lips swollen, her eyes open, connecting with mine. Neither one of us looks away as satisfaction—complete, all-consuming—ripples through our hips and over our skin.

Tying us up in pleasure together.

CHAPTER THIRTY-THREE

Cadence

A sliver of morning light prods me to wake just after dawn. Sydney sleeps on her side, her cheek pressed into the cool white bed linens. Her hair falls over her naked shoulder, streaming across her exposed breast. Her pink nipple, soft and supple, looks delicious enough to lick. I'm overcome with a flood of memory from last night, desperate for more of her, but also deeply aware of my morning breath and my full bladder. I slide out of the bed, running to the bathroom before she wakes up.

As soon as I pad across the floor, Chicken's head pops up from his bed.

"Hold on, hold on," I whisper. "Let me pee and then I'll take you out."

I'm not convinced he knows what I'm saying considering Sydney told me that he's hard of hearing and my low tone is probably outside his range. I close the door behind me, making fast use of the toilet. My breath can wait, I guess. I'd hate for him to have an accident before I can get him outside.

When I walk back out of the bathroom, I rummage in the

suitcase for sweats, throwing them on, braless and underwearless, then slipping my feet into my boots. I grab Chicken's leash from the dresser by the door. He's at my heels immediately.

"You have a full bladder, too." I bend down to hook him up with the leash, rubbing his ears a few times before we scoot out the door.

It's a clear, crisp morning. The courtyard shows the remnants of yesterday's revelers, with abandoned glasses of wine and marshmallow-roasting sticks stacked haphazardly around the firepits. Chicken sniffs at the edge of a shrub that lines the sidewalk, his little black nose twitching as if suspicious of the scent.

I am grateful for this moment alone with Chicken, even though I feel assured he isn't paying any attention to me now that his world has opened up to a host of new smells. Sydney loves this little creature, and anything she loves, I want to know better, because I want to know her better.

Last night with Sydney was more than I hoped it would be — more feelings, more longing, more heat. The closeness wasn't just about sex; at least it didn't feel that way to me. I am self-aware enough to know that I'm not readily in touch with my emotions, but being around her makes me feel a release like a dam is opening inside my chest. I *could* feel more, it *could* be safe to let my guard down.

I want to let her in all the way, to every hidden, secret place.

"There you are" comes my mother's voice. My stomach leaps, feeling caught in the act even though I'm an adult and also I'm not doing anything wrong. Chicken jumps, his tiny paws all lifting off the ground at once. I turn around to see she's approaching, dressed in a matching silky top-and-pants set that looks like elevated loungewear. As she nears, I see that the bright pattern is actually a tarot card print. The deck cascades, with the major and minor arcana overlapping each other in brightly dramatic jewel tones.

"There *you* are," I say, unable to pull my gaze from her outfit. Searching, maybe, for the Ten of Cups, though I can't admit that out loud.

She preens, spinning around to reveal that the back of her shirt has one large tarot card printed on top. The Magician, number one in the major arcana and one of her personal favorites.

"Custom-made," she says. "Gifted by a designer I read for once." She wants me to ask her the rest of the story, so clearly I can't.

"This is from REI," I say, yanking on the hem of my sweatshirt. "Bought and paid for." Chicken tugs at the leash. Her eyes scan down, landing on him.

"Sydney is still sleeping," I reply to her unasked question. I start to move, beholden to the whim of a six-pound dog. She follows, easing into stride as Chicken chases a scent across the courtyard.

"He likes you," she says. "Me he mostly tolerates."

"*Mostly* tolerates, or . . . ?" I jest. It's a slippery slope, bantering with my mother. It's too easy for her to take advantage of my unguarded walls when I'm trying to match her wit.

"All right, he despises me." She smiles, unashamed. "But I'm not much of an animal person."

"To put it lightly." I snort, thinking back to the time I rescued a litter of kittens from the canyon, likely after being dumped there by some hideous human. She let me keep them in the garage for one night before taking them to the shelter.

"You're thinking about those kittens," she says with a snarl.

"And I stand by the decision." She says that second part in a tone that is almost defiant.

"As if I would expect anything less." I cut her a look, but she's looking at Chicken again. We've stopped at another bush, where he's busy marking up a storm.

"I've tried with him, though. For Rick. He just loves the little menace." She's watching as Chicken now moves on to smell a patch of perennials planted in the flower bed at the edge of the courtyard. "Do you think it's something about me?"

I have to bite back a guffaw. "It's definitely personal," I say, lips twitching, throat wobbly. "And you should take it that way."

Her brow hooks. She likes this game, whatever it is, but she's surprised I'm willing to play.

"Oh, I do, no question. But Rick is in denial."

She talks so casually about Rick, the man she's marrying, the man she met just a few months ago. She talks of doing things for him, caring about what he cares about—Chicken, his friends, his daughter, and his magic tricks. She talks like someone who understands selflessness. Without ever saying it explicitly, Moira has set out to turn over a whole new leaf. She'll self-edit the parts that don't fit from the past, and no one around here will be the wiser.

She's a psychic by trade, but *this* is her superpower.

The spike of pain that unleashes in my chest makes me want to run all the way back to Acadia. To hide in the mountains, in crags on cliffsides, in a cave she would never dare to venture inside. Where she won't see me. Where I won't have to think about how her existence has eclipsed every part of my own and the only way to forge my own autonomy was to leave her world behind.

"Cadence." She says my name, the name she gave me, a name I love, and it yanks me out of my spinning thoughts. Our eyes meet. "I have to go to the winery in a couple of hours to finalize a few details before the engagement brunch tomorrow. Would you like to come along?"

Me. Alone with my mother. On purpose.

Me, alone with my mother, finally.

CHAPTER THIRTY-FOUR

Sydney

I wake slowly. My internal clock never really adjusts to time zones, so I almost always expect to either oversleep or wake up at some random, odd time in the night and think it's morning. The light is cool and bright as it slips through the partially opened slats in the blinds. I slept well for the first time in days, and I know the reason why.

As my eyes adjust to the room, my mind skates back over the adventure of last night.

Cadence throwing the perfect bull's-eye axe.

Our clandestine escape from the tent.

Every part of her body; her lips, my fingers, her moans, my orgasm.

And then I become aware that I am alone in this room. Not only is Cadence missing, but Old Man Chicken is gone, too. She must have taken him out for his morning potty break.

I slide out of bed and wander, naked, to the bathroom for my own pee break.

And all I can think about is how I don't want to run away at all. Not from this love affair, not from the strange challenge of my dad's engagement and all the change that will inevitably bring to both our lives. Not from my feelings.

And especially not from Ranger Girl, who I wish was still in that bed.

As I'm brushing my teeth, I throw on her t-shirt and my underwear, and I prop up my phone against the mirror, calling Joe on FaceTime.

After a few rings, he picks up. "Thank fuck, you finally called."

I spit the toothpaste into the sink. "You could have texted to check in," I reply with a scowl. I bend down to rinse.

"Since when has that ever been our dynamic?" he questions. He's dressed in his scrubs, walking his way to work as he sips on his green smoothie.

"Joe, you didn't get the Hailey Bieber smoothie again?" I am stalling. Maybe he won't notice.

"Spill the tea," he says, glancing at his Apple Watch. "I literally have less than a third of a mile left to reach work. Crunch, crunch." He walks stupid fast. Mall walker–level fast. Olympic-fast-walker fast.

"It's Saturday. Why are you working?" I ask. Still stalling.

"Ambition," he says. "Tea!"

"I don't know what you mean by tea." I play dumb. I called to spill—he knows I did—I just like to draw it out for the thrill of suspense.

"You're on location for Daddy's engagement party, and last I checked you were panicking about some soulmate shit, so I can only imagine that you have plenty of updates."

I sometimes loathe myself for the level of honesty that Joe is able to get out of me. And then I remember that I've seen his dick and have pictures in case he ever pisses me off.

"I fucked my future stepsister." It sounds so messed-up to say it like that, but it's true. If our parents actually stay engaged and get married, we will technically be related. Though, as far as I know, there's no law preventing marriage. At least not right now.

Fingers crossed it stays that way.

He stops dead in front of the Equinox entrance. He always tries to sneak in a sweat session before work.

"Ranger Girl?" he asks, incredulous and extroverted about it. A man exiting the gym glares daggers, but Joe is too busy ripping off his shades and screaming to notice. "What happened—holy shit?!"

I sit cross-legged on the bed. He waggles his brows.

"Ooooh, you need to get comfortable for the tale," he says, starting to walk again.

I tell him about the connection we feel despite being polar opposites and trying to keep shit platonic. The tarot reading with Moira—how, despite my determination to take all things she said with a bucket of salt, it hit me like a ton of bricks. I tell him about the Ten of Cups card Cadence pulled when she was with that tarot reader and her fiancée in the bar.

"She's complicated, but I like it." The words drop out of my mouth like little bombs.

"You want to see where it could go," he says. It's the one thing I never, ever care about usually. The endgame of it. The what-if scenarios. But with Cadence, I long for infinite possibility.

Not another goodbye.

Give me strings, baby. Tie me the fuck up.

"But I'm terrified," I say, allowing the wobble of nerves in my voice, the vulnerability of this confession.

"Dramatic." He smiles. Winks. He isn't one to go for sappy.

"I don't know if that's what she wants."

"You're Sydney Sinclair. Who wouldn't want you forever?" he says, and I snort at the irony coming from him. "Well." He laughs. "Besides me."

It's not that Joe is wrong about the way it has historically gone with people vying for the role of romantic lead in my life. I know I can capture the imagination, and because of that, people think it means they want to settle down with me. Start a family. Have a future. Even after just a string of dates or a single hookup. I am never the one fantasizing about babies and marriage and roots.

"Syd," he says, breaking into my thoughts. He's stopped in front of his work building. I can see a woman in a set of dark Prada glasses, with lips that definitely do not need any more filler, entering the glass doors behind him. "If you want her, just tell her." His eyes soften when they meet mine through the phone. "No games, no schemes."

"Just the truth."

"Fucking scary as that is."

We hang up, him kissing at the screen and me cringing at the tenderness I feel as his proposition slices through my rib cage, puncturing my heart.

Us against the world was an excuse. My job is scaffolding holding up the crumbling walls of a life that hasn't felt authentic for a long time, but I couldn't see it that way until this weekend. Flying commercial planes is steady work, and the fact that it keeps me in the sky, away from building a well-rounded life, hasn't worked for years.

Even when I'm not in the air, work requires hours outside the plane for detailing flight plans, prepping the crews, assessing weather patterns. The work is never monotonous but somehow still tedious. It's work that drains me as much as it feeds my need for adventure.

I've used work to explain away my reticence about long-term love.

But if Cadence wants to make a go of this thing, work will have to change.

For one of us, at least.

And it's not just work that will have to change. I can see how every part of my life will be touched by falling in love with Ranger Girl.

Isn't that also the meaning of the Sun and the Moon in tarot? I looked up the meaning for myself, hoping for some other take besides Moira's. The internet said that when these two cards are together, the uncertainty of the Moon is given the warm light of the Sun, leading to clarity, change, and vision for the future.

Being with Cadence is like walking through the dark and out into the light. I feel capable of asking myself big questions and not steamrolling a half-truth as my answer.

This whole train of thought gives me another one.

If I only have a couple more days with her guaranteed, I want to make sure I make them count. I flip over onto my stomach, reaching for the brochure on the nightstand that details all the "romantic and relaxing" activities that Solvang and the surrounding area have to offer.

I'm going to take Ranger Girl on a real live date.

Just the two of us.

CHAPTER THIRTY-FIVE

Cadence

Meet me in the butterfly garden at the
Victorian Inn. Come hungry. ☺

I followed Sydney's instructions to a location I have never been, not in any of the times I've visited Solvang. When I pull up outside the bed-and-breakfast, I'm taken in by what I see. A beautifully restored Victorian home, three stories tall, painted yellow with white trim, the intricate trim's woodwork details popping out in a deep rusty red. I cut the engine on my rental car and step out.

I follow the map I found online that shows the grounds around the inn. There are multiple gardens, but the butterfly garden is at the edge of the grounds near the greenbelt of trees that lines the boundary of the property. I take the path that leads away from the Victorian house, winding through a rose garden, past a small cobblestone seating area where a few guests eat brunch. Eventually I come up to a small gate with a curved trellis overhead. It's been planted with passionflower, which blooms in bright burnt orange.

A small wooden sign that reads JUNE'S BUTTERFLY GARDEN tells me I'm in the right place.

I press through the gate and round a slight bend in the path where, on a deep green knoll of grass, stands Sydney. Beside her is a yellow-and-green picnic blanket with a basket I assume contains food. Staked into the ground beside the blanket is one of those wooden wine holders with two cups secured inside and full of what look like mimosas.

But my eyes don't want to focus on the scene around me.

They want to focus on her.

Her blond hair is down, long and straight and shiny. She wears a deep orange dress that ties at the neckline and cinches in to accentuate her curves. Pearl earrings catch the light, and her fitted denim jacket is rolled up at the cuffs.

"What's this about?" I ask her, swallowing the frog of nerves in my throat. I adjust my deep purple button-down, hoping I am dressed appropriately for whatever she has planned. I close the gap between us.

"Just a little brunch date," she says, bending to grab our glasses. "Ranger Girl."

I don't bite back my smile at the nickname. I want her to see that I like it.

I like her.

We cheers with our glasses and take a sip, but just as I'm about to sit down, she reaches for my waist and tugs me against her. Her hand slides into the back pocket of my jeans, I feel her breath on my cheek, and my lips open.

She covers them with a kiss.

Deep and passionate, but also tender and sweet.

I let my free hand slip around her, fingers splaying out over her back. Her ample curves meld with my more solid frame, and my knees almost buckle at the sensation. Her mouth lifts from mine, and I let out a whimper. I need to get ahold of myself.

She practically has me panting.

We drop to the blanket, and Sydney proceeds to pull out two sandwiches, one a caprese on a ciabatta and the other chicken salad. She knows I don't eat pork or beef, was a vegetarian for years, but I never told her that even now I often can't stomach chicken, though occasionally I'll eat it if there are no other options.

Birds are my favorite creatures. I even like chickens.

I take the caprese sandwich. "Thank you. This is really thoughtful."

"I have ulterior motives, I'm afraid," she says, a small smirk playing on her lips. I quirk my brow, waiting for the rest. "I thought I'd get you a little tipsy and then make out with you surrounded by nature."

My cheeks warm. "You don't need me tipsy for that."

I set the sandwich aside and then secure my wineglass back in the holder.

The heat in her gaze is matched by the warmth I already feel between my legs. I take her glass, never unlocking my eyes from hers.

I press up to kiss her. Just a light brush of my lips at first.

Sydney is a pilot, the head of her flight crew. She's used to being in charge, and I think she mostly likes taking the lead, but even the most strong-willed type A person sometimes wants to surrender. My hand finds the curve of her neck as my fingers move her jaw up, angling her face toward me. I deepen the kiss, and she opens her lips for me to let my tongue explore.

We drift back to the blanket. Everything else melts away.

I feel the curves of her beneath my hands. Soft and yielding, not an ounce of tension in her muscles, just surrender. It's easy to let go with her. To let myself soften. All the hard edges I'm so used to get worn down in all the right ways. I find the hem of her dress and then the flesh of her thigh right beneath it.

I let my instincts do the rest.

⌒

Later, we're lying on the blanket, nibbling on the remains of our sandwiches, and laughing, when it hits me.

I also made a date with my mom.

"Fuck," I exclaim.

"We did." Her voice is all mischief, and it almost derails me completely.

I yank up my phone from the edge of the blanket to check the time.

"Moira asked me to go with her to the winery." I sound like I'm in pain. "I said I would go."

Sydney sits up. She hovers over me, lit from behind by the sun.

"You're gonna hang out with your mom one-on-one?" she asks, a smile spreading her lips, turning her voice bright, too.

"Apparently," I reply, chagrined.

"This is good," she says. "At least attempt to let it be good."

Her eyes search my face. I can't help but notice the longing in them. Maybe I'm just seeing my own longing reflected back at me.

I don't hate my mom, no matter how much I want to.

"That's a big ask, Sydney." I lift up, reaching out to brush the hair off her shoulder. She removed her denim jacket earlier and hasn't put it back on.

She shifts, scooting closer. Her hands cover mine.

"I never talk about my mom," she says, her voice tentative. "Not to anyone."

"You don't have to—"

"I want to." Her eyes trip up to mine. The softest, sweetest blue. "I had this goldfish when I was younger. My mom had gotten it for me before she got sick, and she helped set up the tank, taught me all the care instructions, everything." I'm listening intently, her eyes never leaving my face. "But her health declined rapidly—maybe she had been sick for a long time and I just didn't know."

Her eyes sheen with tears she's trying not to cry.

"And even though she could hardly stay awake, she'd still bring up the fish. Every day—did you check the filter? Don't forget to feed Flounder—"

"Excellent name," I break in. Tears tug from my eyes to skate down my cheeks.

"I couldn't keep her from what was to come, but the goldfish— I could do everything right, follow the rules of care. I could show her I could handle it on my own. I could show her I was fine, fully capable." Her thumb brushes the tears from my cheek. "But I wasn't. And Flounder died the same week my mom did, because I forgot a simple step in his care. I was so determined to show her I could do it on my own that I killed him."

"Goldfish are surprisingly difficult to keep alive," I reply. I chuckle, but it's small and embarrassed.

"We need people, Cadence. As scary as it is to be vulnerable." Her voice cracks. She takes me in her arms. "I push people away, too. It just looks different on me. But if she's reaching out, and you think you can handle it to reach back—"

I press my lips to hers, but not to silence her.

To thank her.

She smiles against my mouth.

"I spent most of my life up until I left LA trying to hold Moira close—or figure out what it was that I could do to get her to hold me close," I say, my voice rough. "I'm just scared that she'll let me down."

Growing up, I knew I was important to my mom. I saw how much pride she took in me. But I also saw how she was always willing to put her needs first. Her agenda. Her wishes. I just wanted her to put me first, even if what I wanted wasn't what she thought I should do.

"I don't know if Moira is going to let you down," she says. "In piloting, we learn to analyze flight paths to seek out the best possible routes given the ever-changing factors of the skies. What if the skies have changed and all you need to do now is look for the best way forward?"

"Forward." I mull the word over in my mind.

"You're almost smiling," she says.

She presses her lips to the edge of mine. She's still holding on to my back with one hand, which she now uses to tug me on top of her. Our bodies crush together as she peppers me with kisses down my neck.

I can't stop the giggle that breaks free.

Her laugh is almost as intoxicating as her eyes.

And then her phone begins to buzz.

She peers around behind me to where it sits on the blanket.

"It's my dad," she says, groaning. She reaches around me, and the move causes me to fall back against the blanket. She hovers over me, boobs mounding from the top of her dress, which is still untied from earlier.

"What a view," I breathe. She cackles as she drops back to a seated position, taking the view away.

"Hey, Dad," she says, the chuckle still in her voice.

I can't make out what he's saying, but I can hear that he's chipper to the extreme. She listens, nodding a couple of times. "Yeah, Cadence is going to the winery with her mom." She grins at me, and I roll my eyes. "A horse ride?" She nibbles her lower lip for a second. "Sure, that sounds nice, Dad."

Looks like we both have dates with our parents.

CHAPTER THIRTY-SIX

Sydney

I can admit that I am rusty in the saddle, and Dad, in his infinite enthusiasm, has definitely overhyped my abilities. Three summers at horse-riding camp in Burbank in my preteens wasn't enough to stick well into my late twenties. The horse I'm on, Rosie, a red-and-white Appaloosa, is recommended for intermediate riders, and less than five minutes in the saddle tells me why. With the slightest pressure from my calves at her side, she speeds up.

"Whoa, girl," I say in a low but gentle tone, lifting the reins so her snout dips and she slows again.

Dad canters up beside me. "You okay there, Birdie?"

"I'm doing better than Pam," I reply as we both turn our attention to the side where Pam's horse has taken her off the trail and in the direction of the nearest vineyard. There's a wooden fence separating this trail and the meadow surrounding it from the vineyards, but something tells me Pam should be nervous.

When I look back at Dad, he's making an *oh shit* face. I laugh, momentarily tightening my calves against Rosie's sides. Again she canters forward, her pace clipping along with extra speed. I get her stilled again, and Dad is able to catch up to me; we settle into a loose walk up the dirt trail that winds away from the vineyard and into the cluster of trees at the base of the hills.

When we got here, I did a quick survey of the routes they offer for their rides. The beginner trail (the one Pam clearly should be on) goes away from the vineyard to a small pond right inside the tree line where you can have a picnic. The trail I suggested was a step up from that, taking you straight into the forest where you can meander around the perimeter of the vineyards until you come out into a clearing where they have archery and other activities that are an upsell. Dad and I just opted for the wine bottle and cheese plate, but I am thinking of suggesting Cadence and I come back sometime for a little moonlit archery. I bet she could handle a bow just as well as an axe.

As soon as I have the thought, I know I should squash it. I can't let myself daydream about a future with Cadence—even just a future date night. Her life is across the country. Mine is here. We just met a few days ago; how could we know if this is something we want to make a go of yet?

Except I feel deep in my bones that I do want to. That I would have the best time of my life if I did.

Soulmates. It feels less strange to imagine actually using the word to describe her than it did when she first told me about Moira's prediction. Then, I wanted to laugh it off. Now, I want to embrace it.

"Birdie?" I can't remember the last time he called me Sydney. I don't know if it's because I was named for the place he met and fell in love with my mother or if it's just because he's jaunty that way.

"Dad," I reply. He looks like he's gearing up for something big.

"Scale of one to ten, how skeptical were you when I told you about Moira?" I'm surprised by the question. Dad isn't usually this direct about stuff. Not a fan of confrontation. I peer at him from behind my shades, like I can investigate his aura or some shit. "They're sunglasses, sweetie, not Annabeth's Yankees cap."

I'm taken aback by the reference. Mom and I read the first couple Percy Jackson books before she got sick, but that was our thing—just the two of us. Dad didn't read them. He shouldn't know that Annabeth's cap makes her invisible.

"I listened to the audiobooks while I was doing flight reports." He smiles. His aviators catch the light. For a second he looks like the picture-perfect pilot, and the sight sends a ping of pain ricocheting around my chest. "And you didn't answer my question."

"Fine," I say. He chuckles. "Scale of one to ten, I was off the charts. Thirteen."

"Oof, unlucky." He cringes. That was one of Dad's flight superstitions. No flight numbers with thirteens, not ever.

"That's how it felt to me," I reply.

"Felt? Past tense?" he asks.

"Maybe I'm down to a seven, now," I say, waving off his gleeful expression with the back of my hand. "But only because I like her daughter." Dad can read whatever he likes into that. Which he will. I can tell by the way his grin grows.

"So Moira's whole *only one room* debacle is working out?" he asks.

"She planned it—I knew it!" I exclaim, the sudden rise in the volume of my voice startling Rosie into a canter. When I get her slowed down again, and when Dad catches up, I add, "I didn't *know* it, but we were suspicious."

"*We?*" I can see his eyebrows rise and lower swiftly a few times behind his aviators.

"That's mastermind shit."

"That's Moira," he says with so much love. I bet his eyes have stars in them.

"And you're okay with her just doing stuff like that? Aren't you worried she'll do that kind of thing to you?"

He shrugs, smiles, looks away from me and back out to the trail ahead.

"It makes me feel taken care of to think she's watching out, making plans, moving, seeing forward, when all I'm used to seeing is right now." His voice gets serious, and my heart rate speeds up. "I know I dropped the ball after your mom passed."

"You did fine, Dad—"

"No, Sydney, let me." The use of my name silences my argument. "For years, living felt like walking through a fog, and there was very little that helped me see clearly. I know I leaned on you, and I know you felt pressured to go into piloting when I retired early." We both know he had to quit. No retirement, just the end of a job he loved.

"You didn't pressure me. I always wanted to be a pilot."

"I distinctly recall you also wanted to be a horse trainer." He looks down at Rosie. "A stuntwoman—"

"I still think that sounds kind of fun."

"—a race car driver, chemist, deep sea explorer—"

"Every kid wants to be a million things when they grow up. Eventually you narrow it down and choose a path." I shut down his list of all my random daydreams.

"I'm just saying, I know it was hard for you, and you stepped up in ways you shouldn't have had to at thirteen."

I don't argue. He isn't wrong.

"I leaned on you, and it wasn't fair. And I still do, and that's not fair, either."

I don't know how to reply to that. So I don't, and he doesn't press the topic any further.

After so many years, you'd think hearing him take ownership like that would be a weight off my shoulders, a relief. But with everything that's happened since I got that invitation in the mail, I'm feeling less grounded than ever before.

I'm also realizing that stability beyond the paycheck is something I actually want.

"There's something I want to talk to you—" he starts.

We're interrupted by a streak of white galloping toward us, a screaming Pam hanging on for dear life.

CHAPTER THIRTY-SEVEN

Cadence

We're standing in the lobby of the hotel, eyes peeled, looking out the doors at the valet, where the shuttle bus to the winery will arrive any minute. I'm watching my mother in my periphery, trying to imagine what it would be like to just be normal and feel normal around her.

It's really hard for me to do.

"Oh, wonderful," Moira says suddenly, and I assume it's because the shuttle has arrived. But when I look up and out through the window, I see that I'm wrong. "I was wondering when you two would arrive!"

I follow the direction of my mother's elated expression to see Kit and Julia walking in with some shopping bags from the Spice Merchant, each holding a Danish in hand. I make eye contact with Kit first, hoping her intuition about the cards isn't the only way she's empathic.

As Kit and Julia approach, their body language couldn't be more different. Kit carries herself with an open ease, fluid, almost like a dancer. She's smiling at us, seems genuinely happy to see us. Julia has the straightest posture I've ever seen.

"We've been here since last night," Kit says. "We've been enjoying the festival. Thank you for the suggested itinerary and guide to the area."

My mother beams.

"We've come a handful of times over the years," Moira says, and I know from experience that this is my cue. She's gearing up to introduce us in what will likely be a gushing display of politeness that is actually bragging in sheep's clothing. "This is my daughter, Cadence."

I am an awkward penguin. "Hey." Julia covers her lips with her Danish to hide her smile.

"Madame Moira's daughter," Kit says, chill in the face of her fiancée, who's almost losing her composure. "It's wild that you have a daughter."

Surprise flickers in Moira's face. "How so?" I hear a razor in her voice that I hope isn't discernable to them.

"You have to know—we all kind of thought you were a witch growing up," Kit says, and I chuckle.

"She is," I say without thinking. Moira cuts me a look. "You literally have an altar in your Reading Room."

"And witches don't have children?" Moira questions. It feels directed at all of us.

"You were more like a fairy tale character to us," Julia replies. Matter-of-fact. "Predicting soulmates, reading futures. We're just surprised you also had this very human, totally normal thing like a daughter."

"I can't decide if I'm flattered by the assessment," Moira says.

She is. There's nothing this woman likes more than her own folklore.

"So how do y'all know Madame Moira?" I ask. If I don't ask, I don't doubt it will occur to my mother later and I'll be cornered.

Kit leaps into the story I already know, animatedly explaining in great detail how she and Julia reconnected at a wedding and fell madly in love, realizing the Twin Flames prediction. But my attention is firmly on Moira as she eats up the praise, confirming to me that she *did* invite them to her party for this reason.

She is still the star of the show.

The shuttle pulls up outside just as Kit finishes and I am stammering through my reaction, trying not to stick my foot in my mouth.

"Enjoy the rest of today," Moira says as we walk away. "The party will hopefully be unforgettable."

Unforgettable.

Engagement parties aren't unforgettable.

But weddings are.

⌒

We climb into the shuttle, and even though it's empty, Moira doesn't put a seat between us.

I fight the urge to move, forcing myself to focus on the concept of a path forward.

But I'm thinking about Lola's theory that the engagement party is actually a surprise wedding, and it's making it really hard to give my mother the benefit of the doubt.

I can imagine Moira doing that for the spectacle, lying to close friends and her daughter just for the plot and nothing more. But it's hard to believe Rick wouldn't tell Sydney. Even if she would be thrilled for him, I don't think she would be thrilled about him lying.

I am not an expert on her yet, but from what I have learned of her so far, she seems like someone who wears the truth on her sleeve — our lies this week notwithstanding. She seems open-hearted. And she really does seem to adore her dad.

"Do you ever think about it?" Moira's voice cuts though my mental chatter.

"Think about what?" I ask, annoyed already even though I don't know what she's referring to.

"Your soulmate prediction," she says. I don't know why it would surprise me that she'd bring that up right after coming face-to-face with one of her success stories. She wants to get a rise out of me, because that was always her way to prod me to open up.

Piss me off and the walls come down.

"What about it?"

"Meeting Kit and Julia doesn't make you wonder, not even a little bit?"

"I've met dozens of your so-called successes, Mom, and never once have I entertained the idea that you should get credit for how I may or may not stumble upon the person I want to spend my life with."

"So you think there could be someone out there you'd want that with?" This question throws me off guard. I feel my face contort and am immediately aggravated that I can't hide it from her.

"Of course I want someone like that," I say, sighing.

"A soulmate?" she presses. She's trying to steer the conversation. I don't have to let her.

"Is Rick your soulmate?" I ask, crossing my arms to close my body off from her. Doesn't mean she can't read me like a book, but at least it makes me feel in control. She smiles, looking away from me, out the window, as if seeing him reflected in the glass.

"Rick is the closest I'll ever get," she says simply.

"What does that mean?" It almost sounds like she's taking accountability for her shitty personality and how it cuts her off from parts of existence she might otherwise have access to. But no, that can't be.

She inhales, nudging me with her shoulder in a playful way that grinds my gears. I lean away from the contact, but she presses on.

"My life, it's not easy for most people to understand." She fiddles absently with the zipper on her purse. "And men—even harder for them than just people." A snort of laughter escapes my lips, and I hate myself for it. God, I really suck at this detached thing. "I can be aloof and manipulative, qualities that you have repeatedly made clear are hard to be around."

"Understatement," I grunt, but the tension in my arms loosens.

"I can't say I know how to be any other way." She sounds exhausted, and for the first time in a very long time, I let myself look at her, see her. The tension in her jaw, the creases around her eyes, the way her hands are always moving. Restless, touching her hair, pinching a crease in her pant leg. For a flicker of a moment, the light touches the top of her head, illuminating the tiniest hint of gray.

For a moment she looks vulnerable, and I feel almost sorry for her.

"But Rick, he doesn't seem to mind that so much," she continues. "In fact, I think he appreciates it. He isn't surprised by much.

He understands the quest for . . ." Her voice drifts. Her expression is dreamy. "Magic. He's not boring—no, he's even surprising."

"Even to the psychic?" My tone is almost playful.

"Even to the psychic." She smiles at me, her eyes steady on mine. "I know you don't believe me, and that's okay. I'm just glad you're here." I roll my eyes and blink to keep the sudden pressure of tears from unleashing. "Cadence, I'm so glad."

"Me, too," I say, instantly, no question. It's like we're playing that game where you clear your mind and say the first thought that comes to the surface. The most honest.

She reaches for my hand, squeezing it. "Mom, stop it." I twitch, not pulling away.

She smiles; I smile. I wonder if we've always looked alike when we do that, and I have just been too stubborn—too hurt, closed off, and angry—to see it.

❧

Whimsy Winery is beautifully quiet this early in the day.

We're standing beneath the broad, worn, and weathered barn doors of the barrel room, where the engagement party will take place. It opens onto a limestone patio, with brightly colored lanterns hanging from the rafters of an arbor. There are ten round tables set up around the perimeter, also in a distressed wood that suits the style of the place.

This is starting to look suspiciously like the setup of a wedding reception.

Moira walks up behind me carrying two small pours of white wine. The clarity and color varies slightly as she swirls them around the bowls of the glasses.

"We have to choose a white for the open bar," she says, holding them up. "You know I'm partial to reds, so."

"You want me to try these and pick one?" I ask, scowling at the glasses. "It's barely after noon."

"Twelve forty-five, fully in the lunch window."

"Alcohol at lunch is served with food."

"Do you want to help or not? You always liked white—"

"No, I'll help." I reach for the glasses, taking one in each hand. "I just had to protest so I don't feel like an alcoholic."

Moira laughs, a husky, full sound in her throat. It's incredibly rare to get that kind of laugh out of her. I've maybe managed it a handful of times in my life. I let myself be pleased at the honor as we drift to one of the high bar tables just inside the barrel room.

"What's this one?" I lift the glass holding the paler white.

"Sauvignon blanc, but a blend. And the other is their chardonnay."

"They're known for the chardonnay, so right off, I'm feeling biased."

She winks. "Let your taste buds choose."

It's so close to something she used to say to me all the time. *Let your intuition take the lead.* I feel those words ripple between us now like water someone has just dropped a pebble into. I let the ripples touch my skin. Feel the ease of the idea wash over me. It's exhausting fighting so hard all the time.

I taste the sauvignon, taking a generous sip onto my palate and swirling it around. It's tart, citrus-led, with hints of peach. I like it immediately, even if it's not what I would choose to drink usually.

"It's pleasant and easy," I say after I swallow. I lift the

chardonnay, their more well-known wine, the one they have stocked all over the country per their brochure. It has a deeper color, but chardonnay can be divisive, less of a crowd-pleaser.

This one is smooth, light on the palate but more robust than the sauvignon. It's got hints of lemon and apple, and none of the buttery notes that I usually despise.

"I don't think there's a bad choice," I say, my eyes traveling from the chardonnay to the sauvignon blanc.

"The budget allows for one," Moira says, and it may be the first time I've ever heard her talk openly about money as if it isn't an infinite, renewable resource granted by the Universe to those who visualize hard enough.

"The chardonnay will be what everyone expects." I look up into her eyes, holding her gaze despite my usual aversion. "Give them something they won't see coming."

"Speaking my language," she replies with a knowing smile.

She's practically saying it with her whole chest. *This engagement party is a wedding! Surprise!* But without some kind of proof, I don't want to freak Sydney out. We're not supposed to be scheming. I'm *supposed* to be detaching and staying open. But if they are lying to everyone, their comfort level with lying makes me all the more suspect of both of them. What else could they be keeping secret, and at what point do we hold them accountable?

"I'll go let them know about the decision," she says, turning away from me and walking in the direction of the visitor's entrance where the event coordinator has an office. When she's gotten far enough away, I empty both wineglasses into my mouth and set them on the table.

Just one more time, just for peace of mind, I'm going to spy on my mother.

I follow her back through the vineyard, trying to be as covert as possible and not draw attention from the staff. There's a flurry of activity around the gazebo set on one of the hilltops, nestled into the vineyards that flow into the hills at the edge of the property.

Gazebos historically point to wedding ceremonies.

The closer we get to the visitor's entrance the more suspicious all this gazebo activity makes me. The main kitchen, utilized only for events, since Whimsy Winery doesn't offer anything more than charcuterie and bread and olive oil on their normal tasting menu, is abuzz with activity.

Sure, they might be prepping food for tomorrow, but I take a quick detour to peek inside. It looks like they're setting up to actually serve today. Platters of tapas are arranged. Silver trays are being polished. Glassware steamed. They're prepping entrées, sauces, and in one corner a pastry chef appears to be putting the final touches on what I can only describe as a full-blown wedding cake.

Two tiers. Rustic. Herbs and flowers wreathing their way down one side.

Why the fuck would an engagement party require a wedding cake?

I whip around from the kitchen, crossing beneath a porte cochere that connects the building with the visitor center, and approach the window at the side of the door. I don't want to burst in and yell *gotcha*. That would just make her double down on the lie. I know Moira well enough to know that. So I peer through the window. She's sitting across from the event coordinator, and in her hand she's holding a small piece of cardstock. Her smile is broad, bright, pleased. The look of a woman who is in on the joke but knows no one else has caught on yet.

I have to find out what's written on that card.

They continue to chat for a few more minutes, until Moira hands back the card and stands to leave. I drop down from the window, hoping that the angle of the door opening will shield me enough that she doesn't see me when she comes back out this way. I try to become one with the outer wall, wishing I were dressed in neutrals and had hair that didn't require its own zip code. But fortunately, when the door opens, she's too absorbed in her conversation—which I barely catch anything from—to glance in my direction.

I slip inside, unnoticed, feeling extremely James Bond.

And a little guilty for how quickly I abandoned the promise I made Sydney to stop scheming and look for a path forward. I hope that if I present her with proof of a con in action, she'll at least direct any anger she feels to our parents and not me.

Her opinion of me matters, a truth I can admit to myself and will have to freak out about at another time.

I make a beeline straight for the event coordinator's desk, where I see a small paperboard box of cardstock sits holding a selection of invitations. My eyes graze them, taking in the simple hunter-green font and the grapevine border. The vineyard's watermark is pressed into the lower right corner, making them look like they come from the winery and not the couple.

Please join Rick and Moira at Whimsy Winery this
evening for a special tour & tasting. Dress to impress.
All expenses paid. Shuttle service begins at five.

Tonight.
This is the confirmation I need to show Sydney.

The next thought bolts through me like a shock of electricity. No longer a tap or a whisper, this is a blast from my intuition, and I can't ignore it. *Together.* We need to decide together what to do about this wedding. We pinky promised we were partners in this, and I want to keep that promise.

We came here thinking Moira was conning Rick, and we were wrong. Moira and Rick are conning us into attending their wedding.

CHAPTER THIRTY-EIGHT

Sydney

They've wrapped Pam in one of those silver foil blankets you always see people wearing after traumatic situations in movies. She's sitting on a bench by a row of hanging saddles, sipping a glass of tepid water. The horse, a usually docile paint mare, is a few stalls over, eating some hay. Dad and Greg are talking to the ferrier and the owner, trying to smooth things over considering Pam adamantly protested the fault of the horse, taking the blame squarely on her own shoulders.

"It's big of you," I say, dropping down next to her on the bench. She snorts. Her eyes still have this wild look in them. More like exhilaration than pure fear. "Taking responsibility like that."

"I have to confess, sometimes I want to just go bananas and throw caution to the wind." She takes a sip of her water, turning her warm brown eyes on me. "I was sitting there on that saddle, trying to gently coax the horse toward the trail. The instructor was nearby calling out orders I should follow to ease the horse back into the direction we were meant to go, and I just snapped." She releases her grip on the blanket to snap her fingers. "I pressed my legs around the horse and said, *Let's go!*" She guffaws. "And she listened!" She shakes her head, grabbing me by the wrist. "Oh, it felt so good, so liberating."

Her laugh is contagious, not just to me but to the horses in stalls nearby. Her horse whinnies, and Pam cackles.

"Sometimes you just gotta say screw it and let go," she adds.

The *screw it* is so Pam, but the words land on me in a very personal way. I wouldn't usually consider myself the kind of person to read into every little thing happening around me as a sign from the universe. But this week has somehow shifted my awareness, broadening the possibility in my imagination that I am not alone in creating the life I want. There could be some force presenting me with guidance, not simply offering me choices. These feelings about my work, Dad's apology for dropping the ball, putting forth the idea that his losses eclipsed my own desires and forced me onto a path I didn't actually choose, which I might not have taken had things happened differently.

Had he just told me that leaving his beloved career had been a choice, not a requirement, I might not have felt so bound to the path of pilot. To following in his footsteps as a way to carry on his legacy. Would I have tried to explore one of those other wild ambitions I had on my list through the years? Would I have felt more grounded in my own life rather than rooted in the life we didn't get to have as a family?

Us against the world. Could I have let others in? Could I have tried to fall in love? Could I have stopped carrying him long enough to heal me?

"I will say, the adrenaline rush made me hungry," Pam says, glancing down at her water with new disdain. I grin.

"I'll see if they're ready to head back." All these questions aren't going to get answered in my own brain, and even if I do find some way to express them, they probably can't all get sorted this weekend. But at least I have to try to bring this out in the open, not brush it under the rug.

I can do hard things. I've been doing them most of my life.

Why should this be any different?

I leave Pam on the bench and walk through the stable toward the office, which is on the other side of this row of stalls. As I near the corner, amid the sounds of horses' whinnies and hooves shifting in hay, I hear Dad's and Greg's low tones. Alerted by the tension in their voices, I slow to peek around the corner before barreling into the mix.

They're alone, no longer talking to the owner or ferrier as they stand outside the office doors together. Dad is taller than Greg, but to me Greg has always felt more intimidating. Not unlikable or mean-spirited, just more authoritative. In charge, where Dad is happy to be a team player. Greg has his hand on Dad's shoulder in a way that reminds me of a coach talking to a player at a critical point in a championship game. His face is stern; Dad's expression is focused.

"I get that you've been digging out of this hole for a while now, and you're trying to make all these big changes—"

"These changes are why I'm finally digging out of the hole, bud, you know that," Dad cuts in, his tone friendly even with Greg's intensity.

"And I'm glad to see it," Greg concedes. "But you do have to understand how this whole weekend looks to Pam and me."

I lean in as Greg's voice drops in volume. My hand grips the curve of a saddle for support.

"I do, I do," Dad says, nodding. He raises his arm to pat Greg on the opposite shoulder. "But the plan is in motion."

"You're sure of that?" Greg sounds skeptical.

"When have I ever lied to you?" Dad asks. It's a loaded question, even if his tone is light. Greg releases his shoulder and barks a laugh.

"Ha!" he says. "We've been friends for over thirty years." And I'm not sure if that means he's never lied in those thirty years or he's lied plenty but never so harmfully as to alienate his friend.

"Here's to thirty more," Dad says, clapping his palm across Greg's back with a loud smack. The sound startles me, and my hand jolts from the saddle.

"Fuck!" I exhale the word in a loud burst as I lose my balance, falling forward and almost right onto the ground in front of them. I manage to course correct, whipping around and stumbling a few feet back from my current position.

"Birdie?" Dad raises his voice. Worry edges into the sound.

"Yeah, just tripped on my own feet," I say, regaining my footing just as they come around the corner. When my eyes meet Dad's, his look nervous.

Startled. Caught.

He's afraid I heard them talking.

Whatever they were discussing, it's connected to the speedy-fast engagement and the conversation he and Greg were having over text when Cadence was with him at Universal. It's not something big enough that Greg and Pam wouldn't attend their engagement weekend, but it is putting a damper on the experience and does seem to have a time crunch.

"I was just coming to see if you were ready to head back," I say, thumbing in the general direction where Pam still sits. "Pam said the adrenaline has her famished."

Dad's shoulders slightly relax. "I can relate."

"I'll go pull around the Denali," Greg says, referring to his vehicle. He tosses Dad another look before walking away toward the barn doors that lead out to the parking lot.

For a second I just stand there, thoughts whirring. This week has shown me just how little I really know my father, the man I've always thought of as my closest friend. Trust is something I just granted him, happily, without really questioning. I was glad to consider Moira a villain in my dad's life, but I never thought maybe Dad was working his own angle and Moira could be the one who's getting the wool pulled over her eyes.

He opens his mouth like he wants to say something. I'm saved by the sound of Pam rustling up behind me.

⌐

Dad was noticeably quiet on the ride back, a rarefied event, and one that made me feel increasingly like I was in trouble even though I hadn't done anything wrong. I didn't mean to overhear their conversation, and even if I did, Dad is keeping something from me that could be related to his decision to get engaged to a practical stranger and a definite con woman. It's not normal behavior for him, someone who is such an open book. It's calling into question that open book status.

Greg pulls up to the valet, and I mumble, "Thanks for the ride" as I shoot out the side door.

I don't want to pounce on Dad without at least getting

Cadence's take on this news. We pinky promised we were in this together, and while this situation could well be something I need to handle myself—or talk to Dad about on my own—that doesn't mean I don't want her help.

I want her in this with me. Whatever *this* is.

CHAPTER THIRTY-NINE

Cadence

I've been pacing the length of this room since we got back from the winery, and I know it's making Chicken nervous. He's sitting up on his bed, the tip of his tongue sticking out through his missing front teeth, watching me with concern in his dark brown eyes. I texted Sydney with an SOS as soon as I was free from Moira's view, but I haven't heard from her yet. For all I know, I could be wearing a hole in the carpet and she could still be riding a horse through the forest.

I look over the weekend itinerary on my phone.

Cheese and Wine at the Hygge 2 p.m.

I drop my phone on the bed and fall back onto the cool linens, closing my eyes and dragging my fingers back and forth over the lids until I see green orbs floating against the darkness. They have to give their guests enough warning so they can get ready and be at the shuttles by five. It's almost two, and my guess is the invites will be delivered to the wine and cheese tasting that is supposed to take place here at the Hygge soon.

A decoy tasting that's probably not even a tasting at all.

Just a way to get their guests in one place to receive their invitations.

It's so fucking theatrical that I almost wonder if Rick came up with the idea. There's a stamp of *magician doing a trick* here. I know he's been training in illusion; maybe this is one he wanted to try out.

I'm freaking out over how to tell Sydney, how she'll react, how it will make her feel, but if I'm being completely honest with myself, I'm also freaking out about how this will change the course of this weekend, popping the bubble we managed to climb inside last night before we even get to enjoy it. There's no way to know if we'll get another chance to hold each other close.

Behind my lids, I can see her now. The soft, sloping lines of her body. The plump pout of her lips. Her hair like sunshine, her eyes like the sky. I want more of her than I've gotten—this wasn't enough, just a few short days. This wasn't enough to hear all her stories, memorize every one of her laughs.

I want more time and space and daydreams and tears.

I want to know her like a best friend and touch her like a lover—

The metallic grind of the lock opening yanks me from my yearning spiral.

I scoot into a seated position as the door opens.

Sydney.

Her hair is windswept, as if she ran here. Her cheeks flushed from sun or exertion, I don't know which. She's dressed in a pair of jeans and a dark blue button-down, sleeves rolled up to the elbows. The shirt is fitted, like it was tailored for her body. It matches her eyes like it was made using a sample of the color.

I shoot up from the bed, closing the space between us. I take her by the waist, tucking my other hand in her hair until I am cradling her head.

I cover her lips with my own.

The kiss is hungry, my tongue fervent.

She smells as good as she tastes, and even with the chaos about to close in, I feel my body ease as my breath and hers mix like a master-blended wine.

Her arms tighten around me as her hands reach for my ass. She tucks her palms in the pockets of my jeans, pressing my hips against hers. I know this can't last—we have to talk—but her kissing me like this is the best salve to any wound.

Chicken's bark breaks us from our bliss. Her lips unhook from mine with a laugh. I drop my forehead to hers, my shoulders shaking in a responding chuckle. Her eyes turn up to peer into mine. The soft light brown lashes, coated with mascara so they stand out, brush her skin.

"He probably needs to eat his lunch," she says with a sigh.

"I think he's just worked up because we're worked up," I reply, grinning over at the little rascal. "I fed him when I got back from the winery." I straighten but don't pull away completely. She doesn't release my ass; I don't let go of her waist. A smile cracks her cheeks, and she leans in to kiss me again.

"You didn't have to do that," she says, tightening her hold on me.

"He was hungry," I say, not sure what this reaction is about but not wanting to stop her from feeling it. "And I don't mind."

We stand there for a moment, just holding each other, a few more breaths inside the bubble, until finally she tugs her hands from my back pockets and I let mine drop from her waist.

"I have to tell you something crazy," I say, just as she says, "I think my dad is the con artist."

Wait, what? I step back. A dent forms between her brows.

"Your dad is the con artist?"

"What happened at the winery?" Her lips kick into the tiniest smirk. "You wanna go first?"

"I think maybe *you* should," I say. She nods, agreeing with reluctance. She paces to the bed and sits, but I am too restless to follow. I turn to face her, noticing as I do that Chicken has lain back down in his bed, his eyes already closing again.

"Where the hell do I start?" she asks, but it's directed more to the room. Or even the Universe, God forbid.

She flips her hair into a deep side part and runs her fingers down the length.

"He brought up all this old stuff like he wanted to get a bunch of new revelations off his chest. I felt like he was building to something, but then Pam's horse went bananas and we had to cut the ride short." As she talks, she's looking away, not right in my eyes. I don't think it's dishonesty keeping her from settling her gaze. It feels more like nerves. The energy of which shoots from her like electricity in a live, frayed wire.

"I mean, that's a good thing, right?" I ask, holding my other thought back so she can finish her story. He might have been trying to tell her about the wedding, in which case, she may not feel this as such a massive blow.

Moira had me on location and still didn't spill. It shouldn't sting as much as it does.

"If I hadn't then overheard Dad talking to Greg about digging out of a hole and how this thing—which I can only assume is the engagement to Moira—is part of what's helping him get out."

It's like someone just dumped a bucket of ice water over my head.

"He's getting something from her, you mean?" I ask, my vocal cords constricted with the chill that's setting in. Am I that out of touch with my own intuition that I couldn't see the signs?

"The documents at the bank with Kismet's name on them," Sydney says, connecting the dots in my head out loud. "They could be refinancing the property to get the equity out. Moira might know Dad needs financial help—"

"And if she doesn't?" I ask her. Sydney doesn't say what we're both thinking.

She will hand over the money because she's in love with him. Moira is cunning; it's hard to imagine she isn't at least aware of his need for cash. I can't imagine she'd go along with him without her own ulterior motive.

"We have to tell her." Her eyes sheen; the barely contained wobble in her voice threatens to break out. I move to the bed and sit beside her. I can't quite bring myself to reach out, take her hand, even though I want to. Too much is spinning in my head, but just being near her helps.

Hopefully the feeling is mutual.

"We have to do it now," I say, dreading the addition of my newly gleaned knowledge. It adds a whole new layer of tension to the situation, especially since we don't know the whole story. "Because the engagement party isn't an engagement party."

She whirls, gripping my hands. The contact slices through my anguish; it's a rudder on my drifting boat. "You mean Lola was right about her theory?" This revelation rattles her despair momentarily.

"I saw an invitation—that they will probably deliver to guests this afternoon at that wine and cheese tasting. It didn't outright say they were getting hitched, but there's no other way to interpret it."

"This is a wedding, and my dad didn't tell me." It's a blow, possibly even bigger than learning Rick may be conning my mother.

"He might have been planning to," I say. The urge to smooth out this uncomfortable situation is strong. Big emotions—especially from other people—twist me up inside myself. I feel like it's on me to settle everything down, remain calm, even when no one else is. A great skill out in the wild but a sucky way to actually live your life. Sydney's fuming. I can tell by the set of her jaw, the flare of her nostrils. She shoots to her feet like she's springloaded.

"That doesn't fucking matter now. He didn't tell me, not about any of this." Her eyes drop to me still stuck to the bed like glue. "I think we need to ambush them."

Confrontation is not my favorite pastime. But at least we have each other's backs.

CHAPTER FORTY

Sydney

I am the one to twine our fingers as we walk. It happens like an instinct—a longing to be close, to feel the heat of her skin. I fit our palms together, savoring the texture of her rough calluses, her deft grip. I don't know if she'll keep holding on when we reach our parents' room or if this thing between us is a secret she wants to keep even as we demand the truth from both of them.

But I do think it won't stay hidden, whether our hands are gripped or not.

The Sun and the Moon and the Two of Cups.

I never told Cadence about the reading—I should stop her now, tug her into a corner and tell her. I don't consider myself a naturally intuitive person, or maybe I've just pushed that part of me so far down in my quest to be the perfect daughter, to live the life I think will make me the least likely to ever actually get hurt, that I can't hear the truth inside me anymore.

Maybe it's sick of me pressing snooze on the truth. Right now, I feel it like a siren scream.

The sun's light touches everything. Your secrets aren't safe.

But it's too late.

Cadence releases my hand to knock on the door. I tighten my fingers into a fist. The string is still threading us together, and I don't fear who knows it.

Moira's laughter cuts through the thickness of the door as she approaches, her voice audible. "We aren't getting one, you goose," she says, I assume to Dad. I assume she's referring to their surreptitious invitations. The handle turns. The door opens.

Her eyes land on us. Cadence first, then me.

I feel a shiver up my spine at the look on her face. Steady gaze, her brow set, her lips curling ever so slightly upward. She can cut through defenses with a look, a heat-seeking missile that never, ever misses its target.

There's no way Dad tricked her into a single fucking thing.

"To what do we—" she begins, her tone as neutral as Switzerland.

"We need to talk to you," Cadence says, and then her eyes shift behind Moira to where Dad sits at the small round table in their room. "Both."

Moira's hip cocks out, but her expression shows no waver. It gives me the distinct feeling that she knew this was coming—planned it to happen this way or, at the very least, expected it. I can't bring myself to entertain the idea that this whole week has been orchestrated by her to play out this way, but I can't deny there have been signs.

There are moves that feel too perfect to be coincidence.

She steps aside to let us in the room. It's bigger than ours, with a seating area and a small dining table. The bathroom, including the mirror and vanity, are in a whole separate room with a door.

Above the bed hangs a watercolor print of the Danish country-side, complete with a windmill and a herd of goats.

Dad has a deck of cards in his hand, which he doesn't set down but shuffles robotically. He was probably practicing some sleight of hand. His eyes are on me, and I'm sure he's picking up on the tension in my body. There's no way he doesn't read it on my face. I just wonder if he's put together that the reason for it is him.

Moira shuts the door behind us and comes around in a fluid movement toward the table. A bottle of wine sits, corked but al-ready opened.

"Is this the kind of conversation that requires liquid courage?" Moira asks, reaching for the glass before she hears our answer. Cadence takes a step forward, her hand clenched at her side. Her body is rigid.

"We know about the wedding," Cadence says without pream-ble. "I saw the invitations. I saw the cake in the kitchens. I saw the gazebo in the middle of the vineyard."

Moira's hand flinches, causing her pour to become uneven. She doesn't spill, and she doesn't stop pouring until her glass is half-full, but she takes these few seconds to get her face under control. I watch it shift into a neutral catlike expression.

Dad, however, doesn't know how to play it cool.

"I was going to tell you today, Birdie," Dad says, standing from the table. He even abandons the cards, freeing his hands to reach out for me.

I step farther away.

"You had all week to tell me, Dad," I say. I press my feet into the carpet, planting them. My knees are weak, and I worry my resolve isn't as strong as it should be. "What happened today with

Pam, it's not an excuse." My voice quivers with anger or sadness, I'm not sure which.

"We wanted it to be a surprise for you." Moira steps in. She literally comes to stand next to Dad, places her hand on his shoulder. His face has fallen into a desperate, apologetic frown, but when she makes contact I see his shoulders straighten.

"So you lied to us?" I ask.

"We . . ." Dad struggles.

"Fibbed." Moira doesn't.

It's surprising how fast the rage bubbles up, explosive and unchecked. "Wow. You really are a fucking mastermind." She smiles at the non-compliment. "Cadence said you were manipulative, but I kept hoping that was personal. Mom shit—not that I'd really know. My mom wasn't like that."

"Sydney, I understand that you're hurt, but Moira isn't to blame here. I was just as much a part of the decision to make this whole thing a little bait and switch. The perfect magic trick."

"And was your scheme to get my mom to refinance her house and her business part of that little trick?" Cadence says, her voice razor-sharp.

Their attention shifts to her. Dad looks bamboozled, but Moira? She's actually *grinning*. Gleeful. This is what she wanted, and I just can't understand why.

"That's why you two were at the bank," Moira says simply. My stomach flips over. I feel seasick.

"You knew we were both there," Cadence says, her own voice even and steady.

"Cadence, I saw you following me. You two are not very good private eyes."

The only sign that her words are affecting Cadence is the slight tinge of pink in her cheeks. "You let us follow you. You let us spy on you."

"And then . . ." Moira takes a sip of wine.

"You gave Sydney a reading." Cadence turns her gaze to me. There's another sign I couldn't see when she wasn't looking my way. Her eyes are bright with tears she's holding back. "You never told me what cards you pulled. But let me guess. She said you would meet your soulmate."

Her words crash over me like thrashing waves in a rough sea.

"I was scared you'd push me away," I say, my voice cracking.

"She really likes you, Cadence," Dad breaks in.

"Your help isn't helping," I snap. He covers his lips with his knuckles.

Cadence turns back to look at Moira. "His friend has been hitting him up for money that he owes him."

"Greg said you've been digging yourself out of a hole, Dad." I don't want to focus on this part, and not just because it sucks for me. I want to focus on Cadence—I don't want her to slip away. But this matters to the pinky promise. I'm in this thing with her all the way. I'm not running from the pact. I'm running into it head-on.

Us against them.

Moira looks to Dad. His face is ashen, but he doesn't look away from me. He doesn't hide behind a broad smile or jaunty tone. He stands there, vulnerable, emotionally exposed.

He says, "I've been in and out of Gamblers Anonymous since I quit piloting."

"Gamblers—" I start, incredulous. "You have a gambling problem?"

"I have it under control," he says, and drops down to the edge of the bed.

"That's like the addict's mantra," I reply, crossing my arms.

"You don't look surprised at all," Cadence says to Moira. I can't tear my eyes from Dad. *How did I not see this?*

"Of course I'm not surprised," Moira replies, waving her off. "Rick and I have been one hundred percent honest with each other since we met."

"That seems to be a sliding scale," Cadence says, and I can't bite back the chortle. It's an actual mindfuck, too bonkers to fathom but also genuinely humorous in a totally screwed-up way. Dad is a gambler and amateur magician; Moira is a literal psychic for money. They're both tricksters and small-time con artists, just not to each other.

These two are perfect together.

Soulmates *and* schemers.

"We have a plan," Dad says, reaching for Moira's hand. She happily takes it.

"I'm selling Kismet. The house and the business. Closing it down. We're going to use the money to pay off the debts and start our next chapter together."

"You're selling Kismet—" Cadence is breathless. This is a blow I wasn't expecting. Neither was she. "But that's your whole life."

Moira's expression softens for the first time. "Not anymore."

"You can't just stop being a psychic," Cadence says. Her voice is wrecked. Her shoulders fall, the news shaking her out of that rigid stance.

"I won't ever stop that part. But I can close Kismet," Moira says. The statement feels unfinished. "I had to go to the bank that day because they're handling the closing, and they needed one last thing before we move forward." She hesitates. Whatever she's about to say isn't something she wants to share. It's not part of her plan, but she's doing it anyway. "Your father was a signer on the deed of the house, and I had to get him to agree to the sale."

Her father.

CHAPTER FORTY-ONE

Cadence

Blood whooshes past my eardrums. Pounding, pounding, pounding from my rapidly beating broken heart. I can't stay here another second. Not in this room with all the secrets swirling around. I whirl on my heels and bolt for the door. I mumble something to Sydney, something like *I need space*, but I'm not even sure how much I say out loud.

She doesn't follow me. She lets me go.

Even with her secret mixed in with the rest, I find myself hoping she isn't letting me go forever.

I get to the end of the row of doors, about to turn the corner into the courtyard near our room, when I hear my name. I don't stop walking. Moira doesn't stop following. The crunch of my boots on the cobblestone, grinding the bits of gravel into the stone, is echoed seconds later by the clack of her sandals following.

"Cadence, wait." Final and firm. I shouldn't turn, but I do.

She's standing alone at the entrance to the courtyard. Her hands hang loose at her sides; her hair catches the breeze. Her eyes are lighter than mine, her freckles, too. She is my mother, there's no denying it, not even if I have this round nose and soft chin and Cupid's-bow lips that I can't see in her.

"His name was on the deed. He wasn't some deadbeat, was he?" She let me believe he was. That searching for him was futile, not worth it.

"Depends on your definition," she says. "He made a choice, and that choice meant he didn't matter to your story." She doesn't step closer, but I do. Not as a concession, more as a threat.

"What gives you the right to decide that, Mom?" I know she likes the name, but it's a flaming arrow on my tongue.

"That," she says, nodding her head toward me. "*Mom*. That's what gave me the right back then."

"When I was a kid and I asked you about him? When I was a teenager? Left for college? What gave you the right then when I was a full-grown adult?"

"I knew how he would react to you finding him. He didn't want a relationship—with either of us." This, at least, looks painful for her to admit. "I wasn't going to give you his name for you to find him and have him"—her voice cracks—"turn you away. I couldn't do that to you." She clenches her jaw, blinking. Tears hover at the edges of her lower lids. "I convinced him to let me keep Kismet by promising I wouldn't sue him for child support."

A thought burrows its way up from the depths of my subconscious, not tapping, not whispering, just appearing like a wild creature on the forest floor.

It's fucked-up, but she really did do this for me.

Kismet.

Was mine. Always.

Full of secret hideouts, surrounded by trees that became

shelter, animals who became friends. For all the ways she used it for herself, she let me have it, too.

"You can't sell the house, Mom."

"You left the house."

"But that doesn't mean I don't still love it." Our eyes lock, and she knows, even though I can't bring myself to say it.

I don't just mean the house.

"It's the only way I can see to get everything Rick and I need," she says. "Everything is different now with the business, with the world. I can't make this work anymore. What I do, the way I do it, it's ending, and I can't stop it."

"You refuse to adapt. That's what would get you what you need." Her jaw is set, just like her mind. Just like her plan. "Lola has relied on that house, that job, since her mother bailed on her. You can't do that to her—at least not without telling her."

"She'll understand. You know she has her own fool's journey to go on when she's ready."

"*You* cryptically claimed she'd know when the time was right to go searching for Lou. That doesn't mean you get to decide that for her—"

"I know you don't see it, but this way everyone gets what they need."

I blink. Even as she's grappling with her plan going awry, she can't just say it. She can't admit it's wrong that she's manipulated us. She pulled me back here from thousands of miles away, and she engineered a love story for me to walk right into.

I let it happen because I wanted it.

Even with the little voice whispering that it was *all because of her.*

"It's not Sydney's fault she's your soulmate," Moira says, as if reading my thoughts from right inside my head. My eyes snap to hers.

Soulmate.

I don't know if she's saying that because of Sydney's reading or because she knows about our initial meeting at Kismet. Right now, it doesn't matter.

"I don't believe in that shit," I bite back.

Liar, liar.

"Even so," she replies. "I see how you two look at each other."

"We barely know each other," I say, even though I feel the flimsiness of the argument as it leaves my lips. "We can't just change our whole lives to be together because of a connection we felt for a few days. That's absurd."

"No, you can't admit that it's what you want because you think that means you'll be admitting I was right."

A guttural growl rises in my throat. "Oh my God, you always have to make everything about you! Some things are not about you, Mom." I snap my heated gaze to hers. I watch the flames light in the dark. She opens her lips to protest, her knee-jerk go-to, but then she doesn't do it. She blinks, then she nods, a quiver rippling her lips.

"You're right," she says, her voice shaky.

"What?" I can't be hearing that right.

Two words I never thought I'd hear her say. It's everything and not enough at the same time. It's a start, but I don't know if I want to stick around to let her finish.

"I shouldn't have come here." I shouldn't have thought I could beat her at her own game.

"But you did. You chose to come here, you chose to stay, and it doesn't matter why. What matters is what you do now." Tears well in my eyes. "What do you want, Cadence?" She asks it as if I were a querent and her cards were in hand, shuffled and ready for me to cut.

"What the fuck does it matter what I want?"

"Everything." She is steady. Sure. The perfect mirror for the Universe. "What you want is what you take action on."

What do I want?

To not be this lonely.

But I can't tell her that without conceding that getting as far away as I could gave me peace, but not happiness. It was an escape from her manipulation, her story of my life, but it didn't give me belonging—that feeling that you matter to someone, that you're known.

Sydney gave me that. This week beside her gave me a glimpse of it, at least. Made me aware of all I was missing and all I could have if I let myself. Despite how angry and hurt I am, I can't deny that—for me—everything I've felt has been real.

Even the part about being glad I came back.

I'm scared of how much I want this story to keep going, despite the catalyst that started it. But I don't think I can accept that I *want* it. That if I lose it, I'll know I chose that, too.

I shake my head. I don't answer her question out loud, I don't say another word. I have to get space. I have to get far enough away from her.

I have to think this through.

Feel it.

What do you want, Cadence?

I don't know the answer to that yet.

CHAPTER FORTY-TWO

Sydney

As desperate as I was to follow Cadence, I wanted to respect her whispered, wounded request. I don't want to be a person who pushes against her boundaries. I don't want to force her to hear me out until she's ready—if she ever is. I didn't tell her about the reading because I didn't want her to push me away, and that was selfish.

But the reading wasn't why I fell for her.

"Say something, Birdie," Dad says. He's still sitting at the foot of the bed.

I'm still trying to process what he said, how it could be true. How could he keep so much from me when it was supposed to be *us against the world*? How had I never seen any of the signs? But I guess I wasn't looking for proof my dad wasn't perfect—I was just looking for a way I could be perfect enough for the both of us.

"Any other lies you wanna get off your chest?" I snipe. "Am I adopted? Are you actually my dad or a doppelgänger switched out by fairies?"

"I think I'm clean out for the day," he replies with none of his usual cheeriness. "The last couple of decades, actually."

"Do you still gamble?"

"Mostly . . . no. Once, a few months ago, which is why I owe Greg. But I have bad credit card debt—" He cuts himself off, looking freshly embarrassed. "And I don't have a membership at the club anymore because of it."

"Good riddance. I hated the club." He balks and so I double down. "It's classist, just like the sport of golf. Historically and even presently, racism and misogyny are the name of the game." His eyes round. As if he's never thought of it in that way and doesn't really want to now.

"I miss the sauna," he says with a sigh.

I snort and drop down to sit beside him on the bed. I should be angrier than I am. I should be more hurt. But overwhelmingly what I feel is relief. Like I can finally drop every ball in the air, let them all bounce out of reach, let them break if they're frail. Being the perfect pilot daughter for my perfect pilot dad was a fallacy in more ways than one.

Dad isn't perfect.

I don't even know if I want to be a pilot.

"I shouldn't have kept the gambling from you. I just kept thinking, *I'll get this under control. I'm just using it to cope*," he says. His eyes trail up and over to the cards on the table. "Magic helped. It mostly curbed the feelings—"

"Did you ever think to just, I don't know, confront your feelings?" I interrupt.

"Did you?" He lifts his brow.

"Fair," I grunt.

He continues. "Then came Moira. And she got it—me. She

saw the flaws and didn't try to change them. She worked with them, and it got a lot easier to believe there was another side to this coin. More than just surviving."

It's silly how much I relate to that feeling. Survival isn't living. Going through the motions isn't happiness.

"You should have told me about the wedding." This is the part that stings the most, stupidly. The fresh lie he chose without thinking twice.

"I should have," he says. "But I hope you don't let all of this sour whatever has started between you and Cadence."

"I don't know if that's up to me, Dad. I lied to her—"

"Omitted a detail—"

"There's less nuance in honesty than you and Moira seem to think there is," I scold him, and I am pleased he appears mostly repentant. "I was happy to let her forget about that reading, to keep the facts of it a secret, because her knowing the truth about it might change her actions. It's like in quantum mechanics. Reality doesn't exist unless observed."

"But observing can alter reality," he adds. "You saw the cards, and you decided you wanted to *see* what would happen if you followed the suggestion."

I swallow the lump forming in my throat. I can see how the meaning in the reading has been playing out between us ever since we met. The clarity that has come from every interaction, for me and for her. That give-and-take that only happens with an equal connection.

The Two of Cups. That cute gay card wasn't kidding.

Moira walks back through the door, which has been hanging open this whole time. Cadence isn't with her.

"I don't want to interrupt," Moira says, but she is going to anyway. "The invites will be delivered to the guests soon." She withers, her face breaking down. The mastermind is not happy with the way the chess game is playing out.

I don't feel bad for her, but Dad rushes to her side, taking her hands between his. Genuine affection and concern pour from his eyes.

The two of them may be a perfect pair of liars, but what they feel for each other is real.

"I don't know where she's gone. I don't know if she's coming back," Moira moans. "I really thought I could give her something she needed and maybe that would fix things between us."

She may not come back. The reality slams into me. I need to go after her. I should. But I am afraid if I do before she's ready, I'll end up pushing her away even further. So I decide to focus on getting more information out of the parents.

"You gotta level with me, Moira." I stand now, too, stepping nearer, wishing I had a height advantage. She's at least shorter than her daughter, though that doesn't make the woman less intimidating. That's something they have in common. "That original soulmate prediction, the one you gave her here when she was a teenager . . . Did you know we met that day at Kismet?"

"I saw you two leaving," she says. "I didn't know you were you, since I only saw the back of your head. But that night at the restaurant I put two and two together."

"Why didn't you say something?" I balk, my temper flaring up. At this point, the idea that she let us scheme and plot with such abandon shouldn't surprise me, but it can still piss me off.

"We've established I like a game," she says with a fluid shrug. "And Cadence hadn't played in years. It was refreshing to see her . . . trying. Even if she was trying to take me down."

"We were trying to protect Dad," I say. He smiles broadly, and it brightens his every feature. "Which was clearly not needed." The smile ghosts.

Moira grins, catlike again. She really doesn't stay down for long, does she?

"Questioning is a good instinct." She repeats her statement from that first dinner that caused me to spiral over so many things that needed questioning in my life.

And asking questions—the right ones, anyway—leads to destiny. *Everything that is meant for you will find you.*

I want Cadence to be my soulmate because of how she makes me feel. The idea that she might be has fueled my actions with her, even if I got the idea to take those actions because of a prediction—a scheme I wasn't even in on. I shift my eyes to hers.

"I have to find her."

She smiles as if she knew I was going to say that.

I bolt for the door, yanking my phone out of my pocket to call her.

"Will we see you at the wedding?" Dad asks. I whip around to see their nervous, expectant faces.

"I don't know yet," I say. "But not without her." I lift my phone, using my face to open it. And then I remember one more thing. "Chicken!"

"We were going to ask you to bring him tonight," Dad says, throwing a puppy-dog face at me. "He's the ring bearer."

"Jesus Christ, Dad, I didn't even know it was a wedding, and now the dog is in it?" I exclaim.

"We hoped you and Cadence would be in it, too," he tries. I hold up my hands in a stop motion. "Moira can just get a key to the room from Sven," Dad edits.

"You can't just do that—"

"Oh, I definitely can."

"Un-be-lievable." I emphasize the syllables, but I don't wait around for her to dismiss my displeasure. "I'll bring him to you."

As I walk, I find her name, *Ranger Girl*, in my phone and tap the little icon. I don't know if she'll pick up, if my calling her will push her away, if it's too much too soon. When the call goes to her voicemail, I hang up. This is not something I want to say in a voicemail. Hell, saying it over the phone is weird enough as it is.

I don't know where to even begin looking for her, but I need to go back to our room for Chicken anyway, so I'll check there. I run down the corridor and through the courtyard to our room, swiping my key in the door. Chicken starts to bark at the sound, but as soon as he sees it's me, he's up, shaking out his tail. My eyes land on a black rectangle nestled in the bed linens.

She wasn't answering her phone because she doesn't have it.

I grab the phone and the dog.

I breathe, a wish in my mind. I don't know who I'm asking, but I hope they listen.

Please let us find each other.

CHAPTER FORTY-THREE

Cadence

I reach into my pocket and realize I don't have my phone.

It's strange, the feeling that washes over me. It's like someone is calling me and I feel the buzz of the vibration.

You are a wild, untamed thing.

I heave a deep breath.

I don't want to be wild and untamed. I want to be normal. Have a normal life where you go to work, you pay your bills, you fall in love with a stranger, and you never think about things like destiny or fate or psychic predictions or soulmates or romances. I tried so hard to shove myself into a life like that. The only part that was true was that I love being out in the wild.

That choice still feels like mine.

Running as far away as possible might have been a reaction to her, but finding myself in the forest wasn't. I don't know how to go back to that solitude now, but it would be so much easier if I could. Sydney has a life here; I have a life there. We can make it on our own.

But we're better together.

I look up at the sky and ignore my inner musings. The sun is on its way west, edging closer to the horizon for the early-evening sunset. It's probably somewhere between two and three p.m. I wonder if the invites have been delivered yet. I hope that whatever is going on, they remember to get Chicken.

Even in the midst of this breakdown, I'm still worrying about Sydney's elderly dog.

I don't have a clue where I'm going, but I need to get as far away from the hotel as possible. I barrel forward through the throngs of people. Tonight's events for the festival and the fact that it's a Saturday have brought out hordes—some even dressed in Norwegian garb and milkmaid gear.

I duck down a side street that looks a little less crowded and notice a small bookstore located in a cute blue-and-white building with a pleasant brick facade. The store is sleepy, not hosting any events today by the looks of it.

I drift around the stacks, calmed by the smell of paper. As a rule, I read electronically—saving precious natural resources. But I've always loved the feel of a book in my hand, the way they look on the shelves, tidily set all in a row.

"I saw that they had the deck." I hear a familiar voice behind me and duck around to hide. I immediately feel stupid. Kit isn't some weird Moira groupie. I don't need to hide from her.

"Let's get a pic fast, though. You saw that invitation thing." Julia comes up behind her. "It's a wedding, right?" Kit stops her motion to look at her. "They're doing, like, a whole surprise wedding." She sounds annoyed.

"Are you upset they didn't ask you to help plan a surprise wedding?" Kit asks, playfully.

Julia rolls her eyes. "I mean, she knows I'm a wedding planner."

"I can't imagine your personalities would gel," Kit replies, turning back around to search the bookshelf of tarot decks. Julia nods, and her eyes trip down to land on Kit's ass. She smiles.

"We could ditch." She presses her hips into Kit's. Her nose nuzzles into her hair. Kit stops searching the shelf, dedicating all her attention now to this covert PDA.

"We can do that"—she spins, hands snaking around Julia's waist—"*and* go to the surprise wedding." She presses her lips to Julia's, lingering, letting her whole body meld into her fiancée.

"You get me," Julia says. "I suppose we should go. She did bring us together."

"She did a little, we did the rest," Kit corrects.

I turn away from the scene, making a beeline for the door as her words conjure up the memory of our reading in the bar. I burst through the front door into the warm light of the early-fall sun.

Catalysts don't decide a lifetime loving each other.

My mom and her invitation—my mom and her prediction—might have been the catalyst for this story. That moment that signaled the start, but it's not what decided how the story would play out. Just like pulling a card isn't a guarantee of that fate coming to pass. That's the whole thing about a tarot reading: The potential is in the cards, the energy of the catalyst, but you are the fool taking the leap.

Your steps decide how the journey plays out.

I understand why Sydney didn't tell me about the reading my mom gave her. I had made such a show of not wanting to be controlled by my mother, pinky promise or not, that I was a flight risk when it came to the mention of soulmates. She wanted a chance, and so did I. How can I fault her for doing what was necessary to make sure we got that chance?

CHAPTER FORTY-FOUR

Sydney

In the sea of people I spot her.

Her hair is a tangle of wild vines. Her body is taut with that coiled, untamed energy. She's walking back toward the hotel with the most beautifully determined expression on her face. I double back, expecting her to be headed to our room. I rush through the lobby leading out to the courtyard, steps behind her.

She stops before I say her name.

It's just us here. Her, me.

No one to predict how this goes, just us to live the story.

"Sydney." She turns around, her hair whipping over her shoulders.

"Cadence." I breathe her name. I want to breathe her in.

I raise her phone in my hand. Her eyes follow the move, and she laughs.

"You tried to call me, didn't you?" she asks.

"It wasn't my first choice of communication."

"Was there something you wanted to say to me?" She doesn't move toward me, keeping the distance between us, but I don't know how much longer I can hold out. She's right there, close enough that if I just took a few steps, I could reach her.

"You deserved to know about the reading," I say, because without her permission I can't go any closer. I won't cross the boundary unless she gives me the okay.

"What were the cards?"

"The Sun, the Moon, and the Two of Cups," I list, unsure if she will know the interpretations off the top of her head. She exhales a laugh.

"You're the Sun," she says, pointing to me. My long golden hair and bright blue eyes.

"You're the Moon," I answer, pointing to her black halo of curls and her practically glowing eyes. "There was a whole story about how we would transform—a light in the dark, clarity, give and take."

"One can't exist without the other," Cadence finishes the idea. "And with the Two of Cups . . ." She nibbles her lip thoughtfully. "Soulmates."

"I don't care about that word," I say, stepping closer. Just one single step.

"That's too bad," she says, her eyes on my feet. I go still. "I do."

She closes the gap between us, taking me in her arms, her lips hovering above mine. Her eyes capture me, holding me with the same sure grip as her arms.

"I would be the worst kind of fool if I didn't fight for you."

I crush my lips against hers to show her that the feeling is mutual. She lets her mouth open to mine, and I invite her tongue to taste me. She clenches my back with her hands, running one down to cup my ass. My body responds to the touch as if it's pulled toward her like a pendulum swinging.

Out lips unlock, but our bodies remain tangled.

"I know we don't have anything figured out," she says.

"Do we have to?" I reply. "Can't we just decide we're doing this and figure it out as we go? No road map, just two fools on a journey?" Her answering smile is all the confirmation I need.

Nailed it.

"There is an elephant in the—" She looks around. "Courtyard . . . that we should figure out."

"The wedding?"

"The wedding." She straightens up, but she still doesn't fully release her hold on me. "To go or not to go?"

"It depends. On a scale of one to betrayal, how much do you want to stick it to your mom?" I ask, playful but no less sincere. She grins—I am awash with relief.

"I think I'd rather have a dinner I don't have to pay for under a blanket of stars than try to prove a point to a woman who has already decided she's as flawless as God." She tugs me back into her, and my stomach turns molten as her curves collapse into mine. "As long as you'll be my date."

I let a slow smile creep up my lips.

She doesn't let me finish before she's back to kissing me again. We twist together toward the room. She unlocks the door, and I kick off my shoes inside.

"I think I need to rinse off," I say, catching her eyes with mine. The door slides closed.

She yanks off my button-down. *Yes.* "I could shower." Her smile is mischief.

I rush to the bathroom, turning the faucet to hot. I make a quick escape of my clothes, and then she's behind me, her hands winding around to cup my breasts, her lips against my neck, tongue titillating my ear. She presses her breasts against my back, and I lean into her flesh. My hand becomes a heat-seeking sensor, searching for the warmth between her legs.

"You feel so good," I growl. She spins me around to kiss me, and we step into the steamy cover of the shower.

I tuck in for a long kiss, sliding with her under the water.

"I'm falling in love with you," I say against her lips. She pulls back to look at me, pushing the wet strands of my hair off my face. Her eyes do an extensive search.

"I think I might already be there," she whispers, leaning down to kiss my forehead, down to my eyebrow, over my cheek. She runs her hands over my hips as her eyes trail down. "Every beautiful landscape, every wonder I've seen, is nothing compared to you."

She scoops me against her, and I lose myself, soft curves all folding into one another. Warm lips working over damp skin.

All my senses, all full of her.

CHAPTER FORTY-FIVE

Cadence

That anyone ever thought this wasn't a wedding just shows how self-involved we all truly are. We arrive at the winery on the final shuttle, almost late and with absolutely zero regrets about it. They're handing out flutes of sparkling wine as an aperitif. A sign shows us the way down the main path that heads into the vineyard and up the hill to where the gazebo sits sturdy.

Almost everyone seems to have gotten the invitations. Turned up in the nicest thing they brought to wear. The only person noticeably absent is Hawthorne. Lola is standing at the gazebo stairs, holding Chicken, her bright copper hair swept up in a bun. She's got on a dark brown jumpsuit, glittery jewelry, and a pair of espadrilles. I give Sydney's hand a squeeze.

"I need to go talk to Lola," I say. "You texting your dad?"

"Nah, I think he should be kept in suspense until the last possible moment," she says with a wicked grin. I smack a kiss to her cheek, glancing down the length of her body. She's wearing a light blue tuxedo dress and white knee-high boots. Her hair is bombshell.

I turn to jelly every time I look at her.

"Be right back." I walk through the crowd, my eyes catching on Kit and Julia standing in a cluster on the other side of the trail leading up to the gazebo. Julia's eagle eye scans the setting, and I wonder what her rates are for wedding planning.

The thought catches me off guard. I don't immediately push it away.

Lola waves Chicken's paw at me when she sees me approaching. There's a distance in her expression, though, like she's not really here at all. Checked out, *God forbid*, about the absence of her toxic pacifist boyfriend.

"Does this make you honorary ring bearer?" I say, trying to break the funk.

"I wasn't sure you were gonna come," she says, cutting her eyes over to Sydney. "Either of you." She looks back to me.

"I wasn't, either," I reply. "It's been a roller coaster."

"You know, don't you?" she says. Her voice is tempered, measured, like she's trying to hold in the bigger, more explosive feelings. I won't play games with her. She definitely deserves better than that.

"Moira's selling Kismet," I say. Her features crumple like a piece of paper in a fist. "It's shitty she didn't tell you."

"No, no—well, yeah, it is—but that's not why I'm upset." She waves me off with one hand, disturbing Chicken's comfortable position. He makes a little peep to indicate his disapproval. "I don't want to go yet, but I'm about to turn twenty-seven, and I've never been on my own. Not from significant others, not from Kismet." She pauses, and I fill in the rest.

"Not from Moira."

She sucks in a sharp breath. "I don't know if I can do it."

I tuck my arm around her shoulder, tugging her close.

"No one ever feels ready," I say. "Even when they are."

Music begins to play. I let go of Lola, but I hope it's not really letting go. I want her in my life somehow, even if it's just random texts, FaceTimes at two a.m. I hope she wants that, too.

I have just made my way back to Sydney when I see Moira, dressed in head-to-toe midnight blue, and Rick beside her, wearing a matching bow tie, as they walk out into the pink glow of the sunset. They don't know we're here, not yet.

"How long until they see us?" she asks, leaning into me as I dip in to kiss her cheek. I can't believe I get to just do that with her. Hopefully forever and ever.

Always.

"Less than sixty seconds," I reply as a swell of music begins to play. I recognize the melody immediately as the classic Etta James song "At Last." It seems fitting for them, two people who have had to wait until later in their lives to find each other. As they start to descend the stairs toward the gazebo, I curl my pinky around Sydney's, and she tightens hers into a promise.

Together we slip between guests who line the walkway until we're right at the edge where they can see us. My eyes meet my mom's. The green in hers matches the green in mine. We are more the same than different, more like mother and daughter than not. She blinks, and I watch as a tear courses down her cheek.

Forgiveness is not mundane magic.

It's not a small thing to change, no matter how old or young you may be.

It's alchemical—it's altering to love someone; it gives them so much power over you. I always wanted power over myself, and I thought the only way to have that was to not let her, not let anyone, really love me. I thought that was what it meant to be untamable.

To be a Connelly woman.

But letting someone love you, that's the real uncharted adventure.

Love is the wildest creature of all.

"Our parents are getting married," I whisper, pressing my lips to Sydney's ear.

"Our kids will think we're so weird." She leans into my touch.

To me, that's perfect. I was always the weird girl climbing high up in the trees, and she was the bird in the sky.

The Sun and the Moon. The shadow and the light.

We no longer exist without each other.

ONE YEAR LATER

Sydney

I remove my sunglasses, handing over my headset to Jodi, the newest, greenest tech at Grand Tours Acadia. She's young and hungry, which I try not to take advantage of, because I don't want to get old and lazy. But today I'm in a hurry, and she offered to put my gear away for me. I'm in no position to argue.

"Anything else you need?" she asks, her bright eyes extra eager.

"Just the headset, Connor has the rest—since you're not flight crew."

"But I'm training to be," she says. I raise my hands in surrender.

"Then watch him, I guess." She moves off in the direction of the plane. I reach out, stopping her with my palm on her shoulder. "After you put away the headset."

She's off with a grin. I walk toward the hangar doors, my eyes catching on the azure horizon. I sign out on the log and I'm golden, but even after six months in Acadia working as a tour guide, I never get sick of the views. Those azure ocean skies may not really be blue, but from where I'm standing, it doesn't matter.

I jog over to my Land Rover, climbing in just as my phone begins to buzz in my back pocket. I yank it out and press the Face-Time button. Cadence pops up on the screen. She's sweaty, her hair a pile of curls coiled on top of her head. I put the phone into my hands-free holder and shove the car into gear.

"They're early," she says, her tone gritty.

"No, they can't be here already."

She spins the phone around to reveal our parents standing out on the porch, each with a large glass of wine in hand.

"I see they opened the wine without me." I grunt, turning onto the highway. "Lovely."

"They brought their own bottle from the Hamptons, along with cheese curds from Wisconsin," she says. "Both of which have a story, and you're not here to help me rate them on a bullshit meter."

I chortle. We created the bullshit meter as a coping mechanism for dealing with Rick and Moira's tall tales about their RV travels around the US. We've yet to hear a tale that isn't a solid six, though most, we guess, are at least eights. For the most part, it's harmless, and we call them on it more often than not.

"Five minutes, babe," I say.

Her eyes soften. "They parked the RV in front of the driveway even though they said they'd be staying at the RV park. The driveway is not built for an RV."

"Remember to breathe," I say, and her expression immediately calms.

"You always know what to say," she says, air-kissing me repeatedly before hanging up.

We're trying, all of us, to do this family thing. It's nice to have a friend in it with me.

Cadence decided not to look for her dad, even though Moira gave her his name and location. That door was closed, sealed shut, no need to open it again.

Closure found us in other ways, too.

Dad's debt—thanks to the sale of Kismet—is all but nonexistent now.

I quit my commercial piloting job and applied to fly tour planes at a company in Bar Harbor so I could be closer to Cadence. It took us all of a month to move in together—we've never looked back. It's been fun getting to know her coworkers—especially Nika and her wife and kids.

Joe got his job in Beverly Hills just in time for me to tell him I was moving. Saved by the grace of the universe from a tantrum I fully expected would come when I told him I was leaving.

"You found your person," he said through tears and chardonnay breath.

I did. A reality I don't know if I'll ever get used to.

I turn onto our street just before dusk and have to laugh at the sight of the giant RV blocking my space in the driveway beside our town house. They went for the biggest one, with the most luxurious bathtub and a king-size bed.

When I reach our front doorway, I can hear Cadence laugh. Something she does a lot, all the time, even when she knows it's what Moira wants her to do. It is my favorite sound in the whole world.

"What did I miss?" I say as I step into the living room. Dad has a top hat out, his cape over his shoulders. "There better not be a bunny in there."

Cadence puts a glass of wine in my hand, plants a kiss on my cheek.

"Just a stuffed one," she says, winking. She's carrying a gray-bearded Chicken in her free arm, and I don't even try to separate them. He's obsessed with her. I can't blame him.

"Where's Moira?" I ask her, blowing a kiss to Dad. Cadence's eyes shift to the patio, where Moira stands, taking in the view of the harbor. We've fallen into a sort of rhythm with them when they visit. Cadence and Dad pair off, him showing her the latest trick he's very nearly mastered, her telling him about the wildlife she's seen on the trails as they cook, setting the scene for our time together. Moira and I are happy to let them take the lead; if you had told me a year ago that would happen, I would have called you a liar.

It's funny how much you can change when you aren't in fight-or-flight mode.

I step out onto the patio that's lit with the glow of the setting sun, backed by the sounds of the marina. I love this view of the water and boats. I love the way the town feels old and rooted in history, but the people here are diverse, full of stories and backgrounds and warmth. I love the winter, cold and curled up beside Cadence on the couch, watching some trash reality TV or some nature doc. I love this life I'm building with her. One day at a time, with no one trying to predict what the future holds except us.

Moira leans against the railing, her hair lightly blowing in the wind. There are a few streaks of silver in it now, more lines on her face. She's settled into her golden years.

"Smells good in there," I say, leaning my elbows on the railing right next to hers.

"They argued over how much garlic, and Rick won."

"Great. Tomorrow morning's tour will *love* that." She laughs, throaty and deep. "One year. How do you feel?"

"I could ask you the same question."

Their anniversary is coming this week, and it's technically ours, too, a fact they both seem to enjoy. But we have a plan to change that with a booking at a hotel in Vegas in a month. We haven't told them just yet, but we have a plan for that, too.

A new little scheme we came up with.

Moira's eyes settle on the lapping water; her smile twitches. "Satisfied."

Safe, I think.

"Everything is just as it should be."

Her words prick a soft spot inside me, dragging forward a question I've had since the very first time I met Cadence. I've been too afraid to ask, unsure if I wanted an answer, and then sure that even though I did, she wasn't likely to give one. She probably won't now.

"Did you know before you sent that invitation that she and I were soulmates?"

The twinkle in her eyes is all the answer I need.

ACKNOWLEDGMENTS

This book will always have a special place in my heart, not only because I wrote it during the roller coaster of my romance-debut year—where it became a joyful escape from the highs and lows that are natural and expected, though no less unsteadying—but because it gave me the space to heal a part of my own heart that had previously been covered over with scar tissue.

Thank you to my editor, Kristine Swartz, for trusting me when I said I wasn't writing the right book. You helped me find my way to the heart of this story. Your guidance, your understanding of me and my work, and your keen eye are unparalleled. It's an honor to have you in my corner—I hope to have you there for years to come.

To the amazing Katie Shea Boutillier, you are a champion. I am in awe of your ability to cut through the noise of this industry, always seeing me and my voice—my purpose here—so clearly. Thank you for talking me off all my creativity ledges. You are a fierce ally and the very best agent there is.

Mary Baker, Tara O'Connor, Anika Bates, Caitlyn Kenny,

Abby Graves, Courtney Vincento, Isabella Pilotta Gois, Bridget O'Toole, and the whole Berkley team: I love getting to be a Berkley author. Thank you for making this experience such a joyful one! Sarah Maxwell: You are a genius. I am honored beyond comprehension that my books are graced with your art.

In this *biz they call author*, community is paramount. I am a lucky girl (or maybe it's just a gift of my fate), because I have found some of the most incredible humans to be part of my author cohort.

Liz Parker: You are my first reader—did you know that? I couldn't tell you how you went from friend to family, but I am thankful that my untrusting Scorpio heart let you make the leap. Thank you for the countless hours of conversation, the years of friendship, and all the spells to make my dreams come true. There is real magic in the world. Our friendship is proof.

Carlyn Greenwald and Mallory Marlowe: Finding you two weirdos made my debut year so much sweeter. Thank you for the honesty and the solidarity, the hours of deep dives into obscure oddities, and photo ops at all the creepy places. Ghost Lovers tour when??

Emily Wibberley and Austin Siegemund-Broka: I am always astounded by the art you both create, and just as astounded that I get to call you friends. Thank you for letting me come for a writing retreat at your house, even if all I *really* wanted to do was play with Bronte.

Bridget Morrissey: truly the best conversation partner a girl could ask for. Thank you for showing me such kindness. You are effervescent, and I am honored I get to hang out with you.

Gretchen Schreiber: Your friendship means the world to me.

Thank you for your generosity in sharing your knowledge, and also for always being down to get oysters and talk story.

Taleen Voskuni: I am so grateful to know you. Emma Alban, Ashley Herring Blake, Jenn Dugan, Dahlia Adler, Jenna Wren, Rachael Herron, *The Incoherent Fangirl, Fated Mates*—your love for *The Lovers* made my romance-debut year feel a little less scary. That is a gift I will cherish forever. To Sarah Fox: Thank you for the tarot deck and all the cheers along the way.

To my agent sib and buddy Matthew Hubbard: Thank you for the text threads of solidarity and enthusiasm. It's always a spot of brightness.

Nika Serras: Your friendship through the years has been a life raft in the deep waters. Thank you for becoming my family in Los Angeles. Thank you for taking me to the Hamptons this year for a writing retreat. And, yes, the Nika in this book is named for you.

Gian Sardar: I am amazed by you and your brain and your process. And also your perfume collection. Being your friend makes me feel fancy.

To my book club: You've inspired me in more ways than you will ever know.

To Val Tejeda: Love you, Scorpio sister. I love our deep dives into all things esoteric and otherworldly. Thank you for your support and friendship. To Catherine and Alice—BTS ARMY forever. Thank you for being true purple-hearted gemstones.

Sara Biren and Tracey Neithercott, my beez. Thank you both for sticking with me all this time. We need a proper writing retreat, with Liz, and lots of time built in for laughter.

The Los Angeles romance author community is especially robust, and it would take up all my words to name you all. But you know who you are, and I hope you know I am grateful to so many of you for showing me such kindness.

Bookstagrammers out there posting about our books—you are the best there is. Thank you for supporting my art and helping others find it. Readers who have found me: Thank you for your love of my stories and the generosity of your time.

The year I wrote this book was more than my romance-debut year. It was also the year I said goodbye to my soulmate dog, Samson. I wrote the character of Chicken because I wanted to always remember the very special gift of an old-man dog curled on your lap or asleep in a bed, missing teeth but never missing a chance to give kisses. I miss you every day, my friend. I am grateful I have your buddy, James, who I think misses you, too.

It's alchemical—it's altering to love someone. There are two people in my life whose love has altered me completely. They turned my hard edges soft; they gave me something to fight for that was bigger than myself. They are why I do this. They are why I do everything. Nathan and Sam, you are my North Node. You are the best of this life. Thank you for believing in me and helping me make my dreams come true.

Keep reading for a preview of Rebekah Faubion's

The Lovers

Available now!

Kit

A sunburst right overhead is the perfect Universe-delivered final touch to this selfie photoshoot at Cabazon Dinosaurs, a kitschy roadside attraction on the way to Joshua Tree. The giant green-and-white T-Rex with the red heart inscribed with "Be Mine" on his chest looms just off-center in the shot. I do a quick "natural" edit and post it on Instagram with the caption, Just a little me time in the desert. #loveyourself #breakingupishardtodo

That will keep fans and foes alike busy for hours. Most of my followers are supportive, light-centered, love-driven humans on a genuine quest for spiritual growth. Some of them are dudes who can't get past Instagram's safety features to send me dick pics but do leave comments on my photos. And a small percentage are people who can't wait to shit on anything I do, no matter how magical or mundane. They like to fight it out in comments or share my posts in stories with derisive asides, but my blue check means I basically never see anything unless it's from people I follow.

Unfortunately, my verified status doesn't protect me from

Mom seeing my post, immediately liking it, and sending me a DM to ask why I'm heading into the desert.

> Are you trying to get away from me, Kitten?
> Is this because I'm bisexual?

Yeah, she spells out the whole word. *Bisexual.* And then she sends three hearts, the colors of the bi flag, and I wish I could bury my phone in the sand right beneath the giant pink brontosaurus on the other side of my white Jeep Wrangler.

My phone then starts buzzing with an incoming call. Dad. A FaceTime.

I message him that I'm driving and I'll text him later.

He hates texting because he's a stickler for grammar and punctuation, can't get past it to send a quick message.

> We still haven't talked about brunch. I know
> you're upset, and you have every right to be.
> This is not ideal, is it, cupcake?

I yank my car door open and throw my phone in the passenger seat.

Ideal.

If I had a nickel for every time my dad has used that word to describe me, Mom, our roles in the rom-com movie of the life he's writing, I'd have a vacation home to escape to and wouldn't have to work this wedding. The word burrowed beneath my skin and tattooed itself on my bones, fusing with my own identity. Dad's definition of the ideal rom-com ingenue is more Meg or Drew than Sandra or Kate. She's dreamy, funny, quirky, cute; she has a creative job and carefree attitude, and girls and guys both adore her.

I snort at the last one.

Closer to home than he thought.

I release a deep breath and wring out the tightness in my upper body, twisting around to the backseat to grab my tarot deck from the inside of my purse. I hold the cards in my hand, closing my eyes and inhaling a few quick breaths. My eyes open and land on the top of the cards. This deck is personal, not one I use with clients or in my "Choose Your Own Tarot Adventure" readings. It was the first deck I ever got, a birthday gift to myself when I was nineteen. Some people believe you should be gifted your first deck, but when tarot came into my life, I needed help understanding my emotional world more than I needed to listen to superstition.

I chose this deck because of its botanical design. A Cali girl through and through, I'm aesthetically inspired by nature in all her wild forms. Even in LA we love a run through a canyon, or a mountainscape at sunset.

The back of the cards is black matte with a winding white vine running over it.

Each card is uniquely designed, though it follows the Rider–Waite structure of traditional decks. I shuffle, *swish swish swish*, and place the deck on my bare thighs. The cards feel warm and heavy, alive with energy. I cut the deck with my left hand and hold my palm over the two top cards. The one that radiates extra warmth is it, always, even when my soul doesn't understand why. I reincorporate the deck with that one on top. Breathe. Turn it over.

The Two of Cups, upright.

A beautiful card featuring two serpents entwining their tails. In the center is an orange poppy. This card doesn't have to mean romance, but it almost always comes to you when there is or will be attraction, partnership, unity.

Romance vibes are so not what I'm sending out, Universe. Please take my hint and act accordingly.

I shake myself out one more time, listening to the chimes of my bracelets rattling together over my wrists, and shuffle the deck again. A single card sticks out askew from the others. I flip it out, turning it over in my right hand.

The Wheel of Fortune, upright.

My heart does a nosedive into my stomach. Spikes of heat shoot over my chest, down the length of my arms, to my fingertips.

I've seen this card combination one other time in my life.

Just one time.

The Haunt O' Ween festival in Old Pasadena is a suburban kid's playground in the week leading up to Halloween. My friends and I had been attending it since we were tiny tots, and the year I pulled those cards, my new, cool best friend had joined us. Julia Kelley had transferred into Forrest Chapel Private Academy the fall of seventh grade. A scholarship kid, a wild card even if she was mostly just sarcastic. Everyone had immediately been fascinated by her.

Fresh meat in middle school always draws a crowd. But while the other girls had mostly lost interest after Julia refused to play any of their mind games, I'd gotten attached.

She was more than fresh. All her dark, sharp edges made my bright, pretty curves feel safe. So when Karen MacMillan, the resident queen bee, dared Julia to visit Madame Moira—psychic reader and neighborhood legend—I couldn't let Julia go it alone.

Madame Moira's tent was set up beside the South Pasadena Historical Museum, a wood-frame building that looked like it was dragged from a ghost town out West. Purple velvet curtains draped over the entrance to her den. Julia and I clutched hands, whispering promises not to abandon each other no matter what Madame Moira's reading revealed.

Madame Moira was not a crone, not even close. She was a pretty woman with raven-black hair, long fingers, nails painted midnight black, and a face that appeared ageless. And not LA ageless. Legit *untouched by the hands of time* ageless. Julia handed over her five dollars, which got her a three-card spread, and Madame Moira got started without much preamble.

Her shuffle was fast. The cards almost looked like they were flying; Julia noted that they seemed to float in the air for a second, and it totally spooked her out.

But I was mesmerized. By the cards *and* the woman who didn't fit in any sort of box. Unmarried, unconventional, and absolutely un-fuck-with-able. She had both of us cut the deck with our left hands, which surprised me since the reading was supposed to be for Julia alone. Julia had been dared; she was the one who paid.

The cards drifted out of the deck, balanced perfectly in Madame Moira's long, trim fingers.

First, the Fool. *The spark of a new beginning.* She looked back and forth between us.

You two, each, both. This. She motioned at our hands, still clasped, dangling unseen at our sides.

Then, the Two of Cups. The art in her deck featured two girls holding their cups up toward each other, smiling, laughing. Full of love. I knew, even without Madame Moira saying it. I knew they were Julia and me.

This bond is special. Unique. The flame of her candle flickered and her eyes sparked with interest. She flipped over the last card.

The Wheel of Fortune.

Twin Flames, two halves of the same soul. Her candle flame sparked and expanded. She smiled, then frowned. *No matter what you do, you will break apart one day. Lose each other, believe it's forever, brokenhearted. But Twin Flames are rare and they can't be extinguished.*

They always find their way back to each other.

I flip the Wheel of Fortune card over now, blinking away the memory.

How long has it been since I thought about that night? Easily, the day comes back to me. I was eighteen. August heat enveloped me as I packed up the back of my car—a Bronco my dad had gotten cheap for me when I got my license. I was leaving for Berkeley, putting space between myself and everything that had happened between Julia and me that summer. I had kissed my parents goodbye, gotten the directions ready to go; the only lingering, unfinished thing was her.

Julia.

She had texted me and called a couple times since that fateful night together. I had avoided her in person, kept the conversation light, noncommittal. She got the drift, and she was angry. *Seething.* That much I knew. Her anger was easier for me to deal with than telling her I wasn't ready would have been. That I couldn't do it. That I had never felt more lost or confused in my life, that I didn't feel like myself anymore and couldn't start college like that.

I just had to put it aside. Push it down.

I had plans; so did she. She'd forget about me eventually.

Twin Flames always find their way back to each other. I heard Madame Moira's words in my head and I ignored them.

What did she know about us?

I reshuffle the cards, my heart doing a dance in my chest. My breathing uncomfortable, unsteady.

Fuck off, I think, directed at the Universe herself.

And I yank my car into gear.

~

I walk inside the Celestial Sands lobby sweaty, my jean shorts riding up my crotch, my silk camisole drenched at my cleavage.

"Hi there," the manager, a sexy Black man with an Afro and a winning smile, says as I approach.

"Hey," I say, and I sound grouchy even if I don't mean to. His bright grin falters. I try again. "This place is gorgeous," I adjust. No need to be a bitch to him; he didn't give me that horribly nostalgic reading. That was all me, myself, and I. "Kit Larson, checking in for the Morgan-Hayden wedding."

His smile is back. "Wedding party or Love, Always staff?"

"Neither. I'm the tarot reader."

"Ah! Then you're staff. Report to Bungalow Ten. It's the *Homebase*"—he places air quotes around the word—"of the operation. They have your room assignment."

He directs me on how to get there by exiting the main house and taking the path toward the bungalows. I snap some shots of the interiors to post in my stories when I leave the hotel next week. As a rule, I never share my location until after I'm well on my way home. One stalker at the Mercer in Soho was enough to teach me that lesson.

I push through the back doors into the breezy garden space, following the winding path toward the bungalow. November in Joshua Tree is my idea of the perfect weather. Warm during the day, chilly at night. You can still sunbathe, and then don a sweater and sit by the fire roasting marshmallows and telling ghost stories, blanketed by starlight.

Bungalow Ten is a small cube with a hammock slung right outside. The door is open, and out of it comes a twentysomething woman with gorgeous black hair and a harried expression on her face.

She nearly bowls me over, barely sideswiping me before stopping short.

"Mystic Maven," she says, her voice a little misty with awe. "Oh my God."

"Oh, yeah, I'm Kit," I reply, and my cheeks feel warm.

"Sorry, that was unprofessional. I'm Zoe. Assistant to the wedding planner—let me know if you need anything." She steps aside. "Room key, et cetera, is inside." She motions back to Bungalow Ten before hurrying along to whatever mission awaits her.

I step up to the entrance and give the open door a courtesy knock. When no one responds, I walk inside. The room is brightly lit by every lamp and overhead light in the place. They've shoved couches and other comfy furniture to the walls and pulled together the tables to form a maze of solid surfaces throughout the room.

A woman—I'm assuming the wedding planner—stands with her back to the door. She looks like she's on the phone, but her voice is low, not audible. Her dark brown hair is swept up in a half-up-half-down do, wavy and thick. She's short, with shapely hips and a tiny waist. She stands like she's got a rod running the length of her body, perfect posture and pretty golden skin.

Jesus Christ. Stop cataloging her body features with such engrossed interest.

She ends her call and spins around.

For the second time today my heart makes a beeline for my stomach. My breath catches in my throat like a jagged pill. My brain short-circuits.

"Julia."

Her name in my mouth is the most decadent forbidden fruit.

Rebekah Faubion is the author of queer rom-coms with tons of heart and more than a little steam. She is also the author of the young adult horror novel *Lost Girls of Hollow Lake*, from Delacorte Press. When she isn't writing books that make her bi soul sing, she enjoys watching anything romantic or scary (or, better yet, *both*), hiking in the Hollywood Hills, and reading tarot by candlelight.

VISIT REBEKAH FAUBION ONLINE

RebekahFaubion.com

RFFaubion

Ready to find
your next great read?

Let us help.

Visit prh.com/nextread

Penguin
Random
House